# Advance Praise for
# The Last of the Blacksmiths

"The writing quality is superb, the historical and geographic detail utterly convincing, the characters well-drawn, and the dialogue persuasive ... Claire Gebben has extraordinary promise. Her prose is quite brilliant; I fully lived within her world."

—William Dietrich, Pulitzer-Prize winning author

"The Last of the Blacksmiths is music and history and motion, love and heartbreak and honest hard work. As Michael Harm—the boy called a "wanderer" at age seven—journeys from Germany to New York City to Cleveland with the dream of becoming a blacksmith, readers travel alongside him cheering in triumph, groaning in despair, nodding in sympathy. Claire Gebben delivers an unforgettable narrator, an intimate glimpse of the immigrant experience, and an ultimately uplifting story."

—Ana Maria Spagna, author of Test Ride on the Sunnyland Bus, winner of the 2009 River Teeth Literary Nonfiction Prize and finalist for the 2011 Washington State Book Award.

"Meticulously researched and lovingly written. Claire Gebben's new novel is both intimate and epic, following one immigrant's journey to America but representative of the journeys of millions. In The Last of the Blacksmiths, Claire Gebben has taken letters and family lore and crafted a compelling story of a nineteenth century immigrant from the political strife of Bavaria to the ethnic communities of Ohio. As a writer who has also researched lost worlds of the past, I was particularly taken with the re-creation of the arts of the blacksmith, and the industrial rivalries in Cleveland when it was a raw and growing city."

—Lawrence Coates, author of The Garden of the World

"An ideal example of living history! Claire Gebben's admirable empathy and imagination turn nineteenth century immigrant letters into a lively and exciting story narrated by the protagonist himself. The precisely researched historical background is embedded in a way that only adds charm. The author makes you believe: it's not fiction, this is the story like it really happened."

—Dr. Hans-Helmut Görtz, author and historian, Freinsheim, Germany

"Rich, intelligent, charming, delightfully earthy, and often touching. I became thoroughly engaged."

—Rev. David B. Williams, author of *Ulu: Bread of Life*

# The Last of the Blacksmiths

For Karen
and Diane,
All the best
with your family
history writing &
adventures.
Claire Gebben 2/18/17

# The Last of the
# Blacksmiths

## A Novel

## Claire Gebben

coffeetownpress

Seattle, WA

coffeetownpress

Coffeetown Press
PO Box 70515
Seattle, WA 98127

For more information go to: www.coffeetownpress.com
www.clairegebben.com

Cover design by Sabrina Sun

The Last of the Blacksmiths
Copyright © 2014 by Claire Gebben

ISBN: 978-1-60381-182-8 (Trade Paper)
ISBN: 978-1-60381-183-5 (eBook)

Library of Congress Control Number: 2013947981

Printed in the United States of America

For Dave, George and Vivian
Craig, Angela and the families

# Contents

# THE HARM-HANDRICH FAMILY TREE

## (Not all family members are represented)

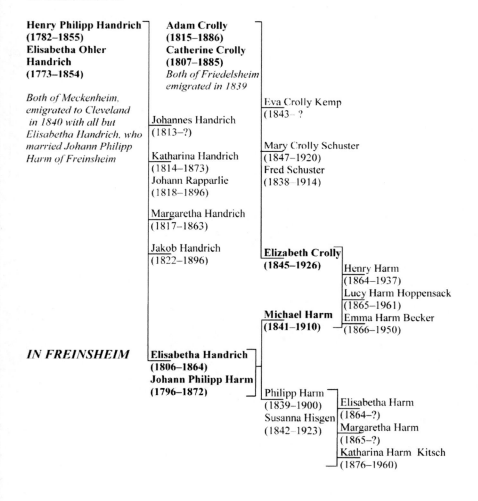

**IN CLEVELAND**

**Henry Philipp Handrich**
**(1782–1855)**
**Elisabetha Ohler**
**Handrich**
**(1773–1854)**

*Both of Meckenheim,*
*emigrated to Cleveland*
*in 1840 with all but*
*Elisabetha Handrich, who*
*married Johann Philipp*
*Harm of Freinsheim*

**Adam Crolly**
**(1815–1886)**
**Catherine Crolly**
**(1807–1885)**
*Both of Friedelsheim*
*emigrated in 1839*

Johannes Handrich
(1813–?)

Katharina Handrich
(1814–1873)
Johann Rapparlie
(1818–1896)

Margaretha Handrich
(1817–1863)

Jakob Handrich
(1822–1896)

Eva Crolly Kemp
(1843– ?

Mary Crolly Schuster
(1847–1920)
Fred Schuster
(1838–1914)

**Elizabeth Crolly**
**(1845–1926)**

**Michael Harm**
**(1841–1910)**

Henry Harm
(1864–1937)
Lucy Harm Hoppensack
(1865–1961)
Emma Harm Becker
(1866–1950)

**IN FREINSHEIM** **Elisabetha Handrich**
**(1806–1864)**
**Johann Philipp Harm**
**(1796–1872)**

Philipp Harm
(1839–1900)
Susanna Hisgen
(1842–1923)

Elisabetha Harm
(1864–?)
Margaretha Harm
(1865–?)
Katharina Harm  Kitsch
(1876–1960)

# Dear Reader

"I READ YOUR NOVEL," ANGELA WEBER, my cousin and friend, told me over the phone, a long distance call from Germany. Angela had translated several dozen nineteenth century family letters, providing me with important insights into Cleveland's German pioneers. "At first I planned to let my daughters read it, but then I came to the part where Michael Harm is together with that cake shop woman. I guess I won't show it to them after all."

We laughed. I might feel sorry about this, but then again, our children, and our children's children, will become adults before we know it. Quite a few of the characters appearing in this novel really lived, but exactly how they lived cannot be known for sure. In a way, it is precisely *because* the book is based on Angela's and my common ancestors that I had to make stuff up. It's the rare family that airs their deepest secrets and misdeeds for the world to censure or savor. So while this book is based on a true story, it is one hundred percent historical fiction, not fact. The truth is, we all make mistakes.

What *are* the facts? For starters, I offer a statistic I learned at the German Emigration Museum in Bremerhaven: in the years between 1850 and 1860, approximately one million Germans left Europe forever, heading for destinations far and wide. Evidence of this mass exodus is present in microfilm records held at the National Archives and Records Administration and can be found by scrolling through passenger lists of ships arriving in U.S. ports during that decade. Millions more left in the decades that followed.

But why? What could have happened to uproot so many? Searching for clues, I encountered the usual textbook topics: "Laws and Regulations," "Unemployment," "Poor Harvests." The heading that really jumped out at me was "Revolution." My great-great-grandfather, Michael Harm, experienced all of these.

*Claire Gebben*

# Chapter 1

---

## New York City, 1857

I WAS LOST, AND HAD NO idea of my way back. To ask for directions would be futile. Even if someone understood me, how could I understand their replies? New York City had seemed a grand entryway for my new life in America a few hours ago. Now I longed only to escape the chaos behind me, people spilling out of doorways, gushing up from underground, staggering, shouting at one another in thick, slurred voices. I could not tear from my mind the shaking of fists at the windows, the raining of bricks from the rooftops. I believed I could find my own way, but I had failed.

I had come too far. In the center of this broad open square a fountain splashed musically, enticing a few families to linger. The clop-clop of horses and rattle of carriages along the broad avenue helped restore my addled senses. I inhaled deeply, the reek of urine and sweat not so strong here. Into my awareness swam the memory of a shop with a German name I had seen a few streets back.

With faltering steps, I returned to the establishment, the shop of a cabinet-maker, the sign painted in both German and English. The windows were dark. At Castle Garden they had warned of this—that no businesses would be open on the festival of American Independence. But they had not warned of the fighting in these streets, more fierce and desperate than any I had witnessed as a child.

As I stood in uncertainty, a man came walking toward me, near to my older brother in age, perhaps eighteen. I drew up the courage and spoke to him.

"*Sprechen Sie Deutsch?*"

The stranger narrowed his eyes. "*Sag mal,* who wants to know?"

Relief flooded over me. "*Bitte,* I am looking for Elizabeth Street."

The beardless man pushed back the brim of his round-topped hat and scratched his forehead. His jaw looked pale and bare, but many men were beardless in this city. He spit on the walkway and wiped his mouth on his sleeve.

"You're a long way from Elizabeth Street." The man peered at me more closely. "Say, don't I know you from somewhere?"

"Not unless you're from the Palatinate, near Freinsheim."

"Freinsheim? Well, what do you know? We're practically cousins. I'm from Dürkheim. Have a beer with me and tell me news of the Old Country."

The man did not have the Palatinate dialect. Would my speech also change over time?

"I'm sorry, I must meet my friends the Beckers," I said, "and hope to arrive before dark. Please point me in the direction of Elizabeth Street, and I'll be on my way."

The stranger frowned, then his brow cleared. "I'll show you myself, for a price."

"A price? You would charge me?"

He shrugged. "You won't be friendly and have a drink with me. Five pennies will buy me a beer after we part. But you must pay in advance."

I had heard rumors of tricksters, so I removed the five coins from my hidden breeches pocket but handed over only two. "I'll give you the other three when we arrive," I said, attempting a voice of authority.

After a moment's hesitation, the man tucked the coins in his vest pocket and doffed his hat. "Karl Finger at your service. And you are?"

"Harm. Michael Harm."

"You don't know the Fingers of Dürkheim? Too bad. What a good time we could've had." Settling his hat back on his head, Karl Finger set off down the street. "You are traveling alone?" he asked over his shoulder.

I swallowed, disturbed by the enormity of the Atlantic Ocean, by the distance that separated me from my family. "I am in America to apprentice as a blacksmith in a wagon-making shop."

Karl nodded and said no more. We walked far, too far it seemed to me, then turned on the street called Bleecker, the roar of the crowd on Bayard growing audible once more.

"This isn't right!" I said, fear making my voice hoarse. "I was told to turn on Canal."

My guide paused. Many buildings surrounded us, but the streets were strangely empty. Twilight had come. Up ahead, a man lit a gaslight, then turned the corner.

"You don't trust me? But look, here is the start of Elizabeth Street."

Karl Finger gestured, and I saw with my own eyes the word Elizabeth painted on the corner building. He picked up his pace and I followed. We went a long way, crossing several streets. Intermittent booms and pops erupted ahead of us. Gunfire? I was so concerned about the riot, I did not notice when my guide slowed his steps. I stumbled right into him.

Karl Finger turned on me, wrapped his leg behind me and shoved. I tripped backwards and fell. As I tried to rise, he leaped on my chest and banged my head hard on the dirt-packed street. Pinned by his weight, I felt him yank and claw at my hidden breeches pocket. He started to tug at my rucksack, then blackness swallowed me.

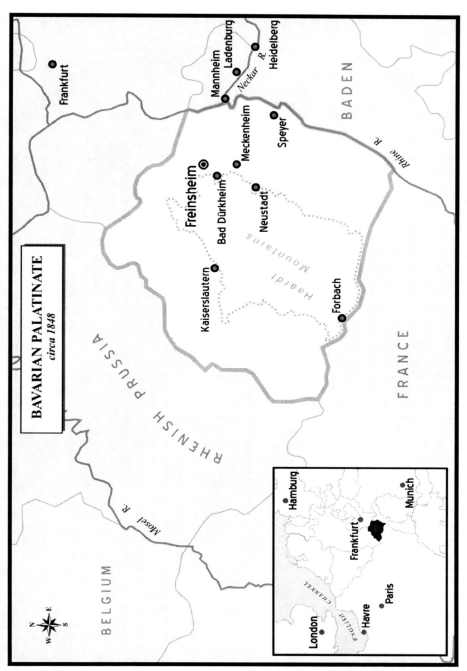

BAVARIAN PALATINATE
*circa 1848*

Frankfurt

Ladenburg
Mannheim
Heidelberg
*Neckar R.*

BADEN

Meckenheim
Speyer

Freinsheim
Bad Dürkheim
Neustadt

*Rhine R.*

Kaiserslautern

Haardt Mountains

Forbach

RHENISH PRUSSIA

FRANCE

*Mosel R.*

BELGIUM

N
E
W
S

Hamburg
Munich
Frankfurt
Paris
Havre
London
*ENGLISH CHANNEL*

Maria Brown, Kroll Map Company

# Chapter 2

## Freinsheim, Bavarian Palatinate, 1848

Is it any wonder that as a boy I yearned to go to America? In 1848, all Europe swelled with the democratic tide, a breaking wave that swept so many across the sea. When the rebellion came to our village, I was but a boy of seven, a farmer's son in the Palatinate, my head full of Indian stories and dreams of adventure.

My family, the Johann Philipp Harms of Freinsheim, owned a modest acreage—fields of grain and vegetables, a vineyard and a plum orchard—but my heart turned in a different direction, toward the bell-like tones of the blacksmith hammer. After all, my name came from my great-great-grandfather, Johann Michael Harm, the first Harm to come to Freinsheim. A blacksmith by trade.

True to my namesake, I could not resist the smithy on Herrenstrasse. I went there often to peer inside at the smoke and flames of the forge, enthralled by the falling sparks, the yellow-white iron at its hottest glow. The smithy gave a glimpse of the world outside our mothers' kitchens, of men working heavy iron, of heat, muscle and grime.

The first rumors of unrest, the rebellion to come, arrived on a February day. That morning I stood with my friend Günter in the open doorway of the blacksmith shop, half my body soaking up the acrid heat inside, the other half exposed to the crisp wintry air. My eyes followed every movement of the master blacksmith Herr Becker, the most powerful man in our village. As usual, he was ordering about two journeymen and Veit Börner the apprentice—at fifteen years old, finished with school and on his way to making a living. Herr Becker was the tallest of them all, his leather apron hanging from his broad shelf of shoulders to the scarred tops of his work boots. In the back, Veit pumped the bellows in sullen concentration.

Herr Becker spied us in the doorway, grabbed a heavy sledgehammer and held it beside us.

"*Guck mal*, they're only as big as this hammer!" he thundered to the other men, his voice grumbling off the stone walls. He dropped the hammer on its head, set his enormous hands on his hips and looked down his thick blond beard at us. "Can either of you lift it?"

Günter stepped forward. He grabbed the handle and bent his knees, lifting it a short distance off the dirt.

"There he goes." The men urged him on with gravelly voices. "That's the way."

Günter backed off and it was my turn. I gripped the handle, straining to raise the leaden hammerhead off the ground, but nothing happened. Were they playing a trick on me? I bent down to examine the sledge. The handle wrenched from my grasp and clunked me in the ear, inflicting a sharp bite of pain. Laughter boomed through the smithy.

"The hammer is beating the boy," Herr Becker said. "You wouldn't know he was a Harm." The men *pffed* and shook their heads. Herr Becker glanced back at Veit, still pumping away at the bellows. "*Bass uff!*" the master shouted, lunging across the room. "You're burning up my iron!"

Günter and I, familiar with Herr Becker's rages, backed out of the shop. In the street, the men's mocking laughter lingered, along with the pain in my ear. What had Herr Becker meant, that I wasn't a Harm? Was it because I was so small? Villagers remarked on this often enough, but I had not thought it mattered so much. I stared at Günter with resentment.

"You could lift that hammer because you're bigger than me," I said, heading off beside him down the paving-stone street.

"I'm not so much bigger. You didn't try hard enough."

"I'll get bigger. I'm going to be a blacksmith."

"You are not. Your father is a farmer, and you must be a farmer, too."

"How do you know?"

"My father says so."

Günter's father was a schoolteacher, so he must have been right. But I did not want to believe him.

"Beat you to the gate," I challenged, the two of us already running.

It was our favorite game, to race down the inner alley of the wall that ringed the village, our feet slapping, our shouts echoing behind us. Houses in Freinsheim crowded up against one another so tightly some even stretched across the second story to meet the fortified wall, forming tunnels.

I touched the corner house first, just barely ahead of Günter, then doubled over, gasping for air. The corner house was the usual finish line, a spot so narrow men had to turn sideways to pass through. Boys assembled here to measure their growth. If we stood squarely in the narrow space and both of our shoulders touched, we could call ourselves men. Günter and I took turns standing in the passage, but of course we weren't big enough. We had not yet started school.

Continuing on to the front gate, we encountered farmers streaming in from the fields, an unusual sight before the noon bell.

"Something has happened," Günter said.

We turned our steps toward the marketplace.

"There is rioting in Paris!" Herr Reibold was saying as Günter and I climbed onto barrels and benches to one side, where other boys had also gathered. In the center of a crowd of men, Herr Reibold held an unfolded newspaper in his hands. Herr Reibold had been a child in the time when Napoleon ruled our region, so he often read the French newspapers aloud, explaining where needed. Due to the rioting, the French King had vanished, Herr Reibold said, probably fleeing for his life. In France, they beheaded their kings.

The blacksmith Herr Becker, still wearing his leather apron, stepped into the center beside Herr Reibold. "The reform banquets have worked," he said, steam rising from his shoulders in the chill gray air. "Let it happen here, too." He gazed at the farmers from under the brim of his cap, making a full circle. "It's time we chased the House of Wittelsbach once and for all to the devil!"

Some men cheered.

With his deep bass voice, Herr Reibold started the men in the "Marseillaise."

> Let's go children of the fatherland,
> The day of glory has arrived!
> Against us tyranny's
> Bloody flag is raised.

Some sang lustily. Others glanced from side to side, wary of the Bavarian police on the edges of the marketplace, who stood observing with their arms folded. To speak against the monarchy was forbidden and could land a man in the tower jail. On this occasion, the police did not intervene.

The Bavarians ruled us in the Palatinate, but we did not welcome them. They ruled from afar, two duchies away, and were separate from us in other ways, too. They ate breaded pork, pretzels and apple strudel. We ate steamed buns with wine sauce, stuffed sow's stomach, and plum cake. They made beer. We made Rhine wines. They were Catholic. We were Protestant. The Bavarian monarchy demanded high taxes and wine quotas with complete disregard for the welfare of the farmers and traders. The idea that we might one day be free of them inspired us and also filled us with fear, a nagging dread that whatever came next might be worse than our present suffering.

As the farmers dispersed, many faces wore frowns.

FEBRUARY TURNED TO MARCH, AND news continued to flow in of revolts in Munich, Vienna, and Berlin. In the vineyards and fields around Freinsheim, the farmers stopped their plow carts to grumble on the road, anxious over what might happen. I was too young to realize the rebellion might also come our region.

One night at supper, Father tugged at his beard as if his mind would not rest.

"Tonight I go to the men's singing club," he said, his wide-set blue eyes serious and clear. He turned to my older brother Philipp. "You and Michael will come with me so your mother has some peace."

I looked over at Mütterchen, seated and trembling at the table, her skin pale as candle wax. I had a vague notion of my mother's illness, the baby girl who did not live. Somehow, the childbirth had weakened her heart. She spent most days at home, except when she went to market or to see if the post coach had brought a letter. Mütterchen wrote to her family in America each year but never received a reply.

"The boys can stay here, *Mann*," she said, tears spilling down her cheeks.

We were unimpressed by her show of emotion. Mütterchen wept for sad things and happy ones, from weariness and, as far as I could tell, for no reason at all. Later I would come to understand this constant sadness, born of separation and loss.

"May I go to Günter's?" I asked.

"*Aha*. You may go to the Glocks," Father said, nodding. "Philipp, you will come with me."

Philipp saw the teacher Herr Glock at school each day, so was just as glad to go with Father. Sometimes I resented how Father chose Philipp, not me, to accompany him. But tonight, another *Pfennig-Magazin* had arrived at the Glocks.

Their rooms weren't far. Our Harm *Hof* stood just outside the village wall. The Glocks rented rooms in the village center. Eagerly, I hopped off in my leather-shod feet down the paving stones of Wallstrasse, so excited about the penny magazine, I did not even pause to pet the stray cats along the way.

As I reached the Glock's door, a white goose beat her wings and honked, driving me around to the back. Günter's father answered my knock. I removed my cap.

"*N'Amend*, Herr Glock."

The schoolteacher's frown relaxed to a smile. "Oho! It's our wanderer friend."

"What is a wanderer?"

"Someone who makes many travels."

"That is not me. I have never traveled anywhere."

"But it's in your blood, *oder*? Seven years old, and already you leave your house after supper to wander the streets."

"I did not wander, I came here directly. Father doesn't get the *Pfennig-Magazin.*"

Herr Glock burst into a hearty laugh. He let me in, closed the door, and went to the table piled high with books and papers. I once overheard my father say that Herr Glock's schoolteacher income did not amount to much. He had to write newspaper articles to bring in extra coin.

Trailing behind him, I kept my eyes peeled for the *Pfennig-Magazin.*

"Günter!" Herr Glock called to the ceiling. "Michael is going to read to us!"

A thump sounded overhead.

"*Nä, nä,* I can't read," I said. "You must read it to me. Is there not a story in the magazine about the Indians?"

"*Doch,* the Indians of the Great West." Herr Glock nodded, his brown eyes studying me until I squirmed under his gaze. "Your Uncle Jakob also had this interest. And your same gray-blue eyes. I can hardly look at you without being reminded of your mother's brother. Such a big personality. Still no letters? I would like to know how it is with the Handrichs, after all these years."

"No letters since the first one."

Herr Glock shook his head in wonderment. "Such a wanderlust with the Handrichs. What an idea your *Oma* and *Opa* Handrich had, to sail across the ocean to America as if it was the Bible land of Canaan."

"I thought it was called Cleveland."

The schoolteacher gave a great guffaw. The air itself seemed to prickle with excitement. I wondered if it had to do with the new freedom of the press ordered by the Bavarian king. All the villagers were talking about it.

Günter thudded down the stairs and landed in the kitchen with both bare feet at once. His straw-colored hair jutted off his head at odd angles as if he'd been lying down. The sight of him made me reach up to smooth down my tangled brown curls. Under his arm, Günter carried the *Pfennig-Magazin.*

"I have read most of it," he said, bringing it over. "It's a good one."

Günter had already learned from his parents how to read. The kitchen had three squat wooden chairs with sturdy backs, one for Günter, the other two for Frau and Herr Glock, but Frau Glock sat in the front room, saying she preferred poetry. Günter and I settled in, and Herr Glock waggled his eyebrows at us, each one bushy as a mustache.

"*Ja, ja,* I know you want to hear the story in the *Pfennig-Magazin,* but tonight, I have a special surprise. I have been waiting for this moment when Michael Harm comes for a visit."

Günter gave a bounce of excitement. "What is it, *Babbe*? What is it?"

"But what about the Indian story?" I asked, my stomach sinking in disappointment.

Herr Glock reached for a parcel on his desk, holding it up with a grin that showed an even row of yellow teeth, only one missing.

"I present to you *The Last of the Mohicans*, a book by the American writer James Fenimore Cooper."

Günter and I leaned forward for a better look. The treasure was bound in smooth black leather with gilt lettering.

"This book too has Indians. It's a story about a frontier man Natty Bumppo and the Mohican Uncas. *Alla hopp*, I'll show you." Herr Glock leafed through several pages and began to read.

> As the frightened deer came first into view the man raised the fowling-piece to his shoulder and, with a practised eye and steady hand, drew a trigger. The deer dashed forward undaunted, and apparently unhurt. Without lowering his piece, the traveller turned its muzzle toward his victim, and fired again ...[1]

As Herr Glock read on, my imagination traveled to this wilderness of America, the deep snow and tall trees, cabins made of logs, horse-drawn sleighs gliding through wind-whispered forests.

The clop of horse hooves sounded outside, and at first I thought it came from the story. A sharp pounding on the door startled me from my reverie. Herr Glock half rose from his chair as Frau Glock appeared, followed by a man in a long riding cape, a feather in his hat like an Indian chief.

"*N'Amend*, Markus! You are far from Heidelberg." Herr Glock strode over to clasp arms with the visitor.

"Konrad, it has happened." The stranger spoke in a dialect I could hardly understand. Behind this man I saw the shadows of others. "The people have revolted. Even now, there is a new parliament forming in Frankfurt. You must join us."

"Great news. Great news indeed!" Herr Glock took the stranger by the arm and they went to the front room.

Gently, Frau Glock laid her hand on my shoulder. "Michael, it's time for you to go home."

BACK AT OUR *HOF*, I went as usual to pray at Mütterchen's bedside.

"Is your father back?" she asked, raising herself up on one elbow.

"*Nä*, not yet. Herr Glock read to us from a book written by an American, about the Indians."

Mütterchen adjusted her nightdress, straightened her cap and laid her head back against the pillow. "Not now, *liebes Kind,* I am tired. Say your prayers and go to bed."

I prayed my usual prayer, the one that goes,

> Lord, let me not wander from thee
> In you may I sleep soft and well
> Give me holy thoughts
> And I'll rest to the fullest. Amen.

After prayers, I went to my bedchamber. In the Harm *Hof,* my brother and I were luckier than most. Other families had old people to care for, and more siblings to watch over as well, most of whom slept on benches used as seats during the day. Since Father's parents were dead and Mütterchen's gone to America, Philipp and I shared a four-poster in a room to ourselves.

I lay awake that night full of questions, waiting for Philipp, my big brother who always had the answers.

"Tonight some men came to Günter's house," I whispered when Philipp came in at last. "Their talk was strange."

My brother changed into his bedclothes and huffed out the candle before answering.

"They came to Father's singing club, too," he said. The covers rustled in the black room as he crawled in beside me. "They are men from the Heidelberg University, smart men who want the rulers to listen to the people. This is a very big secret, Michael. Father says it is dangerous. Father and Herr Becker and many of the other farmers and artisans were at this meeting."

"To sing songs?"

"They sing songs because there is a rule against political meetings. But the men of this singing club also talk of democracy. The men from Heidelberg said we must elect a representative for a parliament. The farmers have asked Herr Glock. At first he said no, but almost all the men voted for him. Only Herr Pirrman had a sour face. I think he wanted to be chosen instead. Herr and Frau Glock will go to Frankfurt together, and Günter will come live with us."

"Forever?"

"While they are gone, *du Dummkopp.* Father has agreed."

# Chapter 3

To honor the Glocks and their journey to Frankfurt, the town council held a *Schlachtfest*. My father offered our pig for the feast, my first memory of the traditional pig butchering—the terrified scream of the sow as the butcher cut her throat. In any event, the sow was little more than skin and bones; at the end of that long winter, the farmer families were living on onions and broth until the asparagus spears rose again in their dark-soiled hills.

At the sight of the steaming pots, the tin plates heaped with blood sausage and potatoes, my stomach rumbled loudly. The bowls of dark, thick soup eased my hunger with rich warmth.

After the feasting, we children played catch with the inflated pig's bladder while the mayor and members of the village council rose one after another to make speeches. In their voices, I heard a new excitement that had not been there before. They entrusted Herr Glock with carrying the interests of wine-makers, farmers, cattle herders, and artisans to the Parliament. The villagers drank wine to the Glocks' health and sang hymns and folk songs.

With the departure of the Glocks, Günter came to live with us, which meant an extra person to help with the farm work. Hour after hour we weeded between the vineyard rows, following along behind Father, who yanked out weeds with such a vengeance, my heart went out to the offending plants. When Father was not looking, Philipp lobbed weeds over the rows so they fell on our heads, raining dirt down the backs of our tunics.

Glumly, I submitted to each task, tending the animals, hoeing, clacking through the vineyard rows to scare the starlings from our ripening grapes. One night as Mütterchen sat spinning her wool and Father pored over his farm ledgers, I could take it no more. I rose from my game with Günter in the front room and stood beside Father at the kitchen table.

"Why must I be a farmer?" I demanded.

Mütterchen paused at her spindle. Father glanced up at me, his blue eyes clear but vacant, perhaps still counting the numbers of his book. "*Wie bitte?*"

"Günter says I must be a farmer because you are a farmer."

"You will make a useless farmer all right," my brother taunted from the front room.

"Hush, Philipp," Mütterchen said.

Father sighed. "To be an *Ackermann* is the Harm living. When I am gone, our lands will be divided equally between you and your brother."

"But what if I want to do something else?"

"Many do not have this good fortune, to own property. You should thank God."

I did not feel fortunate, but I knew better than to say so.

September arrived, and with it, the task I hated most—cleaning the insides of the barrels. Every wine barrel had a small opening, just where the tap was attached at the bottom. When that little door was opened, a powerful stench of grape-skins and yeast erupted from within, burning the eyes, choking the breath.

Father made Philipp, Günter and me go down to the cellar, where we used a long-handled boar-bristle brush to scrub out what we could from inside. I had been doing this since I was five already, but Günter had never cleaned a cask before.

"You have to squeeze your whole body into the barrel to clean it from the inside," I instructed. "It's the blackest blackness you can imagine in there. Someone outside lights a candle and hands it in so you can see what you are doing. You must watch the flame carefully, because if it blows out, that means danger from suffocating air, and you must go right back out again. But if the candle stays lit, you should crouch in there scrubbing with water and the boar bristle brush until all the yeast and coating of the wineskins is off. I am warning you, the smell is as bad as the foul breath of a monster."

Günter nodded, eyes wide. Just then Philipp pushed me aside from the barrel. For an instant, I thought he was going to clean it for me, but he moved on to the larger barrel and leaned against it, arms folded, a smirk on his face.

The saying goes, "If the head fits, so will the man." I sucked in my breath and stuck my head inside the barrel's tiny opening, twisting my shoulders to worm into the yeasty grape-skin ooze. Philipp handed in the candle, and as the light bloomed in the barrel, a skull appeared inches from my face. I let out a scream, kicking and thrashing, backing out of the barrel so quickly I ran into Günter. He stumbled backward, hitting the lantern on the post. We stared in horror as the lantern toppled into a pile of Mütterchen's lamb's wool, causing it to burst into flame. Philipp cried out for Father. The fire was climbing toward the cellar beams by the time Father reached us.

"What's going on down here?" he shouted, grabbing the lantern from the fire. He dove for the crate of potato sacks, threw a pile of them on top of the blaze and stomped down to snuff it out.

"Someth-thing is d-d-dead in there," I stammered, pointing. My throat and nose stung in the sooty air.

Father reached into the wine barrel and groped around. A moment later, he pulled out a fox skull, small and not so frightening after all. Guilt and shame rushed through me. Philipp had only been playing a prank on us. Father turned on Philipp in a rage.

I had no choice but to stand by, helpless, as Father gave Philipp a thrashing. Afterward, Philipp's face was dirt-streaked and wet with tears, but we still had to scrub the barrels. I could not look my brother in the eye. I had been a baby, and I had failed him. I became determined not to let him down again. With sincere zeal, I made a silent vow to be as obedient as possible from now on, hoping to stay out of trouble.

A FEW DAYS AFTER THE BARRELS were cleaned, the grapes reached their perfect ripeness and the annual *Weinlese* began. Villagers gathered at dawn, grunting "*Moahje*" to one another in the dim morning light. Each man strapped a *Logel* on his back, a long, open barrel, narrower at the bottom than the top. It was very heavy, even without the grapes in it. The women and children were given hooked knives and carrying sacks. At the first bell of the day, villagers filed out to the vineyards—men, women and children alike.

The chill morning air soon warmed. Near the ground, yellow wasps hovered above the sun-baked crushed fruit of fallen grapes. People called to one another across green-gold vineyard rows, the older people grunting from the effort, the young full of singing and banter. Women worked in dark aprons and white headscarves, men in their tunics and caps. The adults sipped water mixed with wine to dull the backaches caused by bending for so long.

Günter and I found a spot to pick side by side in the Harm family rows. The clusters of grapes were so heavy they nearly dropped of their own weight into our sacks. As usual, the hours were long and dull.

"I can't wait for freedom to come," I said. I had the vague notion that once we earned our freedom, I'd be released from farm work.

"It won't come for us – soon we'll be stuck in school," Günter said. He did not look forward to school as much as I did, probably because his father taught it.

"So you've heard from your father? You know he's coming back?"

"*Nä, nä.* Stop asking me."

But I had a genuine reason for my concern. Rumors were circulating the schools should close. Of late, as the Parliament dragged on, the people were becoming disillusioned. Word came there had been unrest in Frankfurt, this time against the Parliament. The villagers said they needed to save their money in such uncertain times.

At church on Sunday, the ancient Protestant Church at the center of our village, Pfarrer Bickes refused to hear of such a thing. "We will continue with business as usual," our pastor proclaimed from his lofty pulpit. "The business of moral teaching to the young is just what is needed in this time of reckless disobedience. We may well experience material poverty, but that does not mean our young must experience poverty of the spirit. The schools will remain open."

When the harvest concluded, Pfarrer Bickes carried on as usual, going door to door in his parish collecting the school taxes. Since Herr Glock had not yet returned from Frankfurt, Herr Nagel was hired to be our teacher. I had been eager to start school, but I did not like the new teacher's pointy Adam's apple, which bobbed up and down with each nervous swallow. Herr Nagel drilled the lessons into us without mercy. Soon I learned to hate school. I often became lost in daydreams of Indians and longed for my former days of freedom playing in the willow grove or visiting the smithy.

The sharp rap of Herr Nagel's stick startled me back.

"Michael Harm, you let your head float in the clouds. Never forget: 'A foolish son brings grief to his father and bitterness to her who bore him.'"

Ashamed, I remembered Herr Becker's words: "You would not know he was a Harm." Was I a disappointment to my family, a useless dreamer?

In school that year, Herr Nagel forced us to memorize Schiller's "Song of the Bell," a long poem that many of the children complained about. For my part, I could not help but be enchanted, drawn in by the descriptions of molten metal poured into a mold to cast the bell. Bells were a constant in our lives, ringing to send men to the fields, to call them home, to summon the faithful to church on Sundays. If someone died in the night, bells tolled solemnly in the morning. Alarm bells rang too, warning of danger, fire and storms.

As I practiced reciting Schiller's poem, Mütterchen listened, never failing to nod her approval at the ending—the promise of everlasting life beyond death.

> Therefore now, with the strength of the rope
> Lift the bell out of her tomb for me,
> That into the realm of sound she may
> Rise, into the air of heaven.[2]

For my part, I cared most for the passage about the fiery liberation of the metal.

MINE WAS NOT THE ONLY imagination that caught fire that winter. Just before Christmas, Herr Glock returned to Freinsheim with the announcement of a completed constitution. It was said King Friedrich Wilhelm IV of Prussia was invited to be the new emperor of a *Kleindeutschland*. The village was a buzzing hive of excitement over this news.

But my interests pointed in another direction, fueled by a special gift from my Uncle Jakob in America.

The parcel arrived just before Christmas. That same day, Father, Philipp and I had left before dawn to travel to the Haardt Mountains, to the place where the gray sandstone marked the Freinsheimer forest. Father brought with him a list of trees to fell—bigger logs to split for firewood, smaller saplings to use for a kitchen stool for Mütterchen and a new ladder for the barn loft. As we worked, the air became spiced with the scent of fresh-cut wood.

As I always did in the forest, I thought of Natty Bumppo and the Indians from the *Mohicans* book. But I knew better than to play when there was work to be done. Even so, my mind wandered.

"*Bass uff!*" Father barked at me often. When doing men's work, the felling of trees with sharp axes, mistakes could not be tolerated. After long hours of toil, at last Father tossed a small green pine on top of the rest of the wood, the pine that would be our Christmas tree.

The thought of my favorite holiday made me glad, but the way home was long. With all the wood on the wagon, Philipp and I had to walk beside it on the way home. Father plodded along beside the oxen, his beard swathed in his woolen muffler. We arrived at our *Hof* well after dark.

"A man came," Mütterchen said, standing in the kitchen doorway that overlooked our small barnyard, a shawl wrapped around her shoulders. "He brought a letter from America, from my brother Jakob!"

Exhausted as we were, at this news Philipp and I made short work of tending to the oxen and other animals. Even Father grew impatient.

"Leave the unloading of the *Leiterwagen* until daylight," he grunted, stomping his manure-coated boots on the steps as he went inside.

A short while later, Philipp and I hurried inside as well. Grateful for the warmth, I removed my feet from the torture chambers of my shoes, already too small for me last spring and limped to the sideboard.

"There is a package, too?" I examined the parcel with delight, unable to believe our good fortune.

Mütterchen nodded. "I have looked at it all day, wondering what it could be. Come, eat your supper so we can open it."

Philipp and I ogled the package a moment longer, then turned to our supper of bread and lard, hot potato soup and grape juice. Under the table of scarred wood, the sharp pain in my toes eased to tingling numbness. Finished with my soup, I stuffed down another slice of *Schwarzbrot*, barely chewing, desperate to fill the gnawing hole in my stomach.

Mütterchen watched us eat, wringing her hands in her apron the whole time. She had grown up during the rule of Napoleon, when girls did not go to school, so she had never learned how to read. Gray-brown hairs escaped from her white head scarf and trembled at her temples. Father slurped his soup and methodically chewed his bread.

"Who brought it?" he asked.

Mütterchen took in an anxious breath. "Herr Selzer, the wine merchant. He said he only passed through Cleveland, so did not have much news to report. I invited him to stay, but he was anxious to go on to his brother's family in Erpolzheim."

At last, Father pushed back his chair, picked up the parcel with its letter set on top, and carried them to the warm tiled-in fireplace in the front room. Mütterchen picked up the letter and handed it to Father, the paper fluttering in her fingers.

"See the drawing of a Bavarian soldier? My brother Jakob used to entertain me with these pictures of himself in the Bavarian helmet. He wanted to be a soldier. He was unhappy when my parents wanted to emigrate before he had the chance to serve. He thought soldiering would be an adventure."

Father set the parcel on the floor in front of Philipp and me and cut the string with his pen knife. My brother and I opened it together. As the wrapping peeled away, an odor of animal hide filled the room.

"What is this?" Philipp wrinkled his nose and held up a leather vest. Strips of cut leather dangled from the bottom of it like rain. With a gasp of excitement, I pulled out another one just below it. Philipp tossed his vest aside and reached for the last item, a pair of leather shoes with tiny beads sewn on top.

"What could this mean?" Mütterchen stared at the objects in confusion.

"The letter will tell us," Father said, opening it with deliberation, his hands chapped red from the outdoor timbering. "Yes, *Frau*, it's written by your brother Jakob Handrich. His signature is at the bottom."

"*Bitte* read it, Father," I begged, hopping up and down with impatience. Father cleared his throat.

Cleveland, 10 November, 1848

Beloved sister and brother-in-law,

With great joy I pick up the quill to let you know about how all of us are here in Cleveland. We have already waited four years for a letter from you—

"What? Four years, he says?" A sharp crease lined Mütterchen's broad, pale forehead. "But we have written every year, with no hope of a reply."

Father gazed over the thin pages at her. "Elisabetha, I will read the letter to the end."

I wish that these few lines will meet you in as good health as they leave us. I have been working now for five years at a place in the factory where steaming kettles and machines for steamboats and railways are being built and I earn one and one half dollars per day. I have my own property in town that cost $600, where I have built a house for the old people, who still have their health.

Tears spilled from Mütterchen's gray eyes. "*Gott sei Dank!*" she breathed. Father did not reproach her.

Johann Rapparlie, our sister Katharina's husband, has his own business with blacksmiths and wagon-making, building the chaises with everything ready so that one can put on the horses. It is the fashion here, to have all the work done by one man. The Rapparlies have two shop buildings and a house. Also a dray wagon and two horses.

Sister and brother-in-law, we read in the newspapers of the trouble from the uprisings. If one day your health allows it, you should come to us here. Start your way to America early in spring and do not do a ship contract at home. Wait until you get to Havre. Then you can get passage faster and cheaper. When you arrive in New York, don't make contracts on the canal farther than from station to station, namely from New York till Albany, from there till Buffalo, from there till Cleveland.

As I have the opportunity here with Herr Selzer, I will send you also a small package that holds vests for your two boys and so I do not leave you out, dear sister Elisabetha, a pair of shoes. These presents, they are the work which the wild people or the brown Indians make.

We all send our greetings: Father, Mother, your sisters and brothers-in-law.

I am now still unmarried and will marry soon and then I am politely inviting all of you to my wedding.

Warm greetings,
*Jakob Handrich*

I smoothed down the leather vest with my hands, enchanted by the picture painted on the back, a scene of an Indian riding on horseback, his bow and arrow drawn to shoot a deer. I put the leather to my nose and inhaled. My fingers glided through the fringe to make it ripple. *Will I ever meet this Jakob Handrich, who has given me this wonderful gift?*

Father picked up Philipp's vest, stroking it with thick, stiff hands.

"Rough, but softer than *Lederhosen*," he said, "perhaps the skin of a deer."

A vest like the Mohican must have worn! My head spun with happiness. I wished Mütterchen would try on her Indian shoes, but she only gazed at them, fingering the beads. All at once, she gave a keening moan and put her hands to her face.

"How I miss my parents. And what of Johannes? Why is he not mentioned?"

"*Alla*, Elisabetha, they tell us they have sent letters which did not come to us. Who knows what news we've missed? I will write to your sisters and inquire."

Through her sniffles, Mütterchen nodded. "Thank God my parents still have their health."

"Why don't we go to America?" I asked. "Uncle Jakob tells us how. I want to see an Indian."

Father glanced at Mütterchen. "We have property here, and a good living."

He handed the vest back to my brother. Philipp curled his lip in disgust.

"The Höhn family gets letters from their relatives in Ohio. Sebastian says the brown people are savages, not civilized."

Anger rose in my chest. "Those are the Mingos, not the Mohicans."

"I don't see the difference. The Indians stole and lied and murdered the women and children in that Mohicans book you love so much. If I met a real Indian, I'd kill him."

"The Mohican is noble and understands the beauty of the wilderness, the wild animals."

Philipp made a pistol with his hand and shot at me. I dove for him. We kicked and fought until Father pulled us apart.

From that day forward, while the other boys in Freinsheim played at fighting Spanish soldiers, Günter and I played Bumppo and Uncas from *Last of the Mohicans*. As the proud owner of an Indian vest, I always took the part of the Mohican.

# Chapter 4

## Freinsheim, Bavarian Palatinate, 1849

AS WINTER TURNED TO SPRING, each Sunday, we Freinsheimers gathered in the creaky wooden pews of the ancient Evangelical *Pfarrkirche,* craning our necks to see our pastor above us preaching hard work and obedience to God.

"Do not be led astray by false enlightenment, following your own arrogance," Pfarrer Bickes admonished, his eyebrows knit together in a dark line. By "enlightenment," he meant the democratic ideals of the Frankfurt Parliament. Pfarrer Bickes ruled our town in this manner, putting duty to Calvinist Christian doctrine and to the Bavarian monarchy side by side, disapproving the raucous nights of celebrating a constitution. "Only in obedience to the duty of work, to the plowing and planting, is man spared the lusts and passions of this earthly life. Merry-making and late-night carousing are a nuisance to the community, leading to gluttony, fornication, and sloth."

I possessed a naïve understanding of fornication, aware of rumors circulating in our little village, whispers about one young couple or another "succumbing to sinful ways" in the haylofts or the tall grasses behind the plum orchard, gossip that made the old people peck and cluck like hens over bits of grain.

On a recent April afternoon, I came across one such couple. Spring had arrived, the time when the storks, our symbols of good luck and prosperity, returned to nest in their centuries-old aeries. The day was so warm I changed out of my woolen sweater into the lighter tunic and stole away to the large stand of willow trees in the lowlands, my favorite place for imaginings. Under the graceful curtain of the willow branches, my mind's eye populated an entire Indian village. My Indian father was the chief, and I had two young braves for brothers.

As I neared the grove, bare toes squishing in the mud, I was brought up short by a girl's giggle. I ducked down beside the tall grasses just as Veit Börner dropped out of the tree before Martha Becker, the blacksmith's daughter. Instead of running, she put her hands to her cheeks and laughed. Veit surrounded her with his muscular arms and they walked together behind a thicket at the edge of the field.

I knew Herr Becker would not approve of his older daughter alone in this way with his apprentice. But the bright green tendrils of the willow tree and the pink blossoms of the plum trees stirred a restlessness in me as well, so I did not tell on them.

The fruit tree blossoms of that May of 1849 mingled with heady hopes for changes to come, but once again, our longings would be denied. I was at Günter's, sprawled out on the floor doing my best to make out the words for myself in the Cooper book, when Herr Glock entered, his eyebrows forming a jagged V on his forehead. He strode right over us into the kitchen.

"We are doomed," he said to Frau Glock. "The Prussian King has refused to sign our constitution. He has betrayed us. He accuses the Parliament of lawlessness."

Günter and I rose and went to stand at the kitchen threshold. Frau Glock had turned from the sandstone washbasin, her blue eyes startled wide. "But how, *Mann*? It was he who permitted the constitution in the first place."

"You saw how poorly we fared last fall during the rioting in Frankfurt. The king has the military force we lack. *Frau,* I fear this is the death knell for our cause."

"It isn't possible, *Mann*," Frau Glock pleaded.

"I have little hope." Herr Glock's voice was brittle, as if he might cry. "We must prepare."

THE DAYS THAT FOLLOWED WERE a time of chaos and dismay. The night the news reached us about King Wilhelm's betrayal, the Bavarian police disappeared from our streets. There were rumors that, fearing a peasant rebellion, they took all their money and hid it in a fort.

With the police gone, Veit Börner and other young men strutted around our village wearing red armbands and red insignia on their caps. They spat in the dirt at the feet of the wine-makers, the wealthier "property-owning class" of Freinsheim. The "reds," as we called them, accused the older farmers and artisans, too, calling them Hambacher liberals, claiming their ideas were outdated, not serious enough to make a difference. The Catholic priest Holderied was beside himself. He organized the Catholic day laborers to rebel against the provisional government. A whole troop of them assembled behind the blue-and-white Bavarian flag and marched as a gang through the marketplace, demanding a return to the monarchy.

Another kind of battle existed in our family. Father disagreed with Herr Becker, his closest friend. The blacksmith insisted we must make a stand, military or otherwise, for liberty and equality. Father did not get along any better with Pfarrer Bickes, who did not let a Sunday go by without preaching against the provisional government, insisting we should keep our allegiance to the Bavarian king. Much to Mütterchen's dismay, Father stopped going to church altogether. Philipp and I did not want to go to church either, but no matter how hard we pleaded, Mütterchen still made us. In those confusing times, when I went out with Father, he would turn down another street if we spotted the black robes of Pfarrer Bickes.

The Bavarians were not welcomed, but they had kept order in our village. They had controlled the taverns, so in their absence, an unending drinking fest began. Even early in the morning on the way to the fields, Father, Philipp and I would pass men arguing in a drunken fervor over whether or not the House of Wittelsbach had the resolve to come and crush the provisional government.

After days of uncertainty, Father brought Philipp and me to an assembly in the marketplace. The tax collector and forester, the judge, the mayor and town council members, and men of the cloth—Pfarrer Bickes and the Catholic Pfarrer Holderied—had all gathered there on the wooden platform reserved for the traveling music bands.

A stranger stood in front of them addressing the crowd, a civil commissioner, villagers said. He gave a lengthy speech about King Friedrich Wilhelm IV, the Prussian king who had refused to sign the constitution. He accused King Wilhelm IV of high treason, causing murmurs among the men.

"Therefore, as a representative of the new constitutional government of the United Germany, I order all Freinsheim officials to declare an oath of allegiance *mit Gut und Blut*. With your fortunes and your lives, I tell you." He paused, his bulbous nose gleaming red in the May sunshine, and stared at the officials gathered on the platform. "Who will be the first?"

Our town officials gazed warily around them. Time stretched in tense silence. Then Pfarrer Bickes stepped forward, his black eyebrows drawn down in a glower.

"I have no intention whatsoever of swearing allegiance *mit Gut und Blut*," Pfarrer Bickes said, his voice raw with anger,

The Civil Commissioner put his hands on his hips. "What, you wish to be accused of treason?" He smirked at the crowd "A man of the cloth cannot lead his flock from jail."

"You can drag me to Kaiserslautern with a rope around my neck, and still I will not swear allegiance."

As villagers began to murmur, Herr Becker stepped forward from the crowd.

"Is that so, Pfarrer? *Doch*, you have stood against us all along." Herr Becker flipped his hands down at Pfarrer Bickes in dismissal and turned to the commissioner. "I am not a town official required to do so, but I swear an oath in any case. I hereby declare my loyalty *mit Gut and Blut* to the new constitution, and to the United Germany." Some shouts of approval arose from Veit's red-armbanded men, but Herr Becker raised his large hands to quiet them. "Freinsheimers, we have been pushed around long enough. When the American colonies wanted their freedom from the English, did the king of England give up his power without a fight? Of course he didn't. The Americans armed themselves and took it! Therefore, I say the only way to show we mean business is to form a militia, to be prepared to fight for our freedom. As our poet Goethe says, 'He only earns his freedom and his life who takes them every day by storm.' So it must be with us. Hear this: at my smithy, I will sharpen all knives and scythes for free."

All the men began speaking at once, some shouting approval, some hissing and whistling in disgust. Herr Becker stepped back into the crowd, and with an exaggerated sweep of his arm ceded the stage to the Commissioner.

After Herr Becker's speech, the town officials began to take the oath one by one, the forester and mayor and councilmen all declaring their allegiance. Only Pfarrer Bickes and Pfarrer Holderied stood apart with scowls on their faces, refusing to swear the oath. Indeed there were such hard feelings against the pastors that day, only a few women sat in the church pews come Sunday.

Other than the pastors, only the tax collector did not make the oath, but the men joked he was out of work anyhow, so what did it matter? A Civil Guard of young men was formed as well. For the following days, in the blacksmith shop, there was the constant ring of metal on metal as farmers streamed to the smithy to have their scythes straightened for battle. The dragon's-breath of the bellows choked the air until I thought only of imminent war, during the day, and also at night in my dreams.

BUT THAT SAME WEEK A different kind of terror visited the Johann Philipp Harms. Mütterchen collapsed on the floor of our kitchen, her face ashen, her lips blue. Father cried out to her and knelt down, begging her to tell him what was wrong, but she would not answer. He lifted Mütterchen in his arms and carried her upstairs to bed.

"I must go for the doctor," Father said, leaping back down in great bounds, his face so stern he looked angry. "Look after her until I return."

Fearfully, Philipp and I went upstairs to do his bidding. Mütterchen's breathing was thin and rasping, and she did not open her eyes. While Philipp held a damp cloth to Mütterchen's forehead, I crouched down against the bed post, clutching my knees to my chest, paralyzed with fright.

When the doctor arrived, my brother and I were sent out of the room, but we hovered by the door anyhow. We watched the doctor spread cloths against Mütterchen's rattling chest and apply the black slick mounds of leeches to her thin white arm. When I saw the leeches, I went to my room and hid beneath the bed covers, believing she would die for certain.

The next morning, thanks be to God, Mütterchen was alive, but she did not rise from her bed.

AND SO OUR LONG VIGIL began, the Harm men living in constant fear Mütterchen would depart this earthly life for the heavenly realm. Philipp would not allow me ever to state my fears aloud, superstitious that if we spoke of them, they would come true. I remember lying stiffly in bed each night, straining my ears for any sound from Mütterchen's bedchamber, my lips clamped together tightly to keep her with us.

At first, church *Frauen* arrived with baskets of food each day, and Pfarrer Bickes came once a week, always at a time when Father was in the fields, to sit by Mütterchen's bedside and read scripture to her from our thick *Heilige Schrift*.

Springtime meant tilling and planting and weeding no matter what else happened, so soon Father called on Frau Becker, the blacksmith's wife and my mother's dearest friend, to come with her daughters Martha and Gretel to care for Mütterchen while he went out to the fields.

At least this year promised a more bountiful harvest than the years of flooding and hunger that preceded it. Philipp and I did our share of work, but I lived through those days in a shadowy daze, hacking my hoe at the sopping, heavy dirt, the threat of losing Mütterchen digging deep in my heart.

On the rainy days I did not have to go outside, as I was still so small and my parents feared I would catch ill. Gretel and Günter stayed in, too. We often played on the floor of Mütterchen's bedchamber. Gretel Becker was my age, her sister Martha much older. Gretel looked strange, with pale blond hair even whiter than her father's, her eyelashes so white she seemed to have none at all. Gretel played with her dolls, while Günter and I set up our collections of horse chestnuts in battle formation, pretending they were real horses ridden by imaginary cowboys and Indians to recreate the stories out of the *Pfennig-Magazins*.

Frau Becker was a devoted healer, feeding Mütterchen hot broth with parsley root, garlic and burnt saxifrage. She made us carry buckets of water from the *Gute Brunnen* sulfur spring to make salves of flour and egg white and vinegar, which she plastered on Mütterchen's chest. I'd watch carefully as she made the sign of the cross over my mother's prone form, intoning, "God the Lord protect you" three times. I always added my own silent prayer to seal the spell.

Mütterchen opened her eyes for the first time at the end of May, on the day of my eighth birthday. In the ensuing weeks as she regained her strength, she sometimes sat up and talked with Frau Becker of their childhood in Meckenheim. During these conversations, I was especially alert to any mention of my name.

"Do you think Philipp or Michael are at risk for *melancholia*?" Frau Becker asked one afternoon. "How terrible it must be, to be so overcome in the mind that you take your own life. Isn't that what happened to Johann Philipp's father? A shame he died so young."

"Hush, Liselotte," Mütterchen said.

Frau Becker lowered her voice. "*Tch*, the children aren't listening. See, they're playing. In any case, it is a sin. There was never illness of that kind in my family, or in Gerhard's, either."

Mütterchen sighed. "The Harm men take things too hard. In the Handrich family, we suffer from the weak hearts."

"*Ja, ja*, the women do."

"Such a burden, this fluttering of the heart and dizziness from child-bearing. Johann Philipp and I would have left for America ourselves if not for the unborn child. With my weak heart, he would not hear of it."

Like a bolt from the blue, I learned in this way that we too might have gone to America, if not for my baby sister. I was only a baby myself when she died and so did not remember. I was sorry indeed that I did not get to see the Indians, and men like Natty Bumppo. Instead, my life was ruled by the farmer's hoe.

THAT JUNE, STRANGE MEN BEGAN passing through our village dressed in all manner of topcoats and tunics, carrying rifles, swords, and scythes. It was said they came from the north, from Dresden, where Prince Wilhelm ordered his troops to drag the rebels from their homes and execute them on the spot. "Against Democrats Use Military Force" was the Prussian prince's motto. He was greatly feared. The men called him "The Cartridge Prince."

Those freedom fighters who escaped Prince Wilhelm's army were gathering in Neustadt, at the foot of Hambacher Castle to join up with the Free Corps army of the provisional government.

Then a Commander Massmann arrived in Freinsheim to knock on the door of the Catholic priest, to arrest him for inciting the Catholic peasants to rebel against the new government. The priest was led in chains to the prison in Dürkheim.

"They lock up a man of God?" the people murmured. "It's an empty cell, without even a bed to sleep on!"

Even worse news followed. Pfarrer Karl Holderied was condemned to death, to be executed a few days hence. Just as we learned this, the Free Corps army began to move. Men marching under the tricolor black, red, and gold flags headed through Freinsheim in ragtag disorder. They resembled outlaws more than soldiers, but even so, my parents and others set out buckets of wine for their refreshment and cheered them as they passed. Many men trickled to a few, then the streets were deserted.

Only then did the news reach us that Prince Wilhelm of Prussia had entered our region from the north with an army of thousands. Our Bavarian King had invited the Prussians to come here to crush the rebellion. The new government's Free Corps had been in full retreat.

I cannot forget the rage mixed with fear on the faces of the villagers, exposed to the dreaded "Cartridge Prince" with no military force to stand in our defense.

Solemnly, Freinsheimers began to prepare for the siege. In our barnyard workshop, Father set about constructing a box from scrap wood left over after building the chicken coop. Just tall enough to peer inside, I observed Father pack in the box his wood-carving tools, the weighing scale, cloth bags of seeds, his prized gold pocket watch, a thick packet of papers tied in string, and a leather pouch lumped out with coins. Laying an oilcloth over it all, he nailed shut the lid.

"We'll bring this to the potato field," he said, as he handed me a shovel.

Father and Philipp hoisted the heavy box off the workbench and lugged it out of the yard.

"We're burying this in the ground?" I asked, trailing behind.

"*Ja*," Father grunted.

"But why?"

No answer. Halfway to our field, we stopped to rest beside a cherry orchard. The box was long enough that the three of us could sit on it, side by side. Loaded wagons and carts passed on the road. After the many days of drinking and carousing, the people had sobered, their mouths set in flat lines.

"We should have used our wheelbarrow," Father said, kneading his shoulders.

"How will you build things if your tools are in the ground?" I asked.

Philipp rolled his eyes. "Hush up with your questions."

Father's worried eyes locked onto mine. "In 1689, Freinsheim was burned to the ground by French soldiers." At the word "soldiers," a thrill of fear went down my spine. "Nothing remained but the walls and the church. Some say we don't have to worry this time. But I say to them, better to be on the safe side."

I had not heard this story, but had heard others, stories repeated time after time at community gatherings. Freinsheim's history was freighted with cruel overlords, the prince-electors who had ruled us since Roman times. One prince beheaded rebellious Freinsheimers in 1525. The peasants were executed in the marketplace before a gathering of the entire village. No one was allowed to clean the ground afterward, so the market was stained for months with their blood. When, over time, the rains washed the blood away, the butcher was ordered to slaughter his animals there so the villagers would not forget what happened when they disobeyed.

Some things, no matter how long ago they happened, remain burned into our memories. Especially bitter things. It took a long time to dig a ditch big enough for the box of Harm valuables. We were returning to town when Günter met me on the edge of the cherry orchard. I stopped while Father and Philipp walked ahead.

"*Babbe* says the members of the Parliament will be imprisoned and tried for treason, sentenced to die like Pfarrer Holderied," Günter said. His straw-colored hair shone bright in the sun, but his brown eyes were somber. "He's not going to wait around to find out. We're going to Switzerland."

"For how long?"

Günter shrugged. "We can't take much with us. Here, these are for you." He handed me a parcel. I took it from him and bid him farewell as if it was any other day. Somehow, I could not believe his words. But at home, as I unwrapped the brown paper parcel, misery washed over me. Nestled in the stiff paper were old *Pfennig-Magazins* and the Glocks' copy of *Last of the Mohicans*. My friend was leaving Freinsheim for good.

That night, long after Philipp's breathing had settled into sleep, I lay staring up into the darkness, terrified of what would become of us when Prince Wilhelm arrived. At a "thock" on our bedroom floor, I leaped from bed, afraid the Prussian soldiers had already come. I tiptoed to the window and, in the light of the half-moon, spotted a small dark form in the street—my friend Günter.

We did not say a word. All the houses on Wallstrasse leaned up so closely to one another, someone surely would have heard us. Günter waved, and I waved back. Then he turned and disappeared down the street. Oh, if only I knew whatever happened to my good friends the Glocks, I would surely thank them for their friendship in my young life.

# Chapter 5

⁓

THE RAUCOUS CLANG OF STORM bells tumbled Philipp and me from bed. Rushing to our second floor window, we saw men charging up the street in the gray dawn light armed with rifles and scythes. Shouts sounded through the din of the bells: "To arms! To arms! The Prussians have come! To arms!"

Philipp and I yanked on our clothes and charged down the stairs. Father already stood in the open doorway yelling up to Mütterchen.

"Elisabetha, I am taking the boys to the marketplace. We will return at the slightest sign of danger."

I felt a pang of guilt leaving our mother helpless in her bed, but was too afraid to stay alone with her. The bells continued to peal as we raced up Wallstrasse.

"But Father," I yelled. "Should we not escape for the fields? Will they not burn us up inside the town?"

I am not sure he heard me. Father's jaw was locked in a grimace, the cords of his sun-browned neck standing out in thick stalks, and he did not answer. In any case, by now we had reached the village center, where young men of the Civil Guard grouped together, weapons sticking up like thorns. Veit Börner and Herr Becker stood at the front, their faces fierce with anger.

A few moments later, the bells stopped ringing, their sonorous timbre still buzzing in the air when Pfarrer Bickes exploded through the door of the bell tower dressed only in his nightshirt.

"Citizens of Freinsheim! Citizens of Freinsheim!" he shouted, waving his arms over his head, his uncombed hair tumbling over his forehead. I had never before seen our Pfarrer out of his black robes. Someone tittered. He leaned over, hands on his knees, gasping for breath, then stood and raised both arms in supplication. "Do not think I rang this bell. I did not order it.

To fight would be madness. The Prussian army has cannons and muskets and many soldiers."

"We're not cowards," Veit Börner called out. "We'll chase Prince Wilhelm to the devil!"

His cry raised a few half-hearted cheers. Pfarrer Bickes gaped in disbelief.

"You think you can go against the Prussian army? You and your little band of peasants? I tell you, it will end up as before. You will be beheaded before our eyes, the stain of red blood soaking these paving stones. *Alla*, in the name of God I beg you, put down your weapons and go to your homes."

Murmurs of uncertainty rippled among us. Herr Becker stepped forward. The oversized blacksmith wore his good black topcoat, his pistol tied to his waist bandit-style.

"The Pfarrer speaks true," he said, directing his gaze to his militia. "For so few to stand against so many will only turn our wives into widows. Those who stay in Freinsheim must surrender, or die. As for me, I refuse to live under mean-spirited rulers any longer. I am going south to join the Free Corps army, our last hope for democracy. I leave this very moment. Who's with me?"

A few men stepped forward, including Veit, while others of the Civil Guard remained in a tight clutch. Herr Becker and his few followers hastened away, exiting our village to the south, toward the old chapel tower. I edged closer to Father and reached for his hand. Without the large blacksmith to defend us I felt even more exposed.

"But what will happen to us?" Frau Reibold cried out to the Pfarrer, her voice cracking.

Pfarrer Bickes adjusted a suspender, *pffed* out his lips, then combed through his hair with his fingers. "*Alla*, we must see what can be done. If the rest of you," he gestured toward the Civil Guard, "agree to put down your weapons, I will go out and talk to this Prince Wilhelm of Prussia. Perhaps something can be negotiated."

For the first time, our pastor looked human to me, a man in his nightshirt, his beard hanging down to his navel. Someone, perhaps Herr Reibold or Herr Pirrman, suggested if the Pfarrer was going to talk to the Crown Prince, he ought to dress in something better befitting a man of the cloth. Looking abashed, the Pfarrer agreed.

We villagers, his dutiful flock, followed behind our shepherd to his parish house, bleating with concern amongst ourselves while he went inside and put on his familiar black robe. When he came back out, he strode away from us through the inner tower. Blindly, we followed.

As for what happened next, I am not sure how it came about. Perhaps the people behind pushed those in front, or curiosity got the better of us.

Whatever the cause, without warning we villagers were all streaming outside the protection of the main gate.

On the hill, the Prussian troops were lined up in strict regimentation, their blue uniforms one dark mass, bayoneted guns and artillery spiked and menacing. At the sight, with a collective gasp we stumbled backward as if the army barreled down on us. But the soldiers held their ground.

Father tried to hold Philipp and me back, but we slipped through his grasp to push up front for a closer look at the famed Cartridge Prince. Prince Wilhelm sat high on his white steed at the head of his army, his heavy metal cross gleaming in the sun. The tall plume of his hat waved in the breeze. Men flanked him on horseback on either side, holding aloft the blue and white Prussian flags.

As Pfarrer Bickes trudged up the road alone, our homespun burr of villagers hung back, awaiting miraculous intervention of Almighty God, or doom. Those who bore witness as Pfarrer Bickes approached Prince Wilhelm that morning had a new respect for our pastor that lasted many years. Because of him, no shots were fired and no blood was shed.

Afterward, the Pfarrer claimed he had merely invited the Prince to enjoy some of our best wine and stay for the night in Herr Mayer's house, the newest and grandest erected outside the wall near the main gate. In our Pfarrer's eagerness to dissuade Prince Wilhelm from invading, perhaps he was over-generous in his praise of our little village. Or perhaps the Prince, of his own right, was taken in by Freinsheim's charms, by our ancient *Eisentor* gate and fortified wall with its seven crumbling towers, by the blanket of fields and vineyards surrounding it in all directions, by the *Gute Brunnen* sulfur spring known far and wide for its healing properties.

However it occurred, when the Cartridge Prince shone in all his glory on the north road into our village, Freinsheimer hopes for freedom were lost.

ALL THAT SUMMER, PRUSSIAN SOLDIERS lived in our haylofts, pissed on our town wall, devoured or trampled our crops, and drank our Rhine wine and *Sekt* champagne, in addition to their Schnaps. It lightened our hearts a little that Pfarrer Holderied was spared, set free from prison and his sentence by the Prussian troops in Dürkheim. A small thing to cheer in the midst of the occupation.

At the Harm *Hof*, our second floor hayloft was commissioned as a sleeping quarters for three Prussian soldiers. Up close, the soldiers were of different shapes and sizes like regular people. I couldn't help but ogle their shiny swords and buttons, their muskets and spiked helmets, which both frightened and attracted me.

These soldiers sang songs I did not know, and spoke of city life, of the wide streets of Berlin, of sculptures and opera, of fancy carriages and fine—and disreputable—women. They were haughty in their manners and way of speaking. Their gruff laughter at the villagers, their stories of standing rebels against trees to be shot and of murderous night-time raids in peasants' homes made me reluctant to eavesdrop on them too often.

Over the weeks, news trickled back to us that the Free Corps army had been vanquished. After brief stands at towns such as Kirchheimbolanden and Rastatt, the remaining soldiers fled, slipping across the border into Switzerland.

By the end of the summer, Prince Wilhelm rounded up his troops and returned to the north. But the occupation was not over. As soon as the Prussian wagons and men disappeared over the rise, our true sovereigns the Bavarians replaced them.

From the end of our vineyard rows, Philipp and I watched these new soldiers march in on the dry August road.

"I suppose we belong to the House of Wittelsbach after all," Philipp said.

"I like the blue of the Bavarian uniforms better than the Prussian ones," I said.

"Good thing. One day you and I must be Bavarian soldiers."

I had heard this before, but even so, I studied these soldiers now with new eyes. Three more took up residence in our hayloft. I eavesdropped on these soldiers, too, listening to their talk of Munich and all its glories. Their stories made me wonder what adventures I might have one day, as a soldier, as a man.

The Bavarian troops encamped around us through the wine harvest, drinking our new wine and gorging on our onion cake. The town council had even started plans to build a barracks, since it seemed as if the troops would occupy us forever. But at the beginning of November, as the farmers sweated in the barns threshing grain, the soldiers departed. Once again, the Bavarian police prowled the streets and once again, Freinsheimers endured heavy taxes on our crops and wines, as if March 1848 and the writing of a constitution had never happened.

Not long after the Bavarian troops left town, I returned home from school for the noon meal to find Frau Becker and Mütterchen sitting in the kitchen, tears streaking both their faces.

"Even now Herr Becker sends for us, instructing us to sell the smithy and our *Hof* and move to America," Frau Becker was saying.

"But the troops have gone. Why can't Gerhard return to us here?"

"He has resolved to go to the land of liberty. There is not enough work to support him here in any case. He writes that he and Veit are working their passage on a ship to New York City. He says for us to come right away, to find them through the Auls."

"But Liselotte, you cannot leave me. How will I manage?"

"Elisabetha, I feel sure you are strong enough. In any event, you know my Martha carries Veit's child. We will cross right away. In New York they'll be properly married."

In any case, without Herr Becker in the smithy these past months, it felt as if the hearth fire of the village had gone cold. A number of villagers gathered in the narrow corridor of Herrenstrasse only a week later to bid farewell to Frau Becker, Martha, and Gretel.

Herr Oberholz extended a hand to help Frau Becker up onto the wagon seat. Martha and Gretel sat on the back, their travel trunk wedged among the casks of wine bound for Neustadt. Some talked of the post coach journey over the mountains, others of the ocean voyage from Havre, France and how it might last as long as two months—if the boat did not sink on the way. Herr Oberholz snapped the reins and his wagon lurched forward.

Herr Reibold began to sing "I Pray to the Power of Love" in his deep bass voice. Others joined in the hymn with their quavering ones. I ran behind the wagon with Gretel gazing at me sorrowfully. Her skin around her eyes was splotchy and red from crying. She burrowed her face down into the bunched wool of her travel cloak, looking so sad I longed to cheer her.

"You should be happy," I panted, keeping pace. "You're going to the land of James Fenimore Cooper, of Indians and adventure!"

"I'm afraid of Indians."

"I'd trade places with you any day."

"Arnica doesn't want to go." Gretel pulled a white, wriggling kitten from beneath her cloak. Held by its neck, the kitten mewed pitifully, its pink hind toes spread apart, its blue eyes wild. "Take care of her for me?"

"I don't want it."

Gretel ignored me. She dropped the kitten mid-air so I had to stumble to catch it.

"Goodbye, Michael," Gretel called, the sound of her voice receding.

"Goodbye," I called back. Juggling the squirming Arnica into a firm handhold, I lifted her high for a last glimpse of our friend. "A thousand times farewell."

The kitten came to live in our stable with our other two cats. I felt sorry for her and saved her bits of sausage and cheese. In any event, without my two closest friends to confide in anymore, Arnica heard a good deal of my troubles and sorrows.

# Chapter 6

―〰―

## New York City, 1857

FIGHTING THE BLACKNESS, I CRIED out for help. Moments later, a female voice rang out.

"You there!"

"Leave him be!" shouted another, as if from the heavens.

Karl Finger's weight lifted off me. I heard swift running feet, but my vision did not clear. Unconsciousness lurked, threatening to overwhelm me. I don't know how long I lay there, my head dizzy, my stomach churning, my awareness sinking as if drowning, a peril I imagined so often those long days on the ship. A sharp stab in my spine kept me from going under. Shifting, I recognized the lump of my rucksack beneath me. Karl Finger had not gotten the letters.

Gradually, a dark brick wall came into focus. I moved my head to a new angle. Pain pierced the back of my skull. Above me rose a tall wall, one of the five-story buildings so common in New York. Two heads peered down, round silhouettes against a dark gray sky.

"*Tch,* another farmer boy fresh off the boat," one said.

"Not enough sense to shun the hard liquor," said the other. "Look where it's got him."

The dialect of these two *Frauen* lifted me back to the orange-tiled roofs and clear night air of the Palatinate. I struggled to sit up. The dirt-caked walkway and brick buildings dashed me hard on American shores. Groping for my cap with one hand, I pressed tenderly against the back of my head with the other. My hand came away moist with my own blood.

I swallowed back a rising nausea. "*N'Amend, Frauen.* Excuse me, I have suffered bad luck—"

"He has the old-country manners," the first said. At the sound of a baby's cry, her head withdrew.

The other woman remained looking down.

"*Bitte*, can you direct me to the Beckers on Elizabeth Street? I seem to have lost my way."

The woman considered me. "This is Elizabeth Street," she said. "What's the number?"

"Eighty-five?"

"Three streets down, other side of Grand."

*Grand.* I remembered the shape of these letters, one of the street names pointed out by Franz Handrich on the map at Castle Garden. Thanking the woman, I tried shakily to stand. I was almost upright when my pants dropped to my knees. Scrabbling to pull them up, I examined the frayed bit of cloth where my money pouch had been. My last twenty dollars. Gone.

Crushed by despair, I pinched my pants closed with my fist and staggered off. The walkway seemed to roll beneath my feet like the waves of the ocean. Could this be the America of the Beckers and all those who went before me? A place of violence and chaos?

A barrage of images flickered through my head—the golden circle of Father's pocket watch, the farmer lifted bodily from his wagon, the explosion of gunshots, the horse that groaned as it sank to the earth. My breeches pouch of money torn from my body. Like a condemned man who walks to the gallows in full knowledge of his crime, I knew my vanity and ignorance had led me here. Just a few hours in this land of liberty, and I had lost everything. What would become of me now?

Blackness reached out, threatening to overtake me, but I struggled ahead. At last, I spotted the street sign for Grand, or what I presumed was Grand. In truth, the letters were as alien as this land. I leaned against a telegraph pole and sank to the ground, the throbbing in my head nearly blacking me out. The few people on the walkway stepped around me without a second glance. Propped in a fog, I thought of my brother. I had fulfilled Philipp's worst fears. He was right; I couldn't be trusted on my own. Was he right too that I wasn't fit to be a blacksmith? I swayed my head to the right and left to shake away my doubts. Ash-like specks danced before my eyes.

Eventually, I came to myself again and noticed the pale white faces in the windows across the street, eyes black and hollow, staring not at me but in the direction of the ruckus on Bayard. I squinted in the blue-white glow of the gaslight. There, across the street, I recognized the number eighty-five just above the middle door.

Hope raced through me. I struggled to my feet and stumbled over to the entry. The door swung open under light pressure. I stepped into a pitch black hall, odors of sauerkraut and pork fat clotting the air. A dim staircase ascended in front of me, barely visible in the gaslight from the street. I groped my way upward, the notes of a piano whirling down. At the first landing, I moved toward a crack of light along the floor, felt for a door, and knocked.

"Who is it?" came a muffled voice in German.

"*Entschuldigen Sie*, I am searching for the Beckers?"

"Other side."

I groped my way across the landing and knocked on that door. The piano music stopped. Moments later, the door opened and I beheld a young woman with whitish-blonde hair, her brow knitted in a frown. My knees nearly buckled with relief.

"Gretel? It's me! Michael Harm of Freinsheim."

Gretel's eyes grew large. "Michael? Michael Harm?!" She pulled the door wide and glanced around me into the dark hall. "But where are Herr and Frau Harm and your brother Philipp?"

"They remain in Freinsheim. Gretel, it's so good to see you."

"Come in, come in," said my old friend. As I stepped into the light, she put her hand to her mouth. "But you're hurt! What's happened? Mother! Father! Come quickly, it's Michael Harm. He's injured."

The Beckers were convinced I had been caught in the mob on Bayard Street. Herr Becker had been keeping anxious watch from their window, as all the residents of their building had. It took me some time to clarify that I escaped the rioting only to fall prey to a German "friend," losing everything.

In the lantern light of the Beckers' rooms, I saw my shirt and jacket were coated in blood. Frau Becker tended immediately to my head injury.

"We have never before seen this kind of fighting," Frau Becker said, her voice full of concern. She looked the same to me as always, perhaps stouter, her gray gaze frank and practical. At her touch, I remembered how tenderly she had cared for my mother long ago. "Fire is such a terrible danger here." She glanced over at Herr Becker, who once again stood lookout at the window. "*Mann*, perhaps you ought to go see after Veit and Martha and the babies."

"Liselotte, they have the good sense to flee if there is trouble."

I thought then of my rucksack with its precious contents.

"I carry letters for you from my parents," I said, standing up to retrieve them. My pants began to slip off, so I quickly sat down again.

The Beckers did not seem to notice my embarrassment. Gretel brought me my rucksack and I pulled out the thick packet of letters. Eagerly, Herr Becker came away from the window to receive Father's letter, so Frau Becker went to take his place.

As he read out loud to us, I noticed the old blacksmith no longer presented the imposing figure he once had. His white-blond hair had thinned a good deal and hung down his forehead in limp strings. His beard was scraggly and gray.

Hearing my father's message, so full of confidence in me, I was seized again with shame at my failures. Truthfully, I was thinking of giving up and going home, until Gretel appeared like a fairy princess bearing a plate of sausage and black bread, some plums, cheese, and a glass of restorative Rhine wine.

Feeling slightly better after the meal, I shared news of Freinsheim, what I could remember of friends they knew. But after a second glass of Rhine wine, I could keep my eyes open no longer. The rooms of their living quarters were small, so my hosts brought out bedding for me to sleep behind the sofa in the main room. Dressed in Herr Becker's nightshirt, with two thicknesses of linen wrapped around my head, I fell immediately into a deep sleep.

I WAS AWAKENED BY A PERSISTENT shake on my shoulder. Frau Becker stood over me in her apron, hands on her hips.

"Before it gets too hot, we must give you a good scouring," she said. "Those ships are infested with fleas and lice—I will not allow them in my house."

I sat up groggily. "But what about the rioting?"

"They say it's over for now. It was mainly in the Five Points, where the Irish live."

She handed me a set of Herr Becker's old clothes to wear, much too large, so we used string to tie the waist. It was a Sunday, the streets relatively quiet. I went out with Gretel to empty the chamber pots. She led me to the communal water pump to one side of the row of overflowing privies. I grew dizzy lugging a bucket of water up the stairs and felt bad when Gretel had to carry the rest. Frau Becker heated the water in the dense and airless kitchen. When the washtub was full, the women vacated the room while I bathed. Afterwards, Frau Becker set to work scrubbing my clothes and bed clothes, her face beet red amidst the hot steam. Gretel and I strung the washing out on a line over the alleyway.

"We could hang it on the roof, but we'd have to stay up there to keep it from being stolen," Gretel said, "and word has gone out Michael Harm is here from Freinsheim. We'll have visitors today."

The first guests to arrive were from the same building two levels up, people I had never met who had emigrated from Mütterstadt. They fretted over the riots in the Five Points slum, over what would happen to the city now that the new police had come. The trouble stemmed, Herr Becker said, from the Republican Governor of New York who wanted to put a law in place that would restrict the sale of whiskey and close saloons on Sundays. It made the Irish, most of whom were Democrats, mad as hornets.

Our guests ate Frau Becker's pretzels and drank glasses of Rhine wine, while also feasting on the tale of my misfortune. They inquired several times if I was sure Karl Finger was German, not Irish.

"In any event, we're too close here to the Irish," Frau Becker said, her body moving forward and back in her chair as if it had rockers. "I wished to live deeper in *Kleindeutschland*, but Herr Becker insisted on buying that piano. We had to pay for it, and the labor of four men to carry it up the stairs. Now there is the added expense of Gretel's lessons."

"Shush, Liselotte, she brightens our spirits with her music," Herr Becker said. "In the old country, we never could have offered our daughter such an opportunity. And she shows great talent."

Next Veit Börner and Gretel's older sister Martha arrived. I was glad to see them and especially delighted in their little son, full of energy, his soft curls an unruly brown like his father's.

"So tell me," I said as the little one's eyes sagged into sleep and the room grew calmer, "I must know from the beginning what happened after you left Freinsheim."

"We were fools to think we could just walk out with the Prussians at our gate," Veit said. "Luckily, Herr Reibold chased after us to warn us more troops lay in wait over the rise. He took us to a secret entrance in the cemetery chapel tower. Once we'd crawled inside he covered it up again with stones. He returned two nights in a row with food and water, and on the second night helped us sneak out through the vineyard rows."

I was amazed. "I thought the chapel tower was sealed up for good."

"Just so. Herr Reibold keeps this secret well," Herr Becker said. "He saved us, and we are forever in his debt. Once we escaped Freinsheim, we tried to catch up with the Free Corps army. But in any case, the cause for freedom was lost. The Cartridge Prince chased us easily into Switzerland."

Veit told me of their Atlantic voyage, and of how he had found a job right away in the carriage shop of Ezra Stratton. I felt a sinking feeling then that I had no money to continue my journey. But I had little time to dwell on this, as the Kirchners of Freinsheim arrived next at the overcrowded rooms. Frau Kirchner asked about every last one of her relatives and friends, and inquired so many times for a letter I was very sorry not to have one for her.

WHEN MONDAY CAME, MY PENNILESS condition sweltered in my soul with the July heat. The air was so stifling hot that as soon as I washed and dried my face, my temples beaded again with sweat. With bandages still wrapped around my head, I lay on the sofa agonizing over how I could get the money to go to Cleveland. The previous evening, Herr Becker had made it clear he did not have ten dollars to spare, as his job with the New York-Harlem railroad paid barely enough to sustain his family. I was ashamed to write to Father, and it would take too long to receive a reply, in any case.

A few evenings later Herr Aul came for a visit to pick up his letters, and I took the opportunity to ask his advice.

"Could I find work in New York, to pay for my lodging here at the Beckers, thereby saving money for train fare?"

Herr Aul was quick to discourage me from this course. "Times are very bad. No one is hiring, as they fear the banks will fail again."

"But you found work easily when you first arrived, *oder*?"

"There is always the need for furniture, especially with more immigrants arriving each day. But doing business in America is nothing like it was in the old country. At first I could not believe I had to make so many tables in one day. But this is the way here. The work is not hard, but you must do it fast."

Herr Becker came in from the kitchen then nodding his agreement. "Many of the artisan crafts, the shoemaking, carpentry and blacksmithing, aren't in much demand in the city. It's better in the countryside."

"*Alla*, at least there is work somewhere," Herr Aul said.

"You are right. But I don't enjoy the blacksmith work as I once did. I am one of many, and it is tedious. A man is a living creature, not a machine, after all."

DAYS PASSED, AND I CONTINUED to recline on the sofa as if ill, but my head ached only a little. *Gott sei Dank* the Beckers were kind enough to give me a roof over my head and food to eat. Herr Becker left early each morning for his job with the New York-Harlem railroad and did not return until very late. Frau Becker cooked and cleaned all day with vigor, still square of hip and bold of tongue, careless of the baking flour that dusted her cheeks. For her part, Gretel rustled about the small rooms as if she, not her mother, was mistress of them, always taking care to remove her apron when she left the kitchen, practicing often on her beloved piano.

In truth, during those hot July days, a *Lesesucht* descended on me, a reading addiction that held me in its grasp. Herr Becker owned many books kept tucked in shelves along one wall of the main room. I read a German translation of *Oliver Twist* by Charles Dickens. The desperate circumstances of this boy in London made me pity him—and myself as well. I could wish that the Beckers were my long lost family, but wishing did not make it so. Indeed, my troubles sat on my chest like the ruffian who had beaten and robbed me.

Herr Becker also owned Goethe's *Elective Affinities*. I devoured these short novels and, as soon as I had finished them, began reading them again, lingering over the passages about the chemical affinity between a man and a woman, the mysterious scientific attraction between the sexes. When Charlotte says, "*I for my part know plenty of cases where apparently inseparable intimacies between two people were dissolved by the arrival of a third party,"* I could not help but think of Emil's interference with my love for Anna Marie.

Even in far away America, I clung to the belief that Anna Marie Neufeld once loved me best.

# Chapter 7

## Freinsheim, Bavarian Palatinate, 1851

AS THE SAYING GOES, THE month of May makes all things new. When the cherry and plum trees blossomed with promise, Freinsheimers said farewell to winter's ice and snow with the Festival of the Maypole. In the chestnut grove outside town, the men erected a beech wood pole, which had been decorated by the women with ribbons, crepe paper, and flowers. The women dressed in the traditional embroidered aprons and wore ribbons and flowers in their hair. The men wore festival clothing of breeches and embroidered vests.

For the Festival of the Maypole, love pollinated the air. Young bachelors left gifts at the doors of their chosen maidens.

It was my particular luck, in the Festival of the Maypole of 1851, to stand beside the town beauty, Anna Marie Neufeld, for the children's dance. As we awaited the signal to begin, I thought to tell her about Gretel's kitten Arnica, who just that morning had snuck into our house. Mütterchen had stomped her foot and beat at Arnica with a broom, screeching, "Shoo-shoo!"

I knew Anna Marie would like the story, as she too had been a friend of Gretel Becker. When Anna Marie giggled, she looked so pretty, her dark brown curls tied up in ribbons. I saw blue violets growing in the meadow and stooped to pick some for her. She accepted them with a blush.

"Now that you have picked these flowers, they will wither," she said.

I leaned down for more, but she put her hand out to prevent me.

"*Bitte* don't pick them. They are pretty there."

"But I'll save them for you," I said. "Wait and see."

"They can't be saved. They only have color when rooted in the soil."

"They're just flowers."

Anna Marie looked at me sadly. "Why did Gretel have to go away? Why are so many from our village leaving? What is so great in America that can't be found here?"

I shared her sorrow. Since the failed rebellion, many more families had left. I reached out to console her and, as my hand touched hers, a shock went from my scalp to my toes. She did not pull away.

The music started, and we wove around the maypole, drawn apart, then closer together, again and again. I always knew exactly where she was among the other children in the ring. As the ribbons braided more tightly, I resolved to convince her America was not such a bad place, to tell her of the Cooper books, the adventures to be had. But as the song ended and I bowed in the traditional manner, she curtsied and scurried off to her friends.

I picked more violets that afternoon and brought them home, pressing them into the family Bible with the vague idea I might one day hang a bachelor gift on Anna Marie's door.

DURING THAT SUMMER OF MY tenth year, I was often left alone to hoe in the vineyards while Father and Philipp went to clear stones from the asparagus patch or prune in the plum orchard.

As I toiled, I thought of a thousand other things I'd rather be doing, perhaps sitting at the *Eisentor* gate to watch the farmers and traders arrive for the *Kerwe* church fair or playing Blind Man's Bluff in the chestnut grove with Matthias Höhn, John Fuhrmann and Richard Pirrman—my comrades and classmates of those years. They often beat me at these games. One by one, my friends had grown big enough that their shoulders touched both walls, while mine had not.

As I weeded and sulked, the faint strains of band music floated over the hill.

"I am taking a break," I said to myself, planting the handle of my hoe in the freshly turned earth, leaving the metal crook of it standing above the vines so I could find it later.

When I found the bandwagon, the musicians had stopped and climbed out to take refreshment by the side of the road. The men wore matching navy blue jackets and white shirts. One gentleman, fatter than any I had ever laid eyes on, took up a whole sandstone bench while the others arranged themselves on the grass.

Their bandwagon was the most fabulous I had ever seen, painted bright green and edged with fabulous golden scrollwork. Like a calf lured by fresh clover, I moved forward to examine the lions and birds and leaf ornaments shining in the sun. I peered inside, too, at the tuba and trumpet, the accordion and violin gleaming on the black leather seats. As I reached out to stroke my finger along the bell of the tuba, a voice came out of nowhere.

"*Bass uff, Bengel!*" A man appeared from the other side of the wagon, his head topped with a fancy velvet blue cap.

"I'm only looking."

"Look then. Don't touch."

I sidled over to admire the violin and the many-keyed accordion. The man observed me with an eagle eye.

"That's a strange vest you are wearing," he said after a time.

"It's from America, from my uncle. It's made by the Indians."

I stared longingly at the white and black accordion keys, fingers itching to see how they felt.

"You're a fan of music?"

"I suppose." In truth, I had not really thought about it. I did get excited about the music for the village church fairs, and the music of the circus when it came to Dürkheim. I had memorized the words and tunes of many songs, but we all did this, joining in the folk songs lustily, especially on the refrains.

"Sing something then."

I didn't have to think long to come up with a song choice: "Upon a Tree a Cuckoo Sat." The courage and silliness of the nonsense verses, with their hidden protest against our rulers, was a sure crowd pleaser.

> Upon a tree a cuckoo
> Simsaladim Bamba Saladu Saladim
> Upon a tree a cuckoo sat ...

When I finished, the musicians cheered, somewhat wearily it seemed to me. It was a muggy, thirsty afternoon.

"Very good," said the man. "Herr Franck," he added, introducing himself.

"Harm. Michael Harm."

Herr Franck asked me about my family and our place in the village. I answered honestly, if warily.

"*Alla*, Michael Harm, don't worry. I ask you so many questions because we need a boy. We travel from town to town all summer, and we need someone to stable the horses, bring bread from the bakery and do other such errands. What with Herr Gormann over there taking up more than his fair share of the wagon seat, we need someone small in stature to fill these duties, someone who won't tire the horses on account of his added weight. In return, I'll feed you, teach you songs, pay a small wage. You might even be a singer for us, with training. What do you say to that?"

I could not believe my good fortune. For once, my small size would be an asset. My head grew dizzy with the idea I might see the world. But Father would never agree. As I realized this, my stomach sank heavy as a bowl of stones. I looked up to see Herr Franck waiting, a trace of a smile lifting the corners of his mouth. I could think of nothing to say.

"You don't have to answer right away. We're here in Freinsheim two nights for the *Kerwe*. For now, how about you help us get settled at the *Rathskeller*?"

Which is how, as the Liedmeisters entered Freinsheim, I came to be riding on that glorious bandwagon, the rhythm of a march swirling around me. From up on my perch, I saw Anna Marie Neufeld stop to let the wagon pass, a basket of sticks balanced on her head as all the *Mädchen* carried their loads. Her jaw dropped at the sight of me and my spirits lifted even higher.

I spent the afternoon running errands and forgot all else. The band needed *Wurst* from the butcher, plus an entire stuffed pig's stomach to be cut into *Saumaa* slices for tomorrow's dinner. Also bread, apples, and wine. Herr Franck questioned me about the exact amount of the bill each time I returned, and as I put the coins in his palm, he counted them carefully. His fingers were callused in odd places, his nails bitten short. The last job Herr Franck asked me to do was polish the road dust off the bandwagon. Eagerly, I grabbed the cloth from his hand.

Herr Franck chuckled. "We will get along just fine, *Junge*."

How happy I was to rub over the fine green lacquer and scrollwork of that bandwagon. The black leather upholstery of the seats gleamed. The wheels had been decorated with a swirling, intricate design. Until then, I knew only the cumbersome wine press wagons and simple ladder wagons. I had not imagined vehicles existed of this type, with such fine workmanship and eye-pleasing elegance.

Herr Franck told me the Liedmeister band had done well on recent travels, well enough to afford this beautiful wagon and uniforms. In one more season, the director hoped to travel with the band to Russia and Ireland. If I worked hard and paid attention to my singing, I might join them.

When I'd finished polishing the wagon, Herr Franck placed two *Pfennig* coins in my hand, my first earnings that were mine alone. But I did not thrill as I might have. Just then the six o'clock bell rang to call the farmers in from the field. Remembering I had neglected my work in the vineyard, I ran home as fast as I could. Fortunately, it did not seem as if Father and Philipp had noticed my absence.

All through supper, I don't know how I kept the cork on my excitement. After the meal, I followed Father to his barn workshop and stood by, watching him pick up his planer to smooth a stout pole.

"What about bedding the hens?" he asked, not turning around.

"Today I met the leader of the Liedmeister Band," I said.

"Is it *Kerwe* this evening?"

"*Ja, ja.* This leader, Herr Franck, needs a boy to run errands and look after the horses and bandwagon."

"Here in Freinsheim?"

"Here, and when they travel the rest of the summer from village to village."

Father set down the planer and crossed his arms over his chest. He turned to me, opened his mouth, then closed it again. We stood this way, face to face, for some time. When he finally started to say something, he paused and squinted at the wall behind me. The lines in his face grew darker.

"Michael, where is the hoe?"

My belly of stones plunged to my ankles. I followed his gaze to the empty hook where the hoe should have been. "I ... I must have left it in the vineyard."

"*Du Taugenichts!* Useless! You wish to go off on your own like a grown man, yet you can't even bring a tool home from the field?"

"*Es tut mir leid.* I'm sorry. I'll get it right now."

I ran from the barn, hurrying to the field as fast as my legs would carry me. There in the vineyard stood my hoe, just where I had left it, its head tipped in sorrow. I grabbed for it, and, in utter frustration, stabbed the sharp end of it into the dirt again and again.

Never had I felt so trapped. It was true I was absentminded, that I did not learn things as quickly as Philipp. I made many mistakes, for which I lived in a state of daily repentance. Still, it was not fair that I had to do farm work. I hated it.

Hot resentment sticking in my throat, I returned to our *Hof* and put away the hoe. Later, when I heard the music start in the marketplace, I straggled in misery to the *Kerwe.* I was standing on the edge of the crowd feeling sorry for myself when Anna Marie appeared at my side.

"I saw you on the Liedmeister Bandwagon this afternoon," she said. Her sparkling eyes pierced my soul.

In spite of my troubles, my chest puffed out with pride. "The band leader Herr Franck asked me to help him, that's why they gave me a ride."

Anna Marie reached out to touch the fringe of my Indian vest, a sweet smile on her lips. "You may ask me to dance."

With these words, Anna Marie pulled me under an enchantment. To be sure, Freinsheim had many pretty girls. The Höhn sisters, cousins of my friend Matthias, were quite pretty. It would have been our luck, should my brother or I happen to marry one of these *Fräuleins*, especially since the Höhn family had so much land. There were also the Lind sisters Margaret and Magdalena. And Rosine Aul. Lovely Rosine.

But none compared with Anna Marie Neufeld, the girl I held in the secret chamber of my heart. How often since the Festival of the Maypole had I hoped to dance with her, yet never dared? I can't say I was a Casanova, that my words of acceptance tripped off my tongue like golden arrows to her heart. I took her arm stiffly as we walked to our places in the dance. The Liedmeisters were playing a mazurka, which I managed with clumsy steps.

Herr Franck winked at me as we made our way around with the other couples. Philipp was dancing with Susanna Hisgen, his tanned jaw still free of whiskers, but at twelve years old, nearly the size of a man. Beneath the brim of his cap, Philipp raised his eyebrows at me as we danced past each other.

I think I would walk across hot coals to relive that moment, my first dance with Anna Marie, the touch of her warm hand, her small waist beneath my soil-scraped fingers. It was my only dance with her. Anna Marie was asked to dance by many others.

For the rest of the evening, I sat to one side on a barrel, tapping my foot to the music, singing along. I thought about asking Philipp to talk with Father about my chance with the Liedmeisters, as Father always listened to him. But Philipp was not restless like me—I doubted he would understand. After careful consideration, I decided Father had not said no. Herr Franck would still be here on the morrow, giving Father a chance to get used to the idea. I'd ask him again tomorrow, right after church.

The next morning during worship, Pfarrer Bickes looked even more dour than usual. Our pastor became especially upset on *Kerwe* weekends, as if church fairs ought to be rites of solemn decorum rather than times of music, fun and laughter.

"To live in God's will—that is the true calling of the faithful. Do you think, 'If I say I believe in the Gospel, that will satisfy God, and I am free to do as I please?' That is as much as the Catholics, who say, 'I am free to do as I please, I'll just ask the priest for forgiveness later.' God asks more of us, to be people of devotion and industry and sobriety. God knows what is in our hearts, our most selfish, unholy desires." The Pfarrer seemed to stare straight down at me. "Merrymaking late into the night leads to sin and depravity."

Or maybe he was glaring at Philipp, I thought, remembering how my brother had come in late and slept in his clothes. Did Pfarrer Bickes know Philipp had been besotted with wine? The church bell tower stood right over the marketplace. Sometimes I wondered if the Pfarrer climbed up there to spy on us.

In truth, our Protestant church had a profound effect on me. As I sat in our *Pfarrkirche* with the rays of daylight filtering in through the bubble-filled glass—light that wrapped us all in an air of sacred peace—I often felt the omnipotence of God. Mütterchen's eyes shone with pious devotion as she gazed up at Pfarrer Bickes, and sometimes I too felt this sensation of sacred awe.

But on this particular morning, my heart spilled over with selfish longing. During the entire service, I prayed to God to let me travel with the Liedmeisters. After church, back in the Harm kitchen, I mustered the courage to ask again.

"*Bitte* Father, have you considered whether or not I can work for Herr Franck?"

"Work for Herr Franck?" Philipp asked. He looked pale, like washed out woolen stockings. "I heard last night you rode up on the back of the bandwagon like a little prince."

"The band leader has asked me to work for him," I said.

"What kind of work?" Mütterchen asked. The suspicion in her voice was not a good sign.

"Stabling the horses, washing the bandwagon, running errands. He'll pay my expenses, and a small wage."

Mütterchen turned a questioning gaze at Father. "What expenses?"

"Last night I spoke with Herr Franck," Father said, his body thin and angular in the morning light. "He says they need a boy to help on the road when they travel from village to village."

I should have let my parents talk, but I could not keep quiet. "You have seen Herr Gormann, the fat one who plays the violin? He takes up the seat of two men, so Herr Franck needs someone small in size. Like me."

Philipp sneered and pawed at the top of my head. "You are a dreamer. Music doesn't fill empty stomachs."

Father wrenched his gaze from Mütterchen to me. "My son, there is too much work for you to do this thing. We can't spare you."

"But you'll have my earnings. Then maybe you won't have to make the wine deliveries for Herr Oberholz this winter."

"Herr Franck won't pay you a man's wages."

"He says he'll teach me to sing."

Philipp's lip curled. "Sure, become one of the *Schnorranten*, a beggar musician? Perfect, and wear your Indian vest, while you're at it."

"For shame, Philipp," Mütterchen said. "The beggars need our charity, not our spite. Father, what do we know of this Herr Franck?"

"He is well-respected," I said, my voice rising. "He has already made enough to buy a fancy bandwagon and uniforms of velvet."

"But what village is he from?" Mütterchen asked.

"West of the mountains, the Kusel region," said Father.

"*Nä, nä*, Michael," Mütterchen said. "We don't know anyone from there. He's not family."

"You may not go. You are only ten," Father said, and would speak of it no more.

Dejected, I left the house without taking my dinner. If Father took the strap to me, I was sure I wouldn't feel it. All caring had crawled up inside me, deeper than the strap could ever reach. That afternoon, Herr Franck had said he expected me to come to the *Rathskeller*, but I no longer felt like it. I went the long route, walking all the way around the inner wall, counting every tower and pausing only once, before the prison tower, to consider its gloomy purpose.

Did I dare run away? So many in our village had left for America, and many more talked of going. Yet I wasn't even allowed to travel on a short tour in this region. I had given up hope of blacksmithing. Now must I also give up hope of adventure? Was this truly my fate, to awaken every morning to the wood shaft of the farmer's hoe? But if I ran away, would my family ever speak to me again?

Disheartened, I turned my steps to the underground *Rathskeller* tavern. Only Herr Gormann was there.

"You danced with a pretty *Mädchen* last night," he said from his seat on the long bench against the wall. As he shifted, the bench creaked as if it might splinter.

Warmth grew up the back of my neck. "She danced with everyone."

"She danced with you first."

"That doesn't mean anything."

"To a beauty like that, you must come out and say what you want. You have curly brown hair and sulky blue eyes. I did not see another boy as handsome."

A scraping on the stone steps announced the arrival of the rest of the band. They brought with them the *Saumaa*, sliced and hot. I was invited to share in the feast and enjoyed such a meal as I never had before, a table of men licking our fingers without a thought about manners. Herr Franck drank straight from the mouth of a wine bottle.

"I cannot work for the band," I told him.

"Uh," he grunted. "When your father came to question me, I guessed as much."

"My mother wouldn't send me away with those who aren't family."

Herr Franck looked to left and right. "Do you hear that? Frau Harm doesn't trust us."

"What's not to trust?" asked Herr Kopf, the one who played the tuba. "We're brother musicians, who speak the universal language. Let me play a serenade for Frau Harm that will melt her heart."

"It's your French ideas she distrusts, Herr Franck," said Herr Gormann.

"Which ones?" Herr Franck wiggled his eyebrows suggestively.

"There is too much work on the farm," I said, too loudly.

The men stopped chortling. Herr Gormann picked at his rotting teeth for stray bits of pork.

"*Freilich, Bengel*, we know," he said. "We have left our wives and children to do the farm work at home while we travel all summer."

After dinner the men brought out their instruments for a practice. They played "*Wanderlied*" and Herr Franck asked me to sing. I knew only one verse, so he taught me the others.

On that last night of the *Kerwe*, I did not see Mütterchen or Father come to the marketplace. Philipp appeared sometime during the evening. I watched him try to get Susanna Hisgen's attention, but she refused his every advance. I sat near the band, swaying back and forth to the tunes, pretending not to care. With the coins Herr Franck had given me, I purchased my first *Krug* of wine. Emboldened by the drink and Herr Gormann's encouragements, I asked Anna Marie to dance twice, and she accepted me both times. All of these things I did in an effort not to think about the torn feelings in my chest.

When I returned home very late, Father was waiting up for me, his farm ledgers spread out on the kitchen table.

"So you still live in this house," he greeted me. Against the kitchen wall, his shadow loomed large.

"I'm sorry, Father," I said, my throat hoarse from all the singing.

"And you'll return to this house again tomorrow, when the Liedmeisters go on their way?"

"Yes, Father. I will not be a good-for-nothing. I'll stay and do the farm work."

Father stood up, lit a candle, then snuffed out the lantern.

Upstairs, Philipp sat on our bed still dressed, his head in his hands. At first I thought he was praying. When he spoke, his voice was as mournful as the lowing of an ox.

"Susanna would not dance with me."

"She probably saw you were drunk."

"I was not. I only drank after she refused me."

"Then why wouldn't she dance with you?"

"She says I act like a *Freidenker*, an unbeliever who doesn't fear the Lord."

I pictured Susanna at school. She always sat with an erect back, never giggling like the other girls. She memorized extra Bible verses. To fear the Lord, did one have to wear a sour face all the day?

"I guess you agree with her, *oder*?"

I searched for the words. "Susanna is not the ruler of you, or of any of us, but she acts like she is."

"You are wrong to say that. She can do whatever she wants. Susanna is the prettiest girl in town."

"*Alla*, Philipp, as you say. In your eyes, she's the prettiest girl in town.

Now go to sleep. You can whimper back to her like the butcher's hound in the morning."

Later, when I was almost asleep, Philipp whispered, "*Guck mal,* I am glad you didn't go with the Liedmeisters."

For my part, I felt heavy with despair. "I'm not like you, I'm no good at farming. I like music."

"No one says you can't sing. But it's not an honest living—work that will feed a wife and children. It's a passing fancy."

At his words, my despair deepened. I could think of no reply.

# Chapter 8

## Freinsheim, Bavarian Palatinate, 1856

IN THE NEXT YEARS, WE suffered many poor harvests. Even worse, like a wine cask that has sprung a leak, the village emptied as its people trickled away. I began to dread each new week of school, never knowing come Monday which benches would be empty, which of my friends would have left Freinsheim forever. "*Kein König da,*" the people said of the New World. In the *Rathskeller* tavern and in the marketplace, people spoke of America, a country with no taxes, with endless acres of empty land for farming and no king to interfere in their lives.

"Pfarrer Bickes said seventy families left the parish last year," Mütterchen said to Father one evening at table.

"*Freilich*, at this rate, our village walls would be put to better use keeping the people in," Father said. "Next time I see the mayor, I'll advise him to lock the gates and let no one out."

"Why don't we go to America?" I asked.

Philipp kicked me under the table. As usual, Father did not reply.

During one of his trips to Heidelberg, as he was making wine deliveries for Herr Oberholz, Father purchased the book *Kosmos*. The large volume was written by the great explorer Alexander von Humboldt. Father read out loud to us descriptions of lava-spitting volcanoes and tropical lands, of salty oceans bathing our planet, of celestial bodies lighting the heavens. These images stirred me with *Wanderlust*. Our biggest adventure happened once a year, when our family went to the ruined Limburg Abbey in the hills behind Dürkheim to enjoy the outdoor theater.

The best play so far had been *Life is a Dream* by the Spanish playwright Calderon de la Barca. How I longed to discover, like Segismundo, that I was secretly a prince. What a wonderful dream, to wake up one morning and learn you were someone else entirely. Such fantasies kept my mind occupied during daily toil.

By 1856, my shoulders had touched both walls, although fewer boys had been there to witness the occasion. That summer it rained as if we would never know sunshine again. In the sodden meadows, herders penned the cattle together knee deep in mud, feeding them hay and boiled horse chestnuts rather than letting them tear up the fields. Father, Philipp and I spent hour after hour in the asparagus patch digging ditches to drain the water. At the evening bell, heavy clods of mud clung to our boots as we trod home.

Gradually over the seasons, Mütterchen had grown stronger. As her health improved, I still believed Father might decide to emigrate after all, until my brother tossed a book in my lap.

"I found this among Father's farm ledgers," Philipp said. "Maybe now you'll stop whining about America."

Flipping through *The Emigrant's Catechism*, I saw Father had marked specific passages, about dangers of the ocean voyage, about ships that had sunk in storms. And this:

> Is it possible for persons in poor health to undertake an ocean voyage?
>
> An ocean voyage is best undertaken by strong and healthy individuals, and sick people could hasten their death in most cases, should they expose themselves to the stresses of such a journey. On the ship with which I traveled to America one sick passenger died fifteen minutes after we had left the harbor and were still in sight of the shore, where he was later buried.[3]

"Do you think Father has had this book a long time?" I asked my brother.

"What do you mean?"

"Frau Becker and Mütterchen once spoke of how we would have gone to America with our grandparents the Handrichs, if not for the unborn child."

"*Ach*, I did not think you knew."

"Knew what?"

"That you were the reason we did not make the *Auswanderung.*"

I stared at my brother. "I thought it was because of our baby sister who died."

"You think you're so smart, but in the end you can't put two and two together. The Handrichs left at the end of 1840. You were born in the spring of 1841. Mütterchen was with child with you when her parents and siblings left. Truthfully, I think Father would have gone."

I braced my hands on the chair. "It's *my* fault we did not go to America?"

Philipp shrugged. "*Doch*, I don't blame you. I'm glad we didn't go. Not everyone hates the farm work like you."

"But look how rich our aunts and uncles have become. Johann Rapparlie owns a dray and two horses."

"Shut up, will you? All anyone talks of is America. I say a good neighbor is better than a brother far away."

"They talk of America because it's a place where a man can make his fortune," I said, my same old argument, though my spirit felt as flat as a punctured pig's bladder.

I could hardly believe my bad luck. All along, I had only myself to blame for being stuck here farming, left behind. I had failed my family even before I was born.

In a foul mood, I headed out to the *Gute Brunnen* sulfur well to hear some music, to solace my deflated heart in melody. The *Gute Brunnen* spring, just on the outer edge of Freinsheim's wall, bubbled into a wading pool, its healthful waters attracting the elderly, cripples, paupers, and aristocrats alike. As people gathered on the sandstone benches to soak their limbs, vagabond musicians, the *Schnorranten*, would congregate to play for whoever lent an ear, and possibly tossed a coin.

By this time, my new friend Matthias Höhn and I met there on a regular basis. Born in Deidesheim, Matthias was not an actual son of the Höhns. Although the Freinsheim Höhns had many sons already, they had taken in Matthias, their nephew, when his parents died, one of illness, the other of injury. We had in common the sense we did not belong to our families, me because I did not want to be a farmer, and Matthias because he was an orphan.

During our frequent visits to the *Gute Brunnen*, Matthias and I had taken a liking to Herr Adler, a musician who stood out as much for his talent as he did for his animated facial expressions and his bright rust-colored coat and yellow silk cravat. Matthias and I first met Herr Adler the summer after my disappointment over the Liedmeisters. When we heard him play, we were enraptured. How did his guitar make such a beautiful sound? As the musician took a break, I could not resist going over for a closer look at his guitar.

"You want to learn to play, *Bengel*?" the musician had asked, wiping his brow beneath his round Jewish cap. He also played the violin, I noticed, as the song or the mood suited.

"Yes, but not the guitar. I should like to get an accordion," I said. "It sounds almost like the organ."

"*Aha*, only hymns and church music for you, *Putte*?"

The *Putte* were those cherubs that decorate German fountains and some churches. I knew he was making fun of me, but I didn't mind.

"I like the hymns, but not as much as Susanna Hisgen. You can't pass the

Hisgen yard without hearing, 'What a Friend We Have in Jesus.' I like folk songs, too."

The musician laughed, a sonorous, pleasant sound.

"I want to learn the guitar," said Matthias.

Herr Adler stopped smiling and considered Matthias. "Well then," he said after a moment, as if coming to a decision, "watch my hands carefully, and after a few songs I will let you try."

Herr Adler must have seen something in Matthias, because he turned out to be a fast learner. By the end of that summer, Matthias was able to strum along while Herr Adler played the violin. Other *Schnorranten* also joined in. Sometimes they'd call on me to sing, as they approved of my tenor voice. Herr Adler left his hat out for coins, but very few people showed their appreciation in this manner.

Sometimes, the police arrived at the *Gute Brunnen* to move the players along. I didn't tell my parents about these times. Nonetheless, tongues wag in Freinsheim, and Mütterchen heard from the church *Frauen* that I was singing folk songs with the Jew Herr Adler and the other vagabond musicians.

"What will people think?" she admonished me. "You must stop at once."

But Father took my side. "Elisabetha, until the town council speaks their disapproval, let the boy sing." In this regard, I think Father took to heart Alexander von Humboldt's ideas that all people, Jews, Gypsies, African slaves, and Indians should be treated as equals.

The evening I learned the truth about my birth, both Matthias and Herr Adler were already making music at the well. The warmth of the summer day still lingered in the sandstone of the benches. More than one couple walked side by side, or paused to lean against a linden tree, listening idly to the music while lost in each others' gazes. I sometimes pictured myself walking side by side here with Anna Marie but did not make so bold as to ask her. Even now that I had turned fifteen, I was forever awkward and shy with girls.

I sat sulking the entire evening, until the sun had set and the listeners began to drift away from the benches.

"The Liedmeisters will be at the Herxheim *Kerwe* tomorrow," Herr Adler told us after the last song as he nestled his violin into its case. "I will go, as I have not seen my friend Herr Franck in many years."

"I know Herr Franck," I said, thinking of yet another instance of my endless bad luck.

"Didn't you tell me once he offered to hire you?" Matthias asked.

Herr Adler gazed at us. "So he's also a friend of yours? Why don't we walk there together?"

The next day, in the cool air of morning, I hurried through my chores. Herr Adler, Matthias, and I met on the road to Herxheim and headed off on foot past the grape rows, the fields of cabbages and broad-leafed tobacco baking in the mid-morning sun. In a fine mood, Herr Adler bowed in an exaggerated way to passing villagers, his black hair flopping around on top of his head like a rooster comb. Matthias and I always felt in lighter moods around Herr Adler, who often behaved as if he were on a stage.

"Herr Adler, if you know Herr Franck, why do you not play in his music band?" I asked.

"*Doch*, I played with them for a while, but I am not a man prone to remain with any group. Besides, I don't have a family to feed as those men do. I found that, with so much travel, it was not easy to find a woman and settle down."

I had not considered Herr Adler might be looking for a wife. "But with the Liedmeisters, would you not have a living and a means to marry?"

"Europe is not a good place for the Jews. I want to live where no human being is the subject of a corrupt duchy. In America there is religious freedom. I have saved my money and applied for the paperwork to emigrate."

At this news, any joy the morning held for me evaporated.

"One day I will go to America," Matthias said.

Herr Adler stopped walking. "So you think of this too, to emigrate and try your luck?"

"We both want to go," I said. "It's so dull here. The farm work never ends."

Herr Adler scratched his bearded chin, studying us with dark eyes. "So, you are finished with Freinsheim? You boys believe you have seen all there is to see? Perhaps there is more here than you realize."

"What are you talking about?" I gazed around at the patchwork of vineyards, fields, and orchards, the orange-tiled roofs of our village in the valley below. Taller even than the Catholic Church, the steeple of the Protestant Church pinned the buildings in place like the point of a truncheon.

"Science. In this modern era, we must be true observers of nature in order to see what is before our eyes. Ernst Chladni, this inventor of the euphone, has shown us this. He experimented with acoustics, how music makes invisible patterns."

"Invisible patterns? If they are invisible, how can he know they exist?" Matthias was the more literal of the two of us.

Herr Adler laughed. "Smart boy. But maybe not as smart as you think. Chladni has made an experiment, by sprinkling small particles of sand on a metal plate, then drawing a violin bow across it to make sound vibrations. He wrote about it in his *Theories of Sound*. Beautiful patterns formed on the metal, revealing the invisible waves around us. Even those calls of the *Eichelhäher* birds, as harsh as they are, make a sound pattern."

Herr Adler took out a linen cloth and wiped the sweat from his neck and forehead.

"But what makes the patterns?" Matthias asked.

The musician set down his violin case and pulled out the instrument and bow. "*Guck mal,* I pull my bow across this violin string. See how the string vibrates? It's what makes the sound in our ears; this string movement pushes waves through the air. Chladni has drawn figures to show us some patterns of the different frequencies."

"So there are patterns? What does it matter?" The news that Herr Adler would be leaving made me dull. "I can't see them. I can't feel them."

"You can't feel them? What about when you sing the folk songs with other villagers? Doesn't that lift your heart with a certain sentiment, an organic unity?"

"If my heart lifts or not, what difference does it make? Either way, I am the cause of my family being stuck here. Either way, I am to be an *Ackermann* my entire life."

Herr Adler chuckled. "Are you having a bad day from the start? I am trying to tell you I think of what happens to us now as having just such an invisible pattern. Chladni studied these patterns, why the sand gathered in some places and not others. He found the sand gathered in the points on the metal that did not vibrate. He called these points 'vibration nodes.' So too with this emigration. Some of us move, some of us stay where we are. Those who remain are just as essential to the music as those who go."

I tried to appreciate Herr Adler's point, but in my opinion, no matter whether the patterns existed or not, I was a victim of life forces beyond my control. My restlessness for great adventure was ever-present in my thoughts. If only it would leave me alone, once and for all. Then I wouldn't feel as if I was always missing out on something.

At the *Kerwe* in Herxheim, we followed our ears to the Liedmeister Band rehearsal in the community hall. Slipping inside, I felt the lilting notes vibrate through me, imagined the patterns they made, a wild idea I had never considered before. The band had more musicians now and played in a new, more elegant style, one with less reliance on the low brass instruments, greater stress on the strings and winds. I looked among the musicians for the large shape of Herr Gormann, but did not find him.

"Adler, it's been too long," Herr Franck said, clasping the violinist by the arms.

"The life of the traveling musician serves you well," Herr Adler said, giving a whistle as he looked Herr Franck's wine-colored uniform up and down. "And now you play Beethoven and Schubert! I especially enjoyed the Polonaise."

Herr Franck took in my presence and his eyes lit in recognition. "Could this be Michael Harm of Freinsheim?"

I could not help grinning at this man's round, pleasant face and brown beard, so familiar after all these years. "Herr Franck, I am glad to see you again," I said, removing my cap.

I introduced Matthias, and as Herr Adler and Herr Franck consulted over sheets of music, the two of us wandered through the room studying the instruments set on the benches. Matthias was drawn to a shiny trumpet with a long tongue of brass. I could not take my eyes off a tall cylinder of wood with many keys and a hooked reed mouthpiece. I was so absorbed, I did not notice Herr Franck at my elbow.

"Fine instruments," he said. "Josef Pfaff makes them, the instrument-maker in Kaiserslautern. With our money from the trip to England, we were able to purchase the trombone and bassoon. The Pfaff shop makes them all—the wood, brass and strings. And that," he said, pointing to the brass instrument near Matthias, "is a trombone."

"I have always been sorry I could not travel with you that summer," I said.

"*Doch*, perhaps it would have been too much. You would have rarely seen your parents. We have played in Spain one summer, Italy the next, then Russia. Last year we went to Holland and Scandinavia. Our booking agent makes arrangements now to send us to America. We will give them a fine taste of German music, such as has never before reached their ears."

"Could you use a helper on the trip to America?" Matthias asked.

"I am afraid not, our ticketing agent has already made the arrangements."

Herr Franck rapped with his stick to call the band back to practice, and Matthias and I went outside.

"*Du Sau!*" I burst out, shoving him on the shoulder.

"What's wrong?"

"What's wrong? You ask Herr Franck if *you* can go to America? If they need a helper, I should be the one to go, not you."

"You can't do it, you said so yourself; your family needs you here. Why shouldn't I take the chance? I'm not needed at my uncle's. I'm another mouth to feed."

"*Leck mich am Arsch*," I said. "Kiss my ass. You are no friend of mine."

I stalked into the crowd, leaving Matthias to do as he wished. Just then, I did not care that Matthias had been orphaned. He did well enough with the Höhns.

In the streets of Herxheim, the festival crowds had begun to gather. Smoke curled from outdoor fires, grills hissed with sausage fat. Even so, I fumed in misery, until I happened upon Anna Marie Neufeld serving wine at the stand of her Herxheim relatives. The long braid of her chestnut hair circled her head like a halo, and the fist in my heart unclenched. If I was going to be stuck in Freinsheim, at least it would be in the company of an angel.

Cheered by the thought, I went over to greet her.

"Have you come with your family today?" she asked, taking my *Krug* drinking jug from me and filling it with Rhine wine. Before answering her, I took two healthy gulps, the golden liquid easing my sore head and heart.

"I came early to see Herr Franck of the Liedmeisters. Philipp might come later."

"Will you sing today? You have a good voice."

My head spun, whether from wine or her compliment, I could not say. "*Nä, nä*, I'd prefer to dance with the pretty girl standing before me," I said.

"Leave the dancing to men with some sense, Harm," Emil Oberholz interrupted. I felt a jolt of surprise. I had not noticed the wine-maker's son standing there. Emil Oberholz was Philipp's age, his family one of the wealthiest in our village. "Anna Marie isn't interested in boys with wild fantasies about Indians," he added with a good-humored laugh.

I did my best to laugh with him. I had not worn the Indian vest in many years, but in any case my childhood fantasies had forever fixed my reputation in the minds of Freinsheimers as that of a romantic dreamer.

"How can you be so sure what Anna Marie likes?" I pulled myself to my full height, still a head shorter than Emil. "Perhaps she cares about the wild beauty of the earth and the heavens, a beauty which graces her own."

Emil doubled over laughing. "Next are you going to spout a verse to us? Some melancholy drivel of Kerner? Harm, you're a nut. Look, we're old friends, and your *Krug* is empty. Let me buy you another."

"Michael isn't so thirsty anymore," Anna Marie said, flashing her eyes at me.

I ignored her warning and accepted Emil's offer. If the wine-maker's son chose to be companionable, who was I to object? I toasted my new friend's health. Emil had long been a bully to Philipp and me and the other farmers' sons, but from what I could see, he harassed us out of boredom more than malice. He had brains enough to go to university if he so chose. No doubt he read French and Greek and Latin. Soon our drinking jugs were empty. This time, when I called for another round, Anna Marie refused to sell to us. Undeterred, Emil and I sauntered over to the Oberholz wine stand, where he proceeded to help himself and me to the family cask. When the Liedmeister band struck up in the distance, I did not budge from my place there.

The evening was growing late by the time Philipp appeared. He charged over to Emil and me at the Oberholz wine stand followed by Sebastian Höhn and Richard Pirrmann and a pack of other Freinsheimer lads.

"A Weisenheimer insulted Magdalena Lind," Philipp said, his voice strained with excitement.

I could tell my brother had been drinking too much again. I stood dizzily. Tonight, I might have outdone him.

"Magdalena is crying," Sebastian said, "and can't be consoled."

Emil raised a hand as if swearing an oath. "It's up to us. We must defend her honor!"

As one, we left the Oberholz stand and trooped through the *Kerwe*, eventually discovering the Weisenheimers in a small meadow at the entrance to the village.

"Who is the pig with the foul mouth?" Sebastian shouted at them.

A big lout stepped away from the others. "You little snot, go bother someone you have a chance at whipping."

"*Bankert!* Keep your pig-eyes off Freinsheimer girls."

The lout smirked in the direction of his friends. "Useless drunk."

Like snarling wolves in rival packs, we charged at one another, clawing for any target. Unfortunately for me, the Weisenheimer ogre stood directly in my path and lifted a rope-knot of a fist to greet me. Philipp jumped in to intercept the blow, taking a clean hit to the side of his head. I saw my brother drop to his knees and pummeled against the Weisenheimer to distract him, but the oaf stiff-armed me with ease. Stumbling backward, I tripped and fell, smacking my head. Sharp pain exploded across my vision. As I rolled free of trampling boots, I knew nothing more.

# Chapter 9

THE NEXT MORNING, I AWOKE to a throbbing ache in my skull, my tongue dry as a molting cattail. Boosting up on one elbow, I saw I lay in my own bed. Beside me, Philipp slumbered on top of the covers, a long purple gash above one eye. I shook him awake. He turned toward me, dried blood ringing his nostrils.

"We should get down to the stables before Father sees you," I whispered.

Philipp smiled, then winced. "He already has. Herr Adler, Matthias, and I rolled you home in a wheelbarrow last night. You did not even rouse when we carried you upstairs. How much did you drink? It's Mütterchen, not Father, you should worry about in any case."

I let his words sink in as my brother groped the bridge of his nose with his fingers.

"You look bad," I said.

"I've never felt better."

"*Aha,* you lie, but thanks anyway, for heading off that ogre last night."

We groaned out of bed and went down to feed the animals in the fetid cloak of the barn. When the bell rang to go to the fields, Mütterchen kept me behind for a scolding, telling me how ashamed she was, how the villagers would all think the Harm sons were *Luftikus,* soft and easy-going, lacking in moral discipline.

At last she released me. Thickheaded and unsteady, I straggled down Wallstrasse toward the fields. I had just passed through the *Eisentor* when Emil Oberholz fell in step beside me, his blond hair and earth-brown eyes bright, his visage merry, as if we would soon be laughing again. He threw an arm over my shoulder. As we walked together, my short legs had difficulty matching his lanky stride.

"Harm, what fun we had last night," he said. Even with a fat lower lip, he looked handsome. "Sebastian saw you go down. How's your head?"

"Harder than a rock."

Emil guffawed. "The next time you come to the *Rathskeller*, you must sit with me."

Emil meant sit with "us," the table where he and his comrades talked politics and winemaking night after night. It was an honor to be included, as a lowly *Ackermann*, among these educated and wealthy *Wingertsleit*. I assured Emil I might indeed join him and the other winemaker's sons. I might join him so often he'd grow sick of me. He laughed and we parted in good humor.

The whole village knew by noontime of our drunken rumble against the Weisenheimers. Philipp may not have gotten in trouble with Mütterchen, but he suffered sorely under the severe silence of Susanna Hisgen. For weeks afterward, my brother mooned at Susanna across the church aisle, but she never once turned her head in his direction.

Philipp changed for good then. He left the *Rathskeller* early and took to studying his Bible before bed. Even so, I did not see Susanna and my brother walking together until the end of the summer, the evening Herr Adler told me his emigration paperwork had come through. After Herr Adler left Freinsheim, Matthias and I became friends again, forgiving one another our harsh words in Herxheim. In any event, it was hard to be left behind.

IT SEEMED THE WINEMAKER'S SON Emil had other reasons for keeping me close, reasons I did not understand until the Christmas dance that year. When it came time for the traditional "Lo, How a Rose E'er Blooming," the mayor invited me up to lead the singing, announcing me as Michael Harm, the Freinsheimer with the "fine tenor voice." I had just finished dancing with Anna Marie. She looked beautiful that evening in a red velvet dress with black-and-white twisted brocade on the collar and cuffs. I squeezed her hand and walked to the front of the hall.

My heart bursting with adoration for my beloved, I stood before the Freinsheimers in their holiday finery and sang only for Anna Marie, my blooming rose. As we started the second verse, I noticed Emil Oberholz at her side. I watched him reach down and clasp her hand. Anna Marie's cheeks flushed as red as her dress, but she did not push him away. I continued singing, but the faces in the community hall blurred as if a fog had entered the room.

I had believed I loved Anna Marie for her beauty and the purity of her convictions, for her piety, her love of family and Freinsheim, and for her love for me, a lowly farmer's son. Now my head swam in jealousy and confusion. Did Anna Marie love Emil, not me?

At the end of the song, I hardly felt the thumps of congratulation on my back. My mind was a chaotic scramble, too busy remembering past encounters with Emil, how he'd gotten me drunk at Herxheim and lured me away from the Neufeld wine stand, how he'd danced with Anna Marie at least as often as I had these past months.

That night the veil of my devotion was torn away, and I doubted everything that had gone before. Was Anna Marie only tolerating me out of the goodness of her heart? Were she and Emil conspiring behind my back as a couple, laughing at my foolish sentiments? My innermost feelings of love crushed to a bitter powder, I left the community hall before the singing of "Silent Night."

Back home, Philipp was already in our bedchamber, jumping up and down in a gleeful mood. I slumped down on the bed.

"What's wrong, little brother?" he asked, pawing at my hair.

I pushed his hand away. "You're an ass."

Philipp took his suspenders from the chair back, bound me up and wrestled me to the floor. "Take it back. You're the ass, braying in front of everyone with your singing."

"Get off me, you crazy drunk."

"Drunk? I am not drunk. I am the luckiest man in Freinsheim."

"*Scheiße!* Must I listen to this?" I sighed in leaden despair. "Fine, tell me. No, let me guess. You proposed marriage to Susanna, *oder*?"

Philipp leaped to his feet with a look that reminded me of the prim Susanna herself. "Of course I did not propose marriage. I have no property to make such an offer. But I am sure of her love."

"*Aha,* your lips have touched hers in a loving kiss?"

Philipp turned red in the neck, clutched at his heart and collapsed on the bed in a swoon. My misery was complete.

# Chapter 10

## Freinsheim, Bavarian Palatinate, 1857

IN THE DARK COLD DAYS of the new year of 1857, life itself seemed to freeze over. To pass the dull evenings, I read Goethe's novel, *The Sorrows of Young Werther,* which Matthias loaned me from Herr Höhn 's library. The book was a fitting match to my gloomy state. Like Werther, I wallowed in the infinite suffering of unrequited love. I came to believe it was my destiny to suffer, the dutiful homespun farmer Michael Harm hoeing alone in the fields, never to be united with his true love. I pined over Anna Marie to Matthias until he begged me never to speak her name again.

Then one day in April, a fresh wind blew in from the West. Philipp and I returned from the still-muddy fields for the noon dinner to find Father and Mütterchen in the kitchen with a stranger. Father held a letter in his hands, skimming it with wide, wondering eyes. Mütterchen sat across from him with a trembling chin. Because my parents were distracted, the stranger stood and introduced himself.

"Handrich. Franz Handrich of Buffalo, New York," he said. He wore clothes of broadcloth, a silk cravat tied loosely at his shirt collar. "I bring greetings to you from your *Onkel* Johann and *Tante* Katharina Rapparlie, in Cleveland, Ohio," he said, sitting back down.

Philipp leaned back against the sideboard with a self-satisfied smile, arms crossed over his chest. Franz Handrich wore his shock of long brown hair combed straight back from his forehead, his blond-hued mustache and beard carefully combed.

"Franz Handrich is the grandson of my father's cousin," Mütterchen said, lines of worry etched across her forehead. She did not take her eyes from Father. "*Bitte* Johann Philipp, what does it say? I fear bad news."

I sat down at the table, where five places were set for the meal. Philipp slogged into the front room to bring in another chair, as the American sat in his usual one.

"This letter is old, dated a year ago." Father gave Franz Handrich a questioning glance.

The American shrugged. "Rapparlie said that what with one thing and another, he'd never taken it to the post office. They've had much trouble this past year."

Father glanced at Mütterchen. "*Ach so,* I will read it."

> Cleveland, 30 April, 1856
> Much loved brother-in-law and sister-in-law,
>
> As I am having a good opportunity to write some lines to you, I want to tell you about how we have been here. I am still alive and have my health like before but my foot has been taken from me approximately 12 inches beneath the knee, and I laid down approximately 21 months on the sick bed. I have needed a special doctor, a professor from the university who never pays a visit to anyone sick or injured for less than $5. He came in the beginning 3 times a day because I was so dangerously sick. At the beginning I did not want to admit my leg had to be removed. I kept saying, better to remove my head than my foot. But when I looked at my 3 young boys and my wife, then my heart became heavy, and I gave in. The doctors have removed my leg as I lay on the edge of life and death.
>
> Dear brother-in-law and sister-in-law, I have supported more than a beast of burden ever could. With all of that my house burned down on me, too, almost burning me alive in my sickbed. Thanks be to God, I am almost as healthy as before but I have to walk with two crutches. I am having an artificial foot made in Philadelphia which will cost $150, not counting traveling to that city for the fitting.
>
> With the old people gone—

Mütterchen moaned into her apron. "Both parents dead? But I knew it! I could feel it, remember Father? The rattling at the window that night? Oh, my dear Mama and Papa. Gone to the heavenly beyond. I pray they did not suffer. I wonder if Mama made it to her 70th year." Mütterchen faded at this last. She looked around in desolation, pale and rocking in her straight-backed chair. I had never met my grandparents, but I felt heavy with grief for Mütterchen. After a long moment, she lifted her handkerchief to dab at her eyes. "*Es tut mir leid, Mann.* Please keep reading. I must hear the rest."

Father found his place and resumed.

With the old people gone, Jakob is working all the more and is still unmarried. He earns a large wage now, 2 dollars a day, working in a place where they make locomotives and steam engines.

Dear brother-in-law and sister-in-law, I must write you news of Johannes. I do not know exactly how to express what happened, he suffered a lassitude of his body, perhaps because the heat is very big in the summer here, so his blood rebelled within him and he has lost his senses. He became melancholic and then, 1 ½ years later suddenly he stopped and said he would make a journey that would be his last. He put on his best clothes and a new coat and that was the last time we saw him.

Last year I have rebuilt my house which had been burned down … $2,700. My business goes quite well. I have now 4 shops with 8 smiths, 5 woodworkers, 3 painters and 2 trimmers.

Our brother-in-law Scheuermann is still quite healthy and he and his wife have two boys. He no longer works in barrel-making—he has gone to work for the same factory as Jakob.

My family is all quite healthy and we stay yours faithfully.

John Rapparlie

As Franz Handrich carries this letter from us, he will tell the rest in his own words. He is a brick mason who has built our new house, and you can believe what he says.

Father set down the letter. Still weeping, Mütterchen rose to her feet and made her way slowly up the stairs. The four of us watched her go in respectful silence, then gazed around at the meats and cheese and bread. After a few moments, Father reached for the plate of *Schwarzbrot* and we began our meal.

"In this letter, Rapparlie signs his name 'John,' " Father observed, passing the rye bread to Franz Handrich.

Our visitor nodded. "It's the American name for Johann."

"So what brings you back to the Palatinate?" Philipp asked. "From our experience, people usually travel the other direction."

"I return here to collect my bride," Franz said.

Philipp froze with his soup spoon mid-air. "*Wie bitte?*"

"A man who does the trimming in the John Rapparlie wagon shop has told me of his niece. This *Fräulein* is older, but pretty enough, he says. But many men have left Bobenheim in the *Auswanderung*, and the others are very poor, so this Barbara Metzger has not found a husband. At Herr Metzger's suggestion, I have written to her. The family has now invited me for a visit to meet her in person. If everyone is agreeable, we shall be married."

Unlike Philipp and me, Father didn't seem to find this pronouncement so remarkable, instead turning the subject to our grandparents and how they had spent their last days. Our cousin told Father what he had heard, that they had died within a year of one another without hard suffering. Of Mütterchen's brother Johannes, Franz Handrich knew the same as what was reported in the letter.

Later in the evening, Philipp and I took our visitor to the *Rathskeller*, which gave me a chance to ask questions of my own.

"If you live in Buffalo, how is it that you carry messages from Cleveland?"

"In America, journeymen don't need a *Wanderbuch* passport to travel. I can ply my trade anywhere I like. I went to Cleveland to work for a summer because I did not find a girl in Buffalo."

"But you did not find a wife in Cleveland either?"

My question was not answered, as we just then entered the *Rathskeller* and headed for our usual table of comrades.

"Franz here has traveled all the way from Buffalo, New York, to fetch his bride," Philipp announced, loud enough for all to hear.

Matthias Höhn sat forward. "This is why you have come here?" He sat back with a dismissive wave of his hands. "I am sorry, you must go back home. All of the *Fräuleins* in Freinsheim are taken. And the ones in Erpolzheim. And in Kallstadt. And Herxheim, and … not in Weisenheim. You may have any of those."

The tavern of men erupted in laughter.

Franz laughed along. "The *Fräulein* I hope to marry lives in Bobenheim. For your information, she invited me here." He raised his *Krug*. "Here's to the German *Fräuleins!*"

We drank deeply and thumped our drinking jugs on the table. Matthias wiped his whiskers on his sleeve.

"A great mystery, indeed. So tell us how this happened."

With a grin, Franz enthralled his new audience with the story.

"Marry a woman you've never set eyes on?" Matthias stared at my American cousin in disbelief.

Franz shrugged. "I'm no dummy. I'll set eyes on her first."

"But what's wrong with the girls in America?" I asked.

"I haven't found any who suited me. There aren't as many German women as men coming to make a new life there."

"But what of the American girls? The English-speakers. Aren't any of them pretty?" Matthias asked.

"*Doch*, they turn up their noses at the Germans." Franz gazed around at us with a bitter smile. "You're surprised? But it's of no consequence. The

American women are outspoken and puritanical, and don't make good housekeepers. They hold their meetings of the women's society. Many forbid drinking and smoking in the home."

"*Pff!* The men go along with this?"

"Some support it. In the last American election there was a man running for President, a Gerrit Smith, who gave a speech in favor of the female sex, how they also should have the right to vote. His Liberty Party got very few votes."

For the rest of the evening, Franz regaled us with stories of America, of fiery smelters in the steamboat factories, of enormous lakes of fresh water, of a Niagara waterfall near his city of Buffalo that thundered like ten thousand horses. Philipp left early, as usual, but I hung on to my cousin's every word until the Bavarian police came to close the tavern.

"So what about this Johann Rapparlie?" I asked Franz. We were making our way home in the moonlit street. "Is he as wealthy as it seems from his letter?"

"He is indeed a wealthy man," Franz said. "Why do you ask? Do you think of coming back with me?"

At this question, I felt the familiar longing but pushed the thought away, joking instead to hide my true feelings. "You forget," I said, "you will have your betrothed, Barbara Metzger to accompany you. If you are confused in any way about this, let me assure you, I am not her."

Franz guffawed loudly.

"*Guck mal,*" I warned in a hoarse whisper. "Be quiet, or tomorrow morning Pfarrer Bickes will knock at our door."

With exaggerated stealth we tiptoed the rest of the way home.

The next morning Franz Handrich went on his way blessed by our well-wishes for good fortune with his future bride. But instead of going to the fields at the first bell, Father called us back to the table.

"Herr Rapparlie has written more in this letter than what I read to you yesterday evening," Father said, his face long and somber. His eyes fell on me, then Mütterchen, then came to rest on Philipp. "Something we must consider. The wagon-maker has asked if I might send my eldest son to Cleveland when Franz Handrich voyages back to America. Rapparlie needs a blacksmith apprentice. With his wooden leg, and his sons not yet grown, the wagon-maker says he needs one. Franz assures me Rapparlie is a master craftsman with an excellent reputation."

I glanced over at my brother, whose beard had grown into a woolly brown wreath under his chin. His mouth was set in a thin line.

"But you said nothing about this to me, *Mann*," Mütterchen said. "Philipp does not have the paperwork to leave. What if he's arrested at the border?"

"Elisabetha, that hasn't happened to anyone in our village. Franz Handrich assures me the French will look the other way." Father gazed at Mütterchen sorrowfully. "We must face the truth. Philipp will soon be liable for military conscription. He should leave before this happens."

"Father, are you mad?" Philipp's eyes were flashing, his face white. "You need me for the farm work."

Philipp did not speak of his love for Susanna, which I believed to be his real reason.

"I will go," I heard myself say, emotions swirling inside me like the spinning spokes of a wagon wheel. Was it possible? Could I change my destiny after all?

Philipp shoved at me. "*Du Dummbeidel.* You're an airhead. Our family doesn't have the money to send either of us. The apprenticeship fee is more than we can afford."

At the truth of his words, I felt overcome by helplessness. It was not meant to be.

Father removed his cap and rubbed a thumb on his forehead. "It's strange, but Franz Handrich tells me the Americans don't require such a large fee. They even pay some apprentices a small allowance. He said Herr Rapparlie will accept a cask of Rhine wine in payment, but we don't have to send it right away."

"But where would Philipp live?" Mütterchen asked, her head scarf trembling around the edges of her pale face.

"At the Rapparlie home, the house of your sister and husband in Cleveland. They offer room and board. Franz also escorts others to America: a brother and sister from Rheingöhnheim, and a son of a carriage-maker from Standenbühl. Each of them pay Franz Handrich eighty *Gulden* for the journey."

"*Tch,* so much." Mütterchen's hands dropped limply to her lap.

"In that price is five *Gulden* for Franz's services, plus all billets and lodging covered. In a fortnight, Franz returns to Freinsheim on his way to France. Philipp will leave with him then."

My brother stared at our father as if he were a simpleton.

"But how will you manage?"

Father would not meet Philipp's eyes. "Michael is here. And the Catholic Herr Raffel has asked for work. If we must, we'll hire a day laborer."

"I will go," I said again. I could not keep quiet. "Philipp should stay. He *likes* the farm work."

Father's face was gaunt above his gray-brown beard. The next words from his mouth stunned us all. "Michael, perhaps you are right. Perhaps it is God's will that you do this thing."

My spirit soared in elation.

"*Wie bitte?*" Philipp flipped his palms in exasperation. "No one must go!

Mütterchen?! Tell Father this is madness."

Mütterchen bit her lip, her moist eyes reproachful. But the cords of Father's neck were standing out, a sure sign he could not be dissuaded.

"*Nä, nä*, Philipp, don't you see? We must face the truth. Our land isn't large enough to support two families. Every season, the farm ledgers bear worse news. Elisabetha, surely you don't believe our grandchildren should live as poorly as the potato eaters. It's lucky for us that we have this chance. It will improve life for both our sons."

Philipp stood and paced about the kitchen. "Perhaps if we planted different crops, grew tobacco for cash, planted another vineyard row?"

Father shook his head. "*Doch,* I have watched the two of you grow into men. I see the restlessness in my youngest son."

"Send Michael alone?" Philipp ran one hand through his hair, then placed both hands on his hips. "He's but fifteen! He can't be trusted on his own."

"I will be sixteen next month," I put in.

"We don't know Franz so well, but he is family," Father said, his eyes following Philipp as he resumed his pacing. "And Rapparlie assures us in his letter that the brick mason is to be trusted. I fear there won't be such a chance again." Father turned to me. "Michael, you must be sure. This is a very big duty you take on."

I looked at Father as if from a great distance, as if I already traveled away from him down the road. The idea of leaving twisted me inside—a mix of excitement, sadness, fear and yearning. It had been so long since I allowed myself to dream.

"I think … I should like the blacksmith work," I said at last.

Father turned to Mütterchen. "If it doesn't work out, he can always return."

"But you can see for yourself he's too scrawny, not fit for blacksmithing." Philipp's eyes were red-rimmed with tears. "And how will we get the money to pay a day laborer, let alone eighty *Gulden* to send him to America?"

"For shame, Philipp," Mütterchen said. "If it's God's will, it's not for human beings to decide."

Father's blue eyes were steady and resolute. "As a blacksmith, a man has a skill that will be of value anywhere in the world. Well, Michael?"

I felt angry at Philipp for saying I was not fit. I clenched my jaw with determination. "I will go. I will serve as Johann Rapparlie's apprentice and learn the blacksmith living."

Philipp opened his mouth again, but Father put up his hand. "Philipp, you have said your piece. You don't want to go, so it is Michael who will go to America. He will leave in a fortnight with Franz Handrich. I will write today to Johann Rapparlie that he should expect him. That we send only one of us is God's doing."

My heart hammered under my ribs as it never had before. Was it jubilation or terror making it beat so fast? My life had been turned upside down in an instant, so I hardly knew what was happening. But I felt in my bones this was the right thing for me. At last I had the chance to claim my own destiny.

The decision made, the most urgent problem the Harms faced was that soon there would be one less man to help with the spring planting. So despite the enormity of changes to come, a short time later, I shouldered my hoe as I had a thousand times before and walked with Father and Philipp through the *Eisentor* gate for a long day's work in the fields.

# Chapter 11

⸺⸱ᵅᵗ⸱⸺

DURING MY LAST WEEK IN Freinsheim, much like Segismundo in the play *Life is a Dream*, I did not know whether I woke or slept. As I coped with the excitement and uncertainty ahead, I had to bid farewell to many good friends.

When I broke the news to Matthias, he gaped at me with a mixture of envy and betrayal.

"Did you ask this Franz Handrich if he'd take me across, too?" he asked.

I felt my face redden; I hadn't thought of my friend at all. "I don't go for free—it's costing Father eighty *Gulden*."

I had not spoken with Father about the money, I realized then, which he no doubt had to borrow on my behalf at a burdensome rate of interest. And that morning as I'd left our *Hof*, Mütterchen had been sewing my new travel clothes. She'd shown me the extra pocket she'd hidden inside my breeches to protect my money from thieves. These clothes were an additional expense we could ill afford.

"*Alla*, I'm coming right behind you," Matthias said, his hazel eyes dark with determination. "I'll save my money and leave as soon as possible."

I dearly hoped my friend spoke the truth. "Come to Cleveland, and I will welcome you. What a great time we'll have in the land of liberty."

What an ache of grief I felt as I imagined parting from my family and friends. And from Anna Marie. I had not spoken to her since I saw Emil holding her hand at Christmas, but of late, I began to wonder if they truly were a couple. They did not act like one, at least not like Philipp and Susanna, who met often to stroll under the blossoming plum and cherry trees.

Had I made a mistake? Did Anna Marie care for me after all, as I'd once believed? The Festival of the Maypole drew near, and all at once, before it was too late, I had to know for sure.

Which is how, on the thirtieth of April, 1857, I came to be walking in my new linen shirt and travel breeches toward the Neufeld home on Hauptstrasse. In my hand, I carried a bachelor gift for Anna Marie, which I intended to leave secretly at her door as was the custom. But just as I came to the front stoop, a face appeared at the window. Frozen on the first step, I watched the heavy door creak open.

"Michael, is that you?" Anna Marie stood on the threshold wearing a beautiful dress made of cloth from France, a colorful pattern of lines and squares with a white collar and cuffs. A wreath of flowers crowned her lustrous braid. "I've been hoping to see you."

I removed my cap, my ears growing warm. "And I you."

"Why don't you come in? Mother will welcome you, and serve us wine and cookies."

"*Bitte* thank her, and greet your whole family, but I only came to tell you, I'm leaving for America soon to apprentice as a blacksmith in my uncle's wagon shop."

A slight smile lifted the corners of her pink lips. "We're a small village. I've already heard this news. That's why I wanted to see you. I didn't want you to go without saying goodbye."

"I'm leaving in a few days' time. I came to bring you this."

Anna Marie accepted the present I handed her. She untied the pink bow, letting the ribbon flutter to the ground, and lifted the box lid. She took the frame and held it up for both of us to see, a scene made of the dried flowers I'd been saving and pressing for years among the pages of our family Bible.

"You made this?" she asked. I read kindness in her gaze, and something else. Sadness? Love? "It's beautiful!"

"Those are the blue flowers from the Festival of the Maypole," I said, pointing them out. "Remember? We were children, and you told me not to pick more? They're the most faded after so many years. But I've included other flowers as well to make the meadow. The little lambs are made from milkweed."

Anna Marie laughed with delight, a silvery ripple that filled me with happiness. "A thousand times, thank you. It is a precious gift by which to remember you." She hugged the oval frame over her heart, a gesture that lit a flame of hope in mine.

"Anna Marie, there's no reason you should care for me, or wait for me to have property and a living, but I can't keep quiet any longer. My heart is yours."

My beloved's face fell. Her eyes darted about as if she were agitated, or embarrassed. "You're declaring your love?"

"My heart has always been yours. Surely, you know this? I love you."

"But you're going to America."

"I can't help it. Father sends me without warning. But say the word and I'll come back for you."

Anna Marie glanced up and down the street, her eyebrows pinching into a crease. "But then you'll be liable for military duty."

"You misunderstand me. If I come back, it will be to bring you to America like Franz Handrich does with Barbara Metzger of Bobenheim." I searched Anna Marie's eyes for a sign of her love. "Could you consider such a thing, for us?"

Anna Marie sighed. "Why are the men who love me so impractical?"

"I'm being practical. If you love me too, why must we wait? I'm going so far away, for at least three years. In America, there are no laws saying one must own property to marry. I promise you, I won't be a good-for-nothing. I will make something of myself."

Anna Marie frowned at me, her cheeks flaming red. "Michael, ever since I've known you, your heart has run away with your head. To me, Freinsheim is the most wonderful place of all." Her face crumpled as if she were in pain. "You have always wanted to leave. I have always wanted to stay. *Geh mit Gott,* Michael."

Anna Marie turned and went inside. She did not look back as she closed the door.

Stung, I made my way home. What could she mean, the men who loved her were impractical? What *men*? Had Emil also declared his love? Of course as a farmer's son I did not stand a chance against Emil. In my passion, I'd once again played the fool.

All at once, I felt an urgency to be on my way, to put this great humiliation behind me.

DURING MY REMAINING DAYS IN Freinsheim, I gazed with nostalgia on the crumbling village walls, the grapevines adorning them, feeling as if I were already gone. I worked hard to help my father and brother finish with the planting, my fingernails caking with mud, the hot spring sun warming my back.

Pausing in the fields to ease the muscle cramps in my back, I relished the sight of Freinsheimer women wearing brown aprons and white head scarves as they walked barefoot, carrying bundles of branches on their heads. I reveled in the hoarse, fluting trills of the starlings, the growls and bellowing laughter of the farmers. Every so often, I even caught a ghost-like glimpse of my childhood self hopping through the grape rows behind Father in my fringed leather vest, dreaming of the wild, untamed places of America. It seemed impossible such a romantic idyll lay in my future.

The farewells mounted, the lingering becoming its own kind of torture. When something must end, it only adds to the pain of everyone to draw it out. I didn't really believe I'd be gone forever, feeling certain I could return after my apprenticeship ended. If I made a wage as large as my uncles in Cleveland, I could return any time I wanted.

FRANZ HANDRICH ARRIVED IN AN overnight post coach with his bride-to-be Barbara Metzger and it was time to go. As I packed my rucksack in our bedchamber, Philipp sat on our bed observing my progress with skeptical silence. Since the news went out I was leaving, Freinsheimers had been carrying letters to our *Hof*—quietly of course, so as not to alert the authorities—for me to deliver in person in New York City and Cleveland. There were so many I was having difficulty stowing them among my other belongings.

"You shouldn't go," Philipp said. "Father has had to borrow the money from Herr Oberholz. We'll be in debt for years to pay for you. Mütterchen has been crying all week. She believes we'll never see you again."

I was not oblivious to the burden of grief I brought to Mütterchen. Then too, Father had shown me the farm ledgers and insisted it would be as big a burden if I stayed.

"Not such a loss," I said, laughing so I wouldn't cry. "Without the useless second son around to ruin the harvest, I predict the Harm family will see a year of abundance."

I did not add that I thought Father preferred to keep Philipp by his side rather than me.

My brother did not smile. "You think you hate farm work, but blacksmithing will be harder than you think. You are scrawny and small, always reading your books and singing in the pubs, dreaming so much you don't know what's real. Johann Rapparlie writes of so many misfortunes. I fear the same will happen to you. In the *Rathskeller,* the men say the banks in America fail every year."

I gazed at Philipp, at my brother's face brown from the spring fieldwork, his shirt and breeches dusty from the fields. His worsted socks had permanent streaks of dirt at the toes. Philipp had always been this way, attached to the soil, with only a faint interest in the wider world.

"Well then, oh Superior One," I said, my voice as hearty as I could make it, "explain to me the many families who have left Freinsheim for the New World and sent back letters of a large, empty land with room for all. And who has returned? Answer me that. The world is not so unwelcoming as you think."

"Uncle's last letter said, 'Things have never been so bad as they are now.' "

"*Pff!* Why do you try to hold me here? My going means more land for you."

"I'm willing to share it. We'd come up with a way to increase the yield. I hope this is not your real reason."

I shook my head, touched that Philipp should care so much. Despite our differences, it seemed he would miss me as dearly as I would miss him. From the open window, greetings rang out in the street as Herr Oberholz arrived with his wagon to bring Franz, Barbara and me as far as Neustadt.

"This is my chance, brother, and I intend to take it," I said. "When I'm gone and can no longer look after you, don't try to fight any Weisenheimer ogres from the Grimm's fairy tales."

We laughed, but I spoke only half in jest. Secretly, I felt reassured Susanna Hisgen would be here to keep my brother in check. In some ways, she was good for him.

Philipp stood and ran a paw across my hair. "Who is taking care of whom here? Don't forget I'm your elder."

"Wait and see, soon I'll be an important blacksmith in America, everyone coming to me to solve their problems, to fix old things and make new ones. I'll have a beautiful woman by my side and children to bounce on my knees. Who knows? If I prove my worth as a blacksmith, Uncle Rapparlie might even teach me in wagon-making."

Philipp snorted. "*Ja*, and you will strike gold, and be elected president of the United States. Ha! I will miss your foolish dreaming." He held out his hoe-callused hand, his blue eyes open and honest, vulnerable and pleading. "Brother, I wish you well in America. Don't forget us here in Freinsheim."

I knocked his arm aside and squeezed him in a bear hug. Pushing away, I felt tears prickling my nose. I blinked to clear my eyes.

"Once you hear what a grand life I lead, I'll convince you to come and join me. Then I'll be happiest of all."

We went downstairs, where Father and Mütterchen awaited me in the kitchen. Father handed me the eighty *Gulden*, which I put in my secret breeches pocket. As I did so, I said a silent prayer to God that the Harms of Freinsheim would not be ruined on my account. Father held out his gold pocket watch in his burly palm, flipped it open, and showed me how it should not be wound too tight, how to reset the time if it stopped.

"It will bring you good luck on the sea journey," he said, pressing the gold circle into my palm.

I pushed it back in horror. "*Nä, nä*, Father! You do not mean to give this to me?"

"This is the one luxury I bought with the extra *Gulden* I received after the death of Grandfather Harm. Don't let the saltwater ruin it. Keep it always wrapped in the oil cloth."

"*Nä nä,* this is too great a gift. I will not be gone forever."

Father closed his large-veined hand over mine that held the watch. "Only God knows for certain. It will be yours someday in any case, son."

Mütterchen came close then and clamped my arms against my body, which was exactly what I needed since I felt as if I might break apart.

"God's grace be with you, Michael," she said. She released me and pulled a black leather-bound book from her apron pocket. "Here is a travel Bible. Promise me you will not forget the Holy Scriptures and the goodness of Christ."

I promised. And so I rode out of Freinsheim on the back of Herr Oberholz's wagon, my leather rucksack containing Father's pocket watch, one change of clothes, several books, a flagon of wine and food from Mütterchen, plus letters for the Beckers, the Auls, the Ritthalers, the Höhns, and of course, our Cleveland relatives.

As the wagon pulled out of the village, Matthias ran after us.

"Remember, I am coming soon," he shouted, stopping at the top of the rise.

On the way to Neustadt, Franz and his wife-to-be sat up on the wagon seat beside Herr Oberholz. I had caught glimpses of Barbara Metzger as we loaded the wagon, her brown eyes calm, her sand-colored hair worn in two neat braids behind her ears. She was plain looking, but nice enough. I admit to a great deal of curiosity about a woman who would agree to marry a man she did not know and voyage so far away from her home. With a rush of melancholy, I regretted that Anna Marie was not by my side. Would I find someone to love in America, or would I be alone the rest of my days?

# Chapter 12

## New York City, 1857

THAT FIRST WEEK ON ELIZABETH Street, as I lay recovering from my injury, Gretel and I fell into conversation about our childhood days in Freinsheim. I shared stories with her about Arnica, who'd grown fat and lazy with age. However, it took me several days to find the nerve to confide my heartbreak over Anna Marie. I complained that Anna Marie cared only for Emil Oberholz, while skipping over the part about my ill-fated proposal. Such an impulsive act, I feared, would not be regarded favorably.

Gretel lent a sympathetic ear but soon lost patience with my moping.

"What you need is outings," she said firmly. "I have so much to show you in *Kleindeutschland*. Won't you escort me?"

At first, I stepped into the street somewhat cautiously, but as Gretel guided me away from the Five Points area, east and north into the heart of the German neighborhood, I began to feel more at ease. The beer gardens lining the streets, the musicians, and multitude of shops with German names, all made the city seem not as alien. Indeed, it struck me in many ways as a place of culture and refinement.

On our first outing, Gretel spent a good deal of time in a shop that carried ribbons, buttons, and other sewing notions while I browsed in a store next door that sold all manner of sheet music, so many choices of songs I was glad I did not have the money to decide on one. We also went to the docks for the breeze, and to observe the busy comings and goings of boats.

The sight of the boats reminded me of my duty to continue to Cleveland, and I knew it was time to act. As soon as I returned to Elizabeth Street I requested from Frau Becker a piece of paper, a quill and a jar of ink in order to write a letter to my Uncle Johann and Aunt Katharina Rapparlie.

"A man claiming to know me has led me around in New York and taken all my last money," I wrote. "I had $20 but now it is gone. If you will send the $10 to Herr Becker of Elizabeth Street, New York, I will repay you once I come to Cleveland."

I wrote this message burdened with heavy guilt for my failures on this trip. For how much I had lost, first on the boat, now in the city. In some ways it felt as if my failings were a message from God, a warning that coming to America was never meant to be. I did not dare to think about what would happen if Uncle Rapparlie refused my plea.

Herr Becker took the letter with him to mail the next morning. For my part, once I had written it, I realized I was breathing my last moments of freedom before starting my indenture. From then on, I escorted Gretel into *Kleindeutschland* as often as I could. She took me past the tall columns of the Bowery Theatre. I listened with great interest to her descriptions of the plays and concerts she'd seen there. We strolled arm in arm through Tompkins Square where many German families gathered with their children to enjoy the benches and shade of tall trees.

Gretel also brought me to a portrait shop where the new tintype photographs were being made, a true marvel, this invention that attached life-like portraits to pieces of metal. Gretel paid for me to have my tintype taken. She meant for me to send it back to my family in Freinsheim, but in the end I could not part with the little black box. Each time I gazed on my likeness in its ornamental copper frame and bed of red velvet, I gained confidence. *This is me in America*, I thought. *If God allows it, I will soon be a blacksmith, and make my living.*

The second Sunday of my stay with the Beckers, Gretel's cheeks blushed pink at the visit of Nikolaus Lindemann, a young man twenty years of age, well-dressed in a dark shirt and blue coat. We sat in the front room as Frau Becker served glasses of Rhine wine for the men and the drink called "lemonade" for herself and Gretel.

"How long have you been in America?" I asked Nikolaus.

"I am American born," he replied. "It's my *parents* who emigrated here, from the Grand Duchy of Baden, in 1833. My father is a grocer, but I study medicine at the university. I plan to be a doctor one day."

Nikolaus had such serious goals, I felt a need to impress him.

"I hope to go into the wagon-making business," I said.

"How so?"

"I am to apprentice at my uncle's wagon shop in Cleveland."

"As a wagon-maker?"

"*Doch*, as a blacksmith, but I intend to learn all aspects of the business. Who can say? Perhaps fortune will favor me."

"Even as a blacksmith, you will do well," Gretel said kindly. "Veit makes a good living at Ezra Stratton."

A FEW DAYS LATER, HERR BECKER came home with a reply from my uncle. Johann Rapparlie had agreed to wire the ten dollars for the train fare and instructed me to come to Cleveland without delay. I pretended not to see the relief on the faces of Herr and Frau Becker at this news.

"Michael, we are happy to see you again after so many years, but your Uncle Johann expects you," Frau Becker said. "I'm sure you will be a help to him in his shop."

I spoke my heartfelt thanks to these old friends for their good care of me. After supper, Herr Becker took out a map for the Erie Railroad and spread it across the table to advise me on the journey.

Two days later, at first light, the Beckers and I walked through the Five Points on the way to the Jersey City Ferry, my first time in the slum since my arrival in America. It had not rained in over a week, and the July heat was so intense that people were lying out on shed roofs, porches, and balconies, sleeping all night under the sky, to escape the stifling heat inside the buildings. Such a strange place, New York City, so much humanity packed together. All at once, I looked forward to the train journey, to entering the green countryside once more.

I still carried my travel rucksack, so much lighter than when I first began my journey from Freinsheim. During my stay in *Kleindeutschland,* I had been wearing Herr Becker's clothes, but now I wore my homespun again, carefully mended by Frau Becker. These clothes felt out of place here where everyone wore broadcloth. I felt my poverty keenly. At the docks, Herr Becker generously went over to buy my ferry ticket while Frau Becker wandered over to the hawkers' carts.

"I will never forget you and the kindness of your family," I told Gretel. "And I believe I have guessed your secret. Soon, I expect to receive a letter announcing your marriage to Nikolaus Lindemann."

Gretel blushed. "He has told me he will talk to Father before Christmastime."

"He's a good match for you. I will write home and tell my parents: Gretel Becker has married a doctor!"

"Hush, not so loud. And he's not a doctor yet."

"Your friend Anna Marie will be glad for you."

Gretel pouted her lips in thought. "I miss her. I did not want to come to America, you know."

"I remember," I said. "I tried to convince you it would be a great adventure."

Gretel laughed. "Some adventure. I haven't traveled farther than this city. It is my turn to envy you."

"Perhaps one day you and Nikolaus will visit me in Cleveland?"

She looked doubtful. "I cannot say. But I wish you well in your life there."

Herr Becker returned, his round hat planted firmly on his head, and repeated again the instructions for obtaining my train ticket to Cleveland. It was a short crossing on the Jersey City Ferry, he assured me, pressing my uncle's ten dollars into my hand.

Frau Becker handed me a cloth sack. "It contains black bread, sausages, and some dried cherries for your journey." She gave my arms a firm squeeze in farewell.

From the deck of the ferry, I waved until the Beckers became mere specks on the pier. Overhead, the sea birds flapped with shrieks and cries, but I did not feel the same exhilaration as I had just two weeks ago, when I'd first landed on American shores.

# Chapter 13

~~~

## Arrival in the U.S., 1857

"*FREIHEIT! FREIHEIT!* FREEDOM!" THE SEABIRDS seemed to cry. We stood at the rail of the packet ship Helvetia drinking in the welcome sight of New York Harbor with flocks of white birds shrieking and swirling around us. Hundreds of ships clogged these waters—steamships with humped side wheels, barges laden with cotton bales, tobacco and iron ore, coastal schooners and bluewater clippers. Forty-three days after setting sail, our three-masted ship steered its prow toward the green swath at the tip of Manhattan Island, dropping anchor on June 30, 1857.

The American city of New York spread before us in a dense, box-like haze. How I longed to leap from the ship and swim for shore, if only I knew how to swim. I remained where I was so my parents would not read in the Freinsheimer *Anzeiger:* Michael Harm, sixteen years old of the Bavarian Palatinate, lost at sea.

"Would you look at that, Angela?" Herr Schneider said to his wife. "New York has grown as large as Paris."

As I descended between decks, the steerage area was bedlam, everyone scrambling, packing, laughing, delirious with joy over the fact that our tedious voyage had finally come to an end. From inside my sea box, I removed my extra set of clothes, kept clean and dry all this time in its oilcloth wrapping. As I unfolded them, a faint whiff of Freinsheim filled the air. *Home*, I thought. *But no more.*

I had just finished donning the sweet-smelling garments over my filthy body when Franz Handrich came over and grabbed my salt-stiff old ones.

"Follow me, Harm. Bring your mattress, too."

He pushed his way through the teeming mass of Germans toward the steerage hatch. Mystified, I followed him into the sunlight, only to witness

Franz rush to the rail and toss my clothes overboard. Aghast, I reached the rail just in time to see them floating in the green-brown harbor amid a raft of other belongings—hats, shoes, garments, bed straw. In an instant, they were gone.

"For the fish!" Franz shouted, throwing his head back with a giddy howl. "Go ahead, your mattress, too!"

I dumped overboard the straw from my mattress and the itchy mattress cover, too, with a growing sense of jubilation. For weeks, my scalp had been crawling with bugs. After a few moments enjoying in the reckless celebration around me, I returned below to pack my rucksack with the remaining items in my sea box, then tossed that overboard as well.

On deck in the hot summer sun, I waited several hours in a long snaking line of passengers before my turn came to be taken across the harbor to the round granite fortress called Castle Garden. As I stepped from the steam tug, the ground rocked beneath me so wildly I had to cling to the rope rail to steady myself. Herded into line for inspection, I watched fearfully as uniformed officials pulled out a man who was missing an arm, two parents holding a baby with a croupy cough, and in addition, a few from steerage who had the misfortune just then to sneeze. I did not see any of them again.

Like a *Logel* of grapes poured into a wine press, we Germans spilled into Castle Garden's pink stone interior, its domed ceilings as high as the *Palais de L'Industrie* in Paris. Most of the Customs-House officials spoke German and treated us with dispatch. The Americans even offered a Bureau of Exchange, where, on Franz's advice, I changed my remaining *Gulden* into twenty American dollars—enough for a train ticket, clothes and a few provisions.

When we filed past an area with large maps spread on tables, Franz hurried us through.

"I lived in New York City several years," he said. "I know how to get around here." In the next area, he motioned to some chairs and benches. "As soon as we're reunited with our luggage and our names are checked off on the passenger register, we'll be free to go."

*Free to go.* The words made me dizzy with relief. I could not wait to meet my old friends Gretel, Martha, Herr and Frau Becker. I could already imagine their surprised faces when they first beheld me.

When Franz's name was called, he went up and engaged in a lengthy discussion with the official. He returned with a frown.

"I'm sorry, wife," he said to Barbara. "They didn't have this Immigrant Center eight years ago. There has been a Yellow Fever. They say we must stay inside this place for three whole days. If we don't keel over dead, we'll be allowed to leave."

I was sorely disappointed, but at least we were given the opportunity to bathe. The water was steaming hot and the dirt leaked down my pink skin in brown streaks. Afterward, in the enormous common room, we Germans were lumped together with the Dutch, Russians, Italians and so on. The Scottish, Irish, English, and French were all sequestered on the opposite side. There were no beds. Everyone had to make do sleeping on or behind benches.

That first night, too excited to sleep, I gravitated over to where some men had gathered by a cast iron stove—a place for boiling water and cooking. The pungent tobacco smoke hung here in thick clouds. I learned some immigrants had been staying in Castle Garden as long as three weeks.

"The employment office told me of a grocer who needs a worker," one man said. "But when I went to inquire, the grocer was not hiring after all. He advised me to wait a week and come back. Another week in this place! He told me there is big trouble in this city. The police are fighting each other—an Old Police and a New Police—some disagreement between the mayor and the governor of this state. No one knows what will happen."

"I have heard of the Irish fighting one another," said a man who looked like his brother. He cast a furtive glance across the cavernous hall. "But not police fighting police."

"Without the police around, the Irish gangs will be free to cause trouble," said a third.

I heard many stories that night about the Irish, a poor class of Catholics who arrived in America with next to nothing, bringing with them crime and prostitution and a powerful thirst for American whiskey. After an earful of this talk, I returned to my spot along the wall and slept soundly.

THE NEXT MORNING WHEN I awoke, the benches were astir, people swallowing down rolls and coffee purchased for a penny at the refectory. Several times during those next days, I ventured to the second-floor gallery, a place where the tall fortress windows provided a view of the glistening waters of the harbor. The sun rose each day heavy and orange, but the air inside the granite dome remained relatively cool.

From this high vantage point, I had a view of the processing center in the Garden, where new boatloads of immigrants streamed in daily, most dressed in homespun, their complexions pale. In three days alone I saw hundreds, perhaps thousands, arrive. The rallying cry of freedom, it seemed, inspired not only Germans but the entire world.

On the second day at Castle Garden, Franz changed the original plan.

"This is taking too long," he said. "Harm, you must pay for our two nights at the Freischütz Inn, or my wife and I will skip New York entirely and be on our way."

"That's not our agreement. I can't pay that. After train fare, I'll have only ten dollars and I need money to buy some American clothes."

"The Beckers won't know the difference if you don't go there."

"What about the letter and greetings from my parents?"

"You have their address. Put a stamp on the letter and put it in the post."

"But I also carry a letter for the Auls."

Franz shrugged. "Post that to the Beckers as well. *Guck mal,* I lose money every hour I'm idle. Summertime is best for brick masons."

In the end, I could not convince Franz to stay, but I refused to leave New York without seeing the Beckers. Besides, I was heartily sick of being led around by the nose. America was the land of liberty and I wished to make my own impression of it.

"I made a promise to my parents to visit our good friends," I said. "Go on without me. I'll make my own way."

Realizing I wouldn't budge, Franz took me to the map room. The Americans had all varieties of maps on the tables and pinned to the walls, showing the city and the whole country, too, all thirty-one states and the expansive Territories. The map of Manhattan Island and nearby Brooklyn and New Jersey looked tangled and dense compared to the empty spaces of the American West. On the Manhattan Island map, Franz tested me over and over about the streets I'd need to take to find the Beckers.

"Look," I said, "I understand. Here is the symbol for the iron rails. From Chatham Street, follow the streetcar rails until I see Canal Street. I'll go down to the next street, which is Elizabeth. There I'll find the house of the Beckers."

Franz curled his lip in scorn. "It is not a house, it's a boarding house. The people in the city live in large buildings the size of your Freinsheim community hall, one family to a room, many stacked one on top of the other."

"I'll manage," I said.

ON SATURDAY MORNING, THE FOURTH of July, a port official examined our papers before allowing us out of Castle Garden. "You might want to stay a couple more nights," he said to us in German.

"Why would we do that?" Franz asked.

"There's been fighting in the Five Points. It's quite dangerous, and with the strike, we can't guarantee police protection."

Franz drew himself up to his full height. "I am a citizen of the U.S., not some naïve country bumpkin."

The official shrugged. "If you're headed to Dutchtown, be sure to avoid the Five Points."

He handed back our papers and waved us out the door.

"Now don't look anyone in the eye, just keep walking," Franz urged in a low voice. "Stick with me, and you'll be fine."

We headed up a path through a green garden. Just outside the fence, a crowd of tattered youngsters, some older men, too, were shouting nonsense.

"Popcorn here. Best ever!"

"Night a lodgin'? Fair price."

"Show you 'round?"

"American victuals, best cookin.'"

It was my first encounter with the runners and tricksters who plagued American cities. They spoke English, so I had no idea what they were saying but Franz and others had warned they meant to rob us if they could. Franz led us hastily through the crowd and out the gate.

As we made our way up the street, I was dazzled by the red-white-and-blue flags and bunting hanging from windows and flagpoles. The colors reminded me of France, and in any case, made a cheerful impression, reminding me of what I had heard in the Immigrant Center. Today was the festival day of American Independence. A fine day to enter the land of liberty.

To our right stood a line of black, two-wheeled hansoms, which catered to ladies dressed in yards of silk. They rustled in and out of carriage compartments, their gentlemen assisting them in their dainty slippers over garbage-choked gutters. To our left were the docks, a forest of masts and rigging rising above a phalanx of bowsprits. Here swarms of merchants, sailors, and dockworkers busied themselves with passengers and cargo.

It was still early in the day, but the mahogany-colored brick buildings were already baking in the July sun. The streets were overrun with paupers, hawkers, and tradesmen. Pigs competed with dogs for refuse and food scraps amid a cloying reek of sewage, seawater, and rot. After many blocks, Franz stopped at last.

"City Hall," he said. The marble building was as magnificent as a palace, a wide set of stairs leading up to the entrance. "Here we part ways. Follow the iron rails of that streetcar."

As Franz pointed in the direction I needed to go, he had such a crease of concern across his forehead that for once I didn't resent his patronizing tone. In truth, by now I felt uncertain I had made the right choice to go alone, but did not want to look a coward. I realized the time had come. I adjusted my rucksack on my shoulder, bid farewell to my friends, turned and headed off up crowded walkway, willing myself not to look back.

As I wended my way up Chatham Street, no one to follow behind, I felt a rush of elation. At last, I'd made it to the land of liberty. Soon I'd arrive safely at the Beckers on Elizabeth Street and be greeting old friends. If the Beckers retained the Palatine good manners, they would surely offer me a cool *Krug* of Rhine wine. My mouth watered at the prospect.

Up ahead, a streetcar was unloading passengers. I watched for a moment as a new wave of people crowded on, wishing I had the extra money to spend on such a luxury. When the car was loaded to bursting, the driver whipped the team of horses into motion through a knot of hansoms, carriages, and wagons. Behind the car, a uniformed horseman followed, blowing a horn to clear the rails.

The streetcar moved so slowly it was easy to keep pace. I glanced often to the side to be sure I stayed with the rails and as a consequence, nearly ran down a mother with two young children who stood waiting to cross the street. The woman looked distressed, one hand gripping each little one, her head whipping frantically back and forth waiting for traffic to clear.

A gap came and she made a dash for it, yanking her children behind, but the legs of the smallest child couldn't go fast enough and he stumbled. Just then, to my horror, a delivery wagon careened out of a side street barreling down on them. Shouting out a warning, I dashed into the street, grabbed up the little boy and raced to the other side. The mother followed, caterwauling like a mad woman. As I handed the child back to her, she continued to shriek as if it had been me, not the delivery wagon, that caused the trouble.

"*Es tut mir leid,*" I apologized, removing my cap, but it did no good. The woman would not stop her ranting.

Out of the corner of my eye, I saw several young men move out from under a storefront awning and head in our direction. My explanations unheeded, I hurried off, the woman's angry voice raining on my back as I fled. After some time, I glanced over my shoulder, relieved to find I was not being followed.

In this part of the city, the stench of sewage was suffocating. I longed to hold a handkerchief to my nose, but no one else did, and after what had happened I did not wish to draw more attention to myself. It was mid-afternoon by now, and the air had become as hot as a bonfire. I continued on, noting as I passed the street names for Mulberry, then for Mott, keeping my eyes open for the sign for Canal.

The houses around here were sagging as if they might collapse, and many were in need of whitewash. Other buildings rose as high as six floors, made of brick and many windows. Crowds spilled from underground cellars, quite a few Negroes with ebony-dark skin mixed among them. People leaned out of windows calling to one another, while those around me staggered about, shouting in thick, slurred voices. Falling down drunk, I realized with a jolt.

Rough-looking men smoked and drank under storefront awnings, ogling passers-by. Women paraded the walkways arm in arm, their bodices cut so low their bosoms spilled out. A *Fräulein* caught me staring, put her hands under her breasts and lifted them up as if serving them on a platter. I averted my eyes, my heart racing like a rabbit's. Everything I had previously imagined, my idea of American freedom, of the wilderness and empty land, was turned upside down in this foul-smelling place.

Finally, I came upon the corner building with the word Bayard and knew I was still on the right path. I remembered the same letters from the map. Canal Street would be just ahead. Down Bayard Street I heard cheering. It sounded as if a carnival was taking place. Or perhaps a parade? Eager for a first taste of the exotic customs in this great country, I went a few steps toward the noise.

But I did not find what I expected. Up ahead, in the middle of the street, two men fought with their fists, a ring of people gleefully urging them on. As I stood trying to make sense of it, I noticed the word Mott on the street corner building up ahead. How could that be? I had passed Mott a few streets back. Alarmed, I pushed through the throngs to the next street—Mulberry—and my stomach flip-flopped in dismay.

As I tried to reason it out, the mood of the mob shifted, the cheers turning to hisses and snarls. People began running for cover, calling out with hoarse shouts, diving into doorways and behind barrels. Others appeared in the windows of the buildings, shaking their fists at something farther up the street. Silhouettes of men appeared on the rooftops, sticks or clubs—or rifles—in their hands. Alarm turning to terror, I retreated the way I had come.

But I didn't get far. Objects began to rain from the sky—rocks, furniture, buckets of slop. Near me, a brick thunked a man on his shoulder. He cried out, spun in a circle to see what had hit him, then collapsed. Afraid to go on, I pressed back against a building. Before me, a farmer and his wagon had become trapped by the crowd. His horse was growing agitated, rearing back and snorting in distress. In the back of the farmer's wagon were two enormous hogs.

The farmer stood and shouted to clear the way, but no one paid him any mind. Then a group of young men noticed him, and one tried to climb up on the seat. The farmer pushed the ruffian off, but two others clambered up from behind, lifting the man up under his arms and dumping him over the side. The horse whinnied and bucked. Hands reached up to unfasten its harness. Horse and wagon separated, the mob heaved the wagon over on its side. As the wagon tipped, the hogs spilled to the ground with great squeals, struggled to their feet and barreled off, knocking several people down in the crowd.

Around the overturned cart, men and women were piling barrels and crates to form a makeshift barrier. The horse continued to rear and buck, its eyes white with terror. A gunshot rang out. The horse dropped to its forelegs with a groan, then lay full out on the ground.

The gunshot woke me from my stupor and I ran, arms over my head, praying to God no brick would drop from the sky to end my life. As I fled from the melee, a few ruffians jostled past me, their arms loaded with bricks and stones. I could not believe anyone would run into that riot. Did freedom drive men mad?

I reached the street with the iron rails, but the street sign said Bowery. What happened to Chatham Street? Frightened out of my wits, I dashed blindly ahead, weaving and dodging the other pedestrians, not slowing until my breath came in huffs and a stitch dug into my side.

Coming to myself, I halted at last at a wide intersection with a fountain in the center. This was a fashionable district unlike anything Franz had described, the paving stones swept clean, the couples and families dressed in fine new clothes, carrying baskets and parasols.

I realized the worst had come to pass. I was lost, and had no idea of my way back.

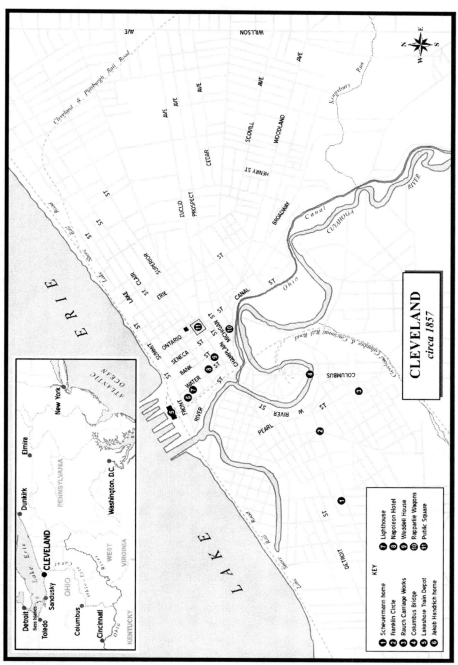

**CLEVELAND**
*circa 1857*

KEY

1 Scheuermann home
2 Franklin Circle
3 Rauch Carriage Works
4 Columbus Bridge
5 Lakeshore Train Depot
6 Jakob Handrich home

7 Lighthouse
8 Napoleon Hotel
9 Weddell House
10 Rapparlie Wagons
11 Public Square

Maria Brown, Kroll Map Company

# Chapter 14

## Train journey to Cleveland, 1857

Fʀᴏᴍ ᴛʜᴇ ᴅᴇᴄᴋ ᴏғ ᴛʜᴇ Jersey City Ferry, New York City looked beautiful and serene to me now, graceful sails billowing in the foreground, the morning sun rising behind a square-and-spire-topped horizon. If only I could erase from my memory the chaos and disaster of that fateful first day on my own, I'd be taking a better impression with me to Ohio.

I only hoped in Cleveland I wouldn't fail so utterly from the start. Determined to put my troubles behind me, I trudged off the Jersey City Ferry with one aim alone—to buy the train ticket on the Erie Railroad exactly as Herr Becker had instructed. At the ticket seller's window, I handed over my ten dollars and a piece of paper Herr Becker had given me stating my destination, which the seller accepted without protest. Then, ticket in hand, I strode directly to an official who pointed out the passenger car where I should board.

The car was crowded to standing room only with a mixed-up assortment of travelers—workers in patched woolen jackets and caps, a fair-haired family with an abundance of children, a group of well-dressed gentlemen with very tall hats, a stout man toting a rifle. Since everyone spoke in English, I had no inkling of their destinations. The men had their cheeks puffed out unnaturally. Every so often, one or another of them would squirt brown juice from his mouth in the general direction of the spittoons. A slimy ooze dripped from these bowl-shaped vessels and puddled on the floor.

Soon we were off, clacking and swaying, leaving the teeming streets and cloying city air behind. Three stations along, the car grew less crowded, so I was able to find a seat across the aisle from a passel of soft-haired, beribboned children. The woman in charge of them was dressed in some kind of uniform—a governess or servant perhaps. The three young children in her care wore elegant finery, a stark contrast to my homespun, oft-repaired clothing. For a moment I met the woman's eyes. She averted her gaze.

As for the children, they squirmed, kicked, and poked one another for a chance to look out the windows. I made faces to joke with them, keeping a watchful eye for burning cinders that floated through the open windows. Whenever I brushed one off, they turned to stare at me with wide, serious eyes. In truth, I felt like one of these children myself, naïve to everything around me.

After five stops, the governess and children exited the train. I slid onto their vacated bench, watching out the window as they crossed the tracks to stand on the platform for the train going in the opposite direction. Had they forgotten something? Or did they ride the train with no destination in mind? I could make no sense of it.

In this landscape of farms, meadows, and forests, the train chugged from station to station, pausing briefly amid small villages of clapboard houses with a church spire or two near the center. For some distance the train followed a wide river, barges and steamships plying the placid waters. My stomach began to growl, but I did not eat, hoping to make Frau Becker's food last the entire journey, however long it might take. On the map, Herr Becker had pointed out Dunkirk, New York, on Lake Erie as the town where I should change trains. By mid-afternoon, the train snaked alongside steep mountain slopes, no lake in sight.

When passengers began to crowd the windows, craning their necks to look, I grew curious as well. I poked my head out my window just as the land dropped away so it felt as if the train was flying. Head reeling, I gripped the edge of the window and stared below me at a river no bigger than a silver thread. Ahead, the locomotive engine rumbled along, suspended above the chasm by airy stone arches. I held my breath until we regained solid ground.

"New York State," the conductor bellowed on his next pass through the car. Delight surged through me. New York? Was this train traveling through the American wilderness written about in *Last of the Mohicans?* Eagerly, my eyes probed the deep woods for signs of wild Indians, for bison, wolves, and bears, but I spied only a few birds, squirrels, and deer. I also saw houses built of logs, which caused a shiver of pleasure down my spine. They looked exactly as I had imagined the cabin of Natty Bumppo, primitive but sturdy.

In contrast, many of the American clapboard houses appeared to be roadside shacks, temporary structures that would not last. The timber beams of these houses were hidden behind the horizontal flat boards. How would a man know if his house was constructed well if he could not see the beams? The durable half-timbered houses of the Rhineland were nowhere in evidence. Gone too were the tightly clenched fists of Rhineland villages. In America, houses were scattered up the hillsides without preserving the forest, every span of farm acreage tended by its own house, far from the towns.

When we arrived at a station called Elmira, twilight was falling, the air turning chilly. Uneasily, I began to wonder if I had missed my stop. I had not expected to travel all night. But the conductor did not question my ticket, so I stayed where I was. All night we propelled westward into the American continent. In truth, the distance felt infinite, as if America was a land not for men, but for the giants of the Grimms' fairytales. The Rhine River and sandstone cliffs of the Haardt Mountains now dwelled in my memory as miniatures, like fairy lands.

Riding into the blackness, I thought of Cleveland and what lay in store for me. I dreaded encountering Charles Rauch, my shipmate on the Atlantic crossing, feeling keenly our disparate circumstances—me a lowly apprentice, Rauch a wagon-maker's son. Would I see Charles Rauch often, making me always aware of my low estate? Had my uncle and aunt spread the word of my misfortunes in New York, so even Rauch had heard of them? If he knew, I felt certain he would gloat over my loss. At this thought, I heard Mütterchen's reprimand in my head, "For shame, Michael. All is vanity."

# Chapter 15

## Coach journey to Havre, France, 1857

Tucked against the foothills of the Haardt Mountains, the town of Neustadt spilled down from the foundations of Hambacher Castle, Europe's ruined throne of democratic ideals. At the train station, Franz instructed Barbara and me to await the arrival of two more traveling companions while he went to see about a coach to Kaiserslautern. The train arrived in good time and when the platform had cleared, a *Fräulein* and a young man remained, a travel trunk between them.

Barbara made bold to speak with them, and indeed, they were Margaret and August Haas of Rheingönnheim, brother and sister, come to meet Franz Handrich who would guide them to America.

Soon after introductions, Franz Handrich arrived, sitting beside the driver of a coach and four that would convey us over the Haardt Mountains. We were to meet one more traveler at Kaiserslautern, Franz said. In the coach, August and I sat across from each other, our knees bumping as the coach rocked to and fro.

"Where is your family?" he asked, staring at me with unblinking blue eyes.

He and his sister were both as pale as porcelain dolls, their hair so black it didn't appear real.

"In Freinsheim. I'm journeying to my uncle's home in Cleveland, Ohio. And yours?"

"Father died of the cholera when we were children," his older sister Margaret said, her eyes as blue and penetrating as her brother's. It was the first of many conversations in cramped spaces, no one getting any privacy. "Our mother has a new husband. My brother and I have decided not to stay."

"You're leaving without their blessing?"

She hesitated. "Our new father did not ... welcome us in his home. Mother thought it was for the best."

"But where will you go?"

"We have relatives in St. Louis," August said without enthusiasm.

August and I were of a similar age, both liable to serve in the military by the age of twenty-one. I assumed that, like me, he carried no official passcard. A jolt of fright passed through me every time I thought of it. "Just keep clear of the Bavarian police," Philipp had advised. "Don't draw attention to yourself and you'll be fine."

The coach journey lasted all night. Franz and I had taken the bumpiest seats in order for the women to have the most comfortable places behind the driver. Pressed into a corner of the bone-rattling compartment, filled with excitement and worry, I hardly slept at all.

As the black night sky turned gray with the dawn, the coach deposited us on the edge of Kaiserslautern at an inn run by a man named Pfaff. As we entered the public rooms, the innkeeper extended a good-natured greeting and informed us that our next coach, to the French border, would not leave until ten o'clock that evening. At first I was disgruntled by the wait, but quickly learned this would be the pattern of our journey, always traveling the cheapest and least convenient way.

We broke our fast with rolls and coffee, the women already murmuring together about sewing, housekeeping, and children as if they had known each other their whole lives. When it came time to meet our final travel companion at the train station, Barbara and Margaret said they wished to stay behind with the luggage. They sat on the benches of the public rooms like roosting hens, their cloaks and skirts fluffed out, so plump I was sure they wore several layers of clothing beneath their top skirts.

At the train station, the locomotive arrived amid dark clouds of smoke and a rain of hot cinders. As the other passengers dispersed, my searching gaze landed on a young man dressed in a ready-made suit of broadcloth, his travel trunk as large as the linen chest that sat at the foot of Mütterchen's bed.

Our guide stepped forward. "Excuse me, are you Rauch of Standenbühl?"

The young man acknowledged him then. "Charles Rauch. You are Franz Handrich?"

"*Aber ja doch!*" Franz clapped his hands together. "We have made our connection." Franz laid a hand on my shoulder. "Charles Rauch, here is Michael Harm. Like you, he's on his way to Cleveland, Ohio."

Charles Rauch's eyes dropped to my bulging leather rucksack. He gave me a cool nod.

"*Tach,*" I said, choosing the familiar greeting. "What a coincidence, that we will be neighbors."

Charles Rauch did not reply, instead giving the pant legs of his suit several brusque swipes to remove the travel dust.

"And here is August Haas," Franz continued, "who travels to St. Louis. His sister and my betrothed await us back at the inn."

I offered to carry one end of Charles Rauch's heavy travel trunk, as I saw no harm in being friendly. "Franz tells me you are the son of a wagon-maker," I said as we trudged along. "I am going to apprentice as a blacksmith to a wagon-maker in Cleveland, my uncle Johann Rapparlie."

"Oh, I will not apprentice," he said. "Father says apprenticeships aren't so common in America any more. He wants me to learn the business so I can take over for him one day."

Apprenticeships weren't so common in America? I wanted to hear more about this, but didn't want to seem like an ignorant fool.

"Your father went ahead of you to America?" I asked instead. "Why didn't you go with him?"

"My mother and siblings remain here—she will not leave her parents, who are too ill to travel."

I confessed to Rauch that my mother was not well enough to travel, either. The very mention of her name gave me a pang of homesickness, so I did not converse with Rauch further.

Back at the inn, over the next several hours of waiting, I noticed a gleaming brass cornet by the music stage and went to examine it.

"This cornet is very fine," I said to Herr Pfaff, who busied himself with a broom at the entry. "Are you perchance of the same Pfaff family that makes musical instruments in this city?"

"*Ja doch*, you mean my cousin Josef Pfaff!"

"I've heard of his shop," I said. "Herr Franck of the Liedmeisters has bought instruments from him."

The innkeeper beamed at me. "Would you and your friends like to visit Pfaff's Instrument Shop? It's not far."

Eager for a diversion, we men agreed. Once again the women declined, choosing to remain with the travel trunks.

As the four of us stepped inside the instrument-making shop of Josef Pfaff, the air was ripe with odors of turpentine and fresh-sawn wood. During introductions, I mentioned Herr Franck and the Liedmeisters to Herr Josef Pfaff. The instrument-maker's eyes lit up in recognition. He invited us behind the counter to where craftsmen worked at tables, sanding, carving, and gluing. One corner of the main room held woods used for instrument-making— spruce, willow, boxwood, ebony. He let me hold a particularly fine violin, and in truth I was entranced. To think I had eighty *Gulden* in my pockets, enough to buy something so fine. I handed the violin back in a hurry, as holding the instrument was tempting me with crazy ideas.

Back in the public rooms of the Pfaff inn that evening, the tables grew crowded with guests who'd come to hear a music band. Singing and forgetting my cares, I drained the last of the wine in my flagon, and, my pockets bulging with coin, called for several more drinks. Our coach arrived late, not until the hour of eleven o'clock, and by that time, my head was reeling.

Once we were again on the road, I fell immediately into a sound sleep. In the middle of the night, jarred awake by a hard bounce, I peered out the window shade. Moonlight spilled over the countryside, a land west of the Haardt Mountains where I had never been before. The patchwork of stubby knolls and steeply terraced farmland looked foreign to me, nothing like the gradual slopes of the Rhine valley. Above us, the stone walls of a castle ruin made a silvery curtain between the black platform of the earth and a star-bedecked sky.

Only a week ago, I had been a farmer, consigned to till the land while others went off on great adventures. Now my own adventure had begun.

As the sky lightened toward dawn and our coach drew ever closer to France, I fretted about the border crossing. In spite of what Philipp said, I was leaving the Bavarian Palatinate without permission of the authorities. Was I tempting God's goodness, to take this risk? I hoped and prayed the officials would not ask for my passcard, sealing my doom.

With such ruminations dominating my thoughts, the first sight of the French tricolor flag caused me to withdraw my head quickly from the coach window. As our driver reined the horses to a halt, a guard yanked open the door and poked his head inside. I squeezed into the corner, trying to make myself as small as possible, but I need not have bothered. The soldier stared through me as if I were invisible. He gave a dismissive wave, and a few moments later our coach rolled into France. If I had timed it by Father's pocket watch, the crossing might have lasted one tick forward of the minute hand.

What an odd feeling it is, to step into a foreign country where people speak nonsense sounds. Over time, I would learn to read facial expressions and listen to the timbre of voices when I didn't understand the language of a place. In this way, I could determine if the speakers were happy or angry or bored. But at this moment, as we stepped out of the coach in Forbach, France, all I could do was gawk around me, uncomprehending, my weary body giddy with relief that I'd made it safely.

When our belongings had been unloaded off the coach, Franz took Charles, August and me aside to wrest our money from us.

"I require sixty *Gulden* each," he said. "They pay with French Francs here. Our agent has told us of an honest place to make the exchange. I will keep your money for you from here on out. It will pay for many things on the rest of the journey through Paris to Havre, and for the billet of passage across the Atlantic."

The thought crossed my mind that Franz might take our money and abscond with it, but I pushed aside this fear and dug inside my secret breeches pocket to produce the notes of exchange. I need not have worried, as Franz returned in only a short while.

"I've made the arrangements. We leave again in the night," he said. "We will travel by coach another two and a half days to Paris. Here at this inn we should pay for a bath."

From then on, the six of us fell into the rhythm of travel. For two long days and nights we bumped along, marking time by coach stops for fresh horses and meals, cleaning up as best we could at a pump or bathhouse. The French countryside expanded before us like a smoothed out skirt. French villages weren't as tidy as German ones, yet not so different, either—the same stucco walls and tiled roofs, similar patchwork fields surrounding them.

At each stop, Franz was solicitous of his Barbara, hopping about like a lackey, bringing her this and that for her comfort while ignoring the rest of us. By the second day, our faces were coated in road dust and sweat. The trip seemed especially wilting for the ladies, their clothing growing rumpled, their hair flattening into strings. Barbara was tidy and complacent at the start, but now her once trim braids wisped every which way and she sat slumped over, looking forlorn. Margaret's features had grown more angular and gaunt, her blue eyes intent, almost feverish, but she sat as erect as ever. Rauch remained cool and aloof, while August proved to be a dull, humorless fellow. No doubt I tired my travel companions as they tired me, but Franz was the worst, with his pronouncements on every subject from his coach seat as if he sat on a royal throne.

When we came at last to Paris, the houses were rundown, the streets littered with garbage, geese, and pigs. Children dressed in rags played in the mud puddles. The farther we penetrated into the city, the more suffocating the stench became. Layers of wood smoke hovered above the tall houses, turning the sunlight to a dingy haze. Clothes hanging on lines made spots of color in the otherwise sunless alleys. Street sellers and beggars wove amid gentlemen and ladies in outlandish finery, the gentlemen in top hats and tails, the women in long silk skirts with parasols. The dresses of the ladies were especially strange, bunched out at the back as if they had baskets tied to their bottoms. From time to time, the filth and crowding was relieved by open parks featuring white marble statues, fountains, and broad walking paths, the sunlit greenery shimmering like a mirage.

At last the coach stopped at yet another inn. This part of Paris flowed with a great river of people, such a fast current that, as I eased out of my confinement, I feared I'd be caught up and swept away. People babbled in sing song notes, through the nose, "lu lu lu lu," like *Amsel* blackbirds, with nothing of the deep gravelly conversation I had known all my life. I began doffing my cap to every finely dressed gentleman or lady who passed. Franz grabbed my hat from my hands.

"Keep your damn hat on, you dumb billy-goat," he said. "We don't do that in the city."

I settled my cap back on my head, my neck and ears flaming hot.

Ever solicitous of his betrothed, Franz negotiated with the innkeeper for a noon dinner. We paid two Francs each for small servings on large, heavy plates. Afterward, Barbara and Margaret arranged themselves on a settee in the public rooms to sit out the hours. August and I borrowed a deck of cards from the innkeeper, since during the coach journey August had promised he'd teach me how to play whist. But Franz had other ideas.

"I have spoken with a man here," he said, "who has told me of Emperor Louis-Napoleon's *Palais de L'Industrie*. He says a great exhibition is underway of paintings and sculpture, the Salon of 1857, a sight not to be missed."

Barbara sighed. "I don't feel up to it. You go if you must. Margaret and I will wait here."

"*Doch*, we're in Paris! And this exhibition is in a new building, with cast iron columns and glass ceilings!" Franz stomped his foot. Barbara's eyes widened and he softened his tone. "There will be plenty of time for sitting around on the boat."

Brooking no argument, Franz paid more coins to the innkeeper to watch our trunks and herded us out to the street. I clumped along in my farmer boots, glancing furtively at the people, understanding hardly a word that was uttered. The black hansoms on the street caught my eye—horse-drawn vehicles with only two wheels, the driver sitting high up outside the back of the coach. As we came nearer to the exhibition hall, street musicians played on every corner.

What a homespun group of peasants we were. I doubted we would even gain entry, but the exhibition officials let us in without protest. Inside the palatial hall, mobbed with hundreds, maybe thousands of people, I stared goggle-eyed at the high, arched ceilings of glass and levels of ornate balconies. Paintings lined every wall from floor to ceiling. Previously, my idea of art involved unsmiling portraits of ancestors rendered in dark colors, which I had seen hanging on walls in Freinsheim's wealthier homes. Here, the colors on the canvas were as bright as summer flower gardens—golds and purples, reds and blues. Wherever my eyes rested, I felt some new shock, a painting of a harbor or a ship in a storm, of hunting dogs or a battle of blood, agony, and death.

And God save me, naked women! At the sight of these large canvases of nudes, I felt a stirring in my manhood but could not look away. Franz kept shoving me along from column to column of paintings, the artworks displayed one above another to great heights. A large crowd gathered before one painting in particular, people peering at it, making animated gestures. Some rolled their eyes and turned away in disgust.

As we came closer, I saw it was a portrait of two peasant women bending over to glean in a farmer's field. I felt a rush of pride. I had never considered such a thing, the farming depicted in paint on a canvas, something glorified to hang on the wall.

Behind me, I overheard two men talking in German.

"There is an outcry over this 'Gleaners,' " one gentleman was saying. I glanced over my shoulder at him, an aristocrat dressed in a fine suit of gray cloth, his beard neatly trimmed.

"An outcry?" His friend wore a pair of spectacles on his nose. "What for? It's only a picture of two peasants in a field."

"Yes, vulgar, isn't it? A waste of good oils." The distaste in the man's voice scraped like a hoe on sandstone. "Who would display peasants on their walls? The subject of a painting ought to be classical beauty, mythology, a glorious battle."

"This Millet has a good reputation. I don't object to his composition and technique. The subject matter is perhaps less objectionable than Courbet's 'Ladies on the Banks of the Seine.' Those were no ladies."

The men snorted with laughter.

"Indeed. The subject matter is beneath good society. I wonder that the Emperor would allow such artwork in his exhibition."

Hearing these gentlemen make a mockery of my family's livelihood, I didn't feel so enamored of this grand Salon any longer. In my village, I had rarely come in close contact with the European aristocrats, but I knew I was of lower standing. Freinsheimers were always saying that in America, aristocrats were on equal footing with the peasants. I dearly hoped they spoke the truth.

OUR COACH LEFT FOR HAVRE at midnight, the spring rain dripping down our windows without cease. At dawn, a gray mist clung like potato soup on the hills. As the sun rose higher, it warmed the puddles, wisps of cloud hovering above them like ghosts. Yellow flowers dotted the green-coated meadows and ditches. Now the coach descended steadily, as steadily as it had risen from the Rhine valley. In the distance, suddenly, there it was, a broad flat line of greenish-blue, smooth and flat as a cloth spread across a table. The Atlantic Ocean. From this vantage, the harbor at Havre resembled a floating city of fishing schooners and merchant ships, barges and three-masted sailing ships.

In the distance, a clipper ship pointed its prow toward the horizon. The sight filled me with both awe and foreboding. I wondered for an instant if I could still turn back, but pushed away the thought. I had made a promise to Father.

As we arrived at the docks, I stared with my mouth agape at swarms of sailors and dockworkers weaving back and forth amid stacks of barrels and crates bearing wheelbarrows and shoulder loads of goods. The black skin of some these dockworkers absorbed the light, so they looked very strange to me. Some of the men wore costumes of white cloth that drooped between their legs, their heads swathed in cloth, as well, something I'd only seen before in drawings of faraway places.

As soon as the coach deposited us. Franz Handrich hopped about as if stung by a ground wasp, inquiring information of nearby travelers then hurrying off to see about our billets of passage. He did not return for over an hour.

"The only packet bound for New York, the Helvetia, sails tomorrow," he said upon his return, sweating profusely. "I've spoken with an agent—there is still room, but we don't have much time."

"Why not wait and take the modern steamship?" Margaret asked.

"It doesn't come for a week. Besides, it costs more money. Barbara and I can ill afford a week's lodging, or the higher fare."

Margaret's bone china face stretched taut and angular. She turned to her brother August.

"I want to sail across quickly. I am afraid of this ocean."

"What does the Helvetia have to recommend it?" August asked.

"It's an American packet, her second voyage. They say she's built to sail fast."

"How fast?" Charles Rauch asked.

"Four to five weeks."

"Four to five weeks?!" He reared back in amazement. "I thought you said it took you three weeks to voyage from America to France."

Franz gave Rauch a withering stare. "That was traveling east, with the wind behind us. It takes longer on the westward journey."

"Helvetia. Higgins. Harm," I said, feeling lightheaded. "All begin with H. Sounds lucky to me."

August chuckled. Franz and Charles did not. Franz turned to Barbara.

"Let's go have a look," he said. "They are loading the luggage this afternoon."

Several piers down, we came upon a knot of homespun Germans—large families, couples, elderly people, men traveling alone. Franz went to the end of the pier and pointed to a three-masted ship in the harbor.

"There she is!"

The Helvetia bobbed on its anchor chain, her sails furled, her three masts draped with a lace of rigging. A red and white swallowtail flag with a black W at the center flapped stiffly from her center mast. Did I dare trust my life to this vessel?

"Are you sure the officials will give me no trouble?" I asked.

"Harm, you and that passcard ... Don't worry so much. Look around. Do you think any other young men have proper papers? Trust me, the agents are only too happy to take our money for the billets."

I did look around, my eyes landing on two old *Frauen* seated on travel trunks, settling black shawls over their shoulders like roosting ravens. I had my doubts, but as usual, Franz was the savant among us.

When it came to buying passage, none of us suffered close inspection of our belongings or papers. Except for the Jews. The Jewish travelers were separated to one side for severe inspection. The customs officials paced up and down, shouting "Moses" and "Abraham" at them, spilling the contents of their provisions on the fresh bird droppings of the pier so they'd have to buy them again. I thought of Herr Adler and wondered if he had been treated in this manner. I hoped for his sake that his violin and guitar—his livelihood—had not been ruined before he even left shore.

As I followed my guide and cousin Franz Handrich away from the docks in search of lodging, I felt unsure of so many things. Could the dockworkers be trusted with our travel trunks? If we arrived late on the morrow, would the boat leave without us? Would we encounter a storm and drown? So many people before me had made this journey—hundreds from my village alone—and arrived safely on foreign shores. I had to believe it would be the same for me. Whether a man lived or died was not in a human's power, but God's.

In Havre, all the inns were full to bursting. We found only one room available, which we reserved for the six of us. Though it was growing late, we trooped out to the chandler's for provisions. Franz knew just what to buy— bags of potatoes to supplement the ship food, small water-tight boxes to store books and valuables, blankets, large cloth bags and straw to fill them to serve as our mattresses. Franz also advised us to buy lengths of rope to secure our belongings when the waves grew large.

Back at the inn, I purchased a large bottle of wine from the innkeeper. What did not fill my flagon, I drank. But I don't believe it was the wine, during my last night on European soil, which made me feel so off balance. Each day that passed had brimmed over with strange sights, people, and ideas. Now I went on the ocean for the first time in my life, to a place I had never seen. In a few short days of travel, I felt nothing like myself, nothing like the Michael Harm who had labored in his father's fields. When I reached the distant shores of the New World, who would I become?

# Chapter 16

---

## Atlantic voyage, 1857

T HE HELVETIA LOOMED LARGER AS the steam tug ferried us across the harbor to the gangway. Her shiny black hull was enormous, the gold scrollwork on her sides and stern elaborate but ominous, like the gilt of a Bavarian funeral wagon. Wavering up the gangway, I saw sailors in the cross-trees, dark silhouettes against the sun. On the tilted deck, I nearly lost my balance as a sack of food provisions was shoved into my hands.

"Damn it, Harm, pay attention," Franz growled. "First we claim our bunks, then we do our gawking."

Chastened, I followed Franz down the ladder into steerage, where passengers were pushing and shoving and crawling over one another in the dim light like an overcrowded nest of mice. Franz elbowed his way through the low-ceilinged area to a group of six empty bunks, the rest of us close on his heels. Margaret and Barbara would be together, he explained in tense, clipped tones, the men of our traveling party flanking them on either side. No one argued. We had all heard of terrible things befalling unprotected women on these journeys. I took the lower bunk to the left side of the women. Charles Rauch took the one above me.

On our other side, two travelers had already settled in. As I stuffed straw into my mattress, my new neighbor looked at me with frank curiosity.

"Sparer. Louis Sparer," he said after a time.

"Michael Harm."

"You people all from the same village?"

"I'm from Freinsheim. Charles Rauch, above me, is from Standenbühl."

"Wiener and I come from Ladenburg on the Neckar." Louis Sparer pounded a fist on the wood platform above him. "Hey, Christian, say hello to our shipmates Michael Harm and Charles Rauch."

"Uh," Christian grunted. "Beware my friend down there. He never shuts up."

Charles Rauch, whom I couldn't see through the solid wood of my bunk ceiling, did not reply.

Nervous and excited and terrified all at once, I hurried to stow my belongings. First, I pulled my mother's Bible from my rucksack. Tucked inside it was the address of the Beckers, who I looked forward to greeting again after all these years. In my water-tight box, I packed the Bible, the *Last of the Mohicans*, a thick packet of letters from various Freinsheimers, Father's prized pocket watch, my wine flagon, and one spare set of clothes, all topped by my empty leather rucksack.

By the time I stowed my tin plate and cup in the shelving along the wall, following Franz's example, the number of people below decks had thinned considerably.

"They're raising anchor soon," Franz said to Barbara, ushering her to the ladder.

Eagerly, I followed. A cannon cracked loud as I emerged from the hatch. Barbara screamed and covered her ears.

"That's the signal—we're on our way!" Franz yelled through the cheers.

I hopped out onto the crowded deck and added my voice to the jubilation, the smoke and gunpowder stinging my nose and throat.

A sailor above our heads sang out a piercing call—others sang in response, swaying together on the yard arms as they unfurled the sails. The heavy sheets of canvas dropped and snapped full of wind. The deck beneath our feet heaved forward. We cheered some more.

Not wanting to miss a thing, I squeezed my way to the rail for a better look. At the Helvetia's prow, smaller boats tacked off, clearing our path. White and gray birds swirled above us with piercing cries. "*Freiheit! Freiheit!*" they seemed to cry. "Freedom!"

After a time, a whistle sounded and all faces turned to the forecastle, where the captain stood erect in his navy blue, brass-buttoned uniform. Captain Higgins extended a terse welcome, first in English, then in halting German. Afterward, the first mate took over in Prussian German, running down a list of the rules. No pipe smoking, lanterns, or phosphorous matches permitted between decks. Passengers were free to move about above decks when it was fair, but during inclement weather must remain below. The cabins and steerage would be cleaned and inspected daily, weather permitting. No one, under any circumstances, was allowed to climb up the masts or to the second class deck. And so on and so forth.

After the first mate dismissed us, I remained above to watch our ship steer for the English Channel. The French shore dwindled at the stern, sunset beams lighting the masts of ships still at Havre, transforming the shoreline to a forest of gold. As the sun sank below the horizon and the coast faded to a thin line, I felt terribly lonely. How far away I was from anything familiar! *God be with you Philipp and Mütterchen and Father. Do not forget me. I'll be back one day.*

Behind me, a somber group of *Frauen* and *Herren*, led by a black-robed *Pfarrer*, began to sing "Jesus, my Refuge," their voices thin in the open sea air. I removed my cap and hummed along. As the sun dropped into the ocean, the wind picked up, the swells deepening as we reached open water. Franz and the others went below, but I had been cooped up so long with Rauch and Handrich and Haas, I put off going down for as long as I could.

The deck began to tilt and plummet. The Helvetia's prow snouted forward, the waves slapping against it, salt spray spitting over the deck. The worshipers finished their prayers and dispersed. As they made their way to the hatch, they gripped one another for balance. Two lost their footing and tumbled down the deck, eliciting laughter and offers of assistance.

Head spinning, I gripped the rail and turned toward the open sea, inhaling deeply to ease my sour stomach. A streak of lightning lit the cloud-banked sky, followed by a grumble of thunder. A sailor grabbed me by the shoulder and rained me with a jangle of foreign words, gesturing toward the hatch. Only then did I realize I was the last one above. As I climbed down into steerage, the sailor thumped down the hatch, snapping the latch tight.

In the black hole between decks, I had to call out to my friends to guide me back to my bunk. A hard rain began drumming over our heads and the ship creaked and moaned, pummeled by waves. Wind gusts howled, and our cramped area was illuminated intermittently by bolts of lightning. I retched several times into the bucket before drifting into a fitful sleep.

When I opened my eyes again, sunlight leaked wanly into our wooden cave and the stench of vomit scraped my nostrils. As the murmur and rustle of passengers grew, I propped myself on one elbow to peep through the tiny porthole for a better glimpse of the morning. The ocean looked like a soft blue blanket on a slightly mussed bed. I sipped wine from my flagon to swish the bile from my mouth, amazed at the sight of the open area of steerage, now a haphazard terrain of trunks and bundles. With chagrin, I realized I had forgotten to tie down my sea box, which had tipped over, spilling its contents. Disheartened, I fumbled to retrieve them.

When the sailors allowed us above, the salty breeze cleared my head a good deal. In the distance, several ships were passing in the other direction, none close enough to hail. As I walked over to the barrels to wash up, a wave slapped on deck as if the sea was unwilling to give up its tempest without one last blow, soaking me through.

Margaret and Barbara prepared a meal, which we ate below to escape the wind and spray. We forked down the mush of peas, bacon, and chunks of boiled potato without enthusiasm. During the entire voyage our food would be bland—biscuits or potatoes, peas or beans, bacon or pickled herring our only source of sustenance.

In the bunks on the opposite side of Franz and August, the Schneider family of Hassloch were our nearest neighbors. They made a good deal of noise, the younger ones jumping around as if they had ants in their pants. Barbara and Margaret befriended Frau Schneider and the three of them started cooking together. Within a few more days, Louis Sparer and Christian Wiener threw in with us as well, Louis having charmed Margaret into cooking for them. Thus, in our little corner of steerage, the semblance of a German village formed.

I DID NOT DEVELOP SEA LEGS for another week. In my never-ending nausea, I found the fresh air on deck suited me best. Above or below, some three hundred of us were packed together like pickles in a barrel. The round-nosed Schwäbish of Württemberg predominated, but plenty were emigrating from Baden and the Palatinate as well. A covered house held the galley and washrooms. On its roof a few young Prussian men sat ogling *Fräuleins* as if they were still in the marketplace of their village.

I heard many stories in these first days, emigrants telling of unhappy conditions in villages left behind, but even more about their plans for what lay ahead. Many of us had relatives we were going to see. Others were farmers moving their whole families, headed for the open country of Illinois, Missouri, and Wisconsin. We farmers bemoaned the years of poor harvests and the dispersal of families as men left to find work in the cities. The *Pfarrer* and his little congregation were Mennonites of Hanau headed for Kansas. In fact, quite a few passengers set their sights on Kansas due to a new Kansas-Nebraska Act, which had opened these territories for settlement.

In Freinsheim in recent years, the men had often argued at length about the political ideas of Marx and Engels and Proudhon—ideas of democracy versus socialism. But on the Helvetia, we didn't talk so often of politics. Instead, the men worried over what it would really be like to live in a land without taxes and kings. In a democracy, could the government leaders be trusted, or was this system as easily corrupted as the monarchies?

With such pressing questions, it did not take long for word to spread that a U.S. citizen was on board—Franz Handrich. Our guide was sought out as an authority on all matters about America, making his head swell even larger. Time and again on deck I encountered my cousin, surrounded by dozens as he pontificated about bank failures, the Gold Rush, the English Know-

Nothings with their disdain for German and Irish immigrants alike. The system of slavery, which we men of moral conscience could not condone. Bar none, Franz's favorite subject was the splendor of Buffalo. According to him, the virtues of his fine city were unsurpassed. I would have preferred to hear him claim Cleveland as the jewel of the Great Northwest.

Early in the journey, several on-board romances began, including one between Louis Sparer and Margaret Haas. Margaret's black hair and wary blue eyes made me uneasy, but Louis seemed to think she was the most beautiful angel on this earth and hovered constantly around her. I steered clear of them both.

Steerage passengers lived separately from those in second class, who kept to an upper deck. I never got a glimpse of their sleeping cabins, but people said second class passengers enjoyed the advantage of a long table and benches, nailed to the deck to keep from tipping over in high seas. On several occasions the smell of roasted pork and sauerkraut wafted down from the upper deck, driving us to unkind remarks about our wealthier counterparts.

A welcome break from the monotony came when ships passed within shouting distance. Some bore exotic names—Queen of the West, Orient, Montezuma. The ship called Ohio sent a thrill through me to my toes. I thought of my relatives then, of meeting them for the first time and seeing Cleveland at long last, of my future still so distant and unreal.

When a school of porpoises appeared for the first time off the starboard bow, I climbed on a barrel the better to see them. Turning back to hop down, I saw two gentlemen descending the stairs from second class. They made a direct path to the base of the mizzen-mast. At that moment for some reason, the Crow's nest was unmanned. Brazenly, they began to climb. I glanced around to see if any sailors saw them. A few eyed their progress, but did nothing. It seemed at sea, as on land, the aristocrats could do exactly as they pleased.

Once the two gentlemen had reached the Crow's nest, they proceeded to wave their arms and call to their friends in second class as if the several hundred of us on the steerage deck did not exist. At last their antics drew the attention of the first mate, who appeared on the forecastle with his arms folded over his chest. I expected him to order the gentlemen down on the spot. Instead, the first mate made an abrupt hand motion, signaling two sailors to scale the mizzen-mast.

The two gentlemen, caught up in making their observations and pointing out to sea, were oblivious to what happened below. But not those of us in steerage. By the time they were ready to descend, we all stood with upturned faces, watching to see what would happen to the rule-breakers.

"*Achtung!*" the first gentleman cried, noticing the sailor below him. "We're coming down now."

The other gentleman swooshed his top hat at the sailor. "Out of the way, man!"

"You aren't going anywhere!" the first mate shouted from his wide-legged stance on the forecastle.

The men looked up, startled.

"Why ever not?" asked the first.

"You haven't paid the fee."

"Fee? What fee?" asked the second, planting his hat firmly back on his head.

"The fee to climb up there. You must pay to get down."

"No one ever said anything about a fee."

"No one said you could climb up there."

"How much is it then?"

The first mate held up a thumb and two fingers, sweeping his hand back and forth for all of us in steerage to see. "Three Thalers."

"Highway robbery!"

"Three Thalers, I say. Three Thalers from each of you."

The first gentleman scratched his chin. "We're not bothering anyone."

"Suit yourselves. It's a fine view. I'm sure you might enjoy it for some time to come."

The two men conferred, apparently aware at last that they'd become part of a spectacle. In any event, to hisses and laughter from the steerage deck, they entered into the spirit of the thing, haggling over the price, making noises about how they might just stay up there after all.

In the end, the gentlemen dickered the price down to one Thaler apiece, making payment by borrowing from a friend in second class. When that man appeared on the forecastle to pay the debt, he was met by a rain of applause and jeers. He placed two Thalers ceremoniously in the first mate's hand, who then called off the sailors, allowing the gentlemen to descend.

The spot of fun gave us something to laugh over in the days ahead. The gentlemen weren't in any financial distress, we all agreed, over the payment of two Thalers. In fact, our general sentiment was that they could have afforded to pay three Thalers apiece. In any case, although the first mate spoke like a Prussian, we decided he was a likable fellow.

ON MY BIRTHDAY, MAY 27, eight days after setting sail, I shared my Rhine wine with Charles Rauch and our two bunk mates, Louis Sparer and Christian Wiener. Steerage was relatively quiet, as many had gone above to enjoy the fine afternoon. As the four of us passed the flagon, we sat across from one another on the top bunks, our heads scraping the low ceiling. In the dim light, a few of the younger Schneider children tumbled and crawled under and over their bunks and those of Margaret and Barbara. Our female traveling companions were currently out of sight. Across the way, four *Junge* played a card game. Two gray-bearded men stared intently at a chess board.

In the past week, I had gotten to know my neighbors Sparer and Wiener only slightly. As to their characters and appearance, they were perfect opposites. Christian Wiener was dark and thin, and paid little attention to his appearance, his hair matted, his clothing stained. Louis Sparer was tall, fair, and broad-shouldered, always brushing and adjusting his tunic, constantly removing his cap to comb back stiff, hedgehog hair with his fingers. Charles Rauch, I did not like to admit, was the most handsome of the four of us, keeping his straight brown hair neatly tied at the back. His blue eyes were intelligent, and his finely chiseled chin did not yet show signs of a beard. He was even taller than Louis, but not awkward and clumsy as the tall sometimes are.

As the wine disappeared, Christian and Louis talked of how they had lived off the charity of the town of Ladenburg because they couldn't find employment. They hadn't known each other until they met at the town council, where they'd gone separately to apply for money to emigrate. The town council had granted their wishes on the same day.

Christian said that, at the time, he'd been sleeping in a livery stable, a luxury granted in exchange for mucking out the stalls. "I'm putting all that behind me," he said. "America is a place where you can remake yourself. If you set your mind to it, you can become a whole new person."

"America may be a free country," said Louis, "but it's going too far to say you can become a whole new person."

Christian shrugged. "Think what you like. If I say my name is something else, if I say I am a German from Pomerania, who in America will be the wiser? But I don't intend to change my country of birth, only my status in society. I will say I am a gentleman from Ladenburg and behave like one of the men who stabled their horses at the livery. On this voyage, I am thinking to myself, things weren't so good for me in Baden, what with my parents dead, and my cousins not welcoming me in their homes. In America, I will change my luck."

It was a strange idea to me indeed that someone could simply change their name to become someone else.

"Do you know English?" I asked. My lack of ability in this area worried me a good deal, for it might hinder my progress in the New World.

"The little I know came from the livery man at the stables. 'Hallo, how are you? I am fine thank you.' He taught me the words for 'horse' and 'food' and 'good morning.' One day, the man laughed at me, saying, 'Your name should not be 'Winner,' it should be 'Loser.' I asked him what was so funny. He explained it was a word play. With a different spelling, Wiener becomes Winner. The word means getting first place in the footrace. I like this for a name. Christian Winner. With such a surname, the manure shoveler will disappear forever."

"My Uncle Johannes disappeared," I said. "But he had *melancholia*. My Uncle Rapparlie wrote about it in a letter. My mother's brother wandered away from Cleveland and no one has seen him since."

"Are you saying I'm crazy?" Christian sat up taller and smacked his head on the ceiling beam. "*Aua!*"

We laughed raucously, the wine coursing through our veins.

Charles Rauch said his father owned a wagon-making business in Cleveland. "He started it five years ago, calls it the Wayside Smithy. He writes he already has more business than he can manage. He has sent for me to come to Cleveland and work beside him. One day, the Smithy will be mine."

Envy cut me like a knife. I had a vision of myself, black with grime at the anvil, while Charles Rauch strutted around as the master of his own shop. The smiles on the faces of Louis and Christian also froze. How could Charles Rauch make such a boast without a care for the rest of us?

Louis broke the silence. "With a business such as that you'll be stuck there always, day in, day out. I couldn't stand such a thing. I plan to work on a canal boat, to see the world and earn my living at the same time."

Christian raised one eyebrow. "And I had you figured for the marrying type. I'll wager *Fräulein* Haas wouldn't want a husband who is so often away from home."

"Margaret has a fine *Hinnere*," Louis said, his mouth contorted in a leer. "To bed her would be a dream, to marry her a nightmare."

"If you bed her, look out, or you'll have to marry her," Christian said.

"I'm not worried about that. I have one of these." Louis looked around to be sure no one was watching, then pulled out a small, flesh-colored scroll from his inside jacket pocket. We leaned in for a closer look.

"What is it?" I asked, strangely titillated by the thin sock of membrane.

"I bought it from a whore in Ladenburg. It's for wearing on the cock, to keep from making babies."

Louis put the thing to his mouth and gently blew so it inflated like an aroused penis. He held it up, then looked at our faces and started to cackle.

"Put that thing away," Christian hissed.

Louis let the air out of the membrane and rolled it up, his shoulders shaking with mirth. For my part, I felt sorry to have shared my wine with him. I made a vow to be more vigilant on Margaret's behalf.

"Rauch and I will both work at wagon shops in Cleveland," I said, to change the subject. "I am to apprentice as a blacksmith for Johann Rapparlie."

Christian snorted. "A blacksmith? You? Blacksmiths are supposed to be large men, *oder?*"

I felt resentful that my birthday had turned sour, but even so, the wine was loosening my tongue. "I'd rather be a singer," I said. "When I was ten, Herr Franck invited me to travel with the Liedmeister Band, to work for them and learn singing. But my family needed me for the farm work."

Charles laughed. "He took us to see the instrument-making shop of Herr Pfaff in Kaiserslautern. You should have seen Harm ogle this one violin, like he was staring at a beautiful woman."

Louis, Christian, and Charles all grinned at me. I decided to laugh along.

"*Alla*, it was a very shapely instrument." I used my hands to illustrate. "Full here, slender at the middle. Sleek and soft. I longed to reach out and caress ..." The faint strains of a violin above decks made me pause. "Comrades, the wine flagon is empty, so now I go up to listen to my beloved."

I scrambled down from the bunk and, with a slight wavering in my steps, made my way to the steerage hatch, my three bunkmates close behind.

Up above, the sea breeze wafted softly and the sun winked through the sails. I followed the sound of the violin to the afterdeck. The violinist was a small woman in a red headscarf. The woman wore her scarf low on her forehead and waved her instrument as she played, as if in a trance. The purity of the notes fountaining from her instrument made me long for Herr Adler and Matthias and our many afternoons at the *Gute Brunnen* well.

Before long, she was joined by a guitar player, a mop-headed youth with a thin pointed nose. I settled down on a coil of rope to listen, closing my eyes to escape for a moment the Helvetia's cramped realm. After a song or two, another joined them, an accordion player with much gray in his beard. The three musicians sounded out tunes they knew in common.

"They play well together," I said to Christian.

"They do indeed. And I just had a brilliant idea. How about a dance this evening?"

"Just so!" Louis said, from his perch on a crate. "A chance to dance with the pretty girls on this boat."

"A sea festival to the God Neptune," I said.

"*Genau!*" Rauch chimed in.

A Neptune Sea Festival! The prospect of a diversion spread like wildfire among the passengers. We asked the three musicians to play for us and they agreed. Captain Higgins was applied to. He granted permission for a dance that same evening.

As sunset arrived, the weather held fine, the blue sea tranquil as a pond.

After the Mennonite *Pfarrer* led his eventide hymn-sing, the sailors lit the whale oil lanterns, casting a clean yellow light. The musicians assembled at the mizzen-mast on a makeshift stage of crates.

And so it happened that, on the balmiest night of our voyage, a sea-faring band of German peasants gathered to dance the waltz and mazurka and stomp our feet to the folk songs. As I stood along the rail, I had my eye on the Schneider's eldest daughter Elise, with her reddish brown hair and bewitching eyes that matched the sea. But I spotted Louis dancing with Margaret and decided to cut in on them instead. I stayed with Margaret for the next dance, and the next, until Louis pushed his way back in.

As I returned to the rail, the moon had risen higher in the sky, a great white lamp over our enchanted evening. Nearby, Franz and Barbara stood very close to each other, Franz nestling Barbara boldly against his body.

"We have planned a diversion for you, Harm," Franz said. "Tomorrow morning, Captain Higgins will marry us."

I grasped Franz's arm. "God's blessings on you!"

Franz grinned and Barbara smiled shyly.

"Will you stand up for me?" Franz asked. "I must have a witness, and you're the closest I have to family on this packet."

"I'll be proud to do such a thing," I said. I pointed up at the moon. "Look! A halo of angels surrounding the moon. I'm sure that your marriage will be long, fruitful, and blessed."

Barbara squeezed my arm gratefully, and the lovebirds resumed their murmurings. Overcome by an urge to honor their wedding eve, I pushed my way through the couples to the musicians.

"Can you play 'Oh, How Is It Possible'?" I asked. "I'd like to sing it for some friends."

The old man fingered out the melody on his accordion. The violinist and guitarist nodded and tuned their strings. I climbed up on some crates.

"*Achtung!*" I called to the dancers. "I have news! My good friends are to be married by Captain Higgins tomorrow." I gestured to Franz and Barbara at the rail, winning them cheers of congratulation. "To Franz Handrich and his betrothed, I dedicate this song."

Oh, how is it possible, that I would ever let you go;
I love you from my heart, do believe me!

It was a slow song, not much in the way of dance music, but one we all knew well. When the notes of the last verse had died away, someone made a request for "*Wanderlied*," so I sang that one as well. Then "*Die Lorelei*."

Afterward, as I climbed down, several Fräuleins moved nearer to dance with me, but I was not in the mood for a dance. Singing those songs had stirred in me a longing for what might have been. On this bobbing tub, Anna Marie seemed very far behind me, but I had not forgotten her. I returned to the rail to stare out over the shifting waters, unfurling into the dark gray night like rolls of black silk. Would I ever find a wife, someone to love, in America? I stared out at the blank horizon that never changed, that never showed if we moved forward or back or in circles. If only I could see what lay ahead, I would no longer feel this void inside, this mid-air space with no landing.

To banish such thoughts, I turned around and scanned the dancers for Elise Schneider. When I spied her, I went to ask her to dance. Then I danced with the younger Schneider girl, Katharina. The deck was so crowded we could do little more than hop in place. Nonetheless, the rest of that night, we all danced with fun and laughter and abandon until the musicians would play no more.

# Chapter 17

A LL OF OUR LITTLE TRIBE—AUGUST and Margaret Haas, Charles Rauch, Herr Schneider and his family of nine, Louis Sparer and Christian Wiener, too—gathered outside the captain's cabin the next morning for the marriage of Franz and Barbara.

The first mate stepped out the door and eyed us warily.

"The Captain will see you in his cabin now," he said to Franz, inspecting the rest of us as if for signs of mold. "Bring only the bride and two witnesses with you."

Margaret and I stepped forward. The first mate turned on his heel and we followed him into the captain's quarters. On a table lay shiny brass instruments, the chronometer and telescope, together with a pile of scrolled charts and maps. The light of the ocean waves refracted through the windows, shimmering on the ceiling and back walls. Franz and I removed our caps.

Captain Higgins sat before a large book and, barely nodding his head in greeting, asked the names of all present. Once the first mate recorded the names, the captain read a few phrases about the bond of marriage. Franz's face was pale, his body trembling. For her part, Barbara was placid and serene, a still pool in Franz's agitated sea. The ceremony concluded, the first mate moved swiftly to see us out.

A romantic at heart, I felt discouraged by how my friends were treated by our captain. Indeed, his compulsory manner indicated that he must not like us much at all. On several occasions I observed my fellow Germans challenging Captain Higgins over how he ran his ship. When there was too strong a wind, we questioned the wisdom of keeping the sails unfurled. When the day was fine, we grumbled over how little progress we made. *Did the captain chart our position daily?* we wanted to know. *Was he sure we were on the right course?*

Perhaps, to the captain, we were a critical, gloomy people.

But who could blame us, after all we had endured? For so many centuries, our dukes, princes, ministers and kings put us in harm's way. And so we possessed a healthy skepticism toward authorities, and toward the vicissitudes of nature and our misfortunes, ever in search of evidence that we would indeed survive the next affliction. We would not mutiny. But it was not in our natures to trust that all would go well. I suspected Captain Higgins preferred the eastbound journey, his cargo holds full of coffee, tobacco, or cotton— cargo that did not complain.

Back outside, the first mate pointed to a small boat dangling at the port bow.

"For the newlyweds to sleep," he said. "One night only."

I chuckled and clapped Franz on the back. He and Barbara blushed crimson. The Schneiders and Charles and August swarmed around, extending their congratulations to the newlyweds, the spirits of our little group momentarily lifted like a canvas at full sail.

But my brightened mood did not last long. That same afternoon I observed a ring around the sun, a sure sign a storm was on its way.

The noon bell rang as I sat on deck beside Rauch, the calm sea belying any threat of bad weather. Pulling out my pocket watch, I flipped it open and noticed once again it ran too fast.

"I don't understand it," I said, showing him. "My father relied on this watch to keep good time, but every day it's incorrect."

Rauch snorted. "It's not the watch, Harm. The rotation of the Earth brings the hour earlier each day."

I stared at him, then gave a weak laugh. "You're right. I'd forgotten about that."

Feeling foolish, I stood and walked over to the rail, where Franz and Barbara were staring intently at turbulent waters off the starboard bow. From the midst of the roughened patch, a whale crested, then another, and another. What a sight, those blue-gray backs wetly polished, plumes of water misting the air in half a dozen fountains. We pointed and exclaimed, drawing others to the railing. Margaret appeared beside me, Louis in tow.

"Monsters of the deep!" Louis growled, leaning in close to Margaret, to scare her or annoy her, I could not be sure.

Margaret shuddered and wrapped her shawl more tightly around her. Louis rested his arm on her shoulder. She shrugged him off and moved closer to me.

"You are too free, Louis," she said. "Once and for all, leave me be."

Louis rolled his eyes in my direction. "Kindly tell *Fräulein* Haas I am the best man she'll find on this ship."

Margaret moved to where Barbara stood on the other side of Franz. I met Louis' gaze.

"*Fräulein* Haas does not find your advances agreeable."

Louis opened his mouth, then clamped it shut again. He looked down and his eyes widened. "Hey," he whistled. "You steal that from Captain Higgins?"

I looked down and saw my pocket watch still open in my hand. "It is a gift from my father."

"What time is it, then?"

I snapped the watch shut. "Time for you to stop bothering *Fräulein* Haas."

Louis sneered out a laugh. "Ha! Big words from a little man. Maybe bigger than you can handle."

I thought Louis was about to use his fists, but instead he set his jaw, turned his back on me, and stalked away.

"We understand now," Franz said to Margaret, his voice consoling. "Harm and I will keep an eye out, so Louis won't bother you anymore."

"Thank you," Margaret said primly, but I saw tears in her eyes. She and Barbara left soon afterward for the women's side of the washroom.

I did not say so, but Franz's words reassured me. I had no desire to stand up against Louis on my own. Nor did I like how Louis had eyeballed my watch as if he had coveted it. That night, when Louis and Christian were away from their bunks, I stowed my watch back in its oil cloth, tucking it beneath the Bible to keep it extra safe.

The storm blew in the next afternoon. In no time at all, it seemed, the waves grew huge as the Haardt Mountains, but nowhere near as dormant. They shifted and roared, their white foaming caps snarling and spitting like famished beasts. As the passengers hurried below, icy gouts of saltwater cascaded down the hatch. I scrambled to tie down my belongings, in the eerie mid-day darkness checking one last time to be sure my pocket watch was safe. Beneath the Bible in my sea box, my fingers groped and groped, but closed around no oilcloth with its circle of gold.

I stood and looked over the top bunk. Rauch lay gripping the bedpost, his complexion greenish-gray.

"Have you seen my pocket watch?" I asked.

He shook his head and moaned. Margaret and Barbara had not seen it either, nor had August and Franz. Grabbing hold of my bunk to keep from somersaulting across the room, I turned to Christian.

"Have you seen my watch?"

"What watch?" Christian flopped to one side, then moments later, to the other.

I was having trouble holding on, but persevered. "My father's pocket watch. It's missing."

"Leave me alone!"

Ducking back down to my bunk, I poked Louis in the side.

"Have you seen my pocket watch?"

"Damn your watch." Louis' body was curled in a ball, his arms cradling his stomach. Suddenly he lunged forward and vomited over the edge of the bunk, missing the bucket.

The ship dipped, then spun violently. The floor swung up and threw me backward into a terrifying nightmare. For the next four days, waves fisted the Helvetia up and threw her down again, raced her forward, then heaved her backward. The ocean pounded down on us with punishing fury. With the others, I moaned and retched and screamed and prayed. *How had it come to pass*, I wondered, despairing, *that my life should end now, when it had hardly begun?* I prayed I could take it all back, that I could at least see my family once more before drowning.

As I suffered in misery and terror, I was hit by a crushing realization. I could never go home. I could never face Father. He had sent me into the world to be a blacksmith, to earn my living. I had begged to go. To return now, without his prized possession and without having ever arrived in Cleveland, would be impossible. Father had believed in me, but I had been vain and foolish and let him down. I deserved to die. I was a failure in any case. I imagined my family receiving word of my death, my brother's grim face, my parents' tears.

Day became night, which turned to day, and still we were tossed in a slick of saltwater and vomit. Finally, on the fourth morning, the mountainous waves softened. A gray light filtered into our beslimed steerage. At long last the sailors threw open the hatches so fresh air billowed in, reviving me some. Weakly, holding out hope, I opened my box and searched it once more. The pocket watch was gone.

Later, when Margaret and Barbara brought down a pot of hot beans, I choked them down like lumps of clay. As I sopped up the last of it with a rock-hard ship biscuit, a woman let out a terrible wail.

"She's dead, God help me, she's dead!"

People rushed to the woman's aid, but it was too late. Sometime during the storm, an old woman had passed out of this life. Now her body lay folded in her bunk like a bag of bones, growing stiffer and colder with each passing hour. I did not know the old woman, but joined others above deck for the sea burial.

In the distance, off the starboard bow, floating islands of white ice were visible, the air chill as winter. Standing by the body, the *Pfarrer* clenched his Bible against his heart. The first mate stepped forward.

"What is the name of this woman?" he asked.

"Anna Bacher," a woman answered, weeping into her shawl. "She was my mother-in-law."

The Pfarrer led us in the 23rd Psalm. We murmured together the familiar words. He prayed to grant Anna Bacher eternal rest and, as two sailors tipped the old woman's canvas-shrouded body into the sea, he led us in singing "Blessed are the Heirs of Heaven." As we sang, I could not help but think of Mütterchen, of how I had begged as a child for our family to emigrate. If the Johann Philipp Harms had made the journey, would Mütterchen have suffered a similar fate? I shuddered to think of her plummeting to the cold depths and prayed to God for forgiveness.

Gradually, my circulation felt restored, and the fog in my head began to clear. However, the sun didn't come out that day. That afternoon, blocked by walls of thick mist, even the icebergs were swallowed from view.

"We're nearing the Grand Banks of Newfoundland," people said.

Consumed by my own fog of self-pity and despair, I peered out the porthole at the gray sea for a glimpse of these Grand Banks. Over and over I berated myself for my vanity, for my good-for-nothing ideas, for losing Father's watch—in truth, regarding the latter, it felt as if a limb of my own body had been ripped away.

As ship life returned to normal, I felt a seething resentment toward my bunkmates. Louis and Christian struck me as men without consciences, who cared only for themselves. As for Rauch, he seemed to have taken offense at my asking about the pocket watch, as if by doing so, I had accused him of stealing it. Why shouldn't I suspect him? What made him so much better than the others? I detested him more openly and felt an irrepressible urge to outdo him. From then on, the four of us feigned courtesy to one another, but I trusted no one.

# Chapter 18

―――~~――――

## Cleveland, Ohio, 1857

T HE TRAIN CHUGGED ON INTO the deepest night. I sat erect in the passenger car as if I alone were responsible for bringing it to Cleveland. I passed the hours planning a speech for my uncle and aunt, to apologize, and to promise to do better. I knew I had started out on the wrong foot with them by borrowing money. I reasoned that I would make it up to them immediately. Hopefully, they would soon forget to hold a grudge.

Around midnight, the train stopped at yet another station. Two men climbed aboard, taking the seat just across from mine. Their faces were grimy with sweat, a condition that matched their filthy, torn clothing, almost rags. In comparison to them, my clean mended homespun looked almost respectable.

One of them rested a jug on his thigh and, as the train whistled and ka-chunked off, he popped the cork, tipped the jug to his mouth and took a deep swallow. Wheezing a cough of satisfaction, he passed the jug to his companion.

Across the aisle, a Frau dressed in black silk tutted her disapproval. The vagabond smacked his lips and leered at her, elbowing his companion as he did so. They chortled and tipped their hats to her. Abruptly, the good lady stood and groped in the swaying car to a seat at the end, by the cold iron stove. Herr Becker had told me of such sour Yankee women, the Puritanical Christian ladies who did not believe in drinking wine and beer.

The vagabond took back his jug from his friend and helped himself to another gulp, then noticed I was watching and tilted the jug toward me in invitation. I did indeed feel a powerful thirst. Ducking my head in thanks, I grabbed hold of the jug's round handle and, imitating the stranger, tipped some of the drink into my mouth. Tears sprang to my eyes as fire raced down my throat. Hacking and choking, I gave a great shudder. When my vision cleared, the men's faces wore huge grins. Had they tricked me into drinking poison?

Hastily, I handed back the jug. The man shook his head and pushed it toward me again, but I signaled an adamant "no." They dissolved into cackling, knee-slapping howls. My face warm with embarrassment, I managed a weak smile. Such was my first experience of American whiskey. A thimbleful numbed the senses faster than a whole *Krug* of wine.

My fellow travelers finished their drink and soon their heads bounced and nodded until they collapsed against each other with lip-rattling snores. For my part, I sat with eyes wide open, unable to shake the fear that I had somehow missed my stop. At each stop for coal and water, I scoured the moonlit landscape for signs we were nearing the town called Dunkirk on the enormous lake, but the view was an infinite landscape of forests and meadows.

I tried to picture the life ahead, and whether what Father had said was true—that it was God's will I should become a blacksmith. I had yet to test myself, to feel the weight of the hammer in my hand, but I had to believe I could do it. The ancient craft was part of my lifeblood. I had been given this chance by fate. In moments of elation, I imagined myself as a great success, able to send money and gifts back to my family in Freinsheim and one day to lure my brother to Ohio to buy a large farm, bigger and more bountiful than the richest men in the Palatinate could own. In moments of despair, I prayed that I would not hate blacksmithing as much as the farm work, that I would not let my family down, as I had so far.

Just as the sun appeared above the treetops, the train arrived at the broad shore of Lake Erie in Dunkirk, New York. I stepped stiff and sore onto the platform and breathed in odors of fish, lake weed, and fresh-sawn timber. From this view, the blue-green waters of the lake were clogged with coal barges, steamers, and sailing ships, but I did not loiter.

"Cleveland? Lake Shore Train?" I repeated anxiously to each uniform-wearing official on the platform. They all pointed to a train waiting on a different track. One of them held up three fingers to indicate several hours before departure. My body tingling with exhaustion. I waited beside the hawkers and carts, my money pouch as empty as my stomach, until at last I was permitted to climb on board. As the train chugged off, in the distance across the lake, thunderclouds built into dark towers. The sky grew ever darker, the heavy July heat nearly choking me of breath.

The train reached the outskirts of a large town by late afternoon. Here wide avenues splayed from the lake shore like the fat fingers of an open palm. The station house spelled out CLEVELAND in block letters above the platform. Finally, I had arrived. The train screeched to a halt just as the clouds overhead gave a boom that shook the earth.

My heart in my throat, I walked out into the pouring rain. Passengers scattered in all directions, pulling their cloaks high and hat brims low. Gentlemen and ladies hailed two-wheeled carriages or dashed up the street under umbrellas. I ran for cover under the first store awning I came to. Sopped through, I stood there for some time, watching as the Lake Shore train whistled, snorted, and snaked off to the west. On Lake Erie, steamships churned through the choppy, gray waters. Horses strained with their loads of passengers and cargo on the mud-river streets.

At last the rainfall began to ease. As I wondered where to go next, a man stepped from the store behind me holding a garden rake. I dared to inquire of him if he knew of Herr Johann Rapparlie, of John Rapparlie wagons. He pointed up the hill and, *Gott sei Dank,* replied in German.

"Up above us, just at the top of this hill, is Seneca Street. Follow it, neither left nor right, until you start to go down again. The shop of Rapparlie stands on the corner with Michigan Street."

I thanked him and set out, slipping and sliding behind the man up the muddy hill toward my new Cleveland home.

The terrain flattened out as I hurried along, past a clean, well-kept public park dotted with young trees. Not wishing to delay any longer, I told myself that I would soon return to explore this part of town. Bordering the greenery of the park were two- and three-story buildings. The Cleveland townsfolk did not dress in such fine silks and top hats as the inhabitants of Paris and New York. A good portion of this populace dressed in dull reds, browns, and blues, the men in odd-looking, wide-brimmed straw hats, the women's heads covered by scarves or decorated bonnets.

When I spotted German lettering on shop signs, I felt considerable relief. The windows in this district displayed stoneware pottery and jewelry, watches, candles, shoes, soap, and cigars. I passed a wagon shop called Black & Co. across from a livery, and another by the name of Drumm, the telltale horseshoe out front. And where, I wondered, would I find the Wayside Smithy in this town? Was my old shipmate Charles Rauch even now walking these streets? But I didn't have time to dwell on the matter. Just as the man at the hardware store said, Seneca Street began to slope downhill. Below me I beheld a cluster of red brick buildings, the words JOHN RAPPARLIE painted boldly across them. Here, at the crossroads with Michigan street, my new life was about to begin.

When hearing the letters from Cleveland as a child, I had often pictured Rapparlie's place of business set in a picturesque forest of towering trees, but this place was one of commerce, no trees in evidence. A short distance from the wagon shop buildings stood a soap- and candle-making factory with tall smokestacks. A tang of lake bracken, sawdust, varnish, and coal smoke bit the air. Rows of squat buildings edged the banks of two waterfront thoroughfares, the first a broad ditch, teams of mules towing cargo-laden barges along its still waters. Beyond this canal flowed a broad river, the tea-colored water stirred with steamers and barges, the air noisy with the shouts of dock workers, the thump of paddlewheels, the shriek of steam whistles and clang of bells.

From the Rapparlie shop came the methodical ring of anvils. Just inside the open doorway I made out a pair of workmen climbing over a wagon bed to heft a wheel into place. To one side of this establishment stood a tall brick house, which I presumed was the residence of my aunt and uncle. It was nearing evening as I crossed the street to the sandstone stoop and knocked at the door.

After a moment, a barefoot, freckle-faced girl opened it.

"It's Michael Harm, the younger son of Johann Philipp and Elizabeth Harm of Freinsheim," I said.

The girl gazed at me blankly. Behind her, a woman appeared, wiping her hands on her apron, her clear, broad forehead reminding me so much of Mütterchen.

"*Gott sei Dank*," the woman said. "He is safely arrived at last. Father, come see, here is the son of my sister Elisabetha."

A silhouette appeared in the kitchen doorway, a man with shoulders tilted to one side, leaning on a cane, young children clustered around his legs.

"Who is it?" the man asked, his voice a low grumble.

"My sister's son, Michael Harm. You sent him train money."

My Uncle Johann regarded me up and down. "He's small," he said to my aunt, then limped toward me. "You are not the eldest, but the younger?"

"I am the younger son of Johann Philipp Harm. My older brother was needed for the farm work. I thank you for your kindness in sending me the train fare. I will repay you at the first opportunity."

Uncle Johann examined me, his hair sticking straight up from his forehead in a stiff, shocking white. "What am I to do with a boy? I don't need another child."

"I'm sixteen!" I said.

His mouth drew down in a scowl.

Aunt Katharina let out a sigh. "Children, meet your cousin Michael. Here is our eldest son John, just turned eight, then Jacob six and Wilhelm four. Sussy is but one year old; she's sleeping in the cradle. Here is our servant Roselie, who helps me on wash day."

Roselie curtsied and went off to tend to little Wilhelm, who was just then climbing on a chair back. Uncle Johann reached out and crushed my hand in his enormous paw. Holding on, he pulled my palm toward him, examined it, then discarded it again and hobbled back to the kitchen.

"Come with me," Aunt Katharina said in an undertone. On the way upstairs to the attic, she pointed out the purpose of several rooms, including a toilet and tub inside the house. In the low-ceilinged top floor, a narrow bed had been tucked along one wall. "Don't mind your uncle. It will take him some time to adjust. We worried about you, as you did not arrive at the same time as the son of Jacob Rauch."

"My parents instructed me to carry messages to the Becker family in *Kleindeutschland*. I became lost in the city and was robbed."

Aunt Katharina nodded, a weary slump to her shoulders. She was a sturdier version of my mother, with the same frizzy brown hair and blue-gray eyes. "It's a hard thing, that you come to us in this manner."

My aunt turned and descended the stairs, leaving me alone. I threw my rucksack on a wooden chair and stretched out on the bed, feeling jostled and numb from my journey. Uncle Rapparlie did not want me. I must have caused him great trouble indeed, to make him so angry. I resolved to devote all my energies to paying him back as soon as I could.

I lay ruminating over the marvels I had glimpsed in this house on the short trip up the stairs. In truth, the Rapparlies did not seem to lack for money. Their house was three stories, in comparison to the Beckers' three tiny rooms, and the furnishings were fine. I had glimpsed leather-bound volumes of poetry, of Goethe, Schiller and Heine on the bookshelves downstairs. They could even afford a servant girl! I closed my eyes and, thanking God for my good fortune, fell into an exhausted sleep.

# Chapter 19

———~~———

E XCITEMENT SURGED THROUGH ME AS I awoke, jarred from sleep by the calls of children. Sitting up, I felt a gnawing hunger in my gut. The last time I had eaten, I realized, was two nights ago when I finished off the last of Frau Becker's provisions.

I peeked out the attic window at the gray-blue morning, at the waterfront docks already swarming with activity. How late was it? I adjusted my homespun shirt and pants and ran my fingers through my hair, anxious now, and a little fearful, to go downstairs and face my uncle. But as I entered the kitchen, he was not there. The woman waiting to greet me was my Aunt Margaretha Scheuermann.

My mother's younger sister didn't have the frizzy light brown hair or the grim set to her chin of Aunt Katharina and my mother. Aunt Margaretha's tresses were smooth dark brown, gathered into a bun at the back of her neck. Her eyes were light blue. Her cheeks—in fact her whole face—was rounder than any I had seen. She had brought her two little children, Georgie and Johnny, to add to the three Rapparlie boys and baby Sussy.

Uncle Johann was already over at the shop, Aunt Katharina informed me as she fed me rolls and sausages, apples, milk and coffee. She said they'd decided to allow me a day's rest after my long journey. While I ate, the little cousins played their games, and Aunt Margaretha peppered me with questions about Freinsheim and my parents.

I described for my aunts how Father had built Mütterchen a stool for her to sit on in the kitchen as she cooked, how some days were better than others. I told my aunts of the wet harvest year of 1856, of the greed of our Bavarian rulers that continued after the uprising. I recounted my sea voyage and the riots in New York City, and the story of how I had been robbed.

At the close of this last tale, Aunt Margaretha frowned. "*Tch,* such a shame." She looked up at Aunt Katharina, who peeled potatoes, dropping them into a pot set on the black iron stove. "Our poor nephew has had a very hard journey and much misfortune. Surely your husband doesn't hold his bad luck against him?"

"My husband has endured much hardship himself and lives these days in his own pain," Aunt Katharina said.

"*Bitte,* how did Uncle Johann lose his foot?" I asked.

"The dray fell on him." Aunt Katharina's forehead creased at the memory. "Three years ago, your uncle went to pick up a load of white oak lumber. A boy threw a firecracker in the street and the horse bolted. The runaway went over an embankment at Lakeview Park. Your uncle was thrown, his foot crushed under the wagon and all those planks. He was long in bed, in such terrible pain, with many doctors coming to see what could be done."

Shaking her head, Aunt Margaretha picked up the story. "After all that, no use, they still had to remove the foot. Johann traveled to Philadelphia for the wooden leg, and when he returned, the very next day, our brother left us. How I wish Jakob was still here! He was always able to talk sense into Johann."

I felt a crush of disappointment. "Uncle Jakob isn't here?"

Aunt Margaretha shook her head. "He's thousands of miles away in California. He took a boat all the way around the tip of South America, a journey of many months. But they say most of the gold has already been claimed, so I doubt he'll have the good luck to find any." She broke off with a laugh, a lilting sound, like a bird. "Such a long face, nephew. With your droopy mouth, you're the image of my sister Elisabetha. We aren't your Uncle Jakob, but we'll do our best to amuse you."

In all our conversations that morning, Aunt Margaretha laughed more readily than Aunt Katharina. I sensed in Aunt Katharina a great weight of some kind, her spirit damp and lumpy, like a pillow left in the rain.

"In any case, nephew, you must be a guest at my house this week," Aunt Margaretha continued, "to see the Georg Scheuermanns on the west side of the Cuyahoga."

Aunt Katharina huffed and flicked a potato peel into the slop bucket. "Sister, you don't know what you're saying. It's not possible. My husband will put the boy to work right away, tomorrow."

"What?" Aunt Margaretha waved a hand in dismissal. "Our nephew has only just arrived. Let him get his bearings a bit."

"But he owes Johann money, ten dollars for the train fare. Johann says he must do chores in our home to repay us."

I felt a jolt of shock. "Uncle Johann no longer wants me as his apprentice?"

Aunt Katharina sighed. "It's not so bad as that. Johann wouldn't go back on his promise to your father. You are to apprentice during the day and repay your debt in the evenings, feed the horses, chop the wood—"

Aunt Margaretha *pffed* in disgust. "*Doch*, that's just like Johann Rapparlie. Listen to me, Katharina, we must not appear mean-spirited. It reflects badly on our family. Let our nephew begin his apprenticeship in August. After all this time, what's two more weeks? Michael must be introduced to the other Freinsheimers here. They'll want to hear his news." Aunt Margaretha turned to me. "What do you think? Come to my house tonight, meet your Uncle Georg, and tomorrow I'll bring you to market to meet more Freinsheimers anxious to hear word of their families."

I glanced back and forth between my aunts. "Will the Ritthalers be at the market? I have letters for them." As I said this, I saw unhappiness cloud Aunt Katharina's face and knew I should not go. Disappointment gathered under my ribs. "Thank you," I said, turning back to Aunt Margaretha, "you are very kind, but I can't go with you. I don't have any money, and I'm obligated to Uncle Rapparlie."

"Never mind that. Georg will talk to Johann."

"Sister—"

"Hush now, Katharina. Your husband isn't thinking right since his injury. We can't treat our own nephew like a slave."

"But I mustn't upset my uncle after he's been so kind to me." I didn't like to be the rope pulled back and forth in this tug-of-war, but even more, I feared shaming my parents.

Aunt Margaretha shook her head. "Don't be afraid of Johann Rapparlie. He's all bark and no bite. It would be better if Jakob were here, but Georg will manage to convince him it's the right thing."

In spite of myself, I thought I might burst with excitement. I didn't deserve this taste of freedom, but the chance was too wonderful to resist. Before the noon dinner that same morning, Aunt Margaretha swept me into her chaise with her two boys and drove us behind a high-stepping, dun-colored horse to her home in Ohio City. My conscience told me I was making a mistake, leaving the Rapparlie home without receiving my uncle's approval. Yet Aunt Margaretha had insisted, and it felt impolite to refuse. I didn't *want* to refuse.

During the drive, I sat high up on the chaise seat, my aunt chattering like a starling about her husband, a machinist foreman in a steamboat factory. I decided my uncle Scheuermann must earn a large wage, because their house in Ohio City was grand indeed, built of red brick with a front porch to sit on in the heat of the day. As I waited for Uncle Georg to return from work, I tumbled and played outside with my two little cousins. Like many German women, my aunt was an excellent gardener, so her yard was bursting with flowers of all kinds. The sweet scents wrapped me in a delicious perfume. It had been a long time since I'd been free to play, with green plants growing all around.

When Uncle Georg came home, unlike my Uncle Johann, he received me in a friendly manner. After supper as it grew dark, he and I drank Rhine wine on the porch, slapping mosquitoes from our necks and hands. As a child, Uncle Georg told me, he had lived in Weisenheim am Sand. I told him of the fight at the Herxheim *Kerwe* between the Weisenheimers and the Freinsheimers, and he cheered so loudly for the Weisenheimers that his boys stopped their play to gawp. In the night air, fireflies sparked in the meadow grasses along the ditch by the road. Georgie and Johnny went with jars to trap them, although they were sorely disappointed that, once captured, the little pulsing lights grew dim.

THE NEXT DAY, A SATURDAY, Aunt Margaretha took me to the Central Market, where I did indeed see many Freinsheimers and received much attention. On Sunday came the best surprise of all. Uncle Georg harnessed the horse and chaise for a drive to the Ritthaler farm in Parma in order for me to deliver my family's letter in person. During the two hour journey, we rode past tidy houses and acres of farmland and grazing animals until I began to feel as if I had arrived in paradise.

The following Saturday, Adam Höhn came to market and took me back with him for a visit to his farm in Columbiana. Here I saw for the first time how, to prevent ruts, the roads were crossed with planks, which rotted easily and caused a rough ride. I also observed the method of girdling trees—farmers ringing the tree bark so the entire forests died, the more easily to plant their crops without felling and stump removal. It was a strange way to treat the trees, I thought. Farmers back in Freinsheim would not believe it if I told them.

Adam Höhn was the uncle of Matthias, so I was especially happy to greet him and give him news of his relatives. These first two weeks, I still wore my homespun clothes, patched in many places. Among the farmers, I didn't stand out so much, but in town, these clothes made me appear doltish, obviously a new arrival from the Old Country. But I felt sure that once I returned to the Rapparlies, Uncle Johann would provide me with new ones.

On my last evening at the Scheuermann's, as I sat at their kitchen table inhaling the heady aroma of corn steaming in a kettle, Aunt Margaretha set an ink jar, paper, and a quill before me.

"You must write to your parents," she said. "Georg will mail it for you."

I looked at my aunt with gratitude, part of me wishing I could stay in this home of laughter forever. Her expressive face passed through many different emotions at once—joy, sadness, serenity, longing. In these two short weeks

I had developed a deep fondness for her. I suspected she gave me the letter-writing task to amuse her children, but a message to my parents and brother was long overdue in any case.

But how to begin? Not only a geographical distance, but also hundreds of strange new experiences and encounters loomed between me and my family. I wanted confess to my parents about my bad luck, how I'd lost Father's watch and been robbed, but these events would come as grave news indeed. Remembering how Mütterchen used to fret so over each item of the Cleveland letters, I resolved to put as good a face as possible on my journey.

With Georgie and Johnny crowding against the kitchen table, Johnny's soft breath tickling the hairs of my arm, I dipped my pen in the jar of blue India ink and started to write.

> Cleveland, 30 July 1857
> Much loved parents and brother,
>
> With joy I pick up the quill to send you the news that I have arrived healthy in Cleveland. First I want to describe the voyage: we were taken aboard the Helvetia on May 18th and our ship left the harbor with good wind. At first there was the seasickness, but after eight days one gets accustomed to the motion. Our ocean journey was not very good, because when one moves around on the water for 43 days, that's not very fast. For days at a time, the wind stopped blowing and the ship rested motionless. When the 43rd day came along, we still didn't see land in the morning at 6 o'clock and at 10 o'clock we had gotten such a good wind we were at anchor at New York.
>
> There I stayed for thirteen days at the Beckers, and met other Freinsheimers too, Veit Börner now married to Martha Becker, with two children and another on the way, and the Philipp Kirchners, they are also very well. I also met the old man Aul, who was very happy about the encounter. I gave them all your greetings and letters.
>
> From there I continued my travel by train on the Erie Railroad to Cleveland. The Rapparlies are all still quite healthy. I have also visited cousin Scheuermann and his family, they are also quite healthy and happy and have two boys. When I was barely two days in Cleveland, it was known to the Freinsheimers all over and I saw many of them on market day.
>
> Adam Höhn comes weekly to Cleveland to the market with his two white horses. He visited me immediately. He asked if I didn't have a letter from his brother. When I told him no he was very sad, he said he had written once before. I later went out with him to his

farm and stayed two days with him. He hosts every 14 days music or a dance in his barn, when all the farmers and Freinsheimers from the surrounding areas come together.

Dear parents, until now I like it very much in Cleveland and wouldn't feel any longing anymore for Germany, if you, dear parents, would be with me. I will learn the blacksmith business, and am thanking our dear God for that.

Now I want to close my writing and I remain your true son and your loving brother,

Michael Harm

Many greetings to all good friends and acquaintances and neighbors.

A greeting to Matthias Höhn and his family and at last to my school comrades and their parents and brothers and sisters.

Write an answer to this letter to Michael Harm at Jo Rapp. Clev Oh.

Back at Rapparlie's, my aunt shook me awake before dawn.

"You must hurry," she said.

Groggily, I sat up. "Are there some work clothes I can wear, so as not to ruin my only shirt and pants?"

"Your uncle cannot spare any. Hurry now."

Determined to make a good impression, I didn't grumble, but dressed and hastened downstairs. Uncle Johann and the boys were already breaking their fast. My uncle didn't even look up to grunt a greeting. I had only taken a few bites of bread and ham when he rose and reached for his cane.

"*Alla hopp*, we start," he said. "At day's end, we sign the indenture papers."

Still chewing, I followed him out the door and across a yard stacked with all manner of wagon parts, tools, and iron. His eldest son Little John came along, on his way to the stable to feed the horses. It was not yet light out. The smithy of the wagon-making shop was on the ground level in the first of four buildings. A man a few years older than me was already there shoveling coal. Uncle Johann pulled a leather apron off a hook and shoved it toward me.

To the other worker he said, "Show my nephew how to prepare the forge fires," then turned and left again for the house.

"Singley. William Singley," the man said. "You must be the nephew, Harm?"

"Michael Harm," I said, tying on the apron, much worn and coated in grease. William Singley was a head taller than me, his chest so barrel-like he appeared to have no neck at all. He had a thick beard of dark brown and small brown eyes in a round face. He showed me how to clean the forge fires of ash from the day before, then line the bottom of the cavity with pine splinters, laying sticks of oak on top, leaving a mound of coal to one side.

"Why don't you light it?" I asked as Singley moved to the next forge.

"The smith does that. Each jour wants his fire just so."

Within the hour, the journeymen blacksmiths—"jours" as we called them—arrived for the workday: Herr Penhoff, Herr Hoffmann, Herr Gesler and several others. Two of them worked at each forge. I watched as they examined their fires, made adjustments, then lit the kindling. As the wood flared up and collapsed, they raked coal into the center.

I stood by, idle, uncertain of my next task. The men ignored me. After a while, Uncle Johann hobbled in and motioned me over to a workstation with two anvils. The second anvil, well off to one side, stood on its stump, old and deeply scarred. Here, my master proceeded to demonstrate my first task. Desperate to memorize every move he made, I watched him select a piece of small iron from a pile and jam it into the fire. Moments later, he took a pair of long-handled tongs and pulled it out, glowing yellow. Laying the bit on the anvil, he gave it four well-placed hammer blows, then held it out to me for examination.

"A nail," he said.

As I looked on, my uncle made two more nails just the same, then handed me the hammer.

"Small work for a small boy," he said, leaving me to the task.

It looked simple enough, but the tongs were heavy and the bit of iron was small. I could barely grip the unforged iron from the fire with the tongs, let alone hold the hot metal in position on the anvil while hammering it. By the time I managed to get one in position, the yellow glow had cooled to a dull orange. I hammered away at it anyway, with mediocre results. With each attempt, my hands seemed to grow clumsier. Often, I fumbled the iron so it fell to the ground.

I labored all morning, and by the noon dinner hour had made only five crooked nails. I feared Uncle Johann would inspect my work and shout at me, but he and the other smiths ignored me. In the long days of idleness during my travels, my muscles had grown soft, so as I crossed the yard to eat the noon meal, my shoulders and forearms ached.

During dinner, neither Uncle Johann nor Aunt Katharina would meet my gaze. I feared I was being tested and felt certain I was failing. I should not have gone to Aunt Margaretha's, I thought guiltily. Uncle Georg must not have convinced Uncle Johann this was the right thing. I knew I was in deep trouble.

The food restored my spirits some, but in the afternoon things did not go any better. Eventually, the apprentice Singley plodded over, hands on his hips, to glower at my labors.

"You're wasting your time," he said.

I gripped a bit of iron firmly in my tongs and poked it into the fire. "It's only my first day."

Singley snorted. "There is a modern machine that cuts the nails. Herr Rapparlie has no need of those nails and no need of you either."

I pulled out the bit of iron and, as usual, the bright yellow glow slipped from my tongs. This time I dropped the tongs, too. As I danced my feet out of the way, Singley burst out laughing. The jours stopped their work to stare. Humiliated, I reached down with my bare hand to pick up the iron, no longer glowing, searing my thumb and forefinger.

"*Aua!*" I shouted, stuffing my burned fingers in my mouth.

"Rapparlie's won a prize with him," one of the men said.

They all laughed.

I suffered through the rest of the day, the fiery pain in my fingers intense. At last, Uncle Johann came over to eye my meager pile of crooked nails. My knees started shaking as if they might buckle beneath me. I did my best to steady them. I had come all this way. I couldn't bear the thought of being sent home.

"You'll stay until the last, you and Singley," he said. "You'll never leave this shop until the forge fires are cold. I've lost two workplaces. Burned to smoke and ash. I'm not about to lose another."

I did as I was told, then trudged home to supper. I sat alone at the table, the rest of the family having already eaten. As I picked at the last of my food, Uncle Johann came into the kitchen and placed the indenture contract before me. Sitting at the head of the table, he watched while I read the dense handwriting.

It was a three year contract, I saw, that would last until my nineteenth year. It contained a list of behaviors forbidden to the apprentice—going to taverns, gambling, fornicating, marrying. It even forbade going to playhouses. Was this how all indenture contracts were written? I had not thought to ask my father how it would be.

I glanced up at my uncle, whose deep-set eyes studied me, one eyelid drooping lower than the other.

"The name Rapparlie has a good reputation in this town," Uncle Johann said, "and will serve you well. What trade secrets you learn, you are forbidden to share with anyone." These words were also written in the contract, so I wondered that he should repeat them. "I pay for your meals and provide room and laundry, plus a weekly allowance of sixty cents, paid every Saturday evening. You'll begin to receive your allowance in November, after you've repaid me in coin and labor the ten dollars owing for the train. Do you understand?"

"In coin and labor?"

"You'll repay me the seven dollars and twenty cents from your weekly wages, your first twelve weeks of pay. The rest—two dollars and eighty cents— you'll earn doing chores around the house. Your aunt and I will assign these tasks and keep careful track so you aren't cheated."

It sounded like something out of *Oliver Twist*.

"What about clothes?"

"I have paid enough coin up front already. I can spare no more."

Normally, apprenticeships included clothing. Did Uncle Johann mean to humiliate me? All at once I felt outraged. I didn't want to do this. I remembered Johann Rapparlie's letter to my father, the words he used to describe my Uncle Johannes' disappearance, how his blood rebelled within him. Was this true, or was this an excuse? Was Uncle Johann a cruel master? My mind racing, I tried to think of any other way to make a living than indenture to this man. Then I pictured my father, thin and pale, the day he said he would send me here. I had promised to do this. I could not go back on my word.

"In August of 1860," Uncle Johann continued, "I'll pay your freedom dues of one hundred thirty dollars." He was leaving many pauses between his sentences. Did he think I was dim-witted? "Then you'll be a journeyman, qualified to work as a blacksmith for hire wherever you choose."

My uncle paused again. It occurred to me he might be having serious doubts about taking me on. That day I'd overheard talk in the smithy of fewer orders for wagons and carriages, of increased uncertainty about the savings banks.

"I told your father I needed an apprentice," Uncle Johann went on, wincing as he shifted the position of his wooden leg under the table, "and so I'm good to my word. My eldest son John is only eight, so I need someone until he is older. My business will be Rapparlie and Sons. I don't look for partners. And I won't abide loafers or idlers. You shirk your duties at your peril. *Verstanden*?"

"Yes, I understand."

Johann Rapparlie came to my side of the table, his breath sour as he leaned down, picked up the quill and dipped it in the ink jar. He pulled the contract from my hand, signed his name, and the words Master Blacksmith. With my burned thumb and forefinger, I also gripped the quill, dipped it into the ink, and signed my name under his.

It was God's will I should do this work.

# Chapter 20

———

THE BURNS ON MY THUMB and forefinger weren't serious, merely the first of many suffered as a blacksmith. Our fingers burned and healed so many times the prints were seared right off them. Our hands and arms became scarred as well. If a burn was bad enough, we would pause to quench our scorched flesh in the cold water of the slack tub. Otherwise, we continued to pound the iron, the nerves of our hands deadened, our skin thick and stretched taut around the bones.

After that first day, Uncle Johann did not allow me near a hammer or anvil, further proof he'd been trying to get rid of me. Each morning began at five o'clock. I'd bolt my rolls and coffee alone then plod over to prepare the forge fires. I was the lowest of the low, filling the coal bins, wearing my legs out on the foot-treadle grinder. Every so often I'd be called to the other departments, to the wheel pit in the wagon yard to pour water on the hot iron of a tire, to assist with stirring the paint cauldron when the painter's apprentice, Fred Fry, was given other duties. My fellow blacksmith apprentice William Singley undermined me at every turn, sneaking bricks under my feet to make me trip, greasing the coal shovel so it slipped from my hands.

One might suppose Uncle Johann, with his amputated foot, would spend fewer hours in his shop, but he was ever-present, penciling wagon specifications on scrap wood, examining a wagon frame in the wood-working department, or forging trickier pieces of hardware with his own hands. The painting and trimming departments were on the second floor of a separate building. A long steep ramp extended from it to move the carriages up and down. It was painful to watch my uncle hobble step by step up that ramp to check on the work of the master painter Herr Fry, but he went anyway. Afternoons he returned to the house at five rather than seven to spend the last work hours with bookkeeping. In the evenings, he went out to call at the homes of delinquent customers.

I returned late to the house each evening, everyone else having finished supper, to a list of tasks—sorting scraps in the woodshed, mucking out the stables, cleaning the paving stones of mud and manure at the front of the house.

ON THAT FIRST SUNDAY, I awoke to the tolling of church bells and realized I had not been to church in a very long time. I went downstairs expecting to find the Rapparlie family dressed in their church clothes, but Aunt Katharina stood washing pots in her housework dress, a scarf wrapped tightly around her head. Jacob and Wilhelm played around her skirts. Baby Sussy lay on a blanket across the room from the hot stove, kicking and playing with her little toes.

"*Aha*, there you are," she greeted me.

My Aunt Katharina reminded me of Mütterchen in appearance, but unlike my mother, she worked with unflagging energy. I sat down at the table to eat my rolls and cheese, while extending my finger for baby Sussy to grab.

"Is there no German church here?" I asked.

"On the contrary. There are too many—the Evangelical Reformed, the Lutheran, the Catholic, the Mennonite. Your grandparents attended the *Zum Schifflein Christi.*"

"The Little Boat of Christ? What kind of church is that?"

Uncle Johann entered the kitchen just then. "Too much squabbling at that one," he said. "Throwing tantrums like little children."

Aunt Katharina ignored him. "Some German sailors started it, a promise to God when they did not drown."

"It sounds right for me since, by the grace of God, the Helvetia also did not sink."

I'd gulped the last of my coffee when, to my surprise, my aunt removed her apron and hung it on a hook. "I'll walk Michael to church," she said to my uncle in a firm voice. "Watch the baby. I won't be long."

My aunt seemed anxious to get out of the house, hastily tying a clean scarf around her frizzy soft brown hair and throwing a lace-edged shawl over her shoulders. Together, we walked up Seneca Street. On this quiet Sunday morning, Cleveland seemed especially sedate compared to New York. We passed a number of churches ringed with horses and wagons, the sound of hymns emanating from within.

As we reached Public Square, I took in the gray sandstone church at the north end, the most European-looking building I'd seen in this town. It reminded me of a church I saw once in Mannheim, although this one had scaffolding around one of the towers.

"Are they just building that one?" I asked.

"That's the Presbyterian church," Aunt Katharina said. "The tower caught fire last spring and the firemen couldn't get the water high enough. It blazed like a giant candle. The tower crashed down right in the street. *Gott sei Dank* the whole city didn't go up in flames."

The *Zum Schifflein Christi* Church was not nearly as grand, a small wooden structure a few blocks down Superior Street. As we stood on the steps, the German hymn "Holy Hour" floated from the open doorway. I'd thought my aunt would join me, but to my surprise, she bid me farewell, turned, and left for home.

I removed my hat and entered as quietly as I could, glad to find an open place in the back pew. The parishioners dressed in their best clothes, I noticed. I had much trouble with only one set of clothes. When Aunt Katharina washed my homespun tunic and pants, I had to sit in a blanket waiting for them to dry.

As if God knew my innermost thoughts, the Pfarrer's sermon that morning emphasized hard work, duty, and obedience, leading me to pray fervently to God for forgiveness for straying toward vanity. With renewed purpose, I returned to the Rapparlies to do my chores.

That evening, the humid August heat forced the Rapparlie family into the wagon yard, where a slight breeze lifted off the river. Uncle Johann ordered me to bring up a pitcher of wine from the cellar cask and shared a glass with me, making me feel welcome for the first time.

In truth, my uncle seemed to be in a good mood. Still for once, he propped his wooden leg on a stool and leaned back with a pensive expression. When his youngest son Wilhelm began ducking back and forth beneath the wooden leg, Uncle Johann captured the boy with his big blacksmith hands, tickling until Wilhelm squirmed and shrieked with delight.

With a glass of Rhine wine to relax my tongue, I asked Uncle Johann about my grandparents. He told me Henry and Elisabetha Handrich came to this country too late in their lives, so they never adjusted to the American way.

"My mother couldn't understand why they remained in town," I said. "She said they'd planned to buy a farm like the Höhns and the Ritthalers."

Uncle Johann made an arc with his cane to take in his four shop buildings and the woodshed overflowing with lumber. "*Alla*, in town, the land values rise fast. All a man has to do is buy a property, live here a few years, and watch his fortune grow. The farming was not for us. Your Grandpa Heinrich was a good carpenter in any case. He worked in our wood shop for some years, until the rheumatism stiffened his joints."

"But how did your business grow so fast?"

Pride sparked in Uncle Johann's slate blue eyes. "When we first arrived in 1840, I took a position in the shop of a German named Drumm as a journeyman blacksmith. I saw right away that here in America it is the fashion for a wagon to be built by one man. People say, 'he has a Drumm wagon,' or, 'that is one of the coaches made by Peter Black.' I brought with me savings from the Old Country, enough to purchase my own property on this street. In my shop, I made a sturdier wagon than Drumm and Black, and Hurlbut, too, and soon had enough business to hire more workers. Even the Yankee Clevelanders come to the Rapparlie shop, though many still prefer the New England carriages."

"What about the shop of Rauch, called Wayside Smithy? Do they make good wagons?"

I had told my aunt and uncle something about my sea voyage, of becoming acquainted with the son of the Cleveland wagon-maker. Uncle Johann leaned against the arm of his chair.

"*Doch,* this Jacob Rauch is a newcomer, only here since 1853. He buys the spokes for his wheels and the steam-bent felloes ready-made from a factory."

"What's wrong with that?"

"How can you guarantee the quality of your parts if they're made somewhere else? And is it honest to put your name alone on this work? The Wayside Smithy has a good location on the Columbus stagecoach line. Otherwise, customers would take their business elsewhere."

Uncle Johann's assessment of the Rauch wagon-making raised my spirits. I had not seen Charles Rauch once since coming here. When I'd asked Singley about the Wayside Smithy, he'd told me it stood well to the west. Cleveland was a town that seemed to stretch in all directions, spread out far, divided in half by the broad, winding Cuyahoga. I realized with relief there was not much danger of running into Charles Rauch at all.

In late September, the days stayed warm and the nights grew cooler, a mixture, as we said in Freinsheim, of *Altweibersommer* and *Goldener Herbst,* of "old woman summer" and "golden autumn." On a Sunday, I was invited again to the Ritthaler farm, where the men hunted in the woods for deer and birds. On this occasion I witnessed for the first time the "passage" pigeons, red-breasted birds so plentiful they blocked out the sun. When the dark cloud of birds swarmed overhead, the Ritthaler men left their harvesting, carpentry, and milling and grabbed their shotguns.

Herr Ritthaler handed me a gun, too, explaining that if allowed to settle on his fields, these birds would eat everything. Their white droppings pelted us from the sky as we lifted our rifles and, with each blast of buckshot, brought down at least half a dozen. The men collected them on a wagon bed in a large pile. With some, Frau Ritthaler baked us American pigeon pies. The rest were fed to the hogs.

In the woods of Parma, the fallen leaves of the oak trees formed a bronze carpet on the forest floor. In a separate acre, Herr Ritthaler had planted a grove of sugar maples, each tree blazing that October with orange, red, and yellow—flaming and miraculous as the burning bush of the Bible.

At the Ritthaler farm I heard the first rumblings of the political trouble then brewing. I was learning that the older German pioneers were for the most part conservatives, members of the Democratic Party. They couldn't understand why so many recent German immigrants supported a new political party called the Republicans. I got an earful about this from Herr Ritthaler, and when I returned to the Rapparlies, learned that Uncle Johann was one of the conservatives.

"That Thieme is such a blowhard," Uncle Johann said one evening, breaking away from his reading of the German *Wächter am Erie* newspaper. I had discovered that if I finished my chores quickly, I could join my uncle and aunt in the kitchen as my uncle read the paper out loud to her. "Here he says: 'the *Wächter* wishes to be a voice of truth. An enemy of all oppression, whether of a black man or a white man, he shall be the consistent friend of liberty ...' What business does Thieme have interfering in American politics? These new immigrants bring their 1848 democratic rebellion here as if there is not already democracy in this country. They make fools of us all."

Aunt Katharina *pffed* and shook her head in commiseration.

"There are 1848 Freedom Fighters in Cleveland?" I was very excited to hear this.

"*Ja doch*, these university students and intellectuals of the 1848 rebellion. They are chased from Germany, but we don't want them here, either."

I felt insulted. I thought of Herr Glock, Herr Becker, and Veit Börner, men with passion for equality and freedom who acted on their convictions. Uncle Johann had been in America so long, he didn't realize all that had happened. In truth, he struck me as an old fool.

"There is a Jacob Müller in this city," my uncle continued, "who brags about the struggle at Kircheimbolanden against the Prussian troops of Prince Wilhelm. He's from Alsenz—the same as this August Thieme, editor of the *Wächter am Erie*. These exiles have taken up with the abolitionists and fight against slavery. I say to them, slavery is in America, whether you like it or not."

"What about those Negroes across the street. Are they slaves?" I was referring to our neighbors, the Warners. Their coal black skin startled me every time I saw them.

"No, they're freemen," Aunt Katharina said. "Mr. Warner works for a wage as a cook. Poor man, a widower with three children."

"*Ja, ja,* there is no slavery allowed in Ohio," Uncle Johann said. "This is the way in America. Each state makes its own laws."

I had already heard plenty about this from Franz Handrich. "How did Mr. Warner get to be free? Did he run away?"

"It would be bad for him if he had," Uncle Johann said. "The Fugitive Law states we have to return runaways to their masters. Some buy their freedom, others are born free."

*Buy their freedom?* How could one buy his freedom if he didn't earn a wage? I remembered how Emil Oberholz used to claim America wasn't the land of liberty as long as Negroes were kept as slaves. I wished to make this point to my uncle, but in those early days, I observed the German saying, *Wes Brot ich ess, des Lied ich sing*—"Whose bread I eat, his song I sing."

Sometime in September, Uncle Johann read in the newspaper about the *Central America,* a steamship carrying many wealthy passengers that sank in a hurricane off the Atlantic coast. When I went to bed that night, a rainstorm pounded hard on the roof and I dreamed I was still on the Helvetia, the ship creaking and lurching, rolling from side to side. I woke gasping for air.

The next day, at the sound of shouts in the street, the men put down their tools and rushed to the shop doors to see what had happened.

"Merchant's Bank is closing its doors!" someone yelled. Men were running up the street toward Public Square.

Just then Herr Fletcher rushed inside. "The gold went down with the ship," he reported breathlessly, grabbing his hat. "Our paper money is worthless!" He dashed back out the door.

Herr Fry thundered down the stairs from his third floor family apartment, bank book in hand. "They're keeping our deposits!" The painter stopped in front of my uncle, who stood blocking one half of the open doorway. Herr Fry peered around his massive shoulders at the street. "Johann?"

At my uncle's grim nod, Herr Fry rushed out the door. The other jours grabbed their hats and followed. Uncle Johann pointed his cane at me and Singley. "Mind the smithy until we return," he growled, limping out behind the others.

Singley and I did our work in silence. So far in our acquaintance, Singley had not shown good humor or friendliness toward me. As we worked, we kept a wary eye on the door, but no one came in.

I had been hearing about this problem in America, the system of banking with *Bildergeld,* "picture money," not uniform in size or shape, issued by any number of banks. The amount printed on it never matched what it was worth. Banks paid less, sometimes next to nothing, especially if the money came from a bank in a different state. Beyond that, some of the money was not *"Bilder"* at all, but counterfeit. Every night Uncle Johann checked the newspaper to learn the worth of this paper money, since it changed from day to day.

When the men returned at last, they were shaking their heads over an Irish brawler named Pat Milligan. Among the Irishmen, who mostly lived in a neighborhood just west of the Cuyahoga River, Pat Milligan was a man of some renown. During the run on Merchant's Bank, Milligan came in waving a horse-pistol. Up at the counter, he pointed his gun at the cashier and demanded his savings in full, an amount of twenty-five dollars. The cashier complied cheerfully, as if Pat Milligan had offered him a bouquet of flowers. The cashier clinked the gold specie—the gold everyone said sank with the S.S. Central America—into Milligan's big palm. The crowd leaned in at the melodic sound. Milligan held the coins out for all to see. Then he smiled at the cashier and handed them back. "So, as you have the money, then I don't want it," he said. The people cheered, and many left feeling confident the bank had their money after all. Indeed, Merchant's Bank did not close that day.

"That's the spirit of America," Herr Penhoff said, his voice full of wonder. "That irrational faith. No matter what, the people do not fear starvation and terror, but instead, see in everything the possibility of better times ahead."

Despite this optimistic spirit, due to bank failures in other parts of the country and trouble with railroad stocks, business slowed at the Rapparlie shop considerably. The only jobs to keep the workmen from standing idle were small ones, such as resetting tires and exchanging wagon wheels for sleigh runners. To pass the time, the jours forged wagon hardware and stacked it in the corners for orders that did not come.

IN THE LAST WEEK OF November, I awoke one morning to an eerie quiet. Out my attic window, the Cuyahoga River was slicked over as flat as a looking glass. Snow coated the roads and roofs in a pristine white. The masts of the ships in dry dock were bedecked, forming a delicate lattice against the gray-clouded sky. It was so quiet it felt as if time itself had frozen over.

Had I overslept? I dressed and hurried down to find the Rapparlie family gathered around the warm iron stove. The pungent smell of baking filled the kitchen.

"Isn't it Thursday, a work day? Why didn't anyone wake me?"

Aunt Katharina slapped a mound of dough from the bread bowl onto a wooden board, her apron sprinkled with flour. "It's a holiday, the Thanksgiving Home Festival." She dug her fists into the dough. "The Yankees go to church on this day, to give their thanks to God."

"We're going out to play in the snow," little Wilhelm said, his blue eyes dancing with excitement. The Rapparlie boys—John, Jacob, and Wilhelm— were just finishing hot rolls. I gulped down my roll and coffee and joined them. We threw snowballs at one another, ducking behind the wagons in an uproarious battle. I was getting quite cold when Uncle Johann emerged from the stables.

"Michael, come here," he said sternly. "We must harness the sleigh."

I welcomed the warmth of the horses. I reached out my hands to the muzzle of the black, who tossed his mane and blew hot breath on my frozen fingers. My uncle showed me how to harness the team, watching with eagle eyes as I affixed the breast collars and bridles.

"Where are we going?" I asked.

Aunt Katharina appeared, carrying a basket of warm food wrapped in cloth. "Didn't we tell you? We're eating at Georg and Margaretha's today."

I helped my aunt load the children into the sleigh, handing baby Sussy up last. As I didn't have a woolen jacket, my teeth had begun to chatter. But I didn't shiver for long. Uncle Johann placed heated bricks on the floor of the sleigh and brought out several animal hides from the shed, dumping them in my arms. Instantly warm, I felt the woolly fur with wonder.

"Bearskins?" I asked.

"Buffalo robes."

Reverently, I tucked these lap robes around the legs of the children and my aunt, unable to resist running my fingers along the Indian designs painted on the face-up leather side. How American I felt as I climbed onto the sleigh seat beside Uncle Johann and pulled a buffalo robe over our knees.

Uncle Johann snapped the reins and the horses trotted forward, the sleigh bells on the harnesses jingling. We glided along the river across a soft blanket of snow. Even the black piles of coal along the riverbank were coated in white, resembling giant white teepees.

We crossed the Cuyahoga River via the Columbus Street Bridge. On the road, families called out to one another from their sleighs, cheerful hails ringing through the air. The Scheuermann house smelled of bacon, apples, and molasses. Aunt Margaretha had roasted two birds—the American wild birds called turkeys. Aunt Katharina had baked *Schwarzbrot* and cooked up an ironstone kettle of root vegetables—carrots, parsnips, potatoes and turnips—basted in bacon fat and sugar.

At this banquet meal I met Herr and Frau Crolly and their three daughters for the first time—Adam and Catherine Crolly of Friedelsheim, a village of the Palatinate just a short hour's walk from Freinsheim. Frau Crolly brought cornbread and pumpkin pie, which she'd learned how to make from a Yankee neighbor.

During dinner, my uncles and aunts reminisced about their first days in Cleveland. Herr Crolly and Uncle Georg met at a cooperage back in 1841, they told me, the first work either of them found in this town. Eva Crolly had been born two years later. Now fourteen, Eva worked full-time at home as a seamstress. Elizabeth and Mary were the younger two. Eventually, Herr Crolly had gone into the barrel-making business for himself. Georg, on the other hand, had found higher-paying work as a furnace man in a steamboat factory.

After the meal the little ones were excused to play. Eva and I remained sitting at the table. I asked about the Thanksgiving Home Festival, and Uncle Georg explained how the states continued to argue about it.

"Each state celebrates it on a different day. Some say the feast began hundreds of years ago, when the first settlers were starving so the Indians had to feed them."

"Where are the Indians now?" I asked.

Uncle Georg swiped at his mouth with a napkin. "The Americans banished them, first near Sandusky, on a peninsula bordered on three sides by Lake Erie. Since then, they've forced the Indians West, across the Missouri River."

"Why? Were they attacking the settlers?"

"You should ask your Uncle Jakob. He was the one who paid attention to the Indians, what was left of them. Many died long ago of disease, when the first settlers arrived."

"Which church do you attend, young man?" Herr Crolly asked. He sat directly across from me and pierced me with his sharp gray eyes. He had not a lick of hair atop his prominent skull.

"Back in Freinsheim, I attended the Protestant Church."

"And here?"

I looked around the table with discomfort. "I've been to *Zum Schifflein Christi.*"

Herr Crolly nodded and said no more. I hoped we'd finished with that line of inquiry, but after everyone left the table, Herr Crolly guided me by the elbow to a corner of the parlor.

"What do you think of *Zum Schifflein Christi*? Do you enjoy the sermons of Reverend Allardt?"

"I've only heard him once," I said, gazing at the carpet.

"But young man, how can you observe the Sabbath if you don't attend church?"

I heard the judgment in his words, but when I looked up, his eyes seemed kind.

"I am saving my wages for better clothes," I said.

Georgie Scheuermann appeared at my elbow just then. "It's time for your English lesson," he said in his piping voice.

He pointed to where the little ones had gathered by the piano bench. My cousins took great delight in teaching me the English words they learned at school, and I didn't mind the lessons. They perched me on the piano bench while Little John paced back and forth, instructing me. From his officious manner, I guessed he was imitating a teacher from his school.

"Holiday," he said, his eyes dark and serious. "Now you say it."

"Howllidei?" I tried.

The children giggled and snorted. "Hah–li–day!" They shouted.

Later Aunt Margaretha played hymns and folk songs at the piano, and I sang along lustily. Rarely did I hear music these days. As I looked around at all the faces singing in the warm firelight, I couldn't help thinking we made a jolly party.

Whisked back home in the sleigh through the blue-black dusk, I felt as if I were in a scene from *Last of the Mohicans*. *If only my brother Philipp could see me now*, I thought with giddy delight. The frigid night wind lashed my cheeks as if trying to wake me from this dream.

# Chapter 21

———

THE BELL-LIKE RINGING OF METAL on metal continued hour after hour, six days a week. Each night, I slogged through my evening chores, then fell into bed numb with exhaustion. Each morning as I made my way downstairs my limbs felt thick as chestnut tree stumps, the sore stiffness not easing for hours.

Over time, I became accustomed to my many tasks—shoveling, pumping, treadle-pedaling, and lugging, so I was freer to observe the work of the other men. I learned to read the gestures and mood of each jour on a given task, to recognize the spectrum of colors of the wrought iron for each degree of heat: orange for fullering, cherry red for upsetting, bright yellow for bending. The hottest of all was white heat, required to weld one piece of iron to another. As much as brute force, the blacksmith depended on timing and acuity and endurance.

It was a man's world—hot, heavy, and dangerous—with few females to grace our days. As such, the appearance of Sonia Sutter took on undue importance. Sonia worked in the trimming department sewing carriage upholstery, dashes, and folding tops. Each morning as Sonia arrived, pulling her strong, capable hands from her muff and hanging her hat and coat on a hook along the shop wall, we men soaked up her feminine aura, the soft glint of her auburn hair, her hazel-green eyes, often teary from the biting Lake Erie wind. If, perchance, Sonia Sutter should look our way, our eyes would dart to our work, but we would furtively glance back again as soon as she turned to go upstairs, hoping to catch a glimpse of her dainty ankles as she ascended.

Like any man in the grit and hard labor of our world, I was susceptible to a dulcet voice and handspan waist. When I was ordered on an errand to the trimming department, my heartbeat would increase in anticipation.

Sometimes I encountered Fred Fry, the painter's apprentice, loitering there, leaning his elbow on the cutting table, angling for a look or smile from Sonia. At the sight, I'd feel a stab of jealousy. Fred was the second son of Herr Fry, the master painter, who oversaw all the work of color mixing and applying the primer, paint, and varnish to the wagons and carriages. There were eight in the Fry family altogether, seven of them living on the third floor above the trimming department, renting their rooms from my uncle. The eldest son, John, had already married and moved in with his wife's family the previous year.

In Fred Fry, I didn't really have much competition. The painter's apprentice was thin and tight as wire, with a pointed chin, so I doubted Sonia Sutter found him handsome. Then again, I had my own shortcomings not necessarily attractive to a *Fräulein*.

One morning as Sonia breezed through the lower part of the shop, I was toting water to the slack tubs. My head turned as if responding to the call of a Siren to follow her figure as she went upstairs. Meanwhile, my legs walked in the opposite direction, right into a row of whiffletrees, toppling them with a loud crash. Losing my balance, I tripped and landed on top of the heap, spilling my water buckets over everything.

"Watch it!" Herr Fletcher cried out, charging toward me with his arm raised.

"I'm sorry," I said, holding an empty water bucket to shield myself from the blow.

My uncle loomed into view just then, his face creased with dark lines. "What's this?!"

Herr Fletcher lowered his arm. "Your nephew made a mess of my whiffletrees!"

"It was an accident. I didn't see them," I said, struggling to disentangle myself.

Uncle Johann scowled down at me, his eyes raking my dripping wet body, the puddle on the ground. "You've lost us time and money. Tonight, you'll go to Herr Fletcher's house and split wood or shovel snow or whatever he orders you to do."

The mess I'd made blocked the path between two carriage bodies then under construction. As I cleaned up, the men bumped and jostled me on purpose. One whiffletree had a gouge in it, I saw, that would require heavy sanding—if it could be repaired at all. I prayed Uncle Johann would not hear about this too and hand out more punishments.

As I finished sweeping up the clumps of soaked sawdust, Herr Hoffmann the blacksmith came through the department and knelt down to hold the dust pan. "It's not as bad as all that," he said, his voice low. "Your uncle looked a fool in front of a customer, so he takes it out on you."

I nodded, grateful for a kind word. In truth, I made many mistakes I couldn't seem to help. My work-thickened fingers fumbled and broke the crockery pitcher when I tried to help my aunt. I tripped over carpets at the house, and once even stumbled down an entire flight of stairs, causing the house to thunder and the children to laugh at me with glee.

"Your head is always floating in the clouds," Uncle Johann would growl. Did he think I'd never heard this before? "You're like the idlers, doing only what you must. Only if a man is willing to work does he get somewhere in this life."

I didn't argue. Like the donkey, I took the flogging. If I just held my tongue, my wages would begin in December. I'd already spent them in my mind, on a new pair of boots and a suit of ready-made clothes, so I could go to church or to the market without feeling ashamed.

Until then, I kept to my attic room on Sundays, staring up at the sloping ceiling, missing Mütterchen and Father, and especially Philipp. My older brother had always been two steps ahead of me, my phalanx for whatever came next in our lives. I had come so far, too far for him to reach me. *If only Philipp were here*, I thought, *I wouldn't feel so alone.* Did he miss me as much as I missed him? How was my brother managing without me? Not receiving any letters, any word from them, left a constant ache in my heart.

The Thanksgiving snow had melted, but in the middle of December, a new snowfall blanketed Cleveland. Then came days of thawing, then freezing again, so huge icicles formed on the houses, hanging from the eaves like ogre's teeth.

Then it was Christmastime. On Christmas Eve, the Rapparlies harnessed the sleigh and we drove again to the Scheuermanns. As we entered their house, my nose was treated to scents of cinnamon, nutmeg, and cut pine. And another aroma, too, sharper on the nose, a marvelous spice called ginger. The Crollys and their daughters had come, and my uncle and aunt had set up a *Tannenbaum* in the parlor, adorning it with candles, *Putte* cherubs, nuts, fruits and ribbons.

It was on this first Christmas I learned how prejudiced the Yankees were against the German custom of the Christmas tree. Only a few years earlier, Uncle Georg told me, the minister of Cleveland's Lutheran Church, a Pastor Schwann of Hannover, was almost dismissed from his pulpit for placing the "pagan" *Tannenbaum* on the church altar.

"The Yankees do not have the tradition of the *Tannenbaum* at Christmas," Aunt Margaretha said, laughing gaily. "As with other things German, they suspect heathenism, or the influence of the devil. Think of it! The devil behind the festive diversion of the *Tannenbaum*."

I listened to the stories of my relatives and laughed along, impressed by their long experience in this country. The skirts on these American *Frauen* were unpatched, sewn out of machine-made silky fabrics and finely woven wool, the collars and cuffs decorated with lace. The men wore coats and vests that looked new, not threadbare. Herr Crolly's great coat sported a black velvet lapel. I had trouble believing that only one year ago, I had sung for Freinsheimers at the Community Hall, where even the wealthiest in the village dressed like peasants by American standards. I had been such a romantic back then, so naïve about my simple life, so unaware of the wider world.

As my aunts prepared the meal in the kitchen, Aunt Margaretha enlisted Eva and me to crack and peel the hot chestnuts. It was women's work, but secretly I enjoyed doing it. It gave me the chance to sit beside Eva, who had dimples in her soft round cheeks. In truth, I did not see how she could be the daughter of Frau Crolly, a woman who sat stiffly erect, her pale eyes set close together like a hawk's.

Peeling the chestnuts also let me listen in on the gossip of the Handrich sisters.

"If only Jakob was here, the party would be truly merry," Aunt Katharina said, mincing the apples with a faraway look. "He's now so many thousands of miles from us."

Aunt Margaretha shook her head. "If only he had married, he wouldn't have run off to hunt for gold."

"Don't be so sure of that," said Frau Crolly.

"Perhaps you're right. I thought he had an eye out for the Burkholder girl. Jakob danced with her many times at the Ohio City ball."

"*Ja, ja,* he was pasted to her side like wallpaper," said Aunt Katharina. "So busy explaining the American ways of doing things, as if he were the mayor."

"But she took up with that Josef Lehring." Aunt Margaretha's hands were busy fluting a pie crust, so she stuck out her lower lip to blow a strand of dark brown hair out of her eyes. "Our Jakob was by far the better choice."

"*Doch,* you knew he had the *Wanderlust.* He had gold fever even then."

"He left so soon after Mama and Papa departed this world…" Aunt Margaretha's hands went still and her eyes filled with tears.

Frau Crolly nodded. "I miss them, too. Your parents were good people, never complaining when times were hard."

The women worked in silence for a while. Finished with my pile of chestnuts, I went to join the men by the hearth fire in the parlor.

"I tell you, Johann, this new Republican Party brings nothing but trouble," said Uncle Georg, puffing his stubby pipe. He still wore his silk necktie, though the other men had theirs untied, their shirt collars loosened. "So much is changing from the days of the Democrats."

"These young Germans are in a fever for abolition, jumping in before they understand American politics," said Uncle Johann.

Herr Crolly looked thoughtful. "They'll get the things they don't want, too, like the Maine laws and women's suffrage."

Uncle Georg laughed. "Well said, Adam. Have you seen the hundreds of business men flocking to the religious revivals? These Puritans are more crazy for their religion every day."

Herr Crolly shifted in his chair. "And this is not a good thing, to turn to the Lord?"

Uncle Johann said, "It's about time someone did." He pulled a footstool closer to prop up his wooden leg, aimed like a rifle at a target. "The bank crisis has knocked the men sideways, so they pray to God for their deliverance. Let the preachers fill them with the fear of God, so that they control their women."

Uncle Georg looked doubtful. "The sermons of the Puritan preachers make me uneasy. The English ladies get so riled, with their moral rectitude and marches for temperance."

"Germans can also benefit from moral instruction," Herr Crolly said. "Some Germans love their beer too much."

Uncle Johann shifted again in his seat. "Perhaps you're right, Adam. No good comes of the Blue Monday idling."

Uncle Georg sat up straighter. "As a citizen of this land of liberty, I'll not be told I can't enjoy my wine. What madness, to blame German beer and wine for America's problems. We don't pour it down their throats!"

"The things of this world are not worth such a fuss. Put first your trust in the Lord God," said Herr Crolly. "Pfarrer Ellenberger used to remind us of this."

It was Uncle Johann's turn to sit up straighter. "Adam, I'll thank you not to make me feel as if I've come to a church service."

My heart beat faster to see my uncle getting riled, but Herr Crolly gazed at him mildly. "No sermon intended, Johann," he said.

My uncle *pffed* and gazed back at the fire.

An outcry about beer and wine and the *Tannenbaum*? I couldn't make sense of it. It seemed to me that America, with its freedom of religion, invited confusion. Different churches stood on almost every corner, each making its own rules, each determined to impose them on others. And new faiths seemed to grow up overnight. Uncle Georg had told me about the Millerites, who disbanded after Jesus did not return on the date expected, and the Mormons of Kirtland, with their strange visions and apostles.

A Christmas feast was served at last, an immense ham in the middle of the table, huge helpings of squash, noodles and plum cake. For the biggest treat of all, Aunt Margaretha handed each of us younger ones a bowl, which we took outside to fill with clean snow. When we came back in, she poured maple syrup over each snowball. The taste of the syrup was sweet, with a trace of wood resin, as foreign and marvelous as this new country.

To end the evening, "St. Nicholas" visited and left presents in the children's shoes by the fire. Among these gifts I contributed an agate marble for each of the little ones, purchased with a few cents of my new wages. Aunt Margaretha carried up a basket of oranges kept cool in the cellar, a treat shipped by train from the State of Georgia. The color alone made my mouth water. I put mine in my pocket to savor later in my attic room. That first Christmas in America, I received from my aunts a woolen coat, a lamb's-wool comforter, a new pair of wool-knitted socks and a muffler to wrap around my ears and neck. But the biggest surprise came from the Crollys—Frau Crolly had sewn me new clothes of machine-made cloth. Although she'd made them without measuring me, they were a perfect fit.

After the gift opening, Uncle Georg stepped out of the room for a moment and reappeared as "Servant Ruprecht." He rattled his cane about and poked at the children, who cowered in terror from his long beard and ash-stained cloak. As I looked on with barely suppressed mirth, Eva sent me a frown, warning me not to spoil it. Much to the children's relief, Servant Ruprecht did not deem any of them worth punishing that Christmas.

# Chapter 22

## Cleveland, Ohio 1858

O N A FEBRUARY EVENING OF 1858, above the howling of a winter gale, we heard the frantic clanging of alarm bells.

"Fire!" Uncle Johann grabbed his cane and lurched from his chair to peer out the window.

Little John and Jacob ran to look out the window beside their father. Aunt Katharina stood up, her ball of yarn falling from her lap and rolling across the room.

"Is it near?" she asked, in a quavering voice. Little Wilhelm clung, wide-eyed, to her skirts.

"I'll go and see." Uncle Johann limped to the foyer and, without donning a coat, stepped outside.

My aunt turned to us. "John, bring down the linens. Jacob, roll up the rugs. Michael, stack the clothes from each room by the doors. Wilhelm, you must bring the sewing basket."

The door burst open again.

"It's the Lake Erie Paper Mill!" Uncle Johann said, his voice tense. "It's bad—there's a great wind. I'll go keep an eye on it, just in case. Michael, come with me. I need your good legs to warn Mother if the fire is spreading."

While Aunt Katharina set the boys to their tasks, I shrugged on my coat and went out with my uncle. Off the river, icy gusts of wind swatted our faces like horsetails. Beyond a row of warehouses along the river, the Lake Erie Paper Mill was one long wall of fire. Charred timbers tumbled from what was once the roof, sparks and burning debris showering a wide area. The firemen couldn't get close. Instead, they trained their hoses on nearby roofs.

"So many fires in this place," Uncle Johann said. "The Americans use too much wood for their buildings. Even with the brick houses, they add wooden cornices, so the roofs go up like kindling."

"I remember from a letter you sent us in Freinsheim, you have suffered many fires."

"The last time, three years ago, we saved our belongings. At the first fire, we lost everything. In 1845, our whole neighborhood burned, all family homes back then. Many didn't rebuild. They gave up and moved West. Our good friends the Bienes moved to Toledo."

I felt a new sympathy for my uncle and saw it as a good sign that he chose to confide in me in this manner. Perhaps he was growing used to me. Uncle Johann and I watched the fire a while longer, until we were sure the Rapparlie property and neighborhood would be spared, then turned our steps toward home.

When I first arrived in America, fires were often caused by camphene, a fuel made from turpentine produced in the Southern states. Camphene was cheaper and more plentiful than whale oil, so people used it despite the danger—the vapors were highly combustible. Often, we read in the newspaper of terrible, sometimes fatal, accidents.

Shortly after the paper mill fire, Sonia Sutter did not appear at work. As the morning wore on, the shop was falling behind on an important order for a dark red chaise. The root-patterned veins of my uncle's temples began to stand out as he looked to the door each time it was opened, always by someone other than Sonia. After the noon dinner, with still no word of her whereabouts, Uncle Johann put on his coat and cap and went out in search of her.

When he returned, he wore such a somber expression that all the workmen gathered to hear his news.

"Sonia Sutter has burned her hands on the camphene lantern," Uncle Johann said. "I've been to the hospital to see her. I don't think she'll have use of them any time soon."

When refilling her lamp, Sonia Sutter had accidentally spilled some camphene. A nearby candle ignited the spill, leaped into the canister and exploded, coating her in burning fuel. Brushing the fire from her apron, her hands had been badly burned. Sonia suffered other burns as well, on her face and arms, but the injuries to her hands were the worst.

Beautiful Sonia. I didn't understand how God could afflict her, of all people. The rest of the day, the men worked with long faces. When the jours left for the evening, Fred Fry hung around William Singley and me as we waited for the forge fires to grow cold.

"I can't believe what happened to poor Sonia," I said.

"It's grave news indeed." Singley's round face looked morose. Until then, I had not imagined him to be a man of much compassion.

Fry grimaced. "*Alla,* this calls for a glass of beer at Schlegel's, *oder?*"

Singley turned to me. "Harm, what about it? If I'm not mistaken, you were sweetest of anyone on our Sonia."

My ears grew warm. I wanted to object that it was Fry who made a fool of himself, but I didn't know these men as I did my old comrades back home. "What is Schlegel's?"

"A better name for it is Jerusalem, a place to drink *Lagerbier.*"

"Shouldn't we go to the hospital?" I did not want to get in trouble for going to a tavern. I'd paid my debt, so no longer had evening chores, but if I didn't turn up for supper, my aunt and uncle would surely wonder at my absence.

Singley shook his head. "You don't want to see our Sonia. It sounds bad. She would not think ill of us for staying away."

I considered the money in my pocket—one dollar and fifty cents saved, after so many grueling months of labor. "I've only just started my allowance."

"I'll stand you a beer," Fry said. "Time to live a little. A man never knows what tragedy is around the next corner."

A great thirst came over me then, for the bubbling amber beer, for the company of friends. I pushed back my concerns and, as the fires cooled to gray ash, grappled for some excuse to give my aunt. As we set out, I asked Fry and Singley to wait a moment.

"I'll eat later," I told Aunt Katharina, popping my head in at the kitchen door. "There's a church meeting."

It seemed a believable fib. Just that week I'd gone again to *Zum Schifflein Christi,* after all these months. My aunt narrowed her eyes at me.

"I'll leave out a plate of food," she said.

I nodded and backed up, right into Uncle Johann, who was just then returning from the stables.

"Watch where you're going!"

"Excuse me, Uncle."

I eased around him and hurried off.

"Did massuh say you could leave?" Fry asked, stomping his feet and blowing on his hands in the wintry night air.

I shrugged, not knowing how to answer. We set off up Michigan Street, our breath fogging from our mouths. At the thought of my escape from another dull night in the Rapparlie home, a thrill of elation and fear rushed through me. What would happen to me if my uncle learned the truth? I hated to think of it.

"We're going to a church meeting," I said.

Singley looked at me oddly. "A church meeting? Perhaps you misunderstood. Jerusalem is no church. Schlegel's has that nickname because many Jews gather there to drink. They have a regular table."

"It says in my indenture contract I'm forbidden to go to taverns. I told my aunt I was going to a church meeting."

Singley snorted. "The language of those contracts is ancient. Rapparlie copies some old document he brought with him from the Old Country. It's different in America; the apprenticeships aren't as strict. Fry and I have been going to taverns all along and never had any trouble. Rapparlie only cares if you drink at his shop, as he puts his beloved wagons ahead of everything else." Singley chuckled to himself. "I keep forgetting you're so new to America, Harm."

"Why? When did you get here?"

"To Cleveland? Two years ago. Before that, I lived in New York for about three. But the Irish ran that town."

"The Irish aren't so bad in Cleveland," Fry said. "My father says John Mulrooney and his lot are all right."

"All right, you say?" Singley snorted again. "All right as far as any blacksmith goes. Let's face it, we're all bastards."

"I guess that makes my Uncle Johann a bastard, too," I said, laughing, feeling more light-hearted than I had in months.

But Singley didn't laugh. "Better not let Rapparlie hear you say that. What did you do to him, anyway? The way he treats you, it must've been something awful."

"You think I did something to him?" To hide my shock, I kept my face tucked in my woolen muffler.

"He doesn't pay you a wage for three months? He makes you go to Herr Fletcher's to do chores for knocking over the whiffletrees? I'd quit if he treated me that way."

"My uncle has done my family a kindness. Worse, I owed him money when I arrived, for the train fare from New York."

"Ah, that's the problem. You owe the old penny-fox money. Still, it seems like something more than that."

"It wasn't my fault, but maybe he believes it was." I told them the story of how I was robbed. "I didn't have anything but the clothes on my back when I got to Cleveland," I concluded as we arrived at the tavern.

Schlegel's saloon was thick with aromas of pipe smoke and beer, the sweat of working men, the woody scent of sawdust. I was relieved to see so many patrons were workers like me, wearing dirt-streaked or paint-splattered clothes, their faces grimy. Gentlemen congregated here as well, their sack coats made of fine wool, their collars sporting silk neckties, their boots polished to a gleam. In the New World, I quickly discovered, it wasn't easy to tell who was a nobleman and who was a pauper. There were both, and many in between, and we all mixed together.

I sat with Fry and Singley at one end of a long table of other craftsmen, listening to the jokes and banter, downing my first cold beer in months in large, thirsty gulps. When our glasses stood empty, I went to the bar to buy the next round. Next week, I reasoned, I'd begin saving my wages.

Singley bought the third round, and at last we sank into the gloomy subject of Sonia Sutter.

"It is indeed a tragedy," Singley said, his broad shoulders slumped. "I wonder if Peter will have her now, since her hands are all burnt up."

I blinked. "Peter? Who's Peter?"

"Sonia's betrothed, *Dummkopf*, Peter Fetzer," said Fry. "Everyone knows of it, and if they don't, they ought to—Peter and Sonia dance together at all the dances."

"Dances?"

"*Ja doch*, the Christmas ball, the Silvester ball. Come to think of it, I've not seen you there." Fry raised an eyebrow. "Are you one of those no-dancing Methodists?"

"Reformed Evangelical," I said, thinking how many lonely evenings I'd spent at the Rapparlie house these past months. "This summer I danced at the Höhn's farm in Columbiana. I heard my aunts speak of an Ohio City ball but didn't think they happened so often."

"*Ja doch*, you miss out. The Germans of Cleveland have a great love of dancing. Every week there's something going on," Fry assured me.

"You meet German girls there?"

"There are many pretty girls, all German—"

Singley put his arm across my chest as if barring my way. "Wait, Fry, what are you saying? Harm, you heard nothing. We didn't invite you."

Fry laughed. "*Doch*, there are too many males as it is, too few *Fräuleins*. I shouldn't have told you."

"Do you have a girl?" I asked Singley.

He shrugged. "I'm not looking seriously until I have a living of my own."

Fry nudged Singley with his elbow. "In the meantime, there is Maggie Roberts to tickle our cocks, yes?" Fry pushed his slight weight against Singley a second time, harder. Singley still didn't budge. "Let's make a visit to Maggie tonight, see if she's willing, *oder?*"

"Maggie?"

Singley nodded solemnly. "*Ja*, Maggie. She's not ... particular."

Fry guffawed. I swallowed, remembering the whores I'd seen on the streets in New York. Fry sat up and leaned forward on his elbows, keeping his voice low.

"*Alla*, she's not particular. She's had us both, *oder*? Perhaps Harm here will take a shine to her as well."

My mind raced in confusion. Drinking at a tavern was one thing, but fornicating? Could this rule, too, be ignored? How I longed to have a woman, to test the strength of my tool. Feeling weak in moral resolve, I pictured Uncle Johann at home, where he remained night after night. He would never have to know. Who would tell him? I had traveled a far distance from the world of Freinsheim, where everyone knew my business and prattled over every misstep.

Weighing desire against fear, I sat silent. Fry's eyes darted back and forth between Singley and me. "I have *Bilder* in my pocket, and Singley, so do you. Perhaps we can bargain with her, get three for the price of two?"

My new comrades drained their beers and rose to leave. In a thick-headed haze, I shrugged on my jacket and followed.

In the month of March, the town of Cleveland was at its ugliest, the sky dulled gray by low-hanging clouds, the snow drifted in piles coated brown-black by coal, ash, horse piss, and manure. My new friends took me through Public Square, where bare tree branches clattered like skeletons in the gusting wind. At the northwest corner, a man stood roasting chestnuts. Two street urchins, perhaps his children, huddled on a nearby bench.

We passed the Drumm shop on Frankfort and descended down the rotting planks of Superior Street to the snaking Cuyahoga. Below us boats hung in dry dock or were frozen at their moorings. Great chunks of ice gathered at the elbows of the river. Music floated up from the Flats from a Melodeon, along with it the sound of men's voices and women's laughter. Were they taking me to a brothel? I began to consider how to escape as Singley and Fry veered down a dark alleyway to a small house. They entered without knocking.

"What is this place?" I whispered to Fry.

"The house of Maggie Roberts," he said quietly, almost reverently.

We stood in a plain, empty kitchen. A rhythmic thump-thumping, impossible to ignore, emanated from the next room. Fry snickered. I felt both petrified and fired with anticipation.

"Maggie runs her own business for less than the brothels charge," Fry said. He leaned in, breath on my ear, adding, "She's fond of the drink."

A few moments later, a man dressed like a boatman from the docks stepped out, still buttoning up his trousers. Without a second glance at us, he let himself out. Singley ducked his head through the open door and mumbled something. A woman's voice answered and Singley went in, shutting the door behind him.

While we waited, Fry paced back and forth, jittery with impatience. For my part, I had sobered a good deal during the walk and now suffered recurring visions of Mütterchen's moist, reproving gaze, of Pfarrer Bickes' piercing black eyes staring me down in condemnation. I had dreamed so often of bedding a woman—but this unhappy place struck me as nothing romantic, a devil's den of iniquity. I worried about catching a disease from whoring, which men muttered about a good deal on the Helvetia. My mind in a turmoil, I waited with Fry, and when Singley came out, I waited with him.

"How much is it?" I asked in a hoarse whisper.

"One dollar," Singley replied.

I had one dollar and five cents in my pocket. Enough.

When Fry came out, the odor of pipe smoke wafted behind him. I stepped inside the room and made out a woman's form in the shadowy lantern light. She leaned against the bedstead puffing a long-stemmed pipe, her bodice low, loosely unlaced, her skirts hitched up to expose the flesh of her thighs. Beneath the smoke, an odor of rutting goats and sour milk rose to my nostrils. I thought of the sex pleasures awaiting me, if I dared.

"You pay first."

I recognized the word "pay" but said nothing, my eyes on her nakedness, my man-part stiffening.

"Let's go, kid. Ain't got all night." She peered through greasy black bangs. "*Schnell.* Hurry up now, *schnell.*" Maggie Roberts' eyes dropped to my bulging trousers. "Jesus," she said, rolling her eyes.

I pulled off my hat, lowering it to cover my crotch.

"Well?"

I shook my head.

"Get out! Scram!" she swept her hand in dismissal. "Damn Dutchies. Whatta they take me for, a schoolmarm?"

My eyes pasted on the woman, I reached behind me for the door handle and eased my way back out. Singley and Fry stared at me. I shrugged. Singley nodded sagely.

"Don't worry about it, Harm," he said. "First time always goes fast."

We let ourselves out onto the rickety porch, where a fog had gathered over the river. Giant sheets of ice aproned the shoreline. We made our way a short distance along the Cuyahoga, then parted ways, Singley slipping up the hill to his boarding house, Fry and me following River Street back to the Rapparlies. Fry entered the side door to ascend to his third floor home as I edged into the Rapparlie kitchen from the wagon yard. I lit a paraffin candle and sat down before a plate of bread, cheese, and meats left out by my aunt.

Uncle Johann appeared in the doorway.

"It's late to be coming home from Bible study," he said.

Scenes of Schlegel's, of Maggie Roberts, mushroomed in my mind, my conscience a jumble of guilt and misdeeds. My uncle came into the room, sat down, and laid his cane across the table, something Aunt Katharina didn't allow when she was around. A long silence passed between us.

"A man's reputation follows him all his life, *oder*?" Uncle Johann said, his face neutral, his voice measured. "If I'm dishonest with a customer, there's a backlash and I lose business, everything I have worked many years to build. This cannot happen. Understand?" I nodded. My uncle continued. "I believe you've lied to me. I do not abide liars and cheaters. Understand?"

I swallowed my half-chewed bread. "I ... I'm sorry. We were sad about Sonia Sutter, and we—"

Uncle Johann held up his hand, his eyes boring into me like a trimming awl.

"As my apprentice, what you do outside of my shop is not my concern—as long as you stay out of trouble. If you gamble, they come to John Rapparlie about the debts. If you fall down drunk in a gutter, it looks bad for John Rapparlie. For this trouble, I'll dismiss you. Otherwise, it is not my concern. But I will not abide liars and cheaters. If I can't trust my own nephew, who can I trust?"

"Uncle, you can trust me. I've paid back the money I borrowed. I'm a hard worker."

"*Oh, oh*, you are small and clumsy, not suited for this work. I wonder if perhaps your parents were trying to trick me, the way they sent their younger, smaller son. It's clear they raised you *Luftikus*, too easy-going. Perhaps they sent you to me to turn you around."

"I am not *Luftikus!*" I said, struggling to keep my voice low. I could not believe he was accusing me and my family in this way. "Since coming here, I've known only the work, at the shop and the house, too. I went out this one night."

"Did you go to the Bible study?"

Shame crept up my spine, but I forced myself to hold my uncle's gaze. If I told the truth, was my apprenticeship at an end? "I went to Schlegel's tavern."

Uncle Johann slammed his paw on the table, making me jump. "You'll pay for this lie. I will charge you next week's wages."

His chair scraped back as he stood. I stood, too.

"But how can I ever—?"

"Should I make it two?"

I forced my eyes to the floorboards, my limbs trembling with rage.

"No. *Es tut mir leid.*"

"If you don't do anything wrong, you don't have to be sorry. Remember that next time."

Uncle Johann spun around and limped out of the kitchen.

I waited until I could no longer hear him upstairs, then slogged the three flights to my low-ceilinged room. I loosened my suspenders and collapsed on the bed. How dare he call me *Luftikus*! I worked longer than anyone, but my uncle only found fault. Did he really believe what he said, that my parents had tricked him by sending me? Singley had said my uncle must hold something against me. Perhaps that was it.

My heart sank. There was nothing I could do about my small stature, or about arriving penniless at my uncle's door. Now, I'd gotten caught in a lie. No wonder my uncle had it out for me. *Gott sei Dank* I didn't have sex with Maggie Roberts. At least in that my conscience was clear.

Now that I saw the problem, I resolved to make it up to my uncle. I didn't need him to turn me around. I could do that myself. I'd work even harder, without complaint. I'd pay attention and do everything anyone asked of me. From now on, I would attend only to work.

# Chapter 23

A WEEK AFTER SONIA WAS GONE, Eva Crolly came to the wagon shop to fill her vacant position in the trimming department. Although I was glad I'd see Eva more often, I thought it was a shame she had to suffer under the heavy hand of Johann Rapparlie. Eva was not yet fifteen, but my uncle insisted she work ten hour days. At least it wasn't twelve hours, like me.

I endured my skipped week of wages without complaint and kept alert for a chance to improve my uncle's opinion of me. Even so, he continued to find fault with everything I did, even when I did more than was asked of me. As the days passed, I came to understand that no matter what I did, I'd never be able please him.

The following Saturday, with my sixty cents of wages in hand, I headed over to Schlegel's Tavern, located Singley and Fry at the table of the craftsmen, and plopped down beside them, a *Lagerbier* already in my hand.

I raised my glass. "Uncle Johann can go to the devil," I said.

Singley and Fry grinned, tipped their glasses, and we drank on it.

And so my regular appearance at Schlegel's began.

In addition to our taste for *Lagerbier* at Schlegel's, we also had a strong thirst for politics. In those months there was a Lecompton Swindle reported in the newspaper, something to do with President Buchanan and the Kansas Territory.

One night as I purchased a round at the bar, the gentleman nearby was complaining loudly about the Supreme Court and also about President Buchanan, whom he declared was nothing better than a panderer to the South. Slavery shouldn't be allowed in the Territories at all, he said.

"*Genau*, it will only bring trouble," I agreed, just as if he'd been talking to me all along.

The gentleman turned to me in surprise. I noticed remnants of his last meal stuck to his beard and mustache. He wore a tattered bowler hat on his head, and his sack coat was stained with sweat and grime. He'd seemed well educated, but perhaps he was of a lower class than I first thought.

"*Doch*, the effort to protect existing slave property opens the way for smugglers and other lawbreakers," he said in reply.

"This is the view in the *Wächter am Erie*, but not everyone agrees. My uncle, for instance. Excuse me, but do you happen to know about this Dred Scott?"

The man shrugged. "If you read the *Wächter am Erie*, how can you not know?

"I am new to America since July."

The man explained in some detail how the Supreme Court had ruled even a Negro who was free could not sue the federal government. He warmed to his subject, which meant I stood listening for some time.

"But if the Negro is free, why isn't he a citizen?" I asked, when he paused at last to gulp his beer.

"The Court ruled the Negro is inferior, and so has no rights whatsoever."

I thanked the man and returned to the table, a good deal worried about my own rights in this country. Since I was not a citizen, did I also have no rights? Was that how this democracy worked? I placed the glasses of beer before my friends.

Fry reached for his and took several swallows. "What did you talk about so long with that man?" he asked, wiping foam from his mouth with his sleeve.

"He was explaining to me about Dred Scott."

Singley nodded. "He would know."

"What do you mean?"

"You don't know who that is?"

I shrugged. "I didn't ask his name. He's a cook somewhere, I think."

Singley laughed. "You fool, that's Brand, the new Justice of the Peace."

I felt abashed that I had spoken so boldly to this important man. Then again, Old Country class distinctions did not exist as strictly here. Territorial distinctions faded as well. The Germans of Cleveland came from all the different German states: Baden, Württemberg, Bavaria including the Palatinate, Hessia, Saxony, and Rhenish Prussia, not to mention Switzerland and Bohemia. The new criteria of one's worth, it seemed, depended on how inventive and resourceful one was about gaining material wealth.

For my part, I remained on the low rung of the ladder. I felt this most keenly at the dances, which I had begun to attend as my savings allowed. Ever shy of girls in Freinsheim, when it came to these German-American *Fräuleins*, I was utterly tongue-tied. These girls adorned their shapely figures in boldly patterned dresses and their braided hair with ribbons and ornaments. I couldn't help but notice how they looked right through me, their eyes peeled for young gentlemen who wore fine suit coats and had horses and carriages of their own. When a *Fräulein's* frank gazes did fall upon me, I felt fully my place as a blacksmith apprentice, rough and dull, lacking in city manners.

In addition to nights at Schlegel's, I began attending the German dances. On the occasion of my third ball, a dance held on Cleveland's west side, I shored up my courage and asked Fred Fry's sister Susan to dance. As she knew me from the wagon shop, she agreed without hesitation. During the dance, I recognized Eva Crolly on the dance floor, and to my surprise, recognized her dance partner as well—none other than Charles Rauch, my shipmate from the Helvetia. Dressed in fine clothes and polished boots, he held himself with the same confident superiority, his head tilted slightly upward to reveal a rust-colored beard dusting his chin.

As the music faded, I parted with Susan and strode over to tap Eva on the shoulder.

"Good evening, *Fräulein* Crolly," I said, in as formal a voice as I could muster. Charles' eyes met mine in a shock of recognition. Before he could speak, I bowed deeply at the waist before Eva. "How nice to see you here. Are you aware of the questionable character of the gentleman with whom you're dancing?"

"Questionable character?" Rauch put up both fists as one would at a boxing match. "Only the lowest reprobate would question my character."

Eva's jaw dropped, and Rauch and I broke into laughter. He clapped me on the shoulder.

"So you came to Cleveland at last!" he said. It was the warmest greeting he had ever given me, and to my surprise, I felt genuinely happy to see him.

"*Doch*, I began my apprenticeship in August. I was sure I'd see you before now."

"Rauch wagons and buggies are made in Ohio City. I don't often cross to the Johann Rapparlie side of the Cuyahoga."

"*Aha*! I see *that* good name reaches far and wide."

The band struck up another tune, so the three of us moved off the dance floor.

"But, how do you two know one another?" Eva asked, looking back and forth between us.

I brandished my arm as if holding a sword. "We were pirates on the Helvetia," I snarled.

She frowned in confusion.

"Harm and I crossed the Atlantic together," Charles said. "Forty-three days at sea on that creaky immigrant packet. But just how do you know Harm here?"

"The Rapparlies and Handrichs are family friends of my parents," Eva said. "And Rapparlie the wagon-maker has recently arranged for me to work at his shop as a trimmer."

Charles looked at her in wonderment. "Oho, so now you are a spy?"

I laughed. "It's more likely you dance with Eva to gain Rapparlie secrets. You haven't divulged any, have you, Eva?"

I was having a grand time, and Rauch struck me as an admirable foe. In the spirit of our verbal joust, giving Rauch a sly, sideways glance, I dipped low at the waist in another bow before Eva.

"Fräulein Crolly, will you do me the honor of this dance?"

Eva giggled and accepted my outstretched hand. Charles deferred, a smile twitching at the corners of his mouth. He looked disappointingly self-assured.

"All right Harm, have your dance, but do come back and talk to me. I want to hear all about New York City."

In truth, I was happy to dance with Eva, not just to annoy Charles Rauch. As we saw each other daily, my friendship with her had grown. She had a stern moral piety like her parents, but also a sense of humor. Each Monday morning she'd inquire how I'd liked Pastor Allardt's sermon, and I'd hem and haw about how I'd been distracted by an ant, or the sprinkling of pipe tobacco on Herr Krug's lapel, so could not rightly recall the precise point of the message. It had become a running joke between us, me always looking for a new, more outlandish excuse. At my feigned discomfort, her eyes would dance with laughter.

I danced with Eva for two songs, not willing to quit until Eva declared her desire to sit the next one out. I helped her find a seat, then dutifully sought out Rauch. He and I recounted our adventures since our last meeting. I even found myself confessing the hair-raising tale of my first day in New York City. Charles seemed taken aback that I told him this, until I got to the part where I paid back my uncle in full. It made me wonder. Had Rauch thought I was going to ask him for money?

Rauch said he was sorry to hear of my trouble, that he'd been envious of me for getting to stay and take in the wonders of New York. He didn't know when he'd have the chance to visit *Kleindeutschland*. Already, his father was building a shop for him to supervise on Pearl Road, which I must visit at the first opportunity.

By the end of our conversation, I knew for certain Charles Rauch had not changed. He still talked mostly of himself. And as before, his bragging dug the knife of envy deep in my ribs. I only hoped that one day I wouldn't feel like such an underling in his presence.

Over the next months, I saw Charles Rauch at other dances, but neither he nor I made further efforts to renew our acquaintance.

# Chapter 24

O N A WARM DAY IN April, after the last patches of slush had melted into gritty puddles, Aunt Katharina flung open the windows to let fresh air circulate through the house. Instead of the rich scents of cherry and plum blossoms so familiar in Freinsheim at this time of year, the breeze stank of anthracite, rust, and sewage, of fresh-cut logs and fish. Even so, around the edges came other aromas—wet earth and growing plants, the fragile perfume of wildflowers. Gratefully, I sucked the air into my lungs, feeling as if during the past winter, I'd climbed through a long, dark cave and finally found the opening.

The ice coating the river and canal melted away, so boats again plied the waters, bearing loads of limestone, salt, coal, and iron ore. The air rang once more with the clang of bells, blasts of whistles, and shouts of dockworkers. In times of fog, boatmen clunked boards hollowly against the hulls to prevent collisions. My attic room provided a view across the river, at the iron locomotives screeching to a halt in the lumberyard, the timber rumbling and shaking the earth as the cars unloaded.

The constant hail of hammers and grating of saws had also returned. New houses were being erected on the edges of town, more going up every week, built by new arrivals in town—people starting commissioning houses, founding businesses of fine hats, tanned leather, cigar-making, and jewelry, new families arriving to overflow the schools with their children.

The ones who came to stay were a mere fraction of those passing through. Minnesota became the thirty-second state to join the Union that May, and two more states—Kansas and Oregon—were vying to join as well. Settlers passed through Cleveland on their way to the interior—to Indiana, Illinois, Missouri, and Wisconsin—their wagons loaded until the canvas tops bulged, cooking pans, coils of rope, and sundries hooked along the outside rails.

The "spring rush," it was called, this sudden surge of demand for new wagons, carriages, and repairs. Many of those who passed through, especially the Germans, sought out the shop of John Rapparlie. I toiled in the shop each day, pumping the bellows, hand-stripping rust and scale from tire strappings, pedaling away at the grinder. My only chance to escape outside came when I was sent with the dray to pick up supplies.

UNACCOUNTABLY, MY UNCLE'S MOOD SEEMED to darken as the weather, and business, improved. One Sunday in May, he looked especially sour, the claw-footed veins standing out on his temples as I sat elbow to elbow with the Rapparlie children at breakfast. Since it was the Sabbath, the rain of hammers and saws had ceased. The Puritanical Americans observed the Sabbath with a Bible-reading piety that would impress even Pfarrer Bickes.

At the opposite end of the long wooden table, my aunt looked wilted. It was quite warm already, one of our first real summer days. Baby Sussy was older now, but could not yet sit at the table on her own, so Aunt Katharina propped her on one knee.

In the strained silence, I noticed Uncle Johann's white shirt had a blue streak running down the front from the shoulder to the tail. Yesterday, my aunt had done the wash, and as the shirts hung on the line in the yard, the blue streaks were visible on most of them. When I'd donned my Sunday shirt, there were blue marks on one sleeve and at the waist, but nothing as remarkable as the stripe across my uncle's shirt.

Uncle Johann raised his hard slate gaze to my aunt.

"What about this shirt, *Frau*? Must I buy a new one each time you do the wash?"

Aunt Katharina sighed. "*Tch,* Father, I'll put the bluing on it next time. I didn't see Wilhelm's navy wool scarf in the washtub until it was too late."

"Is it so hard to run an orderly house with this family? Must things be ruined?" Uncle Johann turned his accusatory gaze from Aunt Katharina to little Wilhelm. "Why was your scarf in your mother's washtub?"

"It had horse manure. I had to clean it," the boy piped. He was so small his chin barely cleared his plate.

"You must ask your mother first, in all things. For this, you will receive the lash."

"It was a mistake," I said. "He's only six years old."

Uncle Johann turned his glower on me. "To spoil these boys will make them *Luftikus*. I teach my children to respect their elders."

"Accidents happen," I said, unable to stop myself.

Uncle Johann's fist landed on the table so hard the dishes rattled. Baby Sussy started to wail.

"You would do well to understand that carelessness causes as much trouble as malice," he snarled above her noise.

I didn't want to argue, nor did I want to hear little Wilhelm's cries as he took the lash. I stood, went to the foyer, donned my hat, and left. As I stepped outside, my senses were swarmed by the aromas of sun-warmed brick and soil, of flower bulbs and meadow grasses. Somewhere to the south, a bird gave a plaintive, long-noted trill. Sometimes I could hardly stand to be in the Rapparlie house. Were I to be so blessed as to have a wife and children, I would never to treat them with such unfairness and cruelty.

It was at least an hour before church services, so I turned south rather than north, thinking it was a fine day to explore the terrain. As I followed the Ohio Canal and the Cuyahoga River, which flowed side by side here, odors of tree sap wafted from the lumberyard across the river. Tall stacks of milled posts glowed blond in the sun. I reflected on the endless tracts of forest I'd witnessed on my train journey here, the dense stands of sycamores and oaks, beeches and hickory. In Cleveland, there were few trees to be found. Singley had told me a mayor devised a slogan a few years back—Cleveland, the Forest City—to inspire people to plant trees, as if saying it could make it so. It seemed to be working. Young trees now grew in Public Square and in orderly rows along the avenues.

I passed docked barges and canal boats and warehouses stuffed with trade goods waiting to be sold and shipped east. Before long I reached the charred remains of the Lake Erie Paper Mill, which stood sentinel at the entrance to a small stream chuckling down between bramble-choked banks. On the opposite slope, a brick works cluttered the rise, geometric blocks of bricks and ovens ascending up Broadway hill.

Farther up the ravine I spied a wilder place, a tangle of trees and deeper woods, gray-brown branches sprouting buds of new green leaves. Abandoning my plans for church altogether, I headed up the gully, soon arriving at a waterfall cascading over a shelf of flat stones. The scene reminded me of Goethe's "May Song": *How fair doth Nature, Appear again!* The last time I had read this verse, I'd been in Freinsheim, my heart consumed with a pure, blind devotion to my Anna Marie. No woman I met in Cleveland tantalized me, or tortured my soul, half as much as she once had.

Above the little falls, the duff of the ravine was speckled with carpets of white, pink, and green wildflowers. From the ridge came a golden glow, hinting at the presence of a meadow or farm. Clawing and grabbing at saplings, wet mud giving way beneath my boots, I slipped and slid up the ravine to arrive gasping for breath at a green rolling meadow. Horses and cattle grazed behind a split-log fence. Beyond them lay a freshly plowed field.

*When I convince Philipp to come here, I'll show him this place*, I told myself. By then I'd be a blacksmith jour and maybe have a wagon shop, and Philipp could have a farm and bring his vegetables to market. I'd advise him not to plant a vineyard. I had heard gloomy reports about the Ohio climate and soil being very poor for grapes.

Hopping the fence, I made my way to the overturned field, crouching down to examine the clay-heavy clods of dirt. Philipp could grow other things—corn and rye, flax and squash and cabbages. Wandering farther, knee deep in the meadow grass, I felt hope lift in my chest for the first time in a long while. One day, perhaps, I could convince my whole family to come here. If they made the journey by steamship, perhaps it would be short enough that Mütterchen could manage it. I'd save enough money and send it to them.

Turning north I took in the gray-green line of Lake Erie behind the square and triangular rooftops, smokestacks and church steeples of Cleveland, my new American home. Feeling redolent, I found an area of soft dry grass and lay down on my back to stare up at the deep blue heavens. Warmed by the sun's rays, I put my hat over my face and dozed for some time. When I awoke, I felt more rested than I had since coming to the New World.

From then on, during Sundays of fine weather, I preferred to visit that little ravine called Kingsbury Run and the meadow above it, rather than the stiff church pews. I found some solace in nature for my loneliness, for my grit and metal-battered soul.

JULY ARRIVED, AND WITH IT, the American Independence Day, with its sharp reports of firecrackers and marching music of parades. I spent my one-year anniversary on American soil with the families—the Rapparlies, Scheuermanns and Crollys—on a picnic, a carefree event entirely unlike the brawl of my first July 4. The month did bring the humid heat I remembered so well, carrying with it a heaviness and torpor. At times it felt as if my blood might rebel within me as it had for my Uncle Johannes. I wondered about that uncle sometimes, about what might have become of him. I never heard my aunts speak of him and was not comfortable asking.

The next Sunday, although the weather was again fine, whining mosquitoes drove me out of Kingsbury Run. As I arrived back at the mouth of the little stream, a strange-looking canal boat hove into view, riding very low in the water. Its upper and lower decks were packed with revelers. The boat was decorated as if for a Festival of the Maypole, the rails and roof entwined in greenery, flowers, and streamers. Even the boatman and mules wore wreaths of flowers. I heard German words issuing from the assemblage. Someone strummed a familiar folk song on the guitar.

"Is there a festival?" I asked the canal boatman. He looked at me blankly and said nothing, slogging past behind his mules. I plundered my brain for the English word. "Holiday?"

The man said something I couldn't make out, so I stood like a dull ox at a fence and watched the boat pass. At the back, a group of young men were cheering and howling.

"Harm!" someone called amid the din. "Is that you, Harm?"

Fred Fry removed his cap and waved, so I could pick him out of the people crowding the lower deck. Then I recognized Singley and other comrades as well.

"Hop on!" Singley shouted.

"There'll be no hoppin'," the canal boatman said. "He'll be walkin', same as me."

Singley did me the favor of translating. "He says you have to walk. We had trouble getting started, so the man's in a foul mood."

"Where are you going?"

"A picnic at Pletscher's Beech Grove, near Newburgh."

I hadn't yet been to Newburgh but had heard of the German town.

"I don't have food to bring," I said.

"We'll share ours," said a female voice from the top deck.

I recognized Brigitte, the friend of Susan Fry, laughing and waving, her soft brown curls swinging loosely beneath her straw bonnet. I smiled and waved back. Singley leaned out over the water for a peek at Brigitte and almost toppled overboard. I had a hunch that Singley was sweet on her, although he'd never said as much.

Falling into step beside the boat, I resolved to join the party. The terrain beside the towpath grew greener as I went along, the boatman and I carefully dodging the episodic manure of the mules. Tall grasses draped the path, and a willow tree here and there brushed my head with its weeping tendrils. Even as hot as it was, the natural world lifted my spirits like rain on a seed, so my chest broadened and my shoulders relaxed. With my hard work at the shop, I had become more muscular. My shirt now stretched tautly across my back. Enough whiskers had emerged on my chin that I sported the semblance of a beard.

At Pletscher's Beech Grove, a stunning forest of thick silver trees and spreading branches, the passengers piled off the boat. As I stood waiting beside the plank for my friends, Charles Rauch hopped off and we greeted each other with civility. Then Brigitte appeared. I reached out my hand to help her onto the canal bank. Once safely across, she looked into my eyes and erupted into laughter.

"We have a hungry one!" she said to Susan, to whom I now extended a hand.

I felt my cheeks redden. Indeed, my stomach cut against my spine, but I didn't realize I wore my hunger so plainly on my face.

The picnickers scattered across the beech grove, mostly young men and women, but older gentlemen, too, surrounded by their wives and young children. Cooking fires were lit for roasting sausages. Fry and Singley and I stayed close to Brigitte, Susan, and their friend Hilda, under the mysterious spell of the female. Hilda and Brigitte were servants, they told us, at the homes of Yankee families on Prospect. They worked six days a week, with only Sundays to do as they pleased.

Fry and Singley had brought along green bottles of Rhine wine. My eyes fell on the label, which read 1848er Dürkheimer Hock, and I grew excited.

"How do you come by this?" I asked, holding it up. "Freinsheim, the village of my family, is just a short distance from Dürkheim."

"Herr Leick sells it. He imports the native Rhine wines," Singley said.

"These must be the ones Herr Selzer trades." I gazed at the bottle as if it contained the nectar of the gods. "I've probably passed by the fields where these grapes were grown."

"Cleveland has its share of Palatines—there's a good market here for Rhine wines."

I savored this connection to my homeland and would have drunk the whole bottle myself if Fry had not wrested it from me. After eating our picnic and consuming the wine, we lounged on blankets or leaned our backs against the sun-dappled tree trunks, the chirping of the cicadas ceaseless in the sultry air.

At some point Charles Rauch stopped by for a visit.

"I hear Rapparlie is not paying you," he said, dropping down beside me to stretch out his lanky legs.

I sat more erect and shrugged, trying to act as if I didn't care. "I owed him money at first. He pays me now, the usual wage for apprentices."

"I don't understand why you signed up for indenture in the first place. It's the old way of thinking. Come work for me—I pay a decent wage from the start."

"To do what? Sort scraps of metal? I'm not yet a jour."

"You don't have to be a journeyman. We run machines with steam, and need men to operate them."

"I'll become a jour first; then you can ask me again. I can't break my indenture contract, in any case."

"What will Rapparlie do if you break it, put you in jail?"

I remained silent, so Rauch turned to Singley, promising to best Rapparlie's wage if Singley defected. Singley's eyes wandered to Brigitte, but he didn't have the opportunity to reply, for a music band started playing. We watched several couples gathering to dance on the mossy forest floor. It was a wilderness idyll as I might have imagined in one of Cooper's books. Rauch asked Hilda to dance, and Brigitte took Singley's arm. Susan might have liked to dance, but I didn't ask her, feeling too relaxed with good food and wine.

"That's Nix, Captain of the Scythe-men of Kirchheimbolanden," Fry said, pointing to a man talking in the ear of the band leader.

"The Scythe-men? Who fought against Prince Wilhelm?" I could not believe my ears.

Fry nodded. "What do you know of it?"

"Prince Wilhelm's army occupied my town for an entire summer. Prussian soldiers slept in our stable loft."

"You saw the Cartridge Prince?"

I nodded, marveling, *Could that boy have been me?* "The Crown Prince stayed at the house of Herr Mayer of Freinsheim."

Susan regarded me with new interest. "You didn't tell us you are a forty-eighter."

Fry shook his head. "Sister, that's impossible. He's a fiftier, like us."

I laughed. This distinction was made among the Germans of Ohio, those who were exiles of the revolution versus those who came later for economic opportunity.

"I was only seven years old in 1849," I said, "but I did lay eyes on the Cartridge Prince."

"Many of these men here are forty-eighters, exiles of that struggle. Over there, the man with the long blond hair, is Jacob Müller, Civil Commissioner of Kirchheimbolanden."

"Of the newspaper? Uncle Johann complains about Thieme and Müller every time he reads it."

Fry told me about these men and their rebellious antics, how they held Thomas Paine festivals to honor the great founder of democracy, and also to goad the Puritans who claimed Paine was an infidel. This surprised me.

"I find it odd," I told Fry, "that the Germans here still care so much for Paine. Back in Freinsheim, the men talked more of the ideas of Engels and the Frenchman, Proudhon, those who claim democracy is a failed system, that a more communal kind of government is needed."

"Ha! Don't mention Engels around Müller. When Müller was Civil Commissioner, he had Engels arrested and taken to Kaiserslautern in chains as a spy. All because Engels thought the rebellion didn't go far enough. It came to nothing, of course. They set Engels free immediately. Müller still talks about the man's arrogance to anyone who will listen."

How amazed I felt, hearing this story. Fry laughed at this as if it were a good joke. I did not think Freinsheimers would find it so. If I wrote a letter to Philipp and told him I knew Jacob Müller of Kirchheimbolanden, would he and the other Freinsheimers even believe me? It struck me again how separated we were, not only by geography, but also by ideas and attitudes.

Near the end of the afternoon, the guitar player began to strum the ballad "*Die Lorelei.*" Everyone in the grove paused what they were doing and joined in.

I know not what it means, that I am so sad ...

Singing the song, I thought of the broad flowing Rhine, of the fabled Lorelei who enchanted sailors. A strong *Heimweh* grabbed my chest, a homesickness for the Palatinate with its hard-working farmers who still didn't have their liberty, for the *Kerwe*, for the barefooted girls, the rows of grape leaves fluttering like flags.

More and more, I realized, I was becoming like the rest of these German-Americans, living out my days in Cleveland without thought of going home, torn by hope, striving, and loss.

# Chapter 25

WHEN SCHOOL LET OUT FOR the summer, at last Uncle Rapparlie's eldest, Little John, came to work in the wagon shop, to haul the buckets of water, to break up lumps of coal, and clear out yesterday's clinker—tasks to which I used to devote my days. At last my chance had come to begin working wrought iron at the anvil. The blacksmith jour Herr Hoffmann started me on small tasks—filing, deburring and such. He demonstrated fitting hinges and making small chains. Anxious to impress my Uncle Johann, I endeavored to learn fast, without error.

For all the good it did. Herr Hoffman would demonstrate a task, which my head understood. However, my hands refused to cooperate. First I would do it wrong, then err a second time and a third, failing again and again. Some men might watch once and then be able to repeat a task with precision, but I didn't have this ability. But if I kept at it, reheating and trying again, eventually the iron would grow pliant, behaving as I willed it. Once I learned a thing in both brain and body, the movements became part of my being. I could perform the tasks ever afterward without fail.

As for Uncle Johann, even when I succeeded at a task, he saw mistakes, throwing my work into the fire and ordering me to do it over again. Or he'd keep me late on menial chores to make me pay for work he claimed he'd have to do over. I felt tempted to give up, to go to the Wayside carriage factory for a decent wage, but in the end, I couldn't bear to bring shame on my parents, to confirm in my uncle's mind he'd been right about me all along. In fact, I feared he might write to my parents to complain, so I gritted my teeth and said nothing, doing everything in my power to keep that from happening.

That July the heat grew ever more oppressive. One afternoon, black towers of clouds formed over the lake. Hot fingers of lightning stabbed all around followed by booms of growling thunder. A strange yellow light suffused the sky, causing us workmen to glance out the windows of our day-lit smithy with trepidation. Suddenly, the clouds burst, pelting a hard rain against the windows, turning the streets to rivers. Men spoke in awed tones of fierce tornadoes ripping up houses and barns in the farm country, of lightning that struck houses so they burned to the ground, only the chimneys left standing like giant grave markers in the charred rubble.

The power of these thunderstorms reminded me of God's awesome might and of his severe retribution for human vanity. I did not dare go too far in seeking my own desires, for fear of the calamities that might bring. But the American courage did not falter. They invented lightning rods to absorb heaven's daggers, sparing houses and their inhabitants. They devised vertical railways to lift people up floor by floor, so men didn't have to climb the stairs. They created a steam organ, the Calliope, pulled by a team of forty horses, a musical instrument of such celestial power it could be heard from a distance of twenty miles. They uncoiled telegraph wires across the storm-tossed Atlantic to tap messages from the Old World to the New in the blink of an eye. Always a new invention, a new marvel, as if one day, man might outwit Almighty God himself.

I was not so sure of this American hubris and the quick pace of change. In that regard, I didn't have much to worry about. My station in life was lowly, my progress measured and slow. That summer, I added to my modest skills by learning hole punching, cutting flattened iron, mending chain, and scrolling hooks for the whiffletrees. Even doing these simple tasks, I suffered great frustration. The other smiths plied their craft with a few deft blows. *What are they doing that I am not?* I would wonder, clenching my jaw against the setbacks.

But the American ambition was infectious. As the days passed, my forearms grew large and roped with muscles. I learned to bend the iron to my will, to solve intractable problems, to produce useful objects from formless lumps of metal. The art of creation turned a key inside me, opening the door of my desire to succeed at this living and go beyond it, to one day produce custom wagons and carriages from start to finish. I formed an opinion about what looked exactly right and what did not, my first understanding of the golden ratio of proportions.

I first felt this sense most strongly one afternoon as I worked alone scrolling wagon hooks. Herr Hoffman had been working beside me, but was called away to help adjust a wagon tongue. Hardly noticing his departure, I continued in a steady rhythm, tapering and curling the iron. As I formed the eye on the last of my hooks, I glanced over at Herr Hoffmann's final hook and noticed it was slightly off in the curve.

Sometime later, Herr Hoffmann returned to find me reshaping his entire pile of hooks.

"Harm, put that down," he growled, eyeing me strangely. "Get to the strap bolts."

I hurried to do his bidding, but from then on Herr Hoffmann relied on me for shaping many of the parts, and some of the finer finishings, while he applied himself to the fittings.

With September came a new sense of urgency, the movers and settlers in a rush to go West before the winter cold and ice. On an especially busy day, Herr Hoffmann was helping Uncle Johann fit a kingbolt for a front axle assembly and in desperation assigned Singley and me to draw out a piece of iron for a side bracket. Singley was to be the smith, I the striker.

I felt a pounding excitement in my ribs; it was my first chance at this job. I had watched often enough how the smith directed the striker's movements, holding the iron on the anvil, tapping his hammer wherever he wanted the blow. The striker's job was to follow the smith with precision, hitting the heavy sledge at the exact place and angle indicated. To call off the striker, the smith would tap the anvil instead of the bar iron. The striker then stood back to await the next heat.

With the formation of each wagon part, the smith belonged to the metal until the task was done. A job might take minutes, or several hours, but regardless, we couldn't stop until it was finished. And so Singley and I began. First, the side bracket had to be flattened and drawn out to considerable length. He and I worked well together for several heats, Singley tapping with his hammer, me swinging down with the heavy sledge. Tap, clang, tap, clang. Tap, clang.

It's not the striker's job to think, but I couldn't help noticing how Singley's tapping was making the metal draw out crooked. Fearing Uncle Johann would be angry at us for wasting his iron, on the fourth heat I didn't pay attention when Singley tapped the anvil to call me off. One last time I swung down the sledge with all my might at the same moment Singley leaned his head in to eyeball his work. My hammer whammed down within a hair's breadth of crushing his skull.

Singley jumped back with a shout. As I lowered the sledge in shock, Uncle Johann appeared out of nowhere and punched me hard in the face. "*Bass uff,* you could kill a man!" he shouted.

Rendered nearly senseless, I wavered over the handle to hold myself upright. My uncle wrenched the sledge from my grasp and raised it as if to flatten me like a rivet. In that instant, I saw the face of my father, his mixture of rage and terror the day he'd rushed down to the cellar to douse the lantern fire. I threw my arms over my head in self defense, but no blow came. A terrible moment of quiet followed in the smithy, punctuated only by the muttering of the fires.

Uncle Johann grunted and lowered the head of the hammer to the dirt. "I'll finish here," he said, nodding to Singley to start the next heat.

"*Es tut mir leid, Onkel*," I apologized, terror-stricken at my error.

Uncle Johann's mouth drew into a snarl. "You are sorry, you are sorry! Don't ever be sorry. Only careful. Careful! Go sweep the wood shavings so I don't have to look at you."

I turned to Singley. "*Es tut mir leid.*"

My friend wouldn't meet my gaze.

THAT SAME EVENING, AS IF the vision of my father had called up a specter, I received the first word from my family since arriving in Cleveland. I was pulling shut the shop doors when Herr Höhn of Freinsheim, his wife, two sons, and three daughters and my old friend Matthias, came walking toward me down Seneca Street.

"Do I see before me the Höhns of Freinsheim?" I cried out, wild with joy at the sight of them.

Matthias ran the last few steps to meet me. "I told you I'd follow you!"

Neither of us could wipe the grins from our faces, although my sore jaw felt thick and lopsided. I broke our gaze to greet Herr and Frau Höhn, the Höhn brothers Hans and Sebastian, and their sisters, the youngest only three years old.

"*Gott sei Dank* it's good to see you. You've come to settle in Cleveland?"

Herr Höhn's face was moist with sweat and road dust. "We're on our way to my brother's farm in Columbiana," he said.

Frau Höhn grasped both my arms and examined me with concern. "*Tch,* Michael, but what's happened to your face? Have you fallen?"

"I'm fine," I said. "I bumped into a post." I hoped desperately they wouldn't learn the truth.

Aunt Katharina and Uncle Johann appeared in the wagon yard just then with their young ones, and I introduced them all around. The Rapparlies spoke for some time with Herr and Frau Höhn, then invited the family to dine with us that evening. The September nights were still pleasant, so I helped my uncle push aside some wagons, bring out a table and chairs, and lug pitchers of cool wine from the cask in the cellar.

Aunt Katharina had been to the Central Market, so we grilled fresh sausages over the wheelwright's pit, a treat we enjoyed in the summers. We also ate corn still on the cob in the American style, and apples, green beans and grilled onions. The neighbor George Weherling joined us. The party resembled a Freinsheimer *Schlachtfest*. The only thing missing was the pig's bladder hanging at the gate.

Throughout the dinner we spoke of the Höhns' steamship crossing, a voyage of only three weeks. After supper, Herr Höhn lit his pipe, exhaling a gray smoke that clung in a cloud around his head.

"*Ach so*, I almost forgot … We bring with us a letter from the Johann Philipp Harms." He removed the letter from his inside pocket and handed it to Uncle Johann. "And something from Johann Philipp Harm to Herr Rapparlie. That waits with our belongings at the docks."

Uncle Johann turned the letter over in his hand, broke the seal and ironed the creases on the knee of his good leg.

29 August, 1858

Dear Brother and Sister-in-law and son,

> We pray daily for your good health.
> We had a good harvest last year and if the fair weather continues, this year's harvest should also be adequate.
> We thank God for Michael's safe arrival with you. As with all other matters, Herr Höhn has seen us often these past months and will tell you how it is with us.
> Brother-in-law, we ordered the wine, that is a payment of the apprenticeship fee, and send it along with Herr Höhn with our grateful thanks for your good care of our son.
> Our heartfelt greetings,

Johann Philipp and Elisabetha Harm, and Philipp Harm

I watched my uncle's expression, hoping this news would please him. He raised one gray eyebrow at Aunt Katharina but said nothing. When he handed the letter to me, I read the brief lines again, then turned to Frau Höhn, who retained the homespun aura of Freinsheim, her hair wrapped in the white scarf.

"How does my mother manage?" I asked.

Frau Höhn observed me with kind eyes. "Satisfactorily, although she doesn't get around as she used to. I didn't see her at the wedding—your father said it would have been too much for her."

I pictured Mütterchen in her chair by the table, trembling, her eyes moist as my father wrote out the lines of this letter, his mouth framed by his wispy beard, the skin around his eyes creased in concentration. No doubt Philipp sat at the table in his homespun tunic, dirt streaks on his neck and forehead from the day's hoeing. What was it like for my brother, with me gone? Had I brought extra hardship on him, as he helped father and faced service in the military? Did he hate me for leaving? I wished he had added a note of his own.

In my mind's eye, the rolling green hills around our village stretched to the pale evening sky. In my imagination, I could smell the ripe grapes of harvest time. Such a different place from here. I touched my sore chin, a small punishment for my terrible carelessness. Was I better at making things of metal than I'd been at helping things grow? After today, I wasn't so sure. Blacksmithing was harder than I thought, just as Philipp had said. My heart clenched with regret. Perhaps I had forced my way into a life where I didn't belong. Where things were destined to go awry.

"*Doch*, the wedding," Sebastian said. "Tell Harm about the wedding. Emil Oberholz has married your Anna Marie Neufeld."

"My Anna Marie?" I echoed. My own voice sounded to me as if it came from a deep well.

"Ha!" Hans laughed. "Everyone knows you were sweet on Anna Marie. It is legend, your desperate proposal to her. But she and Emil were always intended for each other."

Sebastian pushed on my shoulder as if it were a great joke, as if I had not a care in the matter. I couldn't deny their accusation, so kept quiet, hoping my face didn't betray my true emotions. Matthias looked sorry for me.

Herr Höhn turned to Uncle Johann. "The Neufeld and Oberholz families were pleased with the match. We attended the marriage—a fine procession through Freinsheim. It was then I felt saddest at the thought of parting forever from lifelong acquaintances. In part it was Michael's letter—his mention of my brother's farm in Columbiana—that made me feel it was time. My brother has been after me to emigrate these many years."

I looked down at the hard-packed dirt, my head spinning. Emil and Anna Marie were now joined in holy matrimony. It came as no surprise, but still …

Sebastian chuckled. "Your Anna Marie was the most beautiful bride in Freinsheim. After her there were no others, so we bachelors gave up on Freinsheimer girls. Squeeze your thumbs for us, that there are brides for us here in America."

"*Ach so*, we wanted to bring you a letter from your Anna Marie," Hans said, "but she was too busy in the bed of her new husband for such things."

He and Sebastian laughed again.

"The wine Herr Harm sends is from the Oberholz vineyard, and of the highest quality," Matthias said.

My uncle and Herr Höhn changed the subject to the poor quality of Ohio wines, of German progress in viticulture here, and I looked with gratitude at my old friend. I was delighted Matthias had come, thinking it meant I'd be less lonely.

Herr Höhn told my uncle he hoped to purchase a wagon, and soon Uncle Johann was giving him a tour of his shop. The Höhns had sold all their property in Freinsheim for a very good price, Herr Höhn explained, so he had the idea to purchase a farm near his brother. My uncle recommended an express wagon his workers had just completed. He would tell the men to add seats to the wagon bed for Herr Höhn's large family. A bargain was struck. Uncle Johann invited the Höhns to stay the week, until the adjustments were made and the paint dried.

The next day, Uncle Johann allowed me to go along with them to the auctioneer at Superior and Seneca to purchase a team of horses to pull the Höhns' wagon. While Uncle Johann dickered over the price, the Höhns stood to one side with the blank expressions of men new to this country. For my part, I understood all the numbers, and much of the vocabulary important to the trade. I had indeed learned a thing or two since arriving.

EARLY ON SATURDAY, CANNON FIRE announced the opening of the Firemen's Parade. Uncle Johann was in a good mood, or he wanted to impress Herr Höhn. In any case, he gave the shop workers a rare holiday. The Höhns, Rapparlies, Scheuermanns, and Crollys all went together to the docks to watch the arrival of the steamers, packed to overflowing with firemen and their families. Throngs of festival-goers crowded Public Square. Firemen demonstrated a new steam engine that could spout great fountains of water high in the air. The Höhns marveled at American ingenuity, and I felt a flush of pride for Cleveland.

Later in the night, Matthias, Sebastian, Hans, and I went to Schlegel's for *Lagerbier,* which they pronounced to be as fine as any in the Palatinate. On the way home, we encountered drunken firemen brawling in the streets. It seemed funny at first, but they beat a man very badly, which sobered us in the end.

What with so many guests, Matthias and I were relegated to sleep in the wagon shop. As we lay prone, each to our own wagon bed among the shavings and sawdust, I told Matthias more about my transatlantic voyage, about Sparer and Wiener and Charles Rauch, about the robbery in New York. I didn't confess to the loss of Father's pocket watch. The mere thought of it gouged the metal of my soul.

"I only wish my parents and my brother Philipp were here. Then the loneliness wouldn't be so great," I said

"When your father saw what a good price Herr Höhn got for his land, I heard him say he might sell his land also and come with us, if only he knew what it would be like here. But Philipp didn't wish to go."

"If only Philipp draws a good lottery number, so he has little chance of conscription."

"Not much chance of that. Hans, Sebastian, and I were all glad to get out, I can tell you."

"I don't think Philipp would leave, in any case."

Matthias agreed, recounting how Philipp still remained under the slipper of Susanna. I couldn't blame my brother for success in love. I stared into the darkness, picturing what my life would have been like as Anna Marie's husband. My devotion to Anna Marie now seemed a naïve fantasy. Would I ever know such love again?

"What you should do," I said to Matthias, "is make your home here in Cleveland. We'd have great fun together, you playing and me singing, serenading the *Fräuleins.*"

"I'll see first how I like the farm country," Matthias said.

"But I won't be able to visit you. I'm chained to Lord Rapparlie like a slave."

"At least you have a trade," Matthias said. "I have no prospect of making a living."

"If I were you, I'd think carefully before signing on for indenture. It's not so common in America, and the loss of freedom is hard."

"Some things never change, Harm. In Freinsheim, you complained of farm work, now it's blacksmithing. It seems to me you have a fine life."

Of course Matthias didn't understand. Uncle Johann had made a good impression on the Höhns, with his wealth and his busy shop.

# Chapter 26

---

LONELIER THAN EVER AFTER THE departure of the Höhns, the following Sunday I made a visit to the Scheuermanns. The flower garden along the paving stone path, my aunt's warm smile, the piano in the parlor, and her fast-growing young boys, all served to remind me of life beyond the stern, hard-working kingdom of Johann Rapparlie.

"It's good to see you, nephew!" Aunt Margaretha said, pulling me into her red brick home. "We were about to send word. We received a letter from my brother Jakob!"

Aunt Margaretha sat me down at the kitchen table to read my uncle's few lines.

18 May, 1858

Dear Brother-in-law and sister,

I am enormously far away from you and don't know yet if I will be able to shake hands with you again. Until only recently I earned each week $62.00 and paid only $7.00 for the week in room and board. But since then times have become very bad in California. I am in Sacramento Buttes and unable to find work. I want to go from here to dig for gold and try my luck. If I don't like it and am unable to find the blacksmith work, I will see you again soon, approximately within two years.

Jakob Handrich

My aunt and I were discussing, based on this short missive, whether Jakob succeeded or suffered from his adventures out West when Uncle Georg came in from his work shed and offered me a glass of Rhine wine. I readily accepted and followed him down to the cool cellar pantry. Soon we'd settled on two straight-backed chairs amidst bushel baskets of apples and potatoes. An oak barrel of shredded cabbage, salted for sauerkraut, stood in one corner beneath shelves containing jars of jelly, tomatoes, and beans. A curing ham hung from the ceiling. This cellar felt as cozy to me as a small piece of heaven.

"How goes it at the wagon shop?" Uncle Georg asked. He kept a thick brown moustache, but his strong jaw was clean shaven. I thought perhaps I might try shaving off my whiskers, as I didn't think my beard grew in thick enough to be very handsome. "Does blacksmithing agree with you?"

With a jolt, I realized Uncle Georg had probably heard of my near-catastrophe.

"In most things, I improve," I said hesitantly. "I didn't mean to be careless with the striking."

Uncle Georg took a pipe from his pocket. "To be honest, I did hear of this accident. It's one reason the apprenticeships are so long. The work is dangerous, and I don't know of a man who hasn't made a serious mistake at one time or another." His expression grave, Uncle Georg fumbled in his vest pocket for a match. "But Jacob Hoffmann tells me something more—how Johann treats you ill. I don't understand it. I've known Johann Rapparlie a long time. In his dealings, he's always been an honorable man."

"Uncle Johann holds a grudge against me. Even the Rhine wine from my parents didn't improve his opinion."

Uncle Georg shook his head. "Hoffmann doesn't understand it, either. He tells me you have a natural talent and will make a good journeyman one day."

My heart filled with gratitude to hear Herr Hoffmann's kind assessment. "I work hard, but Uncle Johann doesn't change his opinion no matter what. Perhaps I could come live with you? Then I'd only be indebted to the Rapparlies for the work, not the room and board, and it might not be so bad."

Uncle Georg puffed his pipe thoughtfully. I watched the smoke stream from his nostrils, feeling it might be possible for me to have a better situation, hoping desperately his answer would be yes.

"I wish we had room for you. But I'm afraid it wouldn't go so well for you at the shop if you moved over to us. Stand it as long as you can, nephew. Learn the *Handwerk* skills to make a living, and the indenture will end in good time."

Feeling despondent, I nodded that I understood.

Uncle Georg sighed. "Maybe Johann is no longer right in the head. If only Jakob were here, he would talk sense into him."

I couldn't imagine Uncle Johann listening to anyone but himself, and was about to say as much, but Uncle Georg changed the subject to talk about the Oberliners who'd chased down slavehunters to free a captured fugitive slave. While Uncle Georg remained a Democrat, the ideas of the 48ers had made an impression on him.

As we mulled over the Fugitive Slave Law, Herr Crolly came to the Scheuermanns. Aunt Margaretha sent him down to the cellar to find us. Herr Crolly announced he'd bought a house on the east side, on Henry Street, several blocks distant from the Rapparlie shop.

"I hate to leave Ohio City, but the women who come to Catherine for the dressmaking all live on the east side now, and Eva must walk very far to work at the wagon shop each day."

I hadn't forgotten Herr and Frau Crolly's kindness to me that first Christmas and longed to help the family. "Do you need a mover? If you ask him, Uncle Johann will probably allow me to drive his four-wheeled dray to help you transport the furniture."

BECAUSE OF THIS OFFER, THE very next Sunday found me harnessing the roan and the black and driving the dray wagon to the west side for the Crolly's moving day. The weather that afternoon was warm—so warm one might have thought it was still summer if not for the brilliant orange and yellow carpet of leaves on the road.

Regardless of what else occurred, the Crollys observed the Sabbath, so as I arrived I beheld Herr and Frau Crolly and their three daughters walking up the lane from church in their Sunday finest, the women in white lace collars, their hair tucked neatly beneath beribboned bonnets.

Of late the second daughter Elizabeth had grown even prettier than her older sister Eva. Elizabeth was still young, just thirteen, but something about her mischievous eyes and playful temperament made me eager to impress her. The third daughter, Mary, was a trial to her parents. At the family holidays she always demanded the best part of everything—the finest china cup, the fat on the pork chop, the first turn at the piano.

It took two trips to load and unload the furniture and baskets and miscellany. As we worked, Herr Crolly treated me like a worthy helper. By the end of the day, the task had been accomplished so pleasantly I regretted I had not gone into the barrel-making profession, if only to have Herr Crolly as my master. Sometimes I allowed myself to entertain such useless reveries, fantasies of how my life could have turned out differently.

AT LEAST THE HOMESICKNESS CAME less often. I suffered only one wrenching reminiscence that fall, when Uncle Johann sent me on an errand to the hardware store. As I was passing a cake shop, I caught sight of a traditional

Palatine plum cake displayed in the window. A flood of sensations rushed through me, images of Mütterchen and Frau Becker arranging the plums in perfect symmetry across the top of the dough, the sweet-tart taste and rich buttery crust of each bite. Lost in the ridges and hollows of memory, I didn't notice at first that someone was watching me. When I became aware of a woman smiling at me through the window, I ducked away and continued on my errand.

I'd gone only a few steps when a voice called out behind me.

"Young man!"

Reluctantly, I turned, bracing myself for the Yankee woman's reprimand. No doubt she'd call me a *Dummkraut* or some other ingenious American insult.

"Excusing me," I said.

She beckoned to me to come back. "You do no wrong. Come here. Taste. *Schmeck.*" She put one hand on her hip and gave a lilting laugh.

Her laughter confused me. Feeling like a dolt, I followed her inside the shop, the air swimming with fragrances of chocolate, vanilla, and sugar. The woman lifted the counter shelf and went behind it. She was older—how much older I couldn't tell. Rust-colored curls escaped along her temples and neck from under her white cap. She brought the plum cake over and set it down before me, cutting a generous slice. She put the cake on a china plate and pushed it toward me with a silver fork. Her eyes, when she looked up, were as deep green as a carpet of moss.

"Dutch," she said, pointing to the cake. I knew she meant *Deutsch*, German. They all pronounced it like that. "Taste. *Schmeck.*" She picked up the fork and put it in my hand, her pink lips curling into a smile.

Was this woman tricking me into buying the cake? I looked around, but the shop was empty. I had no money, as I'd spent my last twenty-five cents the previous night at another ball.

"Free," she said. "Free taste." The "r" rolled thickly off her tongue.

"*Frei?*"

She nodded encouragingly. Hesitantly, I hefted a forkful into my mouth, my tongue instantly singing from the mingled sweet and sour.

"*Schmeckt gut?*" she asked.

"*Gut,*" I said, bringing my hand up so as not to spit crumbs.

My hand was filthy, coated in coal dust and metal filings, so I quickly dropped it again. The woman kept smiling, though, and gestured for me to continue. I picked up the plate from the polished counter, held it close to my mouth, and used the gleaming fork to shovel the cake in. As I scooped up the last bite, she reached out, presumably to take the plate, and brushed my hand with hers.

Startled, I glanced up to mumble an apology, but her eyes held mine and her gaze intensified. The shop bell rang and a customer entered. The woman whirled around to set the plate behind her, then turned to the newcomer.

"Good morning, Mrs. Chandler," she said.

The *Frau* wore a black wool cloak, her eyes focused on the pastries. The cake shop woman turned back to me.

"*Auf Wiedersehen*," she said in dismissal.

I let myself out and continued in a daze toward the George Worthington Company hardware store. In the store basement, I spent overlong examining different lengths of iron stock, my mind still back in the cake shop. Had the woman touched me on purpose? Had she been making an invitation? But no, it was impossible. She'd fed me as you would a stray dog, probably because I looked the part.

On my return to Rapparlie's, I altered my path to pass the store with looking glasses, to stare into the rectangles and ovals of silver glass that hung in the window. Standing before a tall one, I set down the bar iron with a clank and stood back to examine my image. I'd forgotten my hat, so my brown hair sat tousled atop my head. Of late, I'd started to shave my beard, leaving a sandy-brown moustache in imitation of my Uncle Georg. My blue eyes were set evenly above a symmetrical nose and square jaw. Except for a streak of coal dust above my left eyebrow, my skin was unmarred. My shoulders were strong and broad, my waist narrowing into heavy work trousers, dusty but with few holes. My work boots were scuffed but sturdy.

Was I pulling the wool over my eyes, or had the shop woman found me handsome? I threw my shoulders back as I picked up the iron and sauntered on, savoring the strength in my limbs. I couldn't stop myself from smiling. By the time I reached the wagon shop, I was humming a tune.

In rhythm with my hammer that afternoon, I found myself singing out loud.

"Save it for the singing society, Harm," the journeyman Herr Penhoff said, tossing aside a dull cold chisel.

"Isn't my voice a wonder to behold?" I asked, bowing with a flourish. "If there were a singing society in Cleveland, it would be lucky to have me."

"*Dummkopf*, there is a *Gesangverein*."

"Truly?" I kept imagining America was a foreign land, but every time I turned around, another German tradition had been transplanted here, roots and all.

"Yes, truly," Herr Penhoff said. "The Cleveland Singing Society is very good indeed. The English claim it is clannish of us to hold German singing festivals and sing music they don't understand." Herr Penhoff examined a glowing bar end with a practiced eye, laid it on the anvil and pounded, then brought it up for another look. "In truth they're jealous. We're the better singers."

Herr Dietz chuckled his appreciation.

As for me, I couldn't believe my good fortune. First, a free slice of delicious plum cake, and second, a cake shop woman with startling green eyes. Third, a German singing society in my new American town. Some days are like that, when all the bounty falls from the heavens at once.

That very night, I inquired of Aunt Katharina about the rehearsal times and location of this society.

"I'll ask Frieda Keppler. Sigfried Keppler, the brother-in-law of your uncle, sings in this club."

"My uncle's brother-in-law?" I had not realized he had family in Cleveland.

My aunt looked over her shoulder to be sure Uncle Johann wasn't nearby. "Johann doesn't like to speak of it. His sister is American born. His parents came here long ago, leaving Johann to be raised in the Palatinate by his grandfather, and so he and his sister only met once he emigrated. His sister lives in Cleveland, but Johann and her husband don't get along. They had a misunderstanding about the wagon shop. Sigfried wanted to be a partner in the business, to call it Rapparlie & Keppler, but your uncle refused. As a consequence, we rarely see them."

THE NEXT DAY, AUNT KATHARINA gave me the information about the rehearsals, held every Tuesday evening. "But I'm afraid you can't do it. The start time is half after six, before the workday is over."

I knew it would cause trouble for me if I asked for special consideration. But Aunt Katherina came to my rescue.

"Shall I tell your uncle you'll run extra errands to make up the time?" she asked. I nodded. "*Alla,*" she said, "I'll talk to him."

How light-hearted I felt the following week as I entered Weidenkopf's Hall. The leader, Herr Abel, aspired to higher musical sensibility, directing us in German folk songs and also in more cultured music—that of Mendelssohn, Haydn, Handel, and Liszt. To afford the membership fee and sheet music, I had to forego three weeks of beer and dances. But each Tuesday night when Weidenkopf's Hall filled with the sonorous voices of singing men, I didn't miss those things at all.

# Chapter 27

———❧———

"HARNESS THE HORSES, MICHAEL," UNCLE Johann said one December day. "The new wagon and sleigh are ready for the Schacks on Columbus Road. We'll load the sleigh on the wagon and you'll follow behind with the chaise, so I'll have a way to get back."

I hustled to do my uncle's bidding. Soon we were driving through a landscape bare and brooding. The first snow in the end of November hadn't stuck, leaving everything gray and brown. The wagon wheels sank nearly to the hubs in water-filled ruts on the road. Teamsters driving loaded express wagons crowded ahead and behind, all wagons moving the same speed in a long, slow line.

With time to look about, I spotted a sign for the Wayside Smithy and felt a start of recognition. As we made slow progress, I took in the details, the smithy larger and more rambling than I had imagined, with several outbuildings. Strewn around the property were heaps of broken wheels, cast off metal parts, strips of rawhide, and rusting farm plows. From within the huge open doorway of a barn-like building came the ringing of anvils and screech of saws, sparks raining to the ground.

We delivered the sleigh and wagon to the Schacks without incident. On the return journey, feeling a deep curiosity to see inside Rauch's smithy, I reminded my uncle about the invitation of Charles Rauch, my old friend from the Helvetia. To my surprise, Rapparlie agreed to visit the place, so we pulled into the yard and found our way to the office door.

Charles Rauch himself was in the office, not in the leather apron of the blacksmith, but wearing a necktie and topcoat. We exchanged greetings, and I introduced him to my uncle.

"*Guten Tag, Herr Rapparlie.* We're honored to have you visit, as your reputation is well-known," Rauch said, showing his usual good manners. "Allow me to show you around our shop."

Not "my father's shop" but "our shop," I noticed, the usual envy digging in my gut. As I passed Rauch's desk, I saw copies of *The New York Coach-Maker's Magazine* piled on one corner. I longed to pause and leaf through them, but Rauch was ushering us through the front area into the blacksmithing department, where six forges glowed at once. My uncle's eyes widened in surprise. The wagons and carriages for jobbing stood five deep.

"My father began with jobbing," Rauch said.

"Winter must be your busiest season," my uncle said, surveying the workshop with an expert eye. "We saw a broken axle and two loose wheels on our way here. Amesbury carriages, every one."

Rauch nodded. The eastern imports were a frequent topic among the wagon-makers. Once I witnessed one of these ghost trains, the shipment sent from the State of Massachusetts, each carriage individually wrapped in white cloth. It was a constant vexation, how Cleveland's citizens preferred to order New England carriages, although ones of high quality were built right under their noses.

"Come to think of it, I've seen only one Rapparlie wagon come in, and that repair was from the owner's carelessness—he let his tires go too long without resetting them."

My uncle nodded with satisfaction.

Rauch guided us through a second set of doors to a day-lit wood shop where workers swarmed around the saw trestles. Numerous coaches and buggies were under construction at the same time, many more than at our shop. A variety of heavy iron machinery seemed to be doing the drilling and sawing and planing. Large belts spun into the rafters, driving the machines from under our feet. The floor trembled with the vibration.

"These machines are steam-powered?" Uncle Johann asked, raising his voice to be heard above the clatter.

Rauch shrugged. "The steam generators are in the basement. The machines reduce the time it takes us to do repairs, so the teamsters especially come to us." Under the hum of the machinery, he lowered his voice so only I could hear. "We pay a high wage, and there is the opportunity to work up, to become supervisor of the department."

I kept my expression neutral. Why did Rauch keep making me this offer? But he was moving ahead, through the trimming department, bragging all the while about his latest purchase, a hand-cranked dash stitcher. In the painting department he pointed out the use of ready-made varnish in lidded containers, eliminating the need for a separate fire and an apprentice to stir the varnish cauldron. In the wheelwright shop, there were stacks of hubs, spokes, and felloes, but no benches for hand hewing.

"I wish Father would let me buy a steam-bender. The initial investment is great, but I think we could save much money in the long run," Rauch said, leading us into a large repository, where a neat row of buggies—lightweight road wagons in the American style—stood lined along the wall. I struggled to hide my amazement at the scope of production.

"But where is your father?" my uncle asked. "I was hoping I might have the pleasure of greeting Jacob Rauch, too."

"He's at a meeting in Cleveland with men from the federal government about an order of wagons for the army."

Uncle Johann reddened. Didn't he know about this meeting? Or had he determined his own business wasn't up to the task? In any case, the news seemed to affect him.

Charles Rauch looked at his pocket watch and began leading us to the door.

"We're not as systematized as some. At the G. & D. Cook & Co. manufactory in Connecticut, they make ten vehicles per day. At the moment, we complete only two or three."

We stood in the yard saying our farewells, and again I noticed how much taller Rauch was than me, how much he looked the part of the shop owner.

The rest of the way to the Columbus Street bridge, my uncle and I sat lost each in our own thoughts. Rauch's expensive pocket watch had triggered a memory of the one I had lost at sea, which seemed so much less grand now that I lived in Cleveland and saw many fine things each day. In some ways, I missed the simple farm boy of the Atlantic crossing, who understood nothing of the relentless drive for material wealth.

These days, I longed to become like Rauch, a man in charge of his own shop, making the American buggies using all the modern methods, a pocket watch of heavy gold bulging from my silk vest pocket. I wished I could obtain a copy of the coach-making magazine for myself, to see what mysteries it revealed, and made a resolution to do so at my first opportunity. If I wanted to be a carriage-maker, I realized, I'd need to keep up with the latest methods.

Once we crossed back over to the east side my uncle sat straighter and snapped the reins on the horses' backs.

"Those quill-wheeled buggies of Rauch's won't stand up to the heavy mud of these roads," he said. "They made a terrible mistake. Their duplicated assembly methods will limit the amount of custom work and lead to shoddy workmanship and customer backlash. With all their haste to make money, the Rauchs will be out of business in five years' time."

"The hand-cranked post drill and dash stitcher were enviable, weren't they? These machines would save us much time and labor."

Uncle Johann shook his head. "*Doch,* the egg wants to be smarter than the hen? The *Handwerker* craftsman doesn't rely on the machines to do the work. Nothing will substitute for quality, for time-honored methods and skills."

I nodded that I understood, but held my own opinion on the matter. Where Uncle Johann saw disaster, I saw opportunity. Of all I had seen at the Wayside Smithy, the farm wagons and fancy coaches, my heart had been won over by the buggies. "Quill-wheeled," my uncle had called them—lightweight, speedy conveyances that cried out only for a trotter and a smart crack of the whip. How I longed to travel light and fast in a buggy one day.

"What are the wheels made of? They didn't appear to be oak."

Uncle Johann spat to the side of the wagon. "Hickory. Those buggies won't do a man's work. They're luxury playthings for the wealthy."

THE 48ERS AT SCHLEGEL'S HAD a name for the early German immigrants to Cleveland, for conservative men like Uncle Johann. The "Grays" they called them. Set in their ways, loyal to the slave-owning Democrats. They would stick to the Democrats, come thick or thin. And the Grays had a name for us, too. The "Greens"—new to the country, naïve to the history of American politics, to the Freesoilers and nativist Know-Nothing sentiments, to the Maine Liquor laws that almost ruined German wine- and beer-making interests in the election of 1853.

Near the new year of 1859, my uncle and I fell into an argument full of bitterness and accusation.

"Slavery was written in the Constitution," Uncle Johann said for the hundredth time in so many evenings. "It's not for the North to say. These Southerners have plantations at stake, their cotton and tobacco. For the government to interfere is as bad as the House of Wittelsbach interfering with all levels of business and family life in the Palatinate."

I felt sick and tired of listening to my uncle barking like a mad dog day and night. "When some men are owned by others, it is not a free country," I said, my voice rising.

Aunt Katharina turned from the sink with a warning frown.

Anger flared in my uncle's slate eyes. "You say it's a good thing, to ignore the constitutional law of this land?"

"It's the Southerners who ignore the Constitution," I said. "They try to keep the system of aristocracy, where the rich live in idle decadence while their slaves toil in chains. That's not the true meaning of American independence."

"So you, too, fall victim to the 'Greens,' these betrayers of the Democratic Party. You have not been in this country long enough to see what I have— Republican is a new name slapped over the old Whig party, the same men who worked against the immigrants. 'Americans must rule America!' That was their slogan. Germans not welcome."

"The Republican party is different than the Know-Nothings. It grows stronger since Fremont."

Sussy began to wail.

"*Bitte*, don't argue." Aunt Katharina said, picking up the two-year-old and holding a wet rag to her mouth to suckle.

Uncle Johann glared at me across his newspaper. "*Doch*, you spend too many evenings at Schlegel's. Thieme and his gang have hoodwinked you." He pushed both hands at me in disgust. "It is a very big change, what the Republicans ask us to believe. Such a new thing cannot happen overnight. A steady drop will carve the stone."

"A constant drip erodes a stone beyond repair. Look at President Buchanan, who does nothing while the Supreme Court turns our Territories into slave soil."

"President Buchanan is a Democrat. That's enough for me."

"If you study their platform, you'll—"

"I am a Democrat!" Uncle Johann thundered, so his three boys appeared, gaping and wide-eyed, at the kitchen entry. "*Du bist ein Narr!* That Fillmore was a Whig—a Know-Nothing nativist!"

"*Doch*, I am not as big a fool as the one who turns a blind eye to the ill treatment of the Negroes."

Uncle Johann examined his clenched fist. "Slavery is a necessary evil."

Eyes flashing, Aunt Katharina set Sussy back down. "Johann, for shame. How can you say that? The slave owners separate mothers from their babies. Families must not be broken up in this manner."

"*Frau*, it's not our fight."

I'd never heard my aunt disagree with my uncle before. I hurried to her defense. "The abolitionists believe the Negroes need help—someone to speak for them."

"The abolitionists are making trouble, not peace, with their speeches and moralizing." Uncle Johann's voice was tense beyond reason. "Those Oberliners were itching for a fight. Do you want to see war in this country? The states each going their own way? This country will break into many little pieces, become like Europe with the trade tariffs and cheaters."

"This is America. A democracy," I said, "where things can be decided by voting, by reasonable men. Thomas Paine won over America with his pen, not his sword."

Uncle Johann gave a sneer of disgust. "A boy as Green as the rest."

"At least I educate myself. I won't vote like a mule wearing blinders."

The root veins on my uncle's forehead grew larger.

"You? Vote?" his voice was low and menacing. "At least we're spared that problem!"

The insult hit home. He meant to call me a child—a man had to be twenty-one to vote in Ohio. Anger roared in my ears as I rose from the table, pushed past the boys to the foyer and shrugged on my coat, thinking only of escape.

# Chapter 28

———⁂———

OUTSIDE IN THE SNOW-DRIFTED STREET, I strode off at a quick pace, desiring only to rid my head of the turbulent anger and hatred I felt toward my uncle. I had no particular direction in mind, but before long found myself on the now-deserted street of the cake shop, staring in at the darkened window. Again.

In truth, the cake shop woman's touch, her steady green-eyed gaze, had worked a hunger in me, a natural attraction I felt powerless to resist. I'd passed this street often since that day, slowing my steps as I came to the center of the block to gaze in the window at the pastries. Now as I stood on the walkway, I thought of Goethe's *Elective Affinities*, his novel that spoke of the mysterious "chemistry" between a man and a woman. I thought how I'd once felt an irresistible attraction to Anna Marie, and to Sonia Sutter, but for some reason didn't feel the same way toward Gretel Becker or Eva Crolly. Now this new woman tormented my thoughts.

My breath clouded the pane as I peered inside. On the back wall I divined a crack of light, a door ajar. Just then a shadow passed before the light. I jerked my face away from the window. Was she here? Was the woman even now doing her baking in the back? I stepped out into the street for a view above at the second story windows. It hadn't occurred to me that she might live just above the store.

Snowflakes tickled my eyelashes and I blinked to clear them. For the thousandth time, I remembered the touch of her hand, her startling green eyes. Like a hunting dog on a scent, I rounded the corner in search of a back alley to the store and found one, the sides lined with garbage and refuse, the aroma faint due to the bitter cold. I ventured forward, my manhood stiffening, belying any innocent reason for my presence. I imagined the shop woman's shock at seeing me in this dark place and made a plan. I'd mutter something in English, like "Excuse me, I look for the singing hall." She would say something unintelligible and I'd nod and hastily take my leave. At least I would know for certain if she had touched my hand by accident, so I could put this gnawing desire to rest.

A door midway down the alley opened, lantern light spilling out as a woman swept snow vigorously off the stoop. She looked up and, seeing me, her hand rose to her throat in alarm. I removed my cap and opened my mouth to speak but she put a finger to her lips, and went back inside, leaving the door ajar. Spellbound, I followed, the aroma of yeast and raisins swimming over me as I entered. The woman examined my face in the light then moved behind me to close the door.

"*Ich heiße Michael Harm,*" I said, repeating in English: "I am called Michael Harm."

"Jean Cody." She observed me a moment in a calculating way, hands on her hips.

"Irish?" I asked.

"Manx."

I glanced around the kitchen in panic. "Max is husband?"

"*Manx,*" she said. "The Manx people, from the Isle of Man, near England. *Kein Mann.* My husband is dead ten years."

I felt shaky with relief. My blacksmith muscles had yet to be tested in a real fight. Jean Cody blew out the lantern by her baking board and, candlestick in hand, brushed past me to a narrow staircase. I stood transfixed as her brown woolen skirt faded into the dimness above. Was this woman inviting me to her bed? All signs pointed to the love-making. I moved to the bottom of the stairs to peer upward. Jean Cody popped her head over the banister.

"Come here," she said, her expression unreadable in the darkness.

I swallowed, my throat scratchy and dry. Hat in my hands, I ascended to the landing and gazed around at the well-kept room, embroidered cloths and dried flowers indicating a feminine sensibility. A bed along one wall. Jean Cody came over and reached for my coat. I extended my arms to her but she pushed them away. At her touch, a thrill rushed from my groin to my scalp.

"Tell no one! Swear an oath."

I stared into her searching eyes and shook my head. "I tell no one. *Ich schwöre.*"

For a moment I feared she might send me away. Then she sighed and let go. I unbuttoned my coat, removed it, and handed it to her. She draped it over the banister then removed the pins from her hair, shaking it loose over her shoulders. She took my hand, raising it to her coiled tresses. Our breathing was audible, huffing, as if we walked up a hill. I let her hair spill over my thick, work-worn fingers in silken strands, balancing precariously at this moment between the fiery heat of desire and the terrible blow that would strike me down, should bad luck, or God's retribution, let Rapparlie catch me in this terrible sin.

Even so, I was lost. If this woman would have me, my loneliness, my aching torment, would not be denied.

Jean Cody stepped back to unbutton her blouse. I removed my shirt, unbuttoned my pants and let them drop to my boots, my man-part protuberant, exposed. She unfastened the hard stiffness of her corset and brought me against the nakedness of her warm, bare skin. We swayed back and forth as if dancing. To stop the room from spinning, I closed my eyes. Jean Cody stepped away again to remove her petticoat and undergarments. I fumbled out of my boots and socks. Naked, we lay down on her bed and she guided my sex to the silken wet heat between her legs. I concentrated, trying not to explode, but erupted in a rush anyhow.

My head swirling in a delirium of what had just occurred, uncertain what to do next, I rolled on my back to stare at the ceiling. Jean pressed her bareness against me, eyes blazing, pulling the quilts up to cover us both. We lay side by side, at first not speaking, then murmuring to each other—she in broken German, me in broken English. I told her I came from Freinsheim alone last year, leaving family behind, to live with my uncle. Jean began to stroke me as I talked, her eyes shining as she studied my face.

She'd been married twice, *zweimal*, she told me, as if to explain her experienced love-making. It didn't take long for my man-part to rise again to an urgent stiffness. Jean guided me inside her a second time. I lasted longer, letting her have her way, hoping with all my heart my sex was pleasing to her.

I did not stay more than an hour.

So I enjoyed my first taste of the delicious plum cake of woman. It was not until I arrived back at the Rapparlies and lay in my attic bed that I experienced a terror like no other. I sat bolt upright, bracing my hands against the attic ceiling to still my rocking heart, praying to God I had not fathered a child.

IN THE DAYS FOLLOWING MY visit to Jean Cody, I worried a good deal about what I had done, about the depravity of my soul. I knew well the terrible sin I'd committed, and the high stakes of my risk. If Uncle Johann found out, I stood to lose my livelihood, to bring shame on my family. A baby would seal my doom.

In spite of these fears, I couldn't suppress my jubilation. Even when I encountered Eva Crolly during the workday and felt most keenly my sinfulness, I could not seem to drop out of the rafters. The loving touch of a woman softened my hard, gritty life. In any event, who were Jean Cody and I hurting? She had made it plain that she desired me as I desired her.

The possibility of this woman bearing a child did clamp my feet to the earth. By the next Saturday, I could stand it no longer. I had to know, one way or the other, if I had ruined my future. In the evening before going out, I called Little John to my attic room and, as innocently as I could, asked him the English word for *Schwanger*. To my despair, he didn't know how to say pregnant in English, but between the two of us, we settled on the word "children" as close enough.

Normally, after receiving my weekly allowance, I'd go to Schlegel's with Singley and Fry, but on this night I went alone instead to the public rooms of Napoleon's boarding house, where I nursed one ale for hours, contemplating my predicament. I couldn't afford to get drunk tonight. My plan was to go again to the cake shop alley and get Jean Cody to open the door. I'd ask her my question of vital importance. Hopefully, her answer would be in the negative, and then, I had resolved, I would tell her our association was at an end.

As the hour grew later at Napoleon's, however, I became consumed with the hope Jean Cody might have me one more time. At midnight, my conscience still wrestling with lustful desire, I left the premises and headed directly for the cake shop. Furtively, I slipped down the alleyway.

A lantern light still glowed dimly behind the iced over glass pane by the shop stoop. I scratched at the door as if I were a stray animal, hoping to draw Jean Cody's attention without alerting the neighbors. When Jean opened the door, she didn't look so pleased to see me. Even so, she let me in, blew out the lantern without a word, and took the candle upstairs. I followed, reached for her, and we fell right away to love-making. In truth I felt desperate for it, as I feared I'd never have the opportunity again. Afterward, while we were lying naked in her bed, I pointed to her navel.

"Children?" I asked, doing my best to sound as if I had not a care in the world.

Jean shook her head no. I nearly evaporated with relief. She gave me to understand she was barren. Her first husband had ended the marriage because of this. She had married a second time, a man twice her age, and immigrated with him to Cleveland. He started this cake shop, and shortly afterward, died of the cholera. That had been in the year 1849, ten years ago. Jean Cody had kept the business going.

As I struggled to understand her, it dawned on me that sex with Jean Cody was not such a risk after all. My mind went wild with imaginings. I was concocting schemes to leave the Rapparlies every night to see this woman, to prowl like a cat along the rooftops. I told Jean Cody I wished to see her as often as possible. She let me know in a trice this wouldn't do. We had to be careful. *Vorsichtig.*

Thus, we devised a method—a bit of paper put on the cake shelf, the letter "M" written in pencil in the corner. I was to walk down the cake shop street every day. If I saw the paper with the "M," I should call on her that night. She would only invite me once or twice a month, no more. Never was I to come to her door if anyone was on the street or in the alley, even if I had seen the "M."

"Tell no one," she said, her green eyes dark and commanding.

So my trysting with Jean Cody began. Only one time, after an evening of lager drinking, did I break her rules and appear uninvited at her door. Jean answered the scratching sound I made, sniffed the air, handed me a stale nut bar and closed the door so fast my forehead bumped against it. Another "M" did not appear in her window for three agonizing weeks.

"Too loud," she told me when I visited her again, chastened, sober, my manpart stirring with longing.

"I am a Palatine," I tried to joke. "We're a loud people."

She looked at me with an odd, questioning gaze. "Someone else has used these same words. I thought of him when I first laid eyes on you."

"My rival?" I wished I didn't see memories of other men so often in her eyes.

"No, he no longer lives here," she said.

At the German balls, I continued to dance with Eva Crolly, with Susan Fry, Brigitte Daheim and other girls of my acquaintance, being careful to think as little as possible about Jean Cody. But I didn't have special feelings for a particular girl. Eva Crolly was very kind, but too severe in her religion. Susan Fry's shrill laugh and her thin, prominent nose reminded me of her brother Fred. Brigitte was pretty enough, with a cheerful disposition, but inclined toward Singley.

I sought out Jean in my loneliness, but not for a wife. I felt guilty over this sin, but could not resist. During the workdays, I pitted myself against the stubborn density of iron, my whole being consumed by heaviness, heat, and grime. On a few precious nights, I reveled in the soft embrace of a woman. I felt tenderness toward Jean, who taught me what gives a woman pleasure and softened the hardness of my days.

# Chapter 29

―――

## Cleveland, Ohio 1859

THE CLEVELAND SINGING SOCIETY WORKED longer rehearsals in the spring of 1859, as we looked forward to a *Sängerfest* in June. The annual German Singing Festival was to be held in Cleveland this year, attracting singing societies from far and wide.

"Wednesday afternoon is the day for try-outs, Thursday for competitions, Friday concerts, and Saturday a big parade," Herr Abel informed us one April night at rehearsal. "We're planning to make it a festival of the highest quality, even surpassing Cincinnati's."

Until I'd heard this schedule, I hadn't realized how impossible it would be for me to participate. I approached Herr Abel at the end of rehearsal.

"I'm sorry, but I can't take off work during the spring rush," I said.

The choir director looked at me in surprise. Most singers weren't working class men; they held gentlemen's jobs with more forgiving hours and employers. He sighed. "*Doch*, ask Herr Rapparlie if he can spare you—it's important that we have every voice."

I didn't tell Herr Abel, but I wasn't optimistic. Herr Hoffmann had recently quit Rapparlie's to open his own wagon shop, one block up on Michigan Street. In front of the other men, Uncle Johann had warned Herr Hoffmann that he took Rapparlie customers with him at his peril. My uncle had been in a foul mood ever since.

I tried to ask for the afternoons off several times, but couldn't muster the courage. In the end, the next Sunday when Uncle Johann went to the stable, I sought out Aunt Katharina as she sat darning socks. Not knowing how to begin, I first played a game of peek-a-boo with the three-year-old Sussy.

"What is it, Michael?" my aunt finally asked.

I feigned a look of surprise. "What do you mean?"

My aunt used her teeth to break the thread and pulled the sock from the darning egg. "Normally you don't linger so long at the house on your free day."

I took a deep breath. "There's going to be a Cleveland Singing Festival, and Herr Abel expects the choir to participate. But I'll have to leave work early for some rehearsals and concerts. I could still work in the mornings."

"How many afternoons?"

"Four."

Aunt Katharina's face fell. "Nephew, you know this will not do."

"Uncle should let me off, just this once. I'm not like the workers who take the Blue Monday. I work all six days, and the hours are longer than in most shops."

"Your uncle believes in this discipline. Since the loss of his foot, he's even less tolerant of idlers."

"The Singing Society isn't for idling, it's for high culture. Our choir director says singing and the other arts should be at the center of our lives—it elevates the spirit." My aunt frowned at me doubtfully. "It could be a holiday for the children," I added.

A wistful expression crossed Aunt Katharina's face. "Johann already has our Little John doing a man's work. Our children are given so little time to be children."

Uncle Johann came in then and my aunt glanced up at him with a flush of guilt. I rose and went out to sweep the walkway along the property, something my uncle had asked me to do. Long experience had taught me not to bring up the subject of music with a chore left undone. When I returned, Uncle Johann and Aunt Katharina were facing each other with set mouths as if they'd been arguing.

"Uncle—" I started to say.

Uncle Johann cut me off with a flick of his cane. "Your aunt has told me of your singing festival." He kept his eyes on Aunt Katharina. "There will be hundreds of singers. They will not miss one voice."

"But Uncle, you and Aunt Katharina should come with the whole family, for the songs and festivities. Herr Abel says it will be a great holiday."

"We attended the one four years ago. That was enough."

"This one will be bigger yet. Singing Societies from Columbus and Buffalo and Toledo are coming."

"Perhaps Herr Biene could travel here with his family from Toledo," my aunt said. "I would so enjoy the company of his wife."

"*Frau*, I am old and have lost a foot, but I haven't lost my wits. I know you say this to give your nephew a chance. But he doesn't deserve one."

Aunt Katharina's voice dropped to a lower pitch, the timbre of truth. "Johann, the wagon business won't become better because the boy spends these four afternoons away from the forge. But it won't become any worse either. Michael has a good tenor voice, like his Grandpa Handrich."

Uncle Johann looked away, out the window to the wagon yard. "I cannot spare him."

"I want the children to enjoy the festival." Aunt Katharina's voice was resolute. "Father, I need the music. This city, this country, it wears on me. Sometimes I see ghosts and hear the babies crying." A tear coursed down her cheek, then another, the first tears I'd ever seen my aunt shed. How sorry I felt for her. "You'll deny us this chance for a holiday?"

Uncle Johann shifted his weight and looked down at his wife. He didn't look so happy himself. "We'll invite Herr Biene and his family for the week and make a festival," he said at last. He turned and pointed his cane at me. "But you don't get whole days off, only the afternoons. None of the other apprentices ask for such leniency. I'll send you out to do other jobs, early and late, to make up the time."

Joy spilled through me, so I didn't care about extra work. I cared only that I would get to sing at this festival.

AT LAST THE FIRST WEDNESDAY in June arrived. My master didn't even notice my early departure from the forge, as he went with his family to the docks to welcome the Bienes of Toledo.

Herr Abel had rehearsed us in songs that we'd sing with other choirs for the opening ceremony. Now assembling for our first combined rehearsal, I heard a familiar voice behind me.

"So they let riffraff like Harm sing on the East Side, oder?"

I turned and saw Charles Rauch also in the tenor section.

"Seeing you here, Rauch, is living proof the West Side has the lowest standards of all."

Rauch and I shook hands, and the men around us chuckled. Rauch and my jocular rivalry had continued during these months, but for my part, it was only half in jest. At least Eva Crolly had recently transferred her attentions to a man named Edward Kemp, a decision I heartily approved.

THAT EVENING AT THE CLEVELAND Theater, we gathered on stage in front of a grand statue of Freedom created for the occasion. As 400 male voices lifted in harmony, my entire being was seized by a deep longing for my homeland. How proud my parents would be if they could be here tonight. I sang for my uncles and aunts in the large audience, for my parents and brother back in the Old Country, for the traditions that held us together.

The applause was thunderous. From where I stood on stage, I could see Uncle Johann and Aunt Katharina and their children standing to cheer with all the others. I hoped something might change now. Surely, these harmonies would remind my uncle of our common origins, would heat up his heart to a golden glow, softening his resolute will toward me. Even if he had turned his back on God, how could the music not elevate his soul?

After the program, I stood among the well-wishers with a permanent grin lifting my cheeks so they hurt. After I saw my aunt and uncle and met the Bienes of Toledo, Singley and Fry searched me out to thump my back in congratulations. Even stout, neckless Singley was grinning ear to ear. I heartily approved their suggestion that we visit the summer beer garden on Erie street, and as soon as we left the noisy crowd in front of the theater, the singing of crickets and cicadas enveloped the night, a treble chorus to accompany melodies still humming in my head.

The moon rose half full over young elms as we stepped through the latticed grape arbor of the garden. As the tables were nearly vacant of customers, the proprietor Herr Freyse greeted us warmly. We took our seats before beaded glasses of ale just as a gang of young Yankee boys came down the road and stopped to stare at us over the picket fence.

"Look, it's the stupid Dutchies," one of them leered, a boy no older than fifteen.

"Dumb krauts. Caged like apes at the circus," said another, rattling the beer garden fence so a fern planter toppled and cracked.

I glanced over at Herr Freyse, who polished a beer glass with extra vigor. It was typical that we Germans did nothing at times like this.

"Say, why don't we go inside the cage," said the first, hopping the fence in one bound.

The other four boys swaggered through the archway, full of youthful confidence and liquor. Singley, Fry, and I kept our gazes down, staring at our beers, tense and alert. Instead of coming to us, though, the boys grouped around an old man and his companion at another table.

"Ha, ha, look at this fellow with the gray whiskers," said the leader. He gave a mocking laugh. "He wears an apron like a woman."

"Speck Zee Inglees?"

"If you don't speak English, you don't belong here."

Two of them lifted one end of the table, spilling the beers.

"*Achtung!*" the old man shouted, leaping up.

"*Achtung! Achtung!*" The boys mimicked, doubling over with laughter.

The rest of the customers, our table and one other, all stood in unison. The Yankee boys stopped cackling.

"Aww, we was just leavin'," the leader drawled.

Glancing back a few times, the boys sauntered out the archway and down the road. They had not gone far before they began to hoot with laughter and bravado once more.

"Feel like going for a walk?" Singley asked, an urgency in his low voice.

Not waiting for our answer, he stood and walked out. Fry and I drained our beers and followed. The old man in the garden tried to get our attention over the fence.

"*Psst*, have a care," he whispered. "You'll bring trouble on us all."

Ignoring him, Singley, Fry, and I strolled off in the same direction as the Yankee boys. Fry stuck his hands in his pockets and whistled a breathy tune. Up ahead, the boys left the gaslight district for the moonlit dimness beyond, so busy with their animated talk that they noticed little around them.

"Do you think they saw us?" Fry asked, ducking his head down so only Singley and I would hear.

"They didn't look back," Singley said. "*Bankerts.* The way they treated that old man."

"They are boys," I said, keeping my voice low as well. "Maybe into some corn whiskey. *Guck mal*, that one is staggering."

"Time they got a proper kick in the *Arsch*," Singley growled. "Do them a kindness, *oder*?"

"They are just boys," I said again. I tried to sound reasonable, but my heart raced with excitement.

Singley was not in a forgiving mood. "It's time they learned respect for their elders," he said.

"Let's throw rocks at them," suggested Fry. "Bait them into the attack. Then the fault will be theirs and they cannot accuse us."

My head spun with the beer I'd gulped too fast. The Yankees, even young boys like these, felt free to make fun of our speech, of our style of dress, of our Sunday enjoyment of beer and wine. Were we finally going to teach them a lesson? I surely hoped so.

By now we'd left the area of the gaslights, and the road was lit only by the moon's silvery glow. Fry edged over to skulk under a row of trees growing on the edge of a large yard. Singley and I followed. A structure stood back from the street here, a clapboard church, one of the many in this town. Singley bent down and scooped up a handful of small stones, handing some to Fry and me. We hurled them in quick succession after the receding boys, ears straining for the distant thup-thup-thup as they landed.

"Hey!" a voice cried out in protest.

"Who's there?" shouted another.

Singley hurled three more stones.

"Yow!"

"It's them dumb Krauts, I'll wager."

Scuffling sounds, then a rain of gravel around us. Something sharp stung my ear, a pebble hitting its mark. Footsteps thudded toward us, then shapeless forms hurtled out of the darkness. Singley stepped up to meet two boys, collaring them in one swift movement. He knocked their heads together and pushed them down as if they were clothes stuffed with straw. A third boy flailed toward me. I ducked in time to avoid his swing, then crushed my fist into his jaw. The boy's head jerked to one side as he sprawled on his back. Another got behind me and jumped on my back. I flipped him over. He landed on the dirt with a sickening crunch. My first assailant had arisen by then and landed a punch square on my left cheek. A blow to his stomach doubled him over and he dropped again, gagging. As he sagged full out on the ground, I looked over at Fry in time to see a boy flop forward on his face.

It had happened so fast. Our breath ragged, we took in the five moonlit mounds at the edge of the yard. I tasted blood in my mouth and swallowed. One boy shifted and groaned. Without a word, Singley, Fry, and I backed up, spun around, and walk-trotted toward town. As we regained the gaslight district, I looked at my companions, both flushed in the cheeks from our recent exertions.

"That'll teach those Yanks!" Fry said.

The sound of his voice startled me. We hadn't spoken during the entire fight, not out of choice, but habit. We Germans avoided talking in the presence of the Yankees, since it often led to getting mocked. Warily, I looked behind us, but no one seemed to have followed. We passed the beer garden, now closed, and I remembered the old man's warning to us. All at once, I felt ashamed. The Yankees had picked the fight, but they were just boys. We'd done the greater damage.

"I'm thirsty! Let's go to Schlegel's," Fry said.

Singley and I required no urging. But I should have known better, should have known that Fry couldn't control his mouth. He was wound tight as a wire. The minute we sat down, he started bragging of our exploits. I was trying to figure out how I might shut him up without drawing more attention to ourselves when a gentleman joined our table, Jacob Müller, known to every Cleveland German by reputation. Fry stopped talking mid-sentence. Herr Müller usually sat at the table of the Cleveland newspaper men and Republican politicians. From his breast pocket, he extracted his handkerchief and held it out to me.

"You're bleeding," he said.

I shook my head in disbelief. Müller pressed the linen to my ear, then brought the cloth away. In wonderment, I looked at the red stains on the cloth, then took it from him to dab at my ear.

"Müller. Jacob Müller," he said, easing back in his chair.

"Michael Harm."

I looked over at my friends, expecting them to make introductions, but they stared into their beer glasses. There was a long pause.

"Did I hear you right?" Müller asked Fry. "Some Yankee boys disrupted your evening?"

Müller's hair was slicked back, falling down to his collar so he appeared fierce, like a wolf. Fry didn't answer. The bar had gone quiet, the other men listening in.

"Let us hope your little brawl did no real injury," Müller said. "We can do without that kind of scrutiny."

"*Doch*, they treated us like beasts," Fry said, sulking like a naughty child.

"We were trying to assist in their education," I said, hoping to cast our actions in a more favorable light.

"Is that right?" Müller appraised me with sharp eyes. "Assist in their education how? Teach them that Germans are beasts just like them? I tell you, we have endured these insults for years. To educate an Englishman, one must show him for the narrow-minded busybody he is. We have done this successfully, and they begin to respect us. Unless you have undone in one night what we have struggled for decades to achieve."

"We weren't so rough on 'em," Singley said.

"They don't even know we were German," I said. "We never said a word."

Fry's face brightened. "*Aha*, Harm is right. We didn't say a thing."

Müller shrugged. "You may have the luck. Maybe not. My advice: talk of this to no one." He rose, speaking offhandedly to the room. "These men were here all evening, I am convinced of it." He lowered his voice and said only to us. "Next time, fight a German. Or join the *Turnverein* for physical fitness. *Verstanden*?"

We understood. Singley, Fry, and I rose to our feet, the men's glares searing into us, and trudged out of the tavern.

Walking down Michigan street, Singley snorted in disgust.

"White collar intellectuals," he said. "What do we need with a *Turnverein*? We exercise every damn day."

"Did I hear you right?" Fry mimicked Müller.

"Shut up, Fry," I said, in complete misery.

My left cheek throbbed, my ear stabbed with pain, and I realized in that moment I still held Müller's handkerchief against my ear. How quickly my proud night had turned sour. I prayed to God Rapparlie wouldn't hear of this. In the wagon yard, I washed up and, since two of the Biene children slept in my attic room, I took a horse blanket from the stable, wrapped myself in it, and slept outside on an unfinished wagon bed.

# Chapter 30

———

ONE GLANCE IN THE FOYER looking glass the next morning confirmed the worst. My left eye had swollen and turned purple during the night.

"What's wrong with your face?" little Wilhelm asked as I entered the kitchen.

The Bienes and Rapparlies looked up to gawk at me.

"I bumped into something," I muttered.

"Does it hurt?"

I shrugged and squeezed onto a stool in the crowded room. I was grateful the Bienes were here, so Uncle Johann had something to distract him.

"These English choose fashion over quality," Uncle Johann said, turning back to Herr Biene. "No matter what carriage odometer I recommend, they make their choice based on looks. They buy it even if I tell them it's overpriced and poorly made."

At the side board, Aunt Katharina and Frau Biene were packing a basket of food for an outing to the park with the children. My aching jaw made it hard to chew my bread and sausage. I swallowed it down in lumps, gulped my coffee and left for the forge. Partway across the wagon yard, Uncle Johann called to me from behind. Sure it meant trouble, I stopped and waited for him.

"Did the singing clubs have a late-night brawl?" he asked, leaning forward on his cane to study my face.

I said nothing. He vised my chin in his hand.

"You took a good punch there, on your left eye," he said, wrenching my face from side to side, "and a cut on your ear." He let go. "Who were you fighting? The Irish? The Yankees?"

I kept silent, staring at the ground. Uncle Johann's fist clubbed my right cheek with such force I staggered and dropped to one knee. Blinded with pain, I tried twice to stand before I managed it.

"When the police come, tell them your employer beats you," Uncle Johann said, his voice hoarse, his breath huffing like a mad bull.

Through dazed, speckled vision, I watched Uncle Johann limp back to the house; then I staggered to the smithy. Singley blanched at the sight of me. I braced myself at the work bench fighting waves of dizziness and nausea. When I'd managed to collect my senses, I kept my head down and began my work. I left my hat on my head, and didn't look up as the jours came in. Instead, I focused all my attention on finishing my tasks so I could leave in time for the afternoon singing competition. Like a stubborn mule not willing to be shod, I convinced myself I could still sing. If I stood in the back row, no one would notice my banged up face—no one in the audience, anyhow.

"*Achtung*, the police are here," Singley murmured, suddenly beside me.

In a panic, I set down my hammer and slipped out the back door. Keeping low behind the wagons, I crossed the yard and entered the house, deserted now, the Rapparlies and Bienes all at the park. From my attic window I watched until the police had left. As I returned to my anvil, the men stood around talking. Herr Dietz saw me come in and his mouth dropped open. The other men turned to stare, but I pretended to search for a tool at my work station and wouldn't acknowledge them.

"The English are always so quick to blame us," Herr Penhoff was saying.

"I hear it was the Yankee boys who started it," Herr Dietz said, hefting a hammer in his hand. "They wrecked Herr Freyse's beer garden. Why don't the police arrest the English?"

"They aren't arresting the Germans, either," Herr Penhoff said. "They have no proof, and no one is talking."

"Boys in a brawl. It happens all the time," Singley said. "Why should anyone be arrested?"

"One of the boys suffered a broken collarbone," Herr Dietz said.

With those words, I knew for certain—my Singing Festival was over. I couldn't risk going out in public. Word would get out of my beat-up condition, and I'd be suspected. The police would come and arrest me. Chained to my anvil the rest of the day, I tried to hammer away all thoughts of the singing competition, all that I was missing. When I wasn't feeling sorry for myself, I did a fair amount of worrying about the boy with the broken collar bone. Could I be to blame? I couldn't wipe from my mind the crunching noise when the one boy had landed. I felt revulsion at myself—to hurt a boy was not in keeping with my Christian beliefs, nor with a music-lover's soul.

Two more days of the *Sängerfest* remained, but I saw none of it. Saturday night, for the final concert, everyone attended but me. In the Rapparlie wagon yard I lay on my back alone, staring up at the night sky. The final song, I knew, would be "*Das Lied der Deutschen*," the anthem of the 1848 struggle for a unified Germany. Straining my ears, I imagined the glory on which I was missing out, 399 voices crescendoing in song.

THE BIENES DEPARTED FOR TOLEDO Sunday morning. I returned to my attic room and didn't leave it once all day, not even for meals. In misery, I lay on my bed dwelling on my sorry existence. I worried over the fight with the Yankees, over my reputation with my uncle, over how far I'd strayed from my faith since leaving home. The leaden blow of Uncle Johann's fist had shaken me to my core. If it was God's will for me to be a blacksmith, did it mean I must be beaten black-and-blue by a tyrant? Like iron reheated too often in the fire, I felt burned up, brittle, and easily crumbled. As if the core of my soul were eroding.

I had no heart, even, for visits to Jean Cody. The last time I'd seen her had cooled my desire in any case.

"I sing in the *Sängerfest*," I'd told her proudly, excited for the upcoming festival.

"I prefer Scottish melodies," she said.

"German music very good. German music best." I started to list the names of the great composers whose songs we would sing, but couldn't finish because Jean had a fit of giggles.

"German music best. German music best," she mimicked, laughing so hard she had to dab tears from her eyes.

I felt insulted. What did Jean Cody know about German music? I doubted she'd ever attended a *Sängerfest*. Of late, I'd begun to feel our differences more keenly, as if the melody line of Jean Cody and Michael Harm drifted ever more off-key. At one time, I'd turned to her as a healer who softened the harshness of my days. Now, she too mocked my clumsiness.

THE FOLLOWING WEEK, I DIDN'T go to the cake shop street to check for the sign of the "M" on the shelf. The black bruises on my face faded, but my eyes remained fixed on the sparking glow of the forge fire. I had not left work early for the *Sängerfest*, but I put in extra hours anyhow, going early to the shop to wander through the different departments, the wood shop to check the progress of coaches and wagons, the paint shop to consider the various pigments that produced the most brilliant colors. I stayed later to fashion axle skeins and door hinges, to finish lamp brackets, to rag step plates.

Whenever I became sleepy, I sang to stay awake. The other men growled at me less often to shut up, and Herr Penhoff sometimes sang along in his deep bass voice. The hammers on the anvils rang in accompaniment. I remembered Herr Adler and his description of the sound vibrations, the patterns invisible to the eye, some traveling, some staying put. I had traveled such a great distance, only to find myself again in one place, weighed down by the heaviness of my toil so that I could barely breathe. But I didn't regret my situation. If I could just hold on and make no more mistakes, I'd finish my apprenticeship and become a jour, able to work wherever I pleased.

IN JULY, THE NIGHTS PUDDLED with stifling heat, driving both Fry and me from our respective attic rooms down to the wagon yard. I'm not sure what good it did, as the mosquitoes drove us under suffocating horse blankets. On such still nights, the "wiggle tails," as the English called them, swarmed in a whining plague.

One night, as the mosquitoes pestered incessantly, I couldn't stop thinking of Jean Cody. Shouldn't I at least go to her and explain my long absence? Perhaps I should beg her forgiveness. I lay tossing and restless until I could stand it no longer. Quietly, I sat up and listened for Fry's heavy, even breathing in the next wagon. Reassured he was fast asleep, I eased down and out of the yard.

In the alley behind the cake shop, I scratched at the door in the usual manner, a thousand confused excuses and apologies jumbling my mind. Jean Cody cracked the door open and peered out. I stirred in my groin as I always did at this juncture. We stood face to face in the dim light of her candle. I would have spoken to her if she'd let me in, but she stood blocking the threshold, her slight figure commanding—much like, I realized with a jolt, my own mother. I don't think Jean Cody approved of what she saw in my face. She clucked her tongue and shook her head.

"*Auf Wiedersehen. Kaputt.*"

The finality of her words echoed in the slamming door. I stood on the porch, stunned, relieved, and more alone than ever. Pensively, I went on my way, toward the lakeshore, thinking to gaze at the waves as they sifted the pebble shore, to feel on my face the cool breeze, to mull over what might yet become of me in this life.

Passing through Public Square I encountered a group of stargazers huddled around a telescope. The sight reminded me of Humboldt's *Kosmos*. A clear memory of my father reading this volume about celestial objects to us washed over me, and I decided to wait in line for a turn. When I squinted my eye in the glass, the perfectly spherical shape of the object in the heavens was startling and wondrous.

"Jupiter," said the man standing by. A planet, not a star at all. I took a long turn, beyond the bounds of politeness, wishing my brother and Father could also behold such a marvel. When I finally stepped aside, the whole of the sky glistened, more impenetrable and mysterious than ever. The explorer

Alexander von Humboldt wrote that all of life is interconnected, the big and the small, the ocean currents and the mosquitoes.

I felt like a mosquito.

# Chapter 31

———

THE NEXT AFTERNOON, I WAS helping Uncle Johann grease a fifth wheel assembly when he glanced toward the open doorway and let out a gasp. I followed his gaze to a strange-looking customer, tanned and rugged, sporting a full brown beard beneath a broad-brimmed hat. The man wore a jacket of tanned leather and carried a knapsack on his back. His pants were an odd, bright blue and jackboots covered his legs to the knee. In his left hand he hefted a long rifle, as if headed out on a hunting trip.

"So you're back!" Uncle Johann said. The stranger folded his arms over his chest with a broad grin. Uncle Johann limped over to him, wiping the grease from his hands with a rag. "For a moment there, I thought we were being honored with a visit from Kit Carson!"

The newcomer burst into a hearty laugh and grabbed Uncle Johann in a back-slapping hug. "So good to see you, brother-in-law," he said. "You seem to get around just fine on that leg."

Uncle Johann put his arm over the man's shoulder and turned to me, his expression more exuberant than I'd ever seen.

"*Komm her*, Michael Harm. At long last you meet the brother of your mother. Here stands your Uncle Jakob."

Stunned and thrilled, I set down my hammer and went over to them.

"I've waited my whole life for this," I said.

"And I've traveled thousands of miles from California to take the measure of you, nephew," my uncle said, winking, giving me no doubt we were already on familiar terms.

"I never took off the Indian vest you sent to Freinsheim. I wore it until it was shredded."

Uncle Jakob chuckled, tipping his broad-brimmed hat in a mock bow.

"*Ach so*, I'd forgotten I sent that. How good it is to meet one of Elisabetha's sons. I will want to hear the news of her."

"Never mind about that," Uncle Johann said. "First you must come with me to the house to greet your sister Katharina. She'll be so glad to see you."

I longed to follow them, to pepper my Uncle Jakob with questions, to listen in on everything that might be said. With eager anticipation, I finished the work day and cleaned up for supper. I was not disappointed. The Rapparlie table that night was a lively celebration. As Uncle Jakob came into the kitchen, he lifted each of the children in the air and spun them around, even Little John.

The boy straightened his shirt as soon as his uncle set him down. "If you please, I am no longer a child. I'm studying in the seventh year at school."

"Forgive me, Johann the eldest," Jacob said. "I understand now we must speak of serious matters. You're attending to your studies?"

"Yes, Uncle."

"Reading, writing, and ciphering?"

Little John made a face. "Who needs all that stuff, anyhow? Papa has us going to *two* schools, German and English."

"As well you should. You must attend to your studies. It gives you opportunities."

"Maybe I want to be an adventurer like you."

Uncle Jakob turned his pants pockets inside out and stuck out his lower lip. "But I come back from California with empty pockets, no gold whatsoever."

Little John was not impressed. "You didn't need that gold in the first place, Uncle Jakob. You own a property here, and Cleveland has plenty of jobs that pay a good wage."

Uncle Jakob smirked and turned to Aunt Katharina.

"Tell your husband to sing a different song for once."

From under her nose, he snagged a hot dinner roll from the counter and bobbled it in his hands. Aunt Katharina smiled without a care. I saw the resemblance between the brother and sister, the Handrich clear open forehead, the round face, the gray-blue eyes. Soon they were talking of people they once knew, the Meckenheimers in St. Louis and Cincinnati, people Uncle Jakob had visited during his travels.

Though it was a weeknight, Uncle Johann changed his habits and brought up Rhine wine to share at the meal. He confided to Uncle Jakob about how it went with the wagon business, and after supper, the two men removed to the hearth to smoke their pipes. I followed, glued to Uncle Jakob like pine resin on a log. He smoked from a peculiar-looking hatchet. He called it a tomahawk and told us he had bought it off an Indian. The children took turns squinting up the hollowed-out handle that doubled as a pipe stem.

For once, taciturn Uncle Johann didn't stop talking. His white hair stuck straight up off his forehead.

"The residents of Seneca Street petitioned the city to grade the street. They say there will soon be a streetcar going up and down it, right past our door. Katharina will appreciate riding to market."

Uncle Jakob nodded, his curly brown hair slicked back, his mustache full and neatly groomed. He gave this news his rapt attention, as he did all of Uncle Johann's reports.

"I have collected your rents for the House Place right along," Uncle Johann continued. "With such a tidy sum you can build an even bigger house."

Uncle Jakob turned his gaze to the fire. "I am only here to collect this rent money, Johann, before going on to French Creek."

"What? For the oil boom?" Uncle Johann almost shouted, bringing Aunt Katharina to the kitchen doorway.

"What's wrong, Father?"

"Your brother only just returns, and he leaves us again for Titusville!"

Uncle Jakob looked apologetic. "I have no job to keep me here. I want to see for myself—I was too late to find gold, but I may not be too late for the oil. They say there is big money to be made."

"*Pff!* See what I put up with?" Uncle Johann turned to me. "Here is the Handrich side of the family, every last one of you, always restless for something besides what's right before you." He turned back to Uncle Jakob. "You're the worst of the lot, always mad for the next get-rich-quick boondoggle."

Uncle Jakob shrugged. "Call it madness, Johann, but the saying goes, 'He who rests gathers rust.' I have traveled thousands of miles these past three years—why not a little farther? I'll see with my own eyes if it's nothing or not, then I'll not always wonder about what others say."

Uncle Johann glowered. I too felt miserable with disappointment but was determined to side with Uncle Jakob.

"When you strike it rich, you'll know where to find us," I said. "We'll still be trapped here, unable to move from the rust in our joints."

Uncle Jakob guffawed, but Uncle Johann didn't crack a smile. Uncle Jakob looked at my master with the kindness of an old friend. "I'm sorry, Johann, but I will go again before the week is out."

The days with Uncle Jakob passed quickly, leading up to Sunday, when the Rapparlies invited the families for an outdoor picnic celebration in the wagon yard. The Scheuermanns came, and the Crollys, to see Uncle Jakob and hear tales of his adventures, to eat grilled sausages and drink Rhine wine. Uncle Johann tapped the cask sent by my parents, and Uncle Jakob made much of it, saying it was the best he'd tasted since he left Meckenheim. The Fry family joined us, and George Weherling, so we made a large party, the children laughing and chasing around the wagons.

Uncle Jakob began telling a story of some Indians in the mountains with whom he smoked his tomahawk peace pipe, then froze mid-sentence, gaping out at the street. Following his gaze, I beheld Jean Cody standing at the gate in her Sunday church clothes and a straw bonnet, her face chalk white, her eyes glinting like steel.

Panic choked my throat. I could hardly breathe as Uncle Johann limped to the gate.

"May I help you, Madam?" he asked in English. "We're closed for business on Sundays. This is a family gathering."

Uncle Jakob stepped forward.

"Johann, she's here to see me," he said in German. He walked to her, switching to English. "Hello, Mrs. Cody. It's been a long time. I'm sad to say I'm busy with family at the moment. Shall I call for you later?"

I thought Jean Cody might faint. She looked at me, and then, for some reason at Fred Fry, who turned bright red. "If you please, Mr. Handrich, will you escort me to my shop? It will only take a moment. I have a favor to ask."

Uncle Jakob held out his arm, which she took, and the two departed up Seneca.

Uncle Johann looked puzzled, but shrugged and returned to the festivities. My heart would not stop pummeling in my ribs. What had happened? Why did Jean Cody come here, and stare with such accusation at me? How did she know Uncle Jakob? I looked over at Fry again, his guilty red face, and a horror rose within me. At my first opportunity, I pulled Fry into the wood shop, away from prying ears.

"Do you know that woman who came here?" I demanded.

Fry snickered, his eyes not meeting mine. "It wasn't fair, after Singley and I shared Maggie Roberts, that you held out on us."

"What are you talking about?"

"I followed you the other night to see what you were up to. Then last night, I went to see her myself, but she wouldn't have me. I suppose she was busy with your uncle." I lifted a fist to punch him. Fry put up his arm, warding off the blow. "Hey, I didn't do anything!"

"You have no idea the insult you give," I spit out. "She's not a whore!"

My insides boiled with anger and fear, but I decided against hitting Fry. The risk was too great. Had Jean Cody come to shame us, to call us out in front of Uncle Johann? Or had she come to see Uncle Jakob, and only then saw us standing there? As I waited for my uncle's return, my emotions dashed again and again like the waves on the rocks at Lake Erie's shore. I had worked so hard and was about to lose everything.

Uncle Jakob gave no sign of trouble when he returned, not even glancing my way. He picked up where he had left off in his story about the peace pipe. The rest of the day, I looked for a private moment to speak with him, but such a chance didn't come until late in the evening. As Uncle Johann and Aunt Katharina at last retired for the night, it was Uncle Jakob who suggested that we go out for a beer.

At Napoleon's public rooms, thick with pipe smoke, I sat across the table from Uncle Jakob, filled with dread. I couldn't think how to begin my questions about Jean Cody without giving myself away. Instead, I asked Uncle Jakob about his job long ago in the Cleveland ship yards. He told me he saw many men injured and didn't recommend it.

"But you weren't injured, *oder*? Once I'm a jour, I need a way to make a good wage. I hope to save money for a wagon shop of my own."

Uncle Jakob studied me, the skin of his face thick and leathery, like a man who has spent much time out of doors. "I don't recommend it, for any wage. Even if you find a job away from the smelter, a man must operate one machine, a drill press or emery grinder, all day long. I could tell you stories, but we don't have the time. I must go already tomorrow, and we have an important matter to discuss." Uncle Jakob removed his hat and combed his fingers through his curly brown hair. "According to Jean Cody, you have been busy while I was away. *Auf alten Pfannen lernt man kochen*—on old pots you learn cooking, eh?"

My uncle kept his voice low and spoke in a mild tone, but his eyes held a frightening intensity. I looked down in shame at the bubbles in my amber beer.

"How do you know Jean Cody?" I asked, keeping my voice low as well.

"For a time, she and I ... It was maybe two years after her husband died. She told me she could not have been more startled to see me today in the wagon yard. She said there was a resemblance between us in appearance, but she had no idea ..."

Jealousy pinched my heart. "So you and she are again together? This is what you spoke of this afternoon?"

"Michael, you are in serious trouble." My uncle's gray-blue eyes bored into me. "She had no such thing on her mind. She's very angry that you treat her like a prostitute."

The look in my uncle's eyes was terrible indeed. I felt overcome by despair. If Uncle Jakob's opinion of me was as low as Uncle Johann's, I'd give up and return to Freinsheim for good.

"You must believe me," I heard myself pleading. "I'd never do such a thing! I swore I wouldn't tell, and kept my word. Fry told me this afternoon he followed me, only I didn't know it. He's an *Esel*, a braying donkey."

Uncle Jakob searched my face, then sat back with a sigh. "I told her something like this, that you wouldn't do such a thing on purpose. Even so, she said she planned to ruin both you and Fred Fry, to expose you to Johann. I've tried to reason with her, to convince her that if she does this, people will learn the truth about her, too. She said she's so angry she doesn't care, but in the end, she has agreed to drop the matter, that is, if you—and that painter's son Fred Fry—never darken her door again. I've given her my word on this, and I warn you, I won't defend you a second time."

An old acquaintance of Uncle Jakob's interrupted us then, welcoming him back to town and inviting him to have a beer. As soon as politeness allowed, I mumbled my apologies and went home, hating Fry, hating myself, sick with worry and regret.

When I awoke in the morning, Uncle Jakob was gone.

# Chapter 32

―⁓―

"**Y**OU HAVE NO IDEA HOW close you brought us to ruin," I hissed at
Fry, confronting him the next morning as he stirred the cauldron of
varnish in the yard. "Somehow, Uncle Jakob made it right with the widow
woman, but he says we'll lose our living if we ever breathe a word to anyone."
To my dismay, Fry didn't look the least bit sorry. Anger glowed in my chest
like hot coals. "My uncle says, if you ever go to her door again he'll cut off
your cock."

At last fear blazed in his eyes. I stalked away, refusing from then on to
speak to the painter's apprentice. During the workday, I also stopped singing.
What was the point of it? I'd always have bad luck, no woman, and few friends.
And I faced another year yet of indenture, a lowly servitude clapped around
me like leg irons.

Then another thing happened to sink my mood even further. The very
next week, William Singley turned twenty-one. No one, not even Singley, had
warned me this was coming. I only learned of the celebration when Singley
brought in half a dozen bottles of wine at the end of the work day and began
to uncork them.

"What's happening?" I asked Herr Gesler.

"Singley is a jour. He turns twenty-one today and earns his freedom dues."

The workmen from all the departments gathered around. Singley filled
our tin drinking cups among the anvils and work benches. Lord Rapparlie
himself came over to fill a cup and make a toast.

"William Singley, you become this day a journeyman blacksmith. Never
mind that when you first started, you fell asleep at your work bench."

Herr Penhoff guffawed. "Nailed him under a cowhide, we did. Only had
to do it once."

To whistles and jibes, Singley stepped forward, grinning and bowing, his arms spread wide.

"*Doch*, we turned you around," Uncle Johann said, "so all you know is the work. You are a skilled blacksmith, and I wish you well. Men, William Singley is taking a job at the rolling mill of Stone, Chisholm & Jones. They will pay him more than I am able to, so we must also, on this day, say our farewells."

No one was laughing now. Singley looked around with a hint of a smile lifting the ends of his mustache.

"Hey, it's my freedom dues, not a funeral. Look, you know what women are like, needing their laces and fine trinkets. I've asked Brigitte Daheim to be my wife, and she has accepted."

The room boomed again with deep-voiced cheers. Toasts were made, one upon another, so the wine raced down our gullets directly to our heads. Herr Fletcher and Herr Fry wrapped their arms around each other's shoulders and danced, raising sawdust as they stomped in a circle.

I felt glad for Singley, but such a loss for myself. With Singley gone, how would I endure the long days?

Uncle Johann didn't take on another apprentice, but instead hired an immigrant jour from Kallstadt, a village right next to Freinsheim, a man named Fred Schuster. He had black hair, a finely chiseled face, and stood a head taller than me, but then, so did all the other jours. He was newly arrived in the country, so I pumped him for news of Freinsheim and helped him adjust to the ways of our shop. Before long, he and I became drinking comrades at Schlegel's.

In truth, as excitement brewed in the end of 1859 regarding next year's presidential election, it was rare that of an evening I didn't go to Schlegel's. The divide between the Northern and Southern states was growing worse, and an increased fervor for the Republican Party simmered among the Germans of Cleveland. When John Brown of Ohio led the insurrectionists, the Democrats flung accusations at the Republicans of plotting to incite the Negroes. Incensed, Müller and other Republicans accused the Democrats of trying to cast the Republican Party in a bad light.

On Sundays, I sometimes went to church, so as not to be a complete shirker in the eyes of Eva Crolly. More often, I took long hikes in nature. In early November, just before the weather turned, I set out for a Sunday stroll and encountered the lone figure of Henry Hoppensack standing on Broadway Hill. I knew the brickyard owner from the Cleveland Singing Society. At that moment, he stood scratching his head over a collapsed wagonload of bricks.

"*Guten Tag*, Herr Hoppensack," I said. "Looks like that wagon will make good kindling."

"*Moin, Moin*, Harm,*"* he said in a distracted way. As a Westphalian, Herr

Hoppensack spoke in the clipped guttural manner of the north. "Shouldn't you be in church, young man?"

"I was going there, but the fine weather called to me."

Herr Hoppensack grunted. "I was also on my way when a man reported this broken wagon to me. I couldn't wait to come see about it, as this load of bricks is due tomorrow. You work for Rapparlie, *oder*?"

"I do at that. Rapparlie makes the sturdiest wagons around."

"What do you say about this one? Can it be repaired?"

I could hardly see the wagon beneath the tumble of rust-colored bricks. Two wheels had broken off the axles on one side. "Not worth the time or money. For such a heavy load you'll want iron axles."

Herr Hoppensack squinted at me. "How much would Herr Rapparlie charge for such a wagon?"

I considered what to say. If I brought my uncle some business, it would reflect well on me. But I knew Herr Hoppensack to be tight-fisted. "You need a heavy wagon for such heavy work. I think my uncle would quote a price of two hundred fifty, but he might come down to two twenty-five."

Herr Hoppensack nodded. "You are a hard worker, aren't you, Harm? I also worked hard at your age, as a serf on the manor of the Estate Kilver."

Herr Hoppensack didn't seem interested. I wondered if I'd quoted too high a price.

"If you need those bricks delivered tomorrow," I said, "my uncle could rent you a wagon until a new one is made."

Herr Hoppensack pushed his hat back on his head. "Is that right? *Doch*, normally, I buy the wagons from Drumm, but tomorrow, I'll come see Herr Rapparlie. Now I must hurry, or I'll miss church entirely. You would do well to turn back as well."

I bid Herr Hoppensack farewell and continued on my hike, thinking I rather liked the old man. If he came to order a wagon, I might yet impress my uncle.

True to his word, Monday morning, Henry Hoppensack appeared at the shop. I kept to my work as he and Uncle Johann fell into consultation. Several times, I noticed they glanced in my direction. Eventually, Herr Hoppensack departed and Uncle Johann came over to speak to me, his expression not as pleased as I'd hoped.

"What have you told Herr Hoppensack?" he asked. The eyelid over his one eye sagged dangerously, a sure sign he was angry.

"I saw him yesterday at his brickyard and examined the sad state of his wagon. I assured him Rapparlie wagons are the sturdiest. Did he order one?"

"He ordered one indeed. That old penny-fox insisted I build it for him at half the price. He said you quoted him one hundred twenty-five dollars for the wagon, and I was cheating him if I charged a dollar more. Are you trying to break me?"

"He misheard! I said two twenty-five!"

"And to sweeten the pot, he said you promised the loan of a wagon free of charge while his new one was being built."

"The old man is deaf. I told him you would let him *rent* one."

My uncle's slate blue eyes drilled into me. "This wagon Herr Hoppensack wants, with the iron axles, will cost me two hundred fifty to build. He said I must make it for him for one hundred seventy-five dollars, plus the free use of a wagon in the meanwhile, or he will spread the word my apprentice calls me a cheater. I ought to dock you seventy-five dollars from your freedom dues!"

"But I said *two* twenty-five!"

But Uncle Johann didn't believe me. Once again I had failed to earn his trust.

"I don't think I can last another year under the boot of Lord Rapparlie," I confided to Eva Crolly the next afternoon. Besides Schuster, she was my only friend these days. "Perhaps it would go better for me if I took a job at the Wayside Smithy."

Eva bit her lip with concern. "It's true that the Rauch and Son business does well. But Herr Rapparlie is a respected wagon-maker. If you break your contract, I fear for your reputation. People would say it was a poor reflection on your character."

I shrugged. "Singley told me it's not so uncommon."

"Susan Fry says you have not been to church lately. Perhaps you should return and pray to God. He will guide you in His will."

Dejected by my lot, I didn't have the spirit to make a lighthearted reply.

# Chapter 33

## Cleveland, Ohio 1860

IN THE NEW YEAR OF 1860, as President Buchanan's term drew to a close, war drums beat out a steady warning. The Southern states threatened to leave the Union if any candidate imperiled slavery. Concern weighed heavily in our conversations. Would this election shatter the laws of the Constitution, the American dream of democracy and liberty? If the people of the North voted their conscience, the secession of Southern states and civil warfare were likely outcomes. Some said President Buchanan was the last president of the United States. No matter who was elected next to the office, they said, the Union of North and South would be no more.

In the Rapparlie household, Uncle Johann clung to the Democratic Party ideal. Meanwhile at Schlegel's, Jacob Müller held forth. A key leader of the German Republicans, he'd been elected as a delegate to the upcoming Republican convention in Chicago. To our gathering of *Lagerbier* drinkers, Müller warmed up his vocal chords in support of the former governor of Ohio, Salmon P. Chase.

"Chase is the friend to all liberal Germans," he crowed with conviction. "Salmon P. Chase for president!"

Müller admitted Chase faced stiff competition against William Seward of New York. But when it came to that, the Republican Party platform mattered most of all. If Seward was the choice of the Party, he would be the choice of Müller as well, and Müller advised us to view it in the same light. It seemed an amazing thing to me that the people could choose a ruler by voting. It also made me uneasy that such strong opinions could be held on different sides, and no one could predict the outcome.

That May, the well-wishes and toasts in Schlegel's Tavern sent Müller on his way to Chicago for four days of speeches and debates, for the laborious pounding of each nail into the Republican platform, and for the all-important nomination of a candidate for president of the United States.

What confusion we felt a week later when Müller steamed back into Cleveland on the heels of the electric news wire: Republican Candidates, Abraham Lincoln for President, Hannibal Hamlin for Vice President. Who was this Abraham Lincoln of Illinois? How had this unknown man denied Salmon Chase the nomination? On Müller's return, we gathered at Schlegel's, expecting to see anger and disappointment in his wolf-like gaze, but Müller was a magnet of excitement, his energy contagious.

"Abraham Lincoln's speeches are simple and clear, so understandable and understanding, so profound and convincing, moved with such humane spirit that they speak like the music of the spheres," Müller declared to us in his usual, flowery style. Müller spoke like a preacher at his bar pulpit, dragging us day by day and hour by hour through the spectacle he'd witnessed. He told us of the nomination process, the glory he felt as a member of the regular citizens of this great country, entrusted to the monumental task of choosing a presidential candidate from three men: Chase, Seward, and Lincoln. Though the women could not vote, they made their presence felt from the gallery.

"The women were even more excited," Müller said. "They threw their handkerchiefs and ribbons about, pelting the delegates with bouquets and candies." Chase and Seward were well in the lead the first three days. Lincoln's bid was not taken seriously. He was too new as a politician, with few political experiences or accomplishments. On the fourth day, Müller said, the convention hall became quiet as a church.

"The balloting began. The various states were called alphabetically by the secretary of the assembly. The chairmen of the various state delegations gave their votes loudly and clearly. During this process you could hear a pin drop. Those present followed every vote with their eyes and ears, and after the result was given, a deafening roar broke from the galleries, so loud no one could tell who the shouting was for.

"Now there followed ballot on ballot—without bringing a decision. A half-hour pause was given, so the delegations could have an opportunity to make new combinations. Until now Seward led the voting, Chase right on his heels, with poor Lincoln far behind.

"To pass the break pleasantly, my colleague and friend Fritz Hassaureck invited me to have a good glass of Rhine wine. My neighbor, David R. Carter, who had talked himself hoarse and needed refreshment with bitters, joined us. We joked about Lincoln taking up the rear, and we three 'statesmen' were agreed that it was either Seward or Chase.

"When we returned to the hall, we found a new ballot in progress, and on the announcement of the balloting we discovered that several votes had left

Chase and gone to Lincoln. The courage and zeal of the Lincolnites increased, and the popularity of their hero grew with every moment. Chase's friends abandoned him and found it proper to withdraw his name.

"Tension rose to the heights then. Each of the delegations tried to win one or another delegate for its candidate through argument. At the next round, the matter was not yet decided. No one had attained the needed absolute majority. Seward was only a few votes ahead of Lincoln. One more ballot followed, the last and decisive. Lincoln beat Seward with a majority of two votes.

"The storm of applause which passed through the hall after the announcement was accompanied by the thunder of cannon planted outside the hall."[4]

We men at Schlegel's gulped down Müller's account with gusto. Here was American politics, the process of democracy, playing out before our eyes. Müller extolled our heroic 48er Carl Schurz, who gave a speech at the Convention to be rid of the former Whig party schemes against immigrants. There were still those who favored denying anyone not born in America from holding political office, those who wanted to extend the waiting period for naturalization to twenty-five years. Schurz was a special friend of Lincoln, and spoke in clear, eloquent tones that inspired all. He made sure his proposal didn't sound like a German effort, which would have prejudiced the English against it. Schurz was a success. The stronger laws against immigrants were not included in the platform.

ONCE ABRAHAM LINCOLN BECAME OUR official nominee, what a heady, tumultuous time ensued in Cleveland! There were so many torchlight parades and rallies; I didn't see half of what took place. Like thousands of other tradesmen, the railroad workers, teamsters, carpenters, masons, and other craftsmen, I worked twelve hours a day, six days a week. We'd come to expect that the ideals of American freedom were something for our children and grandchildren, not for ourselves.

Müller and his Republican party seemed cognizant of our plight. They worked up a rags-to-riches account of Abraham Lincoln's humble birth, telling the story of the poverty of his parents, of his childhood as a rail-splitter. We working-class men emerged from our sweat and grime and long hours to hear stump speakers reiterate this inspiring tale, how Abraham Lincoln rose from humble origins to be a teacher and lawyer, now destined for the highest office in the land.

Our hopes of victory increased as the Democrats held their convention in Baltimore and suffered a terrible setback. On the nomination of Stephen A. Douglas, who didn't hold a clear position on slavery, Southern Democrats broke away to hold a separate convention in South Carolina. These men nominated Breckinridge as their candidate. Even Uncle Johann saw this as a bad sign.

"If this Lincoln is elected, there will be a war," he predicted.

"If this Lincoln is elected, it is the will of the people," I said, inhaling the heady promises of the stump speeches. "America is a democracy, where people can go to the ballot box to resolve their differences."

My uncle glared at me, and I stopped myself from saying more. If I could just hold on, I would receive my freedom dues and be released from his rule. At nineteen years of age, I'd be a journeyman blacksmith, saving for a wagon shop of my own. As it was clear Uncle Johann couldn't wait to be rid of me, I kept my ears open for positions in other shops.

But times were bad. Many businesses had closed, with thousands looking for work. It wasn't as bad for the wagon shops in Cleveland, with the settlers still making their way West. From time to time I stopped in at the shops on the East Side—Lowman's, Drumm's, and Hoffmann's—for a glimpse of their operations. I especially admired the shop of Jacob Hoffmann, as he kept the standards of first class materials and sturdy quality like my uncle.

In July, with my indenture due to end in a fortnight, I attended a torchlight parade held in support of the Republican Abraham Lincoln. There I ran into Charles Rauch. The two of us stood side by side to listen to the speeches and the fervor of the spectacle prompted us to reflect on our Palatinate homeland, on our families who continued to struggle under the tyranny of the Bavarian monarchy.

"Is your mother still there?" I asked Rauch.

A shadow crossed his face. "I begin to understand she won't come to America, after all."

"I have faint hopes as well," I said. "I've written to my parents and brother, but they don't answer. My friend Matthias Höhn says my brother doesn't want to leave and my father will only come if my brother does."

I longed to see my family again, especially Philipp. Of late, I'd begun to wonder if, once I was a jour, I might take time off and spend my freedom dues returning home to Freinsheim. I'd been away such a long time I could hardly remember their faces. I could probably find work as a jour in a shop, in our village or another nearby, but owning a wagon shop of my own would be much more difficult to achieve. Our newspapers informed us that the political situation remained repressive. In general, with heavy taxes and trade tariffs to pay, such things as new businesses grew more slowly in the Old Country. I couldn't help thinking how much farther ahead I'd be if I saved my money and stayed here, earning the wage of a jour. I could even send money to my brother, to pay for him to come for a visit.

"Listen," Rauch said as we were about to part, "if you ever grow tired of the old goat Rapparlie, we're short of blacksmiths at our new smithy. My father's business has expanded. We now call it the Rauch & Company and have completed the new shop on Pearl Road. We have many workers, but few real blacksmiths in our employ. I could use a man with your skills and experience."

"Thank you, but to be honest, I'm partial to the custom work of a smaller shop."

"I could offer you more than Rapparlie pays, I assure you. And time off to go to the *Sängerfests*." A look of surprise must have crossed my face, as Rauch hastened to explain. "Yes, I missed you at the Buffalo Singing Festival last spring. Herr Keppler stood next to me and informed me Rapparlie wouldn't allow you the time off. At Rauch & Company, I'll pay you one dollar and fifty cents a day to start, and if you do well, your income will rise quickly to two dollars."

"Thank you, I may yet come to you," I told Rauch, "but I think I have another opportunity." In fact, an idea had just then taken shape in my mind. I turned away from the political speechifying and smoky torches to make my way home, praying to God I'd spoken the truth.

# Chapter 34

━⁓⁓━

M Y FREEDOM DUES JUST TEN days away, I left the shop at the noon dinner to see Jacob Hoffmann, my old blacksmith foreman. I found him shoeing a horse, a job Rapparlie sent out to the farriers. Hoffmann's hair was graying, his leather apron much used and heavily stained. But when I stated my reason for coming to see him, his brown eyes held the kind intelligence I remembered.

"To be honest, I was hoping you would come to see me, as I'm just now shorthanded for a blacksmith," he said. "But how is it that your uncle lets you go? Doesn't he count on you for one more year, until his eldest is twelve?"

"He never said anything about that to me. I want to be more than a blacksmith in any case. Herr Hoffmann, my dearest wish is to learn the wagon business and one day own a shop of my own."

Herr Hoffmann reached for the bridle and clucked to lead the chestnut-colored horse from the shoeing station. "Can't Herr Rapparlie teach you this?"

"He said from the beginning not to think of it, that he would train only his sons in the business. You've seen for yourself. We don't get along."

Herr Hoffmann sighed. "It's right for you to want to advance yourself. You are already a skilled blacksmith and you have it in you to be a fine wagon-maker. *Alla,* once you are a jour, come here to work for me. I can only afford a low wage, but I'll teach you all aspects of the wagon business."

Elated, I returned to the shop and went directly to Eva Crolly in the trimming department, bursting with my good news.

"I regret I must abandon you," I told her in a whisper. "Come next week, I'm going to work for Herr Hoffmann."

Eva arched her brown eyebrows at me. "You will break your contract?"

"Didn't I tell you? My apprenticeship ends August first. You must keep it a secret, if you please. Before I tell my uncle, I must find another place to live."

"I'll miss your visits to my sewing machine, but not for long." Daylight through the window pane cast a clear light on Eva's blushing cheeks. "I'll also be quitting my work here. Edward Kemp and I are to be married in two weeks time, so I will be going to live in the home of his parents."

I grabbed both her hands and shook them vigorously, laughing. "*Doch,* then I'll not have to worry about you slaving away for Lord Rapparlie."

She gave me a reproachful look, but I refused to feel guilty. Floating on air, I hastened down the stairs to my anvil.

I had found a job as a jour but still faced the problem of locating a place to live. Uncle Georg had already said he didn't have room for me. Until I found a situation, I'd have to stay in a boarding house, but I didn't want to suffer the expense. Seven days passed, and still I had not thought of anyone to ask for a living situation. The night of July 28, I came home from a Singing Society rehearsal thinking I must tell my aunt and uncle my plans. As much as I hated the thought of it, perhaps they might allow me to stay on in their home, paying rent, for another month or two until I found a room.

"Good evening, Aunt, Uncle, I—"

"What's this I hear?" Uncle Johann's voice boomed in the quiet house. All the children had by now been sent upstairs to bed. "You're going to work for Hoffmann?!"

"What? I—"

"I learn this not from you, but from my brother-in-law Sigfried?"

I looked to my aunt for help, but she stared down at her embroidery hoop, her knuckles white.

"*Es tut mir leid,* Uncle, I was going to tell you. I only decided myself a few days ago, and was not sure—"

"Your parents sent you into this country without any money or discipline, expecting me to turn you around, and this is how I'm thanked?"

"I thought you didn't want me! We get along so poorly—"

"It's typical of you, sneaking around like this. Another blacksmith can't be found in three days. I should expect no less of someone who stays out every night for the drinking, or the singing, or the singing and the drinking."

"You never said you expected me to stay in."

"Would it have made a difference? You do as you please, listening to no one, still as ungrateful as the first day you arrived."

"That is a lie. I have worked three solid years, at the shop and in this house, for a pittance. You didn't even provide me with proper clothes."

"You call me a liar in my own home? You come empty-handed—in debt— to me, your father providing nothing but a cask of Rhine wine. Small payment for a small helper. *Doch,* you shall leave with nothing."

As I digested this latest outrage, I looked up and saw the four Rapparlie children at the banister, their faces pressed to the wooden rails as if through bars of a jail.

"How dare you!" I shouted, overcome. "The indenture contract says you owe me one hundred thirty dollars."

"You owe me for the shortfall on the Hoppensack job. Seventy-five dollars plus the lost rental charge of eight dollars."

"If you don't pay my freedom dues in the full amount, I'll tell everyone you are a cheat and a liar!"

Uncle Johann's voice lowered to a snarl. "Try it, Michael Harm, and it will lead to your ruin. You are no longer welcome in our home."

I opened my mouth, then closed it again, not trusting myself to say more. I turned on my heel and charged up the stairs, the Rapparlie children scurrying ahead of me to hover in their bedroom doorways, gaping in fright. Grief rushed through me that I must abandon them to such a cruel father. I slowed my steps, pausing to rest a hand on each warm little head. I came to little Sussy last and leaned over to kiss her blonde curls.

Then I ascended to the attic, collected my belongings, and left for good.

THAT FIRST NIGHT OF MY exile, I spent one dollar for one night's lodging at Napoleon's. I knew that if I was forced to live in such a manner for long, my savings would be depleted within the month, but what choice did I have? I would have preferred never to set foot in the Rapparlie shop again, but feared my uncle would hope for this. If I didn't show up for the last three days, he could accuse me of breaking my contract and not pay my dues.

The next morning, I rose early, bolted down rolls and coffee in the public rooms and proceeded to the shop. When Uncle Johann entered the smithy, he looked to my bench and saw me at work but gave no greeting. The noon hour found me sorting through my tools, setting aside those I had not made myself, when Eva Crolly stopped at my station.

"Come outside," she said in a low voice. "My father wishes to speak with you."

Herr Crolly waited for me one block up Michigan, out of sight of the wagon shop. "Your Aunt Katharina has come to our home and told my wife what happened," he said. "Please, you are welcome to stay with us. I could use another man in the house."

"Thank you, but I cannot. Rapparlie is angry beyond reason. If you shelter me, you risk ruining your friendship."

"I don't worry about losing his friendship. That's his choice. In any case, there's something you don't know. Won't you come to our house for the noon dinner so we can discuss the matter?"

I gratefully accepted his offer. As we sat down at the Crolly table on Henry Street, I was brimming over with curiosity.

"Herr Crolly, what do you mean, there's something I don't know?"

Herr Crolly glanced at Frau Crolly. "It seems your uncle and aunt have not discussed with you their plans to move to Toledo?"

I shook my head.

"Johann Rapparlie and Wendell Biene have planned for many years to go into business together," Herr Crolly said.

"But what will happen to the Cleveland shop?"

"Johann will sell his land and buildings and begin again in Toledo. He told me a month ago he's resolved to do it. Herr Biene sells the wagon supplies, the carriage mats, odometers, coach blankets, and such. They intend to locate their stores side by side."

I thought of Aunt Katharina, of how tired she looked, and my heart sank to my toes. I should not have gone out so often, or she might have confided in me. I felt sorry for all the trouble I'd caused her and hoped this change wouldn't bring more hardship.

"Frau Crolly and I both agree it would be a help to us if you came to live on Henry Street. Now that our eldest daughter will be married, we have room for one more."

Eva's cheeks turned pink at this announcement. I looked from her to Elizabeth, so grown up and beautiful, and then to the youngest daughter Mary, also quite pretty. My heart quaked in awe and trepidation. What would it be like to live among the female sex? I hardly knew.

"Won't you consider it, young man?" Frau Crolly asked, her stern voice a contrast to the enchantment her daughters gave.

The Crollys reminded me so much of Father and Mütterchen, I realized, with their Calvinist discipline, the Christian virtues of prayer and piety guiding their lives. At this moment for the first time, I had the power to step into a future of my own choosing. If I could have asked Father and Mütterchen, I felt certain they would approve.

"I'm very grateful to accept your offer," I said.

The time spent at dinner was overlong, so Eva and I made haste back to the shop.

"It's very generous of your parents to offer me a place to stay," I said as we hurried along Prospect. "Last night, I became so very angry and said terrible things to Uncle Johann. I'm sorry for my aunt and the children, that I said these things."

"'Better an end with pain than pain without end,'" Eva said, quoting the old adage. "I've known Herr Rapparlie since I was a little girl, but have never seen him as angry as you make him."

"What have I done wrong?"

"Perhaps he's jealous."

"Jealous? What could he be jealous of? He has all the money and the craft and the good business."

"You laugh, and you sing. You have your youth and both your legs."

"Two legs to run from his fists," I said, letting the bitterness creep into my voice.

"Rapparlie would never admit he needs you," Eva said.

"Needs me like a hole in the head. Sometimes I wonder if Lord Rapparlie drove my mother's brother Johannes mad, and that's why he had the *melancholia* and left. In truth, I have felt at times as if I'm losing my mind."

Eva frowned. "I was young when your Uncle Johannes left, but I remember him. It is true, something was not right with his spirit, but I can't believe Herr Rapparlie was the cause of it."

I was not so sure, but appreciated her honesty. "In any case, it seems I now have two reasons to look forward to your wedding day. I am glad for you, and Edward Kemp must feel himself a very fortunate man. But I'm most fortunate of all, as your marriage assures me a roof over my head."

That evening as I left work and headed for the Crolly house on Henry Street, I felt a lightness in my chest. My indenture was coming to an end, and a new life awaited.

# Chapter 35

———～～———

THE CELEBRATION OF MY FREEDOM dues held little of the sentimentality of William Singley's. On the morning of August 1, Uncle Johann came to me with $130 in bills—the full amount of my freedom dues—wrapped in a packet of brown paper.

"I pay you this not because you deserve it, but because I signed a contract that obligates me. I still am owed recompense for the Hoppensack job, so I'll keep all tools you have made."

"What?!" I began to argue, then thought better of it. If I hadn't found a position with Herr Hoffmann, I'd have felt this hardship keenly, but my new employer would understand.

Still, I didn't feel so philosophical about it. The whole of my last workday, my insides churned a molten orange heat, burning up over the loss. I'd spent the past two years of my apprenticeship fashioning my own tools to my particular hand. It was understood I would own them when the indenture concluded. The loss wouldn't be easily recovered. But I dowsed my anger in the quenching tub and refused to fight any longer. I had fulfilled my promise to my parents, had received my freedom dues in full, and that would have to be enough.

That evening, as the ringing of the anvils ceased for the day, I uncorked bottles of Rhine wine and passed them around to the jours. The workers from the other departments also came to congratulate me and tip a cup. I stood amid the grime of the smithy, the scarred work benches, the array of tongs, hammers, and barrels, each anvil on its stump, the forge fires expired to white ash. The shop appeared nearly the same as the day I set foot in it so long ago. The faces had altered, however. Singley was gone, Herr Hoffmann, too. Earlier that same month Herr Penhoff's aching joints had finally gotten the better of him, so now he stayed at home. Herr Fry and Herr Gesler were still here, more grizzled than ever, as was Fred Fry, although he too had almost completed his indenture. Fry and I had lapsed to civility but never regained our earlier camaraderie. As for Fred Schuster, I felt confident I would see my new friend around town.

When it became clear Uncle Johann wouldn't be joining us, Herr Gesler stepped forward to make the toast.

"Harm, we all like you. All present in this room, in any case. You've become a skilled blacksmith, you've worked hard. We're proud to know you."

The men lifted their cups and drank.

"I'll miss everything about you," Fry said, "except that infernal singing."

Some men chortled and nodded agreement. Others protested that I had a fine voice, but the attempt at humor didn't enliven us for long. Herr Gesler cleared his throat as if to say something more, but he was a man of few words and the silence persisted. Men shifted from foot to foot and glanced toward the door. It felt strange to be gathered here in the shop without Rapparlie present to bless the proceedings.

Herr Gesler put an arm over my shoulders. "Come, Harm, it's time for your first taste of freedom."

He urged me toward the door, and with relief, I stepped outside. A slight breeze riffled up from the river, where a steamship shoveled its way upstream. I did not as feel elated as I thought I might, but sorrowful and uncertain. I wondered if I'd done enough in this country, if I should now go home. But I didn't have time to dwell on these thoughts. Once Herr Gesler had bolted the door, we workmen hiked en masse uphill to Schlegel's to celebrate my freedom dues in earnest.

A FEW DAYS AFTER I MOVED into the Crolly home, the wedding of Eva Crolly and Edward Kemp took place in the Henry Street parlor. Eva moved to the Kemp home in Ohio City, and I moved from the parlor sofa to Eva's former bedroom, which I rented for $2.00 each week.

What a difference life with the Crolly's made! Herr Crolly didn't raise his voice in the home, nor did he rule it like a tyrant king. Frau Crolly and Elizabeth and Mary were well-known seamstresses, their nimble fingers sewing the most even of stitches. Their days were spent on dress-making and sewing handwork of all kinds. Wealthy ladies from the Greek Revival homes on Prospect ordered many fine dresses from them. Elizabeth especially excelled at tatting Battenberg lace for the elaborate dress collars. Though the women had much work, it was a pleasant atmosphere. I rarely heard the sisters squabble.

In those first mornings on Henry Street, I sometimes woke with a jolt, the specter of Johann Rapparlie still haunting my dreams. As I regained consciousness, I'd nestle farther into the warmth of the bed, reveling in my good fortune to be working now for a jour's wage, in training to be a wagon-maker.

The economic times were not so strong, and the vitriol between North and South only increased, causing us all to fear what might happen. As a jour with prospects for a wagon-making future, I strolled about town with a new bounce in my step, ogling the spry locally-made buggies that held the eye both coming and going.

As a newly opened shop, Hoffmann's Wagons still struggled to build a reputation, so we weren't as busy as we might have been. In the lulls, I forged the tools I needed to replace the ones Rapparlie had kept—the tongs and hammers, fullers and chisels, punches, hardies and top swages. I was less sure how to go about learning the carriage business, and at first, Herr Hoffmann gave me no guidance.

Then one afternoon, a few months into my new employment, I went in to see Herr Hoffmann in his cluttered office about a coal order and spied a copy of *The New York Coach-Maker's Magazine* on his desk. Forgetting my original errand, I picked up the publication and pored over its pages.

"Why don't we make this one?" I asked, showing Herr Hoffmann a plate drawing of a phaeton.

Herr Hoffmann pressed his lower lip over his upper one, made a pencil notation on his column of figures, then took the magazine from me.

"I think it's possible," he said at last. As he continued to study the plate, his snowy eyebrows veered up at each end like the wings of a gliding bird. "We'll have to purchase steam-bent hickory for the felloes. A good beginning for you as a carriage-maker. *Aha,* I was looking for something to get you started, to expand the Hoffmann line. I'll give you a corner of the wagon yard to build this buggy. If it turns out well, perhaps we'll make more."

We got started that very moment. On a scrap of wood, Herr Hoffmann helped me sketch the design to calculate the dimensions. Together we went to the lumber shed to choose the woods from the seasoned timber, the hickory for the wheel spokes, elm for the hubs, basswood for the body panels. From then on, I thought only of my phaeton.

Meanwhile at the Crolly home, another kind of passion grew to consume me. When I moved to the house on Henry Street, I hadn't foreseen the impression Elizabeth Crolly would make. Being near this *Fräulein* morning and night created a leaping in my heart like a wild horse untethered. I longed for her to turn her broad, honest gaze on me, did everything in my power to spark her amusement, to say or do something clever to bring the mischievous glint to her eyes.

"*Guten Morgen*, Elizabeth," I'd say each morning, swallowing my heart back down to my rib cage. "*Guten Abend*," I'd say each evening when I returned to the house. In the backyard I'd scrub with vigor at my hands and neck to remove the coal dust and metal filings, but the black grit still clung under and around my fingernails. In the Crolly house, the white lace covers on the chair arms and tabletops, the immaculate order of the rooms, made me feel like a brute, but Elizabeth's smile was kind and her laughter heart-warming, which eased my embarrassment.

I didn't dare jeopardize my situation or show disrespect after the kindness the Crollys had shown to me. I acted the part of a dignified gentleman, treating the women of the house like ladies as best I could. From my freedom dues, I ordered a new topcoat, a silk vest, two white shirts and a new pair of pants, which the Crolly women sewed for me. The cloth was of the highest quality, the seams well-made. Wearing these clothes, I felt like a new man.

I began to attend church with the family, but had an even grander time escorting Elizabeth and Mary to the dances. The two young ladies wore their brown hair in a matching style, tied back at the neck in a bun. But here the similarities ceased. Mary was thin as a rail, with an eager, girlish interest in everything around her. Elizabeth was shorter and plumper than Mary, with sky blue eyes. Her clothes were just as well-designed, but somehow not as vain and showy. She didn't worry so much about what others thought, but held herself with poise and confidence.

We joked and teased and had great fun. To be seen in their company was for me a sheer pleasure. At the balls, I longed to dance only with Elizabeth, but I was shy as always, and reluctant to make a wrong impression. I would ask Elizabeth to dance a few times, but also Mary and other girls. I tried not to reveal my singular interest, but when Elizabeth wasn't dancing with me, I couldn't help but look over my partner's shoulder to locate her in the room. I suffered special discomfort when she danced with Charles Rauch, as he seemed to take more of an interest in her since Eva Crolly had married. But fortunately, this didn't happen too often.

NOVEMBER ARRIVED AND, ON THE morning of the long-awaited Election Day, the sunlight brought a sparkling glow to the yellow leaves. The red-orange brick of the buildings glistened from the previous night's hard rain. Boats scudded across the blue-green, white-capped lake.

At nineteen years of age, I was still ineligible to vote, but I went to our ward precinct to witness the proceedings. Truly, I wouldn't have missed it. What a hubbub to behold: such calling, crowing voices, such giddy, drunken fervor. I witnessed the practice of "vote-fishing," quite common then, where a man arriving to cast his vote was grabbed and held tightly by the arm by a professional ticket peddler. The ticket peddler walked the voter all the way to the ballot box, pressed a ballot into the man's hand and watched like a hawk until he'd dropped it in the box. Even in a democracy, Müller and others impressed on us again and again, there can be much corruption. To be part of a free government always means keeping on guard, to prevent our rights from being taken away from us again.

The majority of Clevelanders were pro-Republican by then, such that, as Lincoln's victory tapped across the electric wires, a great festival filled the streets long into the night. My only regret was that I didn't see the crestfallen face of Johann Rapparlie anywhere in the crowd, so that I might gloat over his Democratic Party's crushing defeat. The head of my new house, Herr Crolly, sided with the Republican Party, so he and I marveled together over the civilized method of casting a ballot to make a change in the highest office in the land. If only my brother Philipp and my Freinsheimer friends could have experienced such freedom, my happiness would have been complete.

At the thought of Freinsheim I felt a pang of guilt, that I hadn't yet written to my parents about the inglorious end to my indenture. In any event, Rapparlie beat me to it.

In the new year of 1860, Herr Crolly appeared in my room looking quite upset.

"Johann Rapparlie has written to your parents, accusing you," he said. "I received this letter today from your parents.."

He handed me the sheet of paper. With dread, I began to read.

25 November, 1860

Dear Adam and Catherine Crolly and daughters, and son Michael,

> To the Crollys of Friedelsheim, whom we have never met, we cannot keep ourselves from writing these few lines to let you know how it goes for us. We are in good health, but much saddened to receive the letter of Johann Rapparlie and learn all that has happened, how we sent Michael alone into this wide world, having done little hard work earlier in his life, so the blacksmithing did not come so easily to him. It was never our intention that the families in Cleveland should suffer on our account. That our son came to Cleveland with no money should not have happened, as the money we gave cousin Handrich was enough for the journey. We do not understand why Michael is angry with Johann Rapparlie about the clothes. Perhaps you can write and explain a little more about this. It's a hard thing, when such news comes, that we cannot speak about it in person. The Lord willing, we

hope one day to repay you for your kindnesses.

Heartfelt greetings in this Christmas time,

Johann Philipp and Elisabetha Harm, Philipp Harm

Crushed with shame, I held my head in my hands. "It's all lies. My parents believe I'm a good-for-nothing. And what must Philipp think of me?"

"Frau Crolly and I don't think your master gives a fair accounting. Your Uncle Georg, too, has heard the truth from Herr Hoffmann, and does not accuse you." Herr Crolly laid a hand on my shoulder.

"But my family in Freinsheim doesn't know this."

"I think they must hear from you."

I did as he suggested that same evening, fighting back the stinging pressure of tears, desperate to convince my parents I had not let them down.

27 January 1861

Much beloved parents and brother,

I received your last letter and regret to see from these few lines that my uncle has written a letter that made you sad. As for the allegations that are such a concern to you, I want to write about it as follows:

First, he has written to you that you sent your child into the wide world, but I came of my own will, you didn't send me, I have asked to go, and I went.

Then secondly, there was no money? This is true because when I came to Cleveland, I had no more money. When I arrived in New York I had 20 dollars left, but I was led around by a man who took the rest of my money, as it happens to so many Germans who are fooled into relying on someone who says they are an "American cousin."

Thirdly, I had no clothes, because my uncle advised you to send me with very little, as the fashions are different here. Although he had written to you he would provide so much for me, he did not buy me any clothes.

Franz Handrich has said my uncle only wanted a cask of wine to pay for what he had done for me, but now Rapparlie writes to you that he has done so much for me and I did so little for him. But that is a lie as big as the others, because he has done little for me, and I've worked so hard for everything. I could still tell you many stories, if my paper would not be so expensive for such things.

Therefore I wish that you would not write him any more letters, because I do not believe he is worth the effort. Amen.

Now I will also write about Uncle Jakob. He has now gone to Titusville and is still unmarried.

As for me I am still pretty healthy and am doing very well. I am working as a blacksmith jour, no longer for Lord Rapparlie, but for Herr Hoffmann. My apprenticeship ended in August, and my current salary comes to nine dollars each week.

Uncle Scheuermann and family are still quite healthy and they do very well. I know no further news except that it looks very warlike in America, and the times are so bad, because many shops are closed and thousands of workers are without jobs.

Now I will close my letter and hope that these lines reach you in such good health as they have left me. I remain your faithful son, and your loving brother,

M. Harm

I salute all good friends and acquaintances and neighbors and all who ask about me—please send my greetings to the Richard Pirmann family, the John Fuhrman family, and a greeting to Anna Maria and her husband Oberholz.

That night, I dreamed of my brother Philipp in the soldier uniform for Bavaria, training and drilling for battle, and awoke praying it was not true. Was Philipp a soldier now? Or was war on my mind from what was happening in America?

# Chapter 36

—⁂—

## Cleveland, Ohio 1861

B ETWEEN THE NOVEMBER ELECTION AND Lincoln's inauguration in March
of 1861, one by one, the slave states of the South seceded. We Republican
Germans didn't understand it, because Abraham Lincoln had vowed not
to interfere with the institution of slavery. So why was this happening? The
newspapers reported rumors of a rebel plot to assassinate Lincoln, which
served to heighten our loyalty and devotion to this gallant man.

The outgoing President Buchanan met with secessionist leaders. Müller
and the others at Schlegel's said it seemed as if he sided with the South, as he
even handed over military resources. Jefferson Davis became the leader of the
"Confederate States" and raised a Confederate flag in South Carolina. Still,
President Buchanan did nothing.

In mid-February, Abraham Lincoln left his home in Illinois to travel to the
Capitol in Washington, D.C. How excited we were in Cleveland to learn that
a stop along the new president's journey would be in our fair city. Officials
planned a huge parade, and it seemed as if the entire state of Ohio descended
on Cleveland to catch a glimpse of the new president. Herr Hoffmann closed
the wagon shop so all of us could go cheer for this great man.

Abraham Lincoln was to arrive by train at the Euclid Station and travel
in a long procession to the Weddell House on Superior, near Public Square.
I wanted to be in the front row for a good look at this great man, so did not
want to wait for the Crolly women to dress in their finery, or we'd be far back
in the crowds.

Early on the morning of Lincoln's arrival, I gulped down my coffee, stuffed
rolls and an apple into my pocket and headed out alone to stand along stone-
paved Superior Street. The weather was terrible, the sky gray and drizzling,
but I held my place at the front, in the shadow of the Weddell House, getting

more and more drenched as the hours wore on.

"Harm!" a voice called out from across the broad avenue. Peering amid the black and gray cloaks and umbrellas, I saw an arm waving back and forth. "Harm! It's Matthias Höhn!"

Joyfully, I hailed Matthias and we bantered back and forth about who would cross the street. At last, Höhn agreed to come to my side.

"You don't come to Cleveland to see me, but you come to see Abraham Lincoln? Now I know where I stand," I laughed.

"I am sorry, old friend." Matthias was dressed in the suit of a gentleman, not like a worker or a farmer. "Much has happened. I now live in the town of Akron and work for an import shop there. I'm only learning the business, but soon I hope to travel back and forth across the Atlantic."

I felt a twinge of jealousy, and sadness, that Matthias wouldn't make his home closer to me. In truth, this happened so often in America, close friends living great distances from each other, until their acquaintance became like that of strangers. We talked of seeing each other often but did not find the time.

"Are Herr and Frau Höhn also in town?" I asked.

"Soon. I traveled by train, but they are coming by wagon. They have business in Randall, at the Forest City Farm, to see about some trotters. Sebastian and Hans are fans of racing."

As we endured the long wait, Matthias and I shared news about Freinsheimers in Columbiana. Some, including his Uncle Adam, had joined the Amish, who believed firmly in separation of church and state and objected to the war-like pronouncements of the English who ruled the government. We worried over the secession of the Southern states, the steady march toward war. On this subject we were of one mind and held out hope that if anyone could find a resolution to this crisis, it would be our new president, the dark-haired lawyer from Illinois.

At long last, faint strains of band music sounded in the distance. A dark-clothed phalanx of dignitaries made its way up Superior Street. When Abraham Lincoln's open carriage—shiny black with bright red wheels pulled by four white horses—trundled past, I recognized the tall black hat and serious, lined eyes of our Republican champion. I felt a warm exhilaration, even standing in the cold and damp, at being so near the "Prince of Rails." A boy sat erect beside him—one of his sons, people said. A slew of horsemen dressed in gray followed behind Lincoln, as well as wagon after wagon packed with brass bands, military, and important personages of Cleveland.

With the rest of the mob, Matthias and I shifted our attention to the Weddell House balcony. As Lincoln appeared above us, we craned our necks and shouted our approval. He gave a brief speech. I was close enough to hear our Republican president, but my English was not good enough to understand it all. I recognized the words "constitution," "liberty," and "common cause," and felt the weight of conviction in his oratory, the momentousness of the task ahead.

When the speech was over, Matthias and I agreed to break our fast at Napoleon's, where the hot potato soup was the best in town. On the way over, weaving through the crowds, we encountered Charles Rauch, who wore a black stovepipe hat as tall as Lincoln's. I lifted my new bowler hat in greeting and introduced Rauch to Matthias. I confessed we were on our way to Napoleon's and invited him to join us.

To my surprise, he readily agreed. The three of us entered the public rooms, treading through the muddy mush of the sawdust-coated floor. We hung our coats to dry amid many others by the large hearthfire.

"Harm, you must come and see our new carriage manufactory on Pearl Road," Rauch said as we dug into a hearty meal and a second glass of Rhine wine. "It's three stories high, and I hire many men. Höhn, do you realize, when I offered Harm a job, he chose to go to Hoffmann's instead? A small family run shop, when he could have worked quickly up to foreman at Rauch & Company."

I rolled my eyes. Why was Rauch always on me about working for him? "I do all right with Hoffmann. His business increases all the time."

"Not as well as you could have. My father's contract with the federal government keeps us very busy." Rauch's tone was dismissive. He turned to Matthias. "So, you're a traveling man? You must convince Harm here, who never goes anywhere, that the old craftsman methods are too slow. If the Cleveland Germans don't keep up with the times, our city will fall behind Chicago and Cincinnati."

Matthias paused to consider, then leaned forward, resting both elbows on the table. "You're right. I have been to these cities, and every time more progress has been made than here." He tore off a chunk of roll and dunked it in his soup bowl. "But the family-run businesses are also still in evidence."

"I think I know what the real trouble is," I put in. "You're tired of catering to the carriage trade, who demand the custom upholstery and such. It slows your production, but you must offer it if we small shops do, *oder*?"

Rauch gave a jovial laugh and changed the subject. He asked Matthias about the future of the import trade, particularly with wines when there was so much temperance sentiment. As he talked, I studied the way Rauch's confidence blazed from him like a bellows-fed fire. I counseled myself not to begrudge him his success. I had my own measured achievements—my freedom from Rapparlie, a position as a jour. In another year or two, I'd have the skills of a master carriage-maker and begin saving money in order to one day invest in a shop of my own. If not exactly a symphony, it was a melody worth singing.

After the meal, we moved with our wine to the fireside.

"How many wagons do you make in a day?" Rauch asked me.

"Hoffmann has four vehicles going at one time."

"*Aha*, but that doesn't answer my question. I'll wager he makes perhaps ten a month? You must realize new machines come onto the market all the time, everything from planing to stitching. Invest in them, or you'll be left behind. In New Haven, they turn out one carriage every hour! My father has located our new shop on the C. C. & C. Railroad, the better to make shipments like the factories in New England."

Rauch's eyes flashed in the firelight. Matthias and I exchanged a glance.

"You say you have a contract with the federal government?" Matthias asked. "What do you build?"

"Heavy artillery wagons."

A shroud fell over our little gathering. I stared into the fire, pondering the flaming inevitability of war. The rumors of assassination schemes against Lincoln were a violent omen. Would this whole, peaceful system of democracy collapse into chaos? Would we become as divided as the German nation-states? I prayed such a thing would not come to pass.

"I'm thinking I will stay up all night," I said. "As I waited this morning for the parade, I overheard some men talking about how they mean to stand outside Weddell House, to keep watch so nothing bad will happen to Lincoln in our city. I've decided to join them."

Rauch smirked. "A noble cause, Harm. I might prefer to stand up to my neck in Lake Erie as stand out all night in the cold and damp."

"I'll wait with you," Matthias said.

We rose to put on our hearth-warmed coats. Once outside, Rauch bid us farewell and turned toward the Columbus Street Bridge.

Höhn and I made our way ten blocks in the other direction, to Henry Street. I invited my friend in, to introduce him to the Crolly family. Over slices of cake and cups of coffee, we explained our plan to guard Lincoln. The women tutted with disapproval, but Herr Crolly was unperturbed. He suggested we wear buffalo robes to keep warm, and we men went out to the back shed to collect them.

"I'm not sure keeping vigil all night will help our president, but I can't find fault with your admiration of him," Herr Crolly said. "If anyone can bring peace in this country, it's Abraham Lincoln. But beware, Michael Harm, you don't make politics your religion. There is only one God."

"I admire Abraham Lincoln but don't worship him," I assured him. "Such a chance to be in the presence of this great man might never come again. I can't stay away."

Seemingly satisfied, Herr Crolly nodded and waved us out the shed door.

And so it happened that Matthias and I—wrapped in brown, wool-furred buffalo robes like two Indian chiefs—joined a corps of admirers at a bonfire outside the Weddell House. Early on, many men in the gathering expressed their wish for Lincoln to make another appearance, to come out and warm his hands by the fire and tell one of his jokes or stories. But as the hours dragged on, those hopeful souls drifted away. In the wee hours, only the hardiest of us remained.

Throughout that dripping night, Matthias and I reminisced about our childhoods, about our relatives and friends in the Palatinate who had yet to see such a dream-come-true as unfolded here before us. If a war happened, we worried, would the idealistic optimism of America vanish forever? Matthias said he thought war would come, but believed it would be over quickly. The Northern states were more organized, while in the South, the slaves outnumbered their masters four to one and would surely rise up against them.

Talking over these matters, I wondered again how long my brother would have to wait for democracy in Freinsheim. Would the separate nation-states ever unite as one under a constitution? Was Philipp even then sitting in the *Rathskeller,* talking over politics with Oberholz and the other *Wingertsleute*? More likely, he was at the table of the *Ackermänner,* discussing crop cooperatives and the latest farming methods. If only Philipp could see me now.

The next morning, Matthias and I cheered Abraham Lincoln on his way from the Weddell House back to Euclid Station. We marched alongside the procession, since Matthias would be departing from that station on the train bound for Akron. After I said my goodbyes to my old friend, I made my way with exhausted but satisfied steps to the Hoffmann shop for another day at the forge.

SOON THE NEWSPAPERS ANNOUNCED THE safe arrival of Abraham Lincoln in the Capitol. But before he was sworn into office, some Southern states had already seceded and others threatened to follow. Within two months, the April attack on Fort Sumter raised Northern ire. Like the rest of the country, Clevelanders prepared for war.

Declaring his intention to preserve the Union, President Lincoln called for 75,000 volunteers for the Union Army. Military marching music began playing in the streets every evening. On that initial call to arms, Cleveland's First Ward had no trouble meeting its enlistment quota. Several men in Hoffmann's wagon shop set down their tools, removed their work aprons, and went off to join the militia. The time of duty was a short ninety days. Everyone assumed the war would be over in less time. I had yet to become a naturalized citizen, so such a decision was not forced on me, but I attended the torchlight rallies, cheering on the men of German, English, and Irish descent who donned the uniform to fight.

At one such rally, I ran into Fred Fry.

"I've done it, Harm! I've signed up," he said, his face animated with excitement.

Even then, officers were herding the new recruits to one corner of Public Square.

My heart clenched with misgivings. "But you must reconsider! Your fine painting skills are needed in Cleveland."

"It's true," Fry said, snorting a laugh, wavering on his feet so I wondered if he had drunk too many *Lagerbiers*. "Rapparlie is in a rage. He blames this war on Lincoln and the Republicans and calls me a Green fool."

I chuckled and shook my head. "I've changed my mind. You are smart to enlist. A regiment is a much more pleasant prospect than spending every hour of every day under the boot of Lord Rapparlie. I wish you God speed and a safe return."

I gave Fry a firm handshake and watched him mingle into the ranks, headed for Camp Taylor.

CONTRARY TO OUR EARLY OPTIMISM, the war did not end quickly, and such farewells became ever more common. In the Crolly home, we lived through these perilous times with grim concern, praying every Sunday at the Reformed Church for fathers and sons who had gone to fight, for the Northern and Southern states to resolve their differences quickly and peacefully.

Often, I struggled in my heart, torn between my Christian beliefs and my urge to prove I was not a coward. One Sunday, as Herr Crolly and I worked together in the shed, repairing a cart for the summer season, I tested out my opinion.

"Next July, I'll be eligible to be naturalized. Perhaps then I'll join the army," I said.

Herr Crolly scraped his emery cloth across the wood handle of the cart with thoughtful strokes. The Crollys used this small wagon to carry home the heavier bushel baskets of fruit and the sacks of flour, sugar, and corn purchased at the Central Market and dry goods store.

"It's a great disappointment to me, that America should be so eager to fight brother against brother," he said at last.

"If I'm a true American, shouldn't I fight for my country?"

"The Christian path is one of humility and nonresistance. This fighting, this struggle for power, makes fertile ground for evil to take root."

"But if I become a citizen, it will be my duty."

"What you do is between you and God. But for my part, I refuse to go to war. If I am called up, I'll move my family to Canada rather than serve."

# Chapter 37

———

E ARLY THAT MAY, A TIME when bad news of the battles grew worse, the Crolly family and I joined the Scheuermanns for a Sunday dinner and had a surprise. As we entered the kitchen, there sat Uncle Jakob Handrich as if he had never left. Joy surged through me.

"So you are back! And how is the oil drilling?" I asked as my uncle clapped his hands on my shoulders in greeting. His long brown hair had thinned some, but with his upright bearing and sparkling gray-blue eyes, he seemed as vigorous as ever.

"*Gott sei Dank*, his wandering days are over!" Aunt Margaretha said from the stove, where she stood frying the old country *Saumaa*. The aroma was heavenly.

Uncle Jakob smiled at her. "*Doch*, I've seen too much spectacular beauty in this life to bury myself in a mountain of slime," he said, settling back in a wood-framed chair that barely contained him.

Uncle Jakob described the oil derricks in Pennsylvania that multiplied over night and the towns that came with them, swarming with rough characters and ladies of ill repute. He had succeeded in getting an oil gusher himself, only to have his neighbor dig a pipe diagonally to tap his well and rob him of his profits.

"I'm not one to shy away from reckless men and hard work. But the muck and foul smell of this enterprise, you wouldn't believe. The men put signs on their drill rigs that read 'Hell or China.' Then it hits me: I don't want to see either place. So I've come home."

Uncle Jakob's presence was a magnet that even Lord Rapparlie could not resist; the Rapparlies arrived at the Scheuermanns' within the hour. Uncle Johann and I kept apart in separate rooms, except during the meal. Uncle

Johann's scowl made me feel a keen discomfort in his presence, until Uncle Jakob announced his intention to work for Uncle Johann. All at once, the stormy furrows in the wagon-maker's brow softened, and I felt the tenseness in my shoulders relax as well.

From that day forward, I saw Uncle Jakob on a regular basis, at the Scheuermanns, or when he stopped by Hoffmann's with news. One warm Sunday in late spring, Elizabeth, Mary, and I heard a call from the street, and came out on the Crolly porch to witness the frontier man sitting bigger than life on the seat of a new chaise, the sunshine bursting from above and within him.

"Nephew, it's a fine day," he called from the road. "I've brought my rifle along with the idea we might go bird hunting."

"You've taken Uncle Johann's chaise and team? You sold him your firstborn, *oder*?"

Uncle Jakob laughed. "*Doch,* Johann Rapparlie can huff and puff, but he does not knock my house down. But where are my manners? See here, what pretty birds with fine plumage have alit on this porch. Good afternoon, *Fräuleins*. Why don't we all take a ride together? I promise I won't shoot you. After I bring you home, you might forgive me for taking Michael away."

Elizabeth and Mary scampered laughing down the path, raising their skirts to ascend to the back seat of the open chaise. I climbed up next to Uncle Jakob, and he urged the horses into a fast trot toward Euclid, heading for the woodland park east of town.

At Doan's Corners, he turned toward Lake Erie, driving along the large property of the wealthy Clevelander Jeptha Wade, founder of the Western Union Telegraph company. The birds sang in the canopy of new green leaves. We were far enough away from the smokestacks that the air smelled sweet and the woodland slopes were carpeted with delicate wildflowers. It was beautiful here, but I couldn't keep my eyes from the members of the fairer sex. I earned a sore neck turning around to see how the sisters were enjoying their ride. Elizabeth pointed and exclaimed at everything she saw, her eyes bright and merry.

Uncle Jakob paused at the far end of the fairgrounds, checked with the Crolly sisters to be sure they were satisfied, then drove back to deposit them at Henry Street. I was loath to part with Elizabeth, but the prospect of a hunting trip was too good to resist. I hadn't been hunting since my visit to Ritthaler's farm the first fall I'd arrived.

My uncle took the winding dirt road up Cedar Glen, passing beside the tall rock shelves that made a lookout over the lake. Up above, the land leveled off, our chaise wheels skimming along graded roads through oaks, elms, maples, and beeches. The quaint brick and clapboard houses of the North

Union Shaker Community were clustered here. The inhabitants had dammed Doan Brook for a woolen mill, creating a pair of picturesque lakes.

Beyond the little village, we eventually arrived in deeper forest, tied up the horse and buggy and proceeded on foot. Uncle Jakob showed me how to aim his long musket and I took a few practice shots, but didn't do much mischief except to scare a few leaves off the trees. Amid the dim stillness of the forest, we moved slowly, careful not to scare off our quarry.

A gargling screech, as terrible as the cry of an injured child, penetrated the stillness. Uncle Jakob put his arm out to hold me back. Hardly daring to breathe, I peered into the forest canopy, imagining some kind of monster about to pounce. Rifle raised to his shoulder, Uncle Jakob stalked ahead. Another screech, and I saw the bird, long-necked and tall, standing at the edge of a ravine. My uncle's rifle cracked. It whipped its head around, then flopped to the ground.

"Turkey," Uncle Jakob said as we walked toward the lifeless bird. "Good thing it didn't see us first. They run like lightning."

As our day in the woods ended, we turned homeward. By the time the horses were prancing briskly down the Cedar Glen hill, the sun had edged toward Lake Erie. It was an unusually calm evening, the water flat and still as sheet iron.

"Uncle, whatever happened to Johannes, your brother who I never met?" I asked. Uncle Jakob and I hadn't talked about my argument with Rapparlie and I wished to know whose side he took. "Rapparlie told my parents in a letter that Johannes had *melancholia,* that his blood rebelled within him. But I thought perhaps his blood rebelled against Rapparlie. I could understand it, if it had."

Uncle Jakob let out a sudden breath, as if I had dealt him a blow. "If only I knew. My brother Johannes didn't take to city life. I urged him to get a farm for himself, but he stayed in town because of a *Fräulein.* When she married another, his sadness got very large indeed, so even in the daytime he didn't rise from his bed. Rapparlie did give him some trouble and called him an idler. He lived with me and your grandparents in House Place then. One day, Johannes came downstairs from his room in his best clothes and said he was making his last journey. None of us knew what that meant. Someone said they saw him take the Columbus stagecoach. I quit my job at the shipyard soon after, and every place I traveled, I asked after him but never learned his fate. I imagine he found a farm somewhere. I like to believe it, anyway. But it wasn't Rapparlie who drove him away. That all happened in the time before Rapparlie lost his foot."

"I'm sorry, Uncle."

"I'm sorry too, nephew. Especially sorry I wasn't around to patch things up with Rapparlie, so he didn't deal so harshly with you. Rapparlie has suffered much, more than we can know, but he shouldn't take it out on you. You've behaved well, what any man would do. In fact, I had a reason for taking you hunting today, to say that now I'm back, you're welcome to move in with me."

I thanked Uncle Jakob, but declined, adding that I was comfortable for now.

He chortled. "*Doch*, I suspected as much. My nest is not filled with such pretty birds as on Henry Street."

"Please don't tease me." The mere hint of my attachment set my head spinning. "I admit, the beauty of the Crolly daughters is soothing to male eyes. But my intentions are honorable. The Crollys are fine people. Herr Crolly has treated me like his own son."

Indeed, I had no idea of leaving their home. With each passing day, my passion for Elizabeth Crolly increased. The sculptured lines of her face, her deft, capable hands, the alluring silk sheen of her hair, beguiled me to heartsick distraction. I could not have been a bigger fool if I'd knelt down at her button-shoed feet and sang "*Ich liebe dich so inniglich*" every morning and night. Elizabeth gave me no encouragement, but I was convinced she felt a regard for me. Such a strange, powerful thing, this love between a man and a woman. The messages race between us, invisible but charged, like an electric current over telegraph wires. Of course, I couldn't declare my love openly. I had next to nothing to offer her as a suitor. All of these thoughts, I did not confess to Uncle Jakob.

"I have been meaning to ask," I said instead, "what it was like when you first came here, when the Indians lived in Ohio?"

Uncle Jakob peered at the road through the moss-dim light. "The Wyandots and Senecas? They weren't a bad sort. I became friends with one or two."

"Where was their village, the one where you bought our vests?"

"There was no village, not by 1840. The Indians would come to the Central Market and sit on their blankets to sell their goods. I tried to talk to an Indian once. He was selling fish, and I asked him in sign language where he'd caught it. That very night he came knocking on my door at House Place. He had two spears in his hands. Scared the old people, your grandparents, half to death. We pointed and gestured, until I came to figure out that he wanted to take me fishing. We went down the Cuyahoga a ways. In the light of a torch, the fish swam right up to our feet. We could stand on the shore and spear their silver bodies with hardly any trouble at all."

I envied my uncle's luck, arriving in America in that earlier time. These days, we didn't fish in the Cuyahoga River. The sewage from the city befouled it. Several years ago, Cleveland had started drawing its drinking water from deep in Lake Erie, so its taste and clarity was much improved.

"What of the many towns you've seen?" I asked. "Do they all have such growth and change as Cleveland?"

"Buffalo is a pretty place. And Cincinnati. St. Louis." I could see the memories flitting in the movement of Uncle Jakob's eyes. "Any of them would do. They all change as fast, or almost. You live now at the center of things, nephew. You must get used to the faster pace."

I nodded. "Cleveland seems to me especially good for a wagon business. Most of the time, we don't even harness the dray. A wheelbarrow is enough to lug supplies from the docks."

"So this is still your dream? To establish a shop of your own?"

"I must save money for many years yet, but I hope one day it will be possible."

Uncle Jakob handed me the reins, took off his broad-brimmed hat and ran his fingers through his hair. "I don't understand it. Your Uncle Johann was set on this, too. As you see for yourself, Johann has chained his life to a business and a family, and it has not made him a happy man. We live in America, nephew. Don't you realize what this means? You are free to travel wherever you want, to work in any profession. Blacksmiths are needed everywhere. *Doch*, don't miss out in this life. Let me convince you there is another way. Go to any place in this grand country. Work there for a time. Spend every free moment exploring the countryside for its canyons and creeks and mountain tops. When you have seen it all, or grow tired of the people, move on. The next place is no doubt more beautiful than the last. It's not a bad way to see the world."

"Don't you long for a wife and family?"

Uncle Jakob leaned an elbow on his knee and gestured toward the houses we now glided past. "There are women everywhere. I haven't felt the lack. Nor, come to think of it, have you."

I didn't like to think of that incident and said as much. "I have lived up to my word. I never bothered Jean Cody again. I don't even go down her street."

"In any case, it seems your heart has strayed to a *Fräulein* who will offer the cage you desire."

No answer leapt to my tongue, but thankfully none was required, as we just then pulled to a stop at the gate on Henry Street, where flowers bloomed up the paving stone path and the tidy well-kept house emanated comfort and caring. Uncle Jakob jumped from the chaise and carried our turkey up the path and through the door, proudly delivering it to Frau Crolly for tomorrow's dinner.

The women served us a late supper of cold meats and dried apples from the cellar, and as we ate, the whole family gathered around to listen to Uncle Jakob's tales of the *Goldmenschen* in California and his many adventures on the long journey home.

# Chapter 38

## Cleveland, Ohio 1862

DURING THE REST OF THAT year and into the next, in the corner of the Hoffmann wagon yard, my phaeton gradually neared completion. I learned to make the gearing—the wheels, axles and suspension. I fashioned hubs of wood under the wheelwright's instruction and learned to shape the spokes to fit the felloes. I already had learned the procedure for tiring at Rapparlie's, the hammer blow on the iron that rang bright and true if the fitting was tight, or sounded a dull thud if it was not. I already knew how to iron the axles and undercarriage. Next I learned from the master woodworker how to properly plane boards for the body panels, to cut the rabbets for the joinery, and carve dado joints to a perfect fit.

It was a bad time financially because the Union government had very large debts and so issued paper money of little value. Many people had unpaid bills, and still others put off buying wagons for the foreseeable future. I used the extra time to work on my buggy. By the spring of 1862, it stood assembled and ready for painting. In the painting department, I worked under a master, Herr Bloyd, mixing colors with the stone and muller. I chose a bright green, as close to the Liedmeister bandwagon as my eye remembered it. My line wavered with the striping pencil, so Herr Bloyd did this detailing, claiming true expertise would come only after much practice. In the trimming department, I sewed the dash, head liner, and seat cushions.

In these various departments, I learned all aspects of the business. But the master carriage-maker must know more. His work is like conducting an orchestra, knowing the exact timing for a linseed oil bath for a pair of wheels, the amount of time it takes paint to dry on a business wagon. The art of wagon-making played out like music, each part like notes falling in succession in a measured rhythm—the frame, the gearing, the wheels, the paint, the upholstery. Any wrong note disrupted the flow. With each passing day, I became more drawn in by the artistry of my chosen profession.

BY 1862, WITH NO END in sight for the War Between the States, the gandy dancers spiked down miles of new railroad to move Union troops, artillery, and supplies. Cleveland's iron foundries belched smoke day and night, disgorging iron rails and plate for the ships of war. Textile mills in Cleveland turned out thousands of blue Union uniforms.

We German-Americans had not worried so much at first about conscription, but by the end of August, after the second terrible battle at Bull Run, a gloom settled over us. Could the North be losing? The Union kept retreating, General Lee advancing. The danger didn't dissuade us, however, only made us more determined. From the Cleveland Singing Society, so many Germans enlisted, including our new director Herr Quedenfeld, that we no longer had a choir. The physical fitness *Turnverein* members joined up in such numbers that they practically formed their own regiment. This club also stopped meeting.

As for me, I grew less, not more, eager to enlist, intent on learning wagon-making, unwilling to part from Elizabeth Crolly. As to the latter, I did nothing to reveal my devotion. It felt selfish during such warlike times to fall in love, to woo and marry, when the boiling of black dye pots filled the air with a mournful aroma. Many families grieved over sons and fathers killed in battle.

The Handrichs, too, lost one of our own, but not in the fighting. One evening, I opened the Henry Street door to Uncle Jakob, whose grim expression gave me a terrible foreboding.

"Your Aunt Margaretha has died," he said. "She fell in the street. At first Georg thought she had tripped over something, but she was gone by the time he lifted her from the ground. The doctor says it was a disease of the heart."

Speechless with sorrow, I staggered back to let him in. Uncle Jakob had come to fetch Frau Crolly, to bring her to the Scheuermanns to help Aunt Katharina wash and lay out the body.

My beautiful Aunt Margaretha, with her ready laugh, her kind, good-spirited manner in welcoming me to this country. How could she leave this life without warning?

All the next day I did not work. Instead, I walked over in my Sunday clothes to Ohio City to gather with relatives and friends in the Scheuermann parlor. Aunt Katharina had laid her sister out in her best black silk, and Aunt Margaretha's face appeared pale blue and mottled beneath the black shroud. Aunt Katharina's eyes were red and raw with weeping as she stood by the casket to receive visitors.

The pastor of the *Zum Schifflein Christi* Church, the new Rev. Schmidt, was one of the first to pay his respects.

"It must be a comfort to us," he said, "to know and remember that what God does is well done."

Aunt Katharina let out a moan and her shoulders shook with sobbing. I was troubled to see her so distraught. As soon as the minister moved on, I went to comfort her.

"I am so sorry, Aunt," I said.

She looked at me with moist eyes and for a moment, Mütterchen stood before me. The vision passed as Aunt Katharina gripped my hands and held them tight. I waited, cloaked in sadness, while she composed herself.

"Nephew, we're moving to Toledo before the winter," she said, her red-rimmed eyes searching mine. Aunt Katharina had grown grayer in these few months since I'd seen her last. "Please don't think harshly of us. I've always been glad you came to America, so I should know the son of my sister Elisabetha."

"God go with you," I said.

"*Tch*, it will be good to begin again. There are too many ghosts in Cleveland."

My aunt folded me in a hug, from which I eased away so as not to break down weeping myself. I sat in the chair by the wall clock, its pendulum weirdly immobile in respectful observance of the dead. I missed Aunt Margaretha terribly and felt a depth of sorrow for Aunt Katharina. So many people I'd never seen before came to tell my aunt how stricken they were by this grand lady's passing. The majority were pioneer Germans who'd settled in Cleveland in its earliest years.

As the minutes turned to hours and people kept trailing through, I realized Uncle Georg was no longer in the room. Guessing where he might have gone, I descended to the cellar to find him and Uncle Jakob sitting in scuffed wooden chairs by the wine barrel, the room dense with pipe smoke.

"I'm truly sorry, Uncle Georg," I said, sitting down on a child's sled to accept a glass of wine from Uncle Jakob.

The machinist's round face wrenched in torment. "She said her heart fluttered like a bird's wings. I didn't think to go to the doctor..."

Uncle Jakob sat forward and placed a large, scarred hand on his brother-in-law's knee. "Now Georg, there was nothing you could have done."

To see Aunt Margaretha lying in her coffin overwhelmed me with a longing to see Mütterchen. In the ensuing days, I felt an urgency to return to Freinsheim, and mentally calculated my worth to see if it was a journey I could afford. I added up what I'd saved of my freedom dues and wages during these recent months, a sum of nearly $110 dollars. But it was a time of war, when transatlantic journeys had all but ceased, and I didn't see how I could make the trip.

One Saturday evening, not long after we lost Aunt Margaretha, my spirits were quite low as I arrived back at Henry Street, only to find a brand new upright piano in one corner of the parlor. I nearly swooned at the sight. Elizabeth sat on the bench, plunking out a tune on its ivory keys. Mary perched on the edge of her caned parlor chair as if she might erupt out of it and push her sister off for a turn.

"God in heaven, what is this?"

Elizabeth played a jarring chord and spun around with a delighted smile. "Isn't it beautiful? Dreher's delivered it this afternoon! Papa has made so much money this year he says we can afford it."

Herr Crolly came in from his study. "What do you think, daughter? Will you play us a hymn?"

Elizabeth pouted. "I've not had time to practice."

"I'll try it," Mary said, but Elizabeth didn't yield her place.

I went over to admire the piano box, the high-gloss sheen and carvings in the walnut, the elegantly scrolled legs.

"Is it the war?" I asked Herr Crolly. "Did you get a large contract with the government?"

"*Nä nä*, it's these oil refineries needing the barrels. The Pennsylvania coopers can't keep up, so orders come all the way to us in Cleveland. I have hired three new workers this month and still, we can't meet demand."

FROM THEN ON AT THE Crollys, we had music to console us, even in the midst of such heavy mourning and loss. Elizabeth practiced every night for hours until her parents insisted she go to bed and give us some peace. From the beginning, her playing held delicacy and sentiment—I recognized in her an artist's soul. Before long we gathered around Sunday afternoons to sing the German hymns, "Whither go, when storms blow?" and other *Kirchenlieder* that brought small comfort in these war-like times.

After Aunt Margaretha died, I tore myself away from the Crolly home more often to go to Ohio City. There I played the American game called base ball in the yard with the Scheuermann boys or, on afternoons when it rained, received English lessons. With Uncle Georg, I'd drink one or two glasses of Rhine wine, a practice not indulged on Sundays at the Crollys.

One such afternoon, as I set out for a visit, I was walking along Franklin Circle when Charles Rauch drove up beside me in his buggy and trotter.

"Harm," he called, reining to a stop, "join me for a ride."

I hadn't shared my plans with the Scheuermanns, so I climbed up on the narrow buggy seat. Rauch snapped the horse into a fast trot, so I had to hold my hat to keep it from blowing off my head.

"I hear you are living at the Crolly home," he said.

"Yes I am," I said, seizing my chance to gloat. "But your Eva no longer lives there. She has married Edward Kemp."

"Eva? Is that why you think I ask? Don't trouble yourself. She wasn't the girl for me. I merely wonder about the family. Herr Crolly strikes me as a humorless sort, but he does well in business, *oder*?"

"I'm proud to be living in their home," I said, bristling at his criticism. In truth, I hoped to model my life after Herr Crolly's. "The Crolly name is a good one. They may not circulate among the highest society, but don't let that fool you. Through rightful behavior and economy, the Crollys have built up a good wealth."

Rauch gave me an amused glance. "There is truth in what you say, Harm. I've had my eye on the second daughter, Elizabeth, for some time. Put in a word for me, will you?"

I sat very still. "I'm a boarder in the home and claim no other influence."

Rauch laughed. "*Doch*, at least be a friend and don't give me away. One of these Sundays, you'll see me at the Crolly door."

It took everything in my power not to jump from the carriage and sprint as fast as I could back to Henry Street, to erect a tall iron fence around the property. I prayed to God that Elizabeth might possess enough common sense not to fall for this braggart and his wealth.

Charles Rauch turned his buggy down Pearl Road, and before I knew it, parked before the Rauch & Company carriage manufactory. The main building was of red brick, three-stories high, taking up the better part of the block. I absorbed the length and breadth of my rival's establishment and felt despondent indeed. Charles Rauch led me into the gleaming repository, a show room for finished vehicles. At the sight of the splendid victorias and broughams, I felt bile rise in the back of my throat.

"Did you hear? My father enlisted with the Union Army," Rauch said. "He does the horseshoeing and wagon repair. He has joined the army to spare me, and promises to keep far from the field of battle so I don't need to fear for his welfare. These days I'm the proprietor, seen by the government as the one on whom this business relies. That way, I don't face the draft."

Charles seated himself before a polished roll-top desk and gestured with his chin to the room full of shiny carriages, buggies, and wagons.

"Go ahead, have a look around," he said. "You may just approve and want to come work for me after all. With so many going off to war, I'm always shorthanded."

Now I understood the reason for his bringing me here. Rauch wished to show off, hoping I might report his success to the Crollys. I was not about to feed his vanity any further and had just opened my mouth to beg my leave when my eye settled on a covered business wagon. "I haven't seen any of those on Cleveland's streets," I said, my voice echoing in the hollow space as I strolled across the wood floor for a closer look.

"You have good taste," Rauch said. "That's our newest design, to carry the large blocks of Lake Erie ice in the summers."

I examined the workmanship. The joinery was passable, but the iron scrollwork on the lamp brackets was asymmetrical. The same disproportion occurred on the lamp brackets of the cabriolet next to it. But the picture of a polar bear painted on both sides of the ice wagon was so realistic, it sent a cold shiver down my spine. There, my critical eye could find no fault.

"Who is your master painter?" I asked.

"*Ja, ja,* you leap to the heart of the matter. Herr Lehr, a portrait painter, came into our employ when photography ruined his business. A true artist, *oder*? Hoffmann can't have him."

"You're calling me an art thief?" I asked, careful to keep my voice jocular. I walked around the business wagon to the other side, where another buggy on display sported white stitching on the dash and folding top. I hadn't seen this style before. "How much do you ask for this one?"

"One hundred twenty-five dollars. Without the top, one hundred ten dollars." Rauch pushed back in his chair and, ever lord of his manor, rested his shoes on his desk.

I examined the buggy wheels. The mortise joints of the hubs were even and true.

"Did your factory make these hubs?"

Rauch brought his feet back to the floor and sat up straighter. "That's the beauty of it! We purchase not only the hubs, but also the wheels. To buy them ready-made is much more cost effective."

"There's a new wagon shop on Champlain Street," I said, "run by Herr Beach and Herr Butler. They have a contract to build ambulances for the army."

"Go work for them then," Rauch said with a shrug. "It's your loss."

At the superiority of his tone, I felt the back of my neck warm. Did Rauch feel sorry for me, believing I was such a failure I couldn't make it on my own? Had Rapparlie besmirched my reputation, spreading the word to other wagon-makers that I was a good-for-nothing? That Rauch kept trying to hire me now struck me as the gravest of insults.

"Factory work doesn't provide a living like the artisan crafts," I said. "There's nothing creative in operating a machine all the day. A man might as well be a machine himself. There's no art to it."

"The old ways hold all of us back. Harm, you must keep up with the times, or you drag everyone down."

"I don't see how it holds a man back to master an art, to keep the shops small and the carriages custom-made."

"*Doch*, go ahead, ruin your prospects to be rich keeping to the 'cut and try' artisan methods. You always were dedicated to worthless old things. It was pathetic on the Helvetia, how broken up you were about that pocket watch of yours." Rauch saw my look of surprise. "Of course I knew Wiener took it. But why should I stick my neck out for something like that? It was not so expensive and fine. Surely you understand, now that you have seen what luxuries we can afford in America."

The varnished floor of the repository shifted under my feet as if we were back on the ship. I could hardly comprehend what I was hearing.

"Christian Wiener took it? You saw this happen?" I asked, striding back across the room.

"Sure, I saw. But why cause a scandal over it? A watch of so little value couldn't make him look like a gentleman. More likely, he sold it to the first huckster he met."

I brought my face level to Charles Rauch's over his polished desktop.

"That is what separates us once and for all," I said, enunciating each syllable. "You don't see the intrinsic value in things, only the science and profit. You are as off kilter as the scrollwork of your lamp brackets."

Rauch's eyes widened as it dawned on him he had fired a cannonball through our acquaintance. He leaned back, lifting both hands. "I'm sorry. I thought you knew that manure-shoveler stole your pocket watch. Look, I'm only trying to help. You'll never get anywhere if you stick to the ways of the Old Country."

"I will remember this about you," I said. "Don't worry on my account. I'll make my own way."

I turned on my heel and left. I stalked back across the river, too foul a mood now to visit Uncle Georg. I found it hard to believe Charles Rauch felt such pity for me. What was he trying to prove? That he could hammer me, bend me, twist me this way and that to his own liking? Did he somehow guess my love for Elizabeth, now that he had set his sights on her? I had come across the Atlantic, yet faced the same plight, the same helplessness against those who lorded themselves above me.

My emotions in disarray, I wandered until my steps carried me to House Place. Uncle Jakob was at home. He said he was on his way out, but even so, he welcomed me with Palatine hospitality. We sat together over a glass of wine. Then he watched me drink another glass, and another. He asked what was wrong, but I couldn't find the words. He accused me of being a dullard and very poor company. Still, I had little to say and didn't budge from my chair. With a grunt, Uncle Jakob stood, put on his hat, and said he was going out to see Hannah Wolff, a Catholic woman he'd been visiting of late. I mumbled that I didn't wish to leave, so he left me sitting there alone.

I spent the night at House Place on the sofa, so sodden with wine I didn't hear my uncle return.

# Chapter 39

———

As September arrived, I lived as if in the middle of a railroad tracks, knowing that a train could come around the bend any moment to flatten me, that Rauch might come calling any moment at the Crolly door. To add to this predicament, my five year waiting period had concluded in July, making me eligible to become a U.S. citizen. Eligible for conscription.

With Herr Crolly, I had long discussions regarding the war. It was his belief that war didn't solve conflicts but gave in to human conceit, that it was a betrayal of our Christian beliefs. I knew my upbringing in this regard, that killing was forbidden in the Ten Commandments. My parents would not approve of me joining the military, after all they had sacrificed to help me leave the Palatinate. It would make no sense to them, that they'd spared me military duty for Bavaria, only to see me serve the Union.

So many Clevelanders, some known to me, had been wounded or killed in battle. Herr Quedenfeld of the Cleveland Singing Society died at Cedar Mountain. Fred Fry had gone missing at the Battle of Perryville. Each day, through the door of the Hoffmann smithy, I watched Frau Fry plod up Michigan Street, her mouth set in a determined line, to the post office to see if word had come about her son.

In the saloons and on the job, we Germans grumbled a good deal about the lack of progress in the war, especially since Lincoln was not fighting for the abolition of slavery, but only to preserve the Union. Most Germans wanted abolition, although some worried that an end to slavery would mean Negroes heading north looking for work, threatening our jobs.

A Depot Hospital for the returning wounded was erected alongside the lakeshore train station. Wounded soldiers were unloaded there every day, a constant reminder of Lincoln's failing to bring a swift end to this conflict and so contain its cost.

As fewer men enlisted, the federal government made a new law to entice us. Any immigrant serving in the army could reduce his five year residency requirement for naturalization to one year. This law didn't matter much to me, but my blacksmith friend Fred Schuster saw his opportunity and joined up. Every time another friend went off to Camp Taylor, I would ask myself, did my Christian convictions keep me from joining the fight, or was I merely a coward? I believed in our great Republican president but was not eager to die at a young age, before I had a chance for a wife and family.

News of the battles trickled in slowly, sometimes reported in the newspapers weeks after they'd occurred. Impatient for news, we turned to the commissioning house on River Street, the Clark, Gardner & Co. This establishment shipped goods from Ohio's interior to points north and east, and as a consequence, had installed their own telegraph office. The men of this company used the wire to receive news of battles. On large wall maps in their front room, they placed different colored markers to show the positions of Union and Confederate troops. Whenever one of us had reason to be on River Street, it became a habit to poke our heads inside the commissioning house and scrutinize the maps for the latest progress of our Union Army.

Singley didn't enlist, so I still saw him from time to time at Schlegel's. He had a small son now, another child on the way. We were in agreement—we had much at stake in our futures and could not bring ourselves to volunteer.

I made the decision to declare my citizenship regardless, to solemnly swear to protect and defend the Constitution and Government of the United States. I did so knowing I would be liable for military duty in order to impress Elizabeth Crolly, who was American born. It wasn't until I stood inside the courthouse swearing this oath that the finality of the act hammered me on the head: I was turning my back on my homeland forever. All those times I'd told myself I could so easily go home if I chose evaporated. Even if I went home, I wouldn't belong there.

As I left the courthouse, a terrible weight descended on me, and for the next several days I struggled against a sluggishness, as if I might take to my bed like Uncle Johannes and not rise in the morning to greet the day. To beat back this torpor, I concentrated on my work, and on lovely Elizabeth Crolly. Gradually the sharp ache of loss eased.

The only bright spot for me in those grim months was that Charles Rauch didn't darken our door. The thought was pushed to the back of my mind so that I wondered if he'd ever said such a thing or if I'd imagined it. I expended all my energy on my buggy and saved as much money as I could, anticipating the time when I could declare my love for Elizabeth.

In September, Uncle Jakob informed me that a man named William Gabriel had purchased the Rapparlie property at Michigan and Seneca. The family would move to Toledo before the snowfall. Uncle Jakob said he didn't intend to work for this new employer, so I begged him to come over to the Hoffmann shop and he agreed. Herr Hoffmann was pleased to have my uncle, as business had picked up with the new greenbacks, and supply wagons were being purchased by the Union Army as fast as we could build them.

By Christmas, in spite of a small success at Antietam, the war was a festering boil that wouldn't heal. At the West Side Christmas Concert and Ball, Charles Rauch was in attendance, his appearance completely altered.

"What's happened?" I asked him by way of greeting. Like many other men, he had shaved his beard so it formed a rust-colored wreath under his chin in imitation of Abraham Lincoln. His face beneath it was chalky and thin.

"Didn't you hear? My father was killed in battle at Antietam."

"I'm so sorry," I said, thinking of these terrible times, how many were losing fathers, young and old. Elizabeth reached out from where she stood beside me to put a gloved hand on Rauch's arm.

"I am so sorry for your loss," she said. "I pray that your father did not suffer?"

"I don't know." Rauch shook his head as if to clear it of a dense fog. "No one who was there has come back to tell me what happened."

Elizabeth listened with deep sympathy, and before I knew it, the two of them had wandered off, arm in arm, for a turn around the edge of the room. Surely, I told myself, Elizabeth was merely being kind? But the lurking dread came again, and my deep resentment over the pocket watch festered, ruining the rest of my evening.

# Chapter 40

## Cleveland, Ohio 1863

I T WAS A SUNDAY AFTERNOON just after the New Year. Elizabeth, Mary and I were singing at the piano when the dim sound of sleigh bells could be heard, followed by a knock at the front door.

"*Guten Tag*, Frau Crolly," Charles Rauch greeted the woman of the house. "I wonder if I might visit your daughter Elizabeth?"

Frau Crolly determined the caller's name, then let Rauch in. Blushing, Elizabeth went over to help him remove his heavy woolen greatcoat, hanging it on the coat rack with his fur-lined hat. Politeness dictated I should leave the room, but I couldn't bring myself to go. Perhaps Elizabeth wouldn't encourage him, and that would be the end of it.

Elizabeth sat back down on the edge of the sofa and picked up her tatting needles. Charles Rauch took a seat in the easy chair by the crackling hearth fire. Mary and I sat side by side on the piano bench. Frau Crolly settled into her rocking chair and examined Charles Rauch with close-set eyes.

"Do you attend church, young man?" she asked.

Charles Rauch glanced over at me, as if for assistance, but I let him drip like the snow melting off his coat.

"I attend the Zion Church," he said, turning back to Frau Crolly.

"There is much straying from the Holy Scriptures these days. It is time to gather in the flock. My husband and the Reverend Benzing even now make progress in this regard."

"*Wie bitte*?" Rauch looked to Elizabeth this time.

"Mama, leave him alone. He has said he attends the Lutheran church. That should be enough. *Entschuldigung*, Charles. Even now, in this deep snow, my father is out with Reverend Benzing visiting Reformed families about starting a new congregation. The subject rests heavily on my mother's mind."

"*Doch,* I understand," Charles Rauch said. "The Reformed Church of Pastor Rütenik is not to your liking?"

Frau Crolly sniffled into her handkerchief. "Herr Crolly was fond of Father Kaufholz."

Of late, there had been more squabbling in the churches. When Pastor Rütenik had come, the Crollys weren't the only ones to fall away. After a prolonged silence, Rauch sighed and placed a hand on each knee.

"I thought perhaps," he said to Elizabeth, "you might like to go for a sleigh ride to Rocky River? The snow clings to the tree branches in such a picturesque way, and the sun is making its presence felt from time to time."

Elizabeth's eyes lit up. "I'd love an outing. Mother, may I go?"

At the eagerness in her voice, my stomach felt as heavy as a wheelbarrow load of pig iron. I rose and went to the kitchen, from where I heard the voices of farewell, the banging of the door as Rauch and Elizabeth went out together, the sleigh bells receding up the street.

What girl would not be swayed by the wealth and status of a man like Rauch? He had inherited his father's business and no doubt owned several horses and carriages in addition to the sleigh. It would be several years before I could be a serious rival to such a man, if ever. Just as Oberholz had stolen away my Anna Marie, I was destined to lose Elizabeth Crolly.

From then on, most Sundays Charles Rauch arrived to sit in the parlor while Elizabeth and Mary sewed or played the piano. I made it a habit to be absent, to help Herr Crolly split logs for the fire or make repairs at his woodworking bench.

"Michael, why don't you stay with us?" Elizabeth asked at the supper table after the third visit. "Charles Rauch is also your friend. I'm sure he comes to see you, too."

"I don't much like to sit around," I said, avoiding her gaze.

She asked several more times in the next weeks, but what could I tell her? My tale of woe about the pocket watch would reflect just as poorly on me, as I continued to hold a grudge against Rauch in such a pathetic, unchristian manner. Yet I couldn't pretend politeness to this man, who mocked me at every turn. I blamed Rauch as if he had stolen my treasure himself. And now he'd come to steal my true love. Doggedly, I stayed away, and Elizabeth stopped asking why.

When the snow melted and spring flowers bloomed, Rauch began pulling up to the gate in his elegant chocolate-brown buggy drawn by his white-footed chestnut trotter. Each time Elizabeth headed off with this wagon-shop owner for a ride, I felt my unworthiness, as unwanted as the excess slag skimmed from molten iron.

It got so that every Sunday, I'd step out immediately after the noon dinner for long rambles, seeking solace in nature. I no longer visited Kingsbury Run for hikes. By 1863, my old haunt had been drastically transformed, the stacks of red brick from Herr Hoppensack's brickyard replaced by cylindrical oil refineries erupting up the slopes like pox on a sailor's back. Uncle Jakob had been right. The Titusville oil was as sought-after as gold. Due to the war with the South, we'd lost our access to camphene, so new kerosene illuminant gained in importance. The air at Kingsbury Run scalded the nose and eyes like burnt rye bread. In order to take my nature walks, I had to ride the new streetcar out to Nine Mile Creek station in Collamer. There the vineyard rows were being staked, and the landscape reminded me achingly of home.

In general, my happiness at the Crollys dimmed considerably. Even when Rauch was not present, I kept my distance from Elizabeth, her beauty more tantalizing each day as I found myself unable to temper my desire.

"What's wrong with you, Michael?" she would ask. "Do you worry over the war?"

"I think of my parents and my brother Philipp. It's been so long since I saw them," I'd answer, dissembling.

There were also sharp splinters of truth in my words. Elizabeth knew, as I did, that I was no longer permitted to leave this country. In the first part of 1863, President Lincoln had ordered a conscription of men ages twenty to forty-five. Such a necessity harkened back to the days of kings and prince-electors in the Old Country, and it troubled us Germans, I can tell you.

"Won't you sit beside me and sing?" Elizabeth said in her kind way. "I'm sure it will lift your spirits."

"I'll listen to you play," I said, and waited until she was lost in the music before rising to go out.

Of course, I couldn't tell Elizabeth what was wrong. Who was I to destroy her innocent happiness with my heavy gloom? I tried to ignore my feelings of love, to forget I'd ever thought of her in this way. In moments of deepest torment, I considered wildly how I might declare my love while I still had a chance. But I was older, more cynical. I found I could no longer act on such romantic impulses as I once had.

Instead, fighting the world-weary *Weltschmerz* always within me, I threw myself into my work. When a lull came at the forge, I'd experiment on bits of scrap metal. Steel was becoming more prevalent in those days due to Bessemer converters, but was not yet in common use. I saw its potential, but missed the grain and ductility wrought iron offered. Thinking I might one day assemble an ornamental gate for the Crollys' paving stone path I practiced scrolling wrought iron into elegant leaf decorations. I crafted graceful hat and apron hooks for the kitchen, such humble offerings to the household bringing me a small satisfaction.

That autumn, from occasional whisperings and glances between Mary and Elizabeth, I sensed that Elizabeth's courtship with Charles Rauch had moved forward. It was on an Indian summer Sunday in mid-October, the air rich with acrid-scented oak leaves, that I happened to step outside the Crolly home just as Rauch halted his buggy at the fence. His rust-colored beard matched his horse's leather collar. His dark green topcoat flashed handsomely against his brown-painted carriage.

"Harm," he greeted me, swinging down from the driver's seat and hitching the reins to the gate post. "Beautiful day for a ride, *oder*?"

I snorted. "I'm sure you aren't here to invite me."

Rauch guffawed and bounded up the porch steps while I kicked and rustled off down the leaf-strewn path. In truth, I should have been in as good a humor as Rauch, since a gleaming new buggy, built by my own hands, now stood finished in the Hoffmann wagon yard. All my spindle-wheeled phaeton required was a horse and driver to ride it out of the yard. That very afternoon, I'd hoped to rent a horse from the livery for a hunting trip with Uncle Jakob. But my uncle had gone on a ride instead to Chagrin Falls, escorting the freckle-faced Hannah Wolff.

As I crossed Euclid, a street popular with the Yankee gentlemen for racing one another in their road wagons, a horse and buggy charged upon me from behind, taking the corner in a swirl of leaves and grit. Dashing for my life, I spun around and saw Charles Rauch high up on the open seat. Next to him, Elizabeth sat gripping the folding top with one hand, her other clamped on her hat, ribbons flying. The turn was so sharp she nearly tumbled out of the buggy.

At the sight, a sense of outrage roared within me. What business did Charles Rauch have, driving so hard? He had raced the horse so fast he had not even noticed me in the road. What kind of coward was I, to let Elizabeth suffer such a lack of consideration? I lived in the land of liberty and was now a smith in my own right, with the power to call the strikes as I saw fit. Why did I still live like a peasant ruled by lords?

As I walked on, I couldn't shake the memory of Elizabeth's pale frightened face as she clung to that buggy seat. I decided to forego the streetcar, heading instead for Lake Erie's shale cliffs, where I stood staring out over waters burnished by the sun to a deep green hue, endlessly shifting in unpredictable swells. It struck me how wrong Rauch was for Elizabeth, his reckless confidence a stark contrast to her gentle, sensible manner. I would not treat her so carelessly. I would extend to her the regard she deserved. Perhaps I couldn't offer such wealth, but I'd be a decent husband and work hard so she would not starve. In fact, that week Hoffmann had praised my phaeton and wanted to begin building more of the same style. He told me I had the choice of keeping this buggy for myself or selling it at a profit. Either way, I was now a man of modest means, poised to build a reputation as a wagon-maker as I had always dreamed.

With a rush of dismay, I saw my stupidity. Here I had my own buggy at my disposal, and what had I thought to do with it? Take it for a hunting outing with Uncle Jakob, like an old bachelor man who couldn't get a girl. Did I have no imagination at all? Elizabeth Crolly had been right to ask what was wrong with me. It was time I stood up for myself.

Stubborn resolve kindled within me. By the end of a long walk along the lakeshore, I had become determined to no longer stand passively aside. Back at Henry Street, all was quiet in the parlor save for the staid ticking of the grandfather clock. Realizing it was already the supper hour, I entered the kitchen and felt a rush of relief to find Elizabeth seated at the table.

"How was your ride today?" I asked her, taking my place.

Elizabeth looked up in surprise. "Oh, it was satisfactory. I think it was the last for the season, as this fine weather will surely not hold."

I held her gaze, thinking of the times I'd seen her with Charles Rauch. How could she love a man who drove too fast and bragged so often? I should have stayed around more, I realized, the better to gauge the affection between them. Elizabeth didn't look down, observing me with her frank, open eyes, one eyebrow raised. Did Elizabeth Crolly care for me, after all? Could it be possible?

For the entirety of that long Sunday evening, I stared at the pages of a book but didn't read a single word. A hope lifted my mind to wild imaginings, to desperate impulses, so I could barely breathe.

The next morning, still bent on my new sense of purpose, I left the house early for the smithy with but one thought in mind: to declare my love for Elizabeth Crolly before it was too late. I had to find out if she loved me, or live the rest of my life as a good-for-nothing coward.

When I arrived at my anvil, several jobs awaited my attention, but I set to work instead on two bars of wrought iron I'd been saving amid the clutter of my workbench. The bars extended as long as my forearm and were an inch square all around. I held the first in my hand, weighing it for balance and heft, seeing inside it the graceful candlestick I aimed to create. I heated the center of this piece to a glowing yellow and chiseled four deep incisions, one on each side. After several heats, the incisions began to separate. I repeated the process with the second bar until it matched the first. Next I heated the center metal one last time to bright lemon yellow, clamped the unheated end in the vise and gripped the other end with the wrench, rotating and leaning my weight in one swift motion, twisting the metal into a bulbous, symmetrical cage. I did the same with the other piece, then heated and reshaped each cage until it lined up exactly with the other, chamfering the edges to final softness with my wooden mallet. I cut the pieces to equal height, then drew the tips to fine, spiked points and attached the drip rings.

As I was fashioning the bases in which I'd set the sticks upright, Uncle Jakob came over, hands on his hips.

"Where are the damned wear strips, nephew?" he asked.

I shrugged.

"The brace for the coach lantern?"

I shrugged again. With my tongs, I held up one still-hot candlestick, eyeing the length of it to be sure it was straight and true. "What do you think?" I asked Uncle Jakob. "It's made of iron, not copper or silver, but the cage is well formed, *oder*?"

"For the love of God."

I looked up at my uncle expecting to see anger but saw a spark of amusement in his eyes. His good humor bolstered my courage.

"Today, I make candlesticks," I said, swallowing down a lump in my throat. Would Elizabeth have me?

Uncle Jakob studied me as if doubting my sanity, then trudged back to his anvil. It was only five o'clock, too early to end the day, but I raked out my forge fire in any case. I oiled and polished the candlesticks to a fine sheen, wrapped them in a scrap of canvas, and departed for home.

ON HENRY STREET, I ENTERED the kitchen and helped myself to the kettle of warm water always at the ready on the stove. Frau Crolly made no comment as I carried it to my bedroom. With the soap and warm water, I scrubbed myself from head to toe, then donned my best starched white shirt and black woolen pants. Over this, I added my waistcoat and, around my shirt collar, tied on a silk tie.

While Mary and Elizabeth helped their mother prepare dinner in the kitchen, I snuck a piece of pink ribbon from the sewing scraps and returned upstairs to tie a clumsy bow around the canvas-wrapped candlesticks. In the parlor, I hid my gift beneath the sofa leg. All the while, I was making sums in my head, one hundred dollars saved from my freedom dues, plus two years of saved wages, and a new buggy to prove my mastery as a wagon maker. One-hundred-and-fifty dollars and a living. Not enough to build a house or start a business. But enough, I hoped, to make me an acceptable suitor.

It was nearly the supper hour as I stood at the door of Herr Crolly's study, where each evening he pored over his business ledgers. The room smelled of leather and bootblack.

"May I speak with you?" I asked.

Herr Crolly glanced up and with a look of puzzlement, took in my Sunday clothes.

"Sit down, sit down," he said, as if my question had finally reached his ears.

I sat, and a long silence stretched between us. All day I'd been turning over elegant phrases in my mind, but now my wits left me entirely. Herr Crolly's eyes dropped back down to his ledgers. I had to speak or lose her forever.

"If you will give your blessing," I said in a rush, "I hope to ask Elizabeth for her hand in marriage."

Herr Crolly's eyes shot up again, his jaw dropping in surprise. Wordlessly, he reached for his pipe, tamped in fresh tobacco, lit the stubby bowl, and inhaled. In the close air of the room I felt faint. After a few thoughtful puffs, he sighed.

"You're diligent and hard-working, Michael. You've shown Frau Crolly and me courtesy and respect." He sat forward, propping one elbow on his desk. "But to be honest, I expected it would be Charles Rauch coming to see me to ask for my blessing. Does Elizabeth have any idea of your feelings for her?"

Herr Crolly's reserve, the doubtful frown on his face, came as a shock. Did he not like me so much after all? I cleared my throat.

"Herr Crolly, we both know I don't compare well to Charles Rauch. I haven't wanted to interfere with his attentions, nor, as a boarder in your home, did I want to show your daughters any disrespect. But I love Elizabeth. I must let her know this, before it's too late."

"Before Rauch declares his love, you mean?"

"I must know if she will have me."

"But how do you intend to provide for her?"

"You and Frau Crolly know as well as anyone that I'm in an uncertain place with my living. But I swear to support your daughter no matter what. God willing, I hope one day to save enough for a wagon shop of my own."

"Will you be going off to war?"

"I'm of like mind with you in this regard. War is an evil that brings much hardship and little gain. I'll not volunteer, but I can't promise I won't be called up for the draft."

Herr Crolly nodded, studying me. "And where will you live?"

I felt sweat gathering under my armpits and collar. "Of course, I have no home to offer," I said, convinced by his serious gaze that he didn't favor me. I stuttered ahead anyhow. "Elizabeth ... Elizabeth is still ... young, and will not want to leave her parents' home so soon. I was hoping ... I thought we might continue to live here. Herr Crolly, I love Elizabeth with all my heart, will be a devoted husband to her and dutiful son-in-law to you and Frau Crolly."

For several long minutes, I melted under Herr Crolly's stare.

"All right, young man," he said at last. "I am a Christian man, so material wealth is not of the utmost importance. I trust God will provide. And I feel already as if you are my son. Make your proposal and see if my daughter will have you. Indeed, I'm curious as to what her answer might be."

When Herr Crolly and I arrived for supper, we received strange looks from the women of the house.

"Is there a concert tonight?" Frau Crolly asked, eyeing my fine clothes.

"No, but perhaps I'll go out later," I said, looking at Elizabeth.

She kept her gaze on her plate. When I looked over at Mary, she burst out giggling.

"What's so funny?"

"You look dressed up to go a-courting."

"*Tch*, Mary," said Frau Crolly.

I do not know how it happened, that I sat all through the supper with this blessing of Herr Crolly on my mind. After we had eaten, Herr Crolly returned to his study, leaving the door ajar. Frau Crolly sat in her rocking chair by the fire, her Bible open in her lap. Elizabeth arranged herself on the sofa for a night of handwork, her fingers nimble as she tatted, the hook flashing in and out of the lace in a blur. Mary practiced a waltz on the piano. I chose a seat beside Elizabeth, feeling a lout beside her evenly stitched beauty.

For five years I had hammered at the forge, six days a week, this restless ache in my heart heated and reshaped, never finding its true form. Now I believed I'd found her, sitting before me in this parlor on Henry Street. I only regretted that my parents and brother did not know her, but perhaps, once this war came to an end, the two of us could travel to Freinsheim so they might behold her loveliness with their own eyes.

Did I dare hope she would return my love? A dizziness came over me and my mouth felt parched. I dearly wished the Crollys might think to serve a glass of Rhine wine at supper once in a while. I remembered the startled expression on Herr Crolly's face when I blurted out my purpose and resolved to introduce my proposal in a gentler way.

"You would love Freinsheim, the town of my birth," I said, pausing to clear the gravel in my throat. "You would understand me so much more if you visited there."

Elizabeth set her tatting needles in her lap and looked up, confusion pinching her brow. "You speak often of Freinsheim. It must be a very pretty place."

"It is! If only you could see it. My brother Philipp, he has a farmer's magic. I'm sure he has helped my father turn a profit with the Harm land. This is the best time of year. Once the war ends, we should go ourselves next autumn, to see the vineyards sparkle with a golden light, like a jar of honey set in the sun."

"My parents have sworn to me they'd never make such a journey again. It's over-bold of you to suggest I travel with you alone."

I faltered, a bead of sweat trickling down the back of my neck. "*Entschuldigung*, I have put the cart before the horse. I don't mean to offend you. What I mean is, I hope to introduce you to my family one day, as someone dearer to me than an acquaintance. I have asked your father, and now I ask you. Will you be my wife?"

Elizabeth's eyes startled wide. Frau Crolly looked up from her Bible. Mary stopped her playing, fingers hovering above the keys.

"I don't understand." Elizabeth looked to left and right. "I had no idea that... that you care for me."

"Elizabeth, I've been in such agony. I believed you would pledge your troth to Charles Rauch."

"The interest is on his part, not mine. Had you asked, I'd have told you as much."

Her tone was reproachful. I felt ashamed.

"Do you care for me?" I thought I might split wide open if I did not quickly get an answer.

Herr Crolly came to stand in the door of his study. Elizabeth looked to him, then to her mother, then down at her hands. My soul trembled, and I grasped for a way to ease her confusion. Remembering my gift, I reached under the sofa to retrieve it.

"Look, I've made this pair of candlesticks as a symbol of my love. I pledge to be a loyal and true husband, to care for you always." I handed the present to her and she nearly dropped it in her lap. I hadn't realized the candlesticks were so heavy as that. "Elizabeth, I've been saving my money and will sell my first buggy for more. If the war ends soon, we can travel together to the Old Country, so you can meet my parents and my brother. I want to show you Paris, France. It's such an amazing place with the art, sculptures, and gardens. I will protect you and care for you always."

Elizabeth gazed down at my present, untied the ribbon, and let the cloth fall away. She examined the candlesticks in her lap. Her mother reached out her hand, so Elizabeth passed one over to her. Then she turned her face to me, a slight smile lifting the corners of her mouth.

"You sound as if you plan to take me to your Freinsheim and hold me captive there, never to return."

At the mischievous sparkle in her eyes, my head swirled in a delirium of love. "Then you will come with me?"

She shook her head in bemusement. "I shouldn't want to leave my parents and my sisters for such a long time, to travel so far away."

Enchanted by her naïveté, I remembered Elizabeth was four years younger than me, just turned eighteen. In good time, I could convince her to travel. What mattered now was that she gazed on me with affection, a love I never dreamed possible.

"Elizabeth, will you marry me?" I asked again.

This time, she didn't hesitate. "Yes, Michael Harm. I will be your wife."

ON FRIDAY, OCTOBER 30, 1863, Elizabeth Crolly and I were married in the Crolly parlor, near the exact spot where I'd proposed to her just two weeks earlier. Uncle Jakob stood as my witness, and Eva Crolly Kemp stood for Elizabeth. The Rev. Benzing performed the ceremony. Uncle Georg came with his boys, and the Crollys and Kemps dressed in their finest clothes. Delicious foods—*Kuchen* and candies—were served on fine china, set out on a pristine lace tablecloth in the dining room. As Mary played hymns on the piano, Elizabeth descended the stairs in a dress she'd made herself, the beads and buttons and lace arranged to perfection, my angel from the heavens.

My Elizabeth was a fine young wife, of whom I was very proud. She had been sewing on her trousseau for many years, so that first night she wore a nighttime garment of purest white, delicate embroidery on the collars and sleeves. She would not come to my bed, and so I went in to hers, where even the pillow cases were edged with filet crochet. In our first nighttime coupling, Elizabeth did not show as eager a sexual desire as Jean Cody. I had to beg her to remove her bedclothes and be naked with me. She worried about the creaking of the bed, that her parents and sister might overhear us.

AFTER THAT FIRST NIGHT, I went early Saturday morning to the livery to see about a horse, a fine white trotter that I harnessed to my shiny green buggy. Elizabeth dressed in a new suit of traveling clothes. We rode out into the countryside to the farm acreage of Adam Höhn in Columbiana. I had sent a wire earlier in the week regarding our arrival, so Matthias was there from Akron to greet us. It was the weekend of the annual fall dance festival in the Höhn barn, with many old Freinsheimers in attendance. Matthias brought with him a *Fräulein* of his own, with whom Elizabeth became immediate friends. And so we enjoyed an evening of lighthearted fun, in the fresh softness of our newly consummated love.

Late Sunday evening, once we'd made the long drive back to the house on Henry Street, Elizabeth told me she would prefer to remain clothed for our lovemaking. I attempted again to give her pleasure, but she recoiled and wouldn't allow it. I didn't force her, acceding to her wishes, however arbitrary and childish they seemed, certain she would grow accustomed to me over time. Elizabeth's world was one of order, of cleanliness and propriety, which stood in contrast to my days of metal, rust, and fire.

In any event, Monday arrived, and the routine workdays resumed.

# Chapter 41

## Cleveland, Ohio 1864

During that first winter of married life, I rarely had time to be at home. The War Between the States floundered on with terrible battles and casualties, and at the shop, we cranked out drays, express and supply wagons from morning till night.

I returned at night seeking the loving embrace of my wife, but Elizabeth was not as passionate as I'd hoped. Thinking it might stir the sensual in her, I gave her Goethe's *Elective Affinities*. To my utmost surprise, she disapproved of Goethe's morals, preferring instead the sermons of Beecher.

As for poetry, she admired the English sonnets, especially those of the woman poet Elizabeth Barrett Browning:

> I love thee with a love I seemed to lose
> With my lost saints—I love thee with the breath,
> Smiles, tears, of all my life!—and, if God choose,
> I shall but love thee better after death.[5]

How Elizabeth reminded me of Mütterchen as she read out these lines.

Although I worked hard and long, we did enjoy moments of fun. On wintry Sundays, she and I went tobogganing with Singley and his family, a time when my bride's penchant for fun and teasing made me fall in love all over again. But the war cast a shadow over all.

"I saw your friend Fred Fry," Elizabeth said to me one night early in 1864.

She had begun to spend hours of each day at the new Soldiers' Home, tending to the sick and wounded.

"*Gott sei Dank*, he is alive! Do Herr and Frau Fry know he has returned?"

Elizabeth's eyes filled with tears. "They know. He was moved from the

Depot Hospital to the Soldiers' Home, and will stay there for some time."

"What happened to him?"

"He lost an arm, and a bit of his senses. They say it happened at the battle in Kentucky, at Perryville. He must have been clubbed hard in the head. He cannot speak."

I went to visit Fry the very next day, and indeed, what I witnessed at the Soldiers' Home—the beds lined with injured men, the atmosphere of misery and loss—tore at my soul. Fred's right arm, the arm he used for painting, had been amputated near the shoulder, so he appeared lopsided, like half a man. The old conspiratorial light came into his eyes when he saw me, but as I sat with him, a spittle of drool formed in the corner of his mouth till I couldn't resist using my handkerchief to dab it for him.

Sitting among these fallen soldiers, I felt overwhelmed by guilt. I'd declared my oath of allegiance to the Constitution but felt no inclination to fight this war. What was the true reason? In my heart, was I still a German? I wondered if these wounded soldiers felt a sense of belonging, a duty to their country, that as a German I was incapable of feeling. After that visit, each morning and night I made a fervent prayer for these men, and for an end to the terrible war.

IN 1864, WE FACED A new presidential election that held none of the Republican fervor of four years ago. The "Radical Republicans" objected to Lincoln's suspension of the writ of habeas corpus. To counter the Republican Party's "Union" Convention in Baltimore, Radical Republicans called their own convention one week earlier in Cleveland, where they nominated J.C. Fremont as their presidential candidate. German-Americans from Missouri came up and made impassioned speeches for their General Fremont, saying they strove to establish a true Republican Party that didn't pander to the interests of the war Democrats and the South. Our loyalties divided, Cleveland Germans struggled between our ideals for a government truly by the people, or sacrificing certain principles to remain unified, thereby keeping our incumbent president for the swiftest possible end to the killing. At this election, most of us still stood by Lincoln, especially once he took the stand to emancipate the slaves.

In the midst of the summer's heat and uncertainty, a telegram arrived bearing a new tragedy. Herr Hoffmann brought it to me as I ironed an axle, handing it over with a long face.

> TO: MICHAEL HARM
> MOTHER DIED MAY 14. FATHER TO SETTLE ALL FREINSHEIM
> ESTATE. COME HOME.
> PHILIPP HARM

Grief and regret showered down on me like hot cinders. Seven long years had passed since I saw Mütterchen. Why hadn't I gone home to Freinsheim with my freedom dues, in order to see Mütterchen one last time? Why had I rushed into marriage? My mother had never set eyes on my bride. I hadn't even found the time to write home about my marriage, as I hoped to bring Elizabeth to them one day in person as a surprise.

Herr Hoffmann put his arm around my shoulders, removed my leather apron, placed my bowler hat on my head, and guided me to the door.

"I am indeed sorry, son," he said. "Go home now and see your family. I'll not expect you back until Monday."

*Come home,* the telegram said. Perhaps I could finally do this. Even in wartime, I'd heard of exceptions being made if a family member died. I could apply to the government for a passport. A rush of hope ran through me. I'd go home and tell Elizabeth, and we would make immediate plans to travel. I hadn't forgotten the sympathy Elizabeth paid to Charles Rauch on the death of his father. Of course, she would show me the same consideration, even if it meant traveling far from her parents.

When I returned home with my sad news, and my plea that we must leave immediately, I was sorely disheartened by her response.

"Husband, I am sorry for your loss, but I will not go with you to Freinsheim," she said.

For the first time in our marriage, I wanted to shout at her, to reproach her for neglecting the housework to spend all her time at the Soldiers' Home, for refusing me in bed now for over two months. But of course I didn't, since Frau Crolly and Mary were nearby in the kitchen. In fact, it seemed as if Elizabeth and I never had a moment to ourselves. Hot with anger, I turned my back on my wife and stalked out of the house.

Outside, the heat of a June afternoon rode over me like a steam locomotive. Beneath the clank of factory machinery, the crunch of carriage wheels on macadam, the incessant pounding of construction hammers, I made out the low cooing of a Mourning Dove somewhere nearby. I hadn't seen my mother since I was fifteen years old. It seemed to me now I had abandoned her. My chest ached and my eyes flooded with tears.

Everything in my life felt suddenly wrong. Perhaps my leaving Freinsheim was not God's will, but my own vanity, my refusal to be a dutiful son. I had stepped into Philipp's rightful place, and since coming here, had made mistake after mistake, losing everything, causing hardship to my uncle, rushing into marriage. Perhaps I struck out on a melody never meant to be played. Now I had a wife who refused to obey me, who had not a care for my homeland or my family. Or for me.

In disconsolate grief, I roamed the streets, eventually finding myself at the docks on River Street, where the steamships belched their funnels of coal smoke, where the piers bustled with workers, cargo, and passengers. At the docks, a schedule of Lake Erie steamer lines was posted, the fares not so high.

It occurred to me that perhaps my wife was only afraid of what she didn't know. If she were to go for a lake voyage, she might see it was not so terrible. Perhaps then I might be able to convince her to make the longer trip to Europe. Matthias Höhn had told me of an Andrew Wehrle of Baden who'd started a vineyard on the Bass Islands, the best place on Lake Erie for growing grapes. Wehrle had made a cellar there, and a dance pavilion many Germans liked to visit. I also wished to see Detroit, a city praised for its pine lumber and thriving German community. Pleased to have come up with a solution, I purchased a passage for two to sail that same evening.

On my way home, I made a detour to House Place to deliver the news about the death of Mütterchen to Uncle Jakob. My uncle now worked as a smelter foreman at the Cuyahoga Steam Furnace Company and had not yet returned from work, so I left a note that he should visit me at the Crolly's that evening and went on my way, my steps enlivened by the prospect of a midnight sail.

When I returned home, Elizabeth stared with such dismay at the steamship tickets that I began to doubt the soundness of my plan.

"Haven't you heard of the Bass Islands, where people make a holiday to enjoy the vineyards?" I asked. "Matthias tells me it reminds him of Freinsheim. Once you see it, you'll also long to visit my homeland."

My wife looked up at me with a pale face, too pale, but she didn't argue. "As we leave tonight, I must go pack," she said, turning to go upstairs.

In that moment I felt a rush of pride, that at last my wife had learned to do my bidding. Perhaps I could also order her to come to Freinsheim with me, if it came to that. Exulting in my victory, I paid little heed to the disapproving looks of Frau Crolly. But my mother-in-law didn't berate me, perhaps in sympathy for my recent loss. Whatever the reason, I felt grateful to be moving forward, to be offering my wife her first experience with sailing so we could make more trips in the future.

When Uncle Jakob came to call, I poured us both glasses of Rhine wine in the parlor and delivered the sorrowful news about the passing of Mütterchen, his sister whom he hadn't seen in so many years. Herr Crolly came home, and, upon hearing of my mother's death, commiserated with us in the kindest manner.

After only one glass of wine, Uncle Jakob stood to leave.

"Nephew, I'd stay, but I had a previous engagement this evening. I'll send a telegram tomorrow to Katharina and Johann in Toledo."

"I understand," I replied. With some excitement, I told him of my travel plans yet that evening. Uncle Jakob wished us fair winds.

AT 11 O'CLOCK THAT SAME evening, Elizabeth and I carried our small travel cases to the steamship docks. As we stepped onto the vibrating deck of the "Queen City," Elizabeth gripped my hand tightly with her small one. I reassured my young wife we were perfectly safe, pointing out that only the lightest of breezes stirred Lake Erie's inky black waters. As the ship left the dock and headed away from shore, on the narrow bed of our cabin, I held her tight. What an adventure, I murmured in her ear, to make this journey together alone, the first of many to come. At first Elizabeth lay stiffly beside me, but gradually her breathing settled into a soft regularity and I too slept.

In the morning, we awoke at the docks of Detroit, having missed entirely the journey past Sandusky and up the Detroit River. Stepping on land once more, my wife's spirits seemed to brighten. Her arm in mine, we made a promenade along Jefferson Avenue like any fine gentleman and lady. On Woodward, we paused to gaze in the windows at the fine dresses and hats, at crockery and tableware and household sundries.

We didn't have a lot of money to spend, and war inflation was terrible just then, but I confided to Elizabeth the possibility that if Father had plans to settle all the Freinsheim estate, I might receive a modest sum in the coming year. I declared I would buy her fine cloth and fancy buttons and sewing notions. While my wife didn't appear won over by my attempts to soften her, she did patiently endure the full hour I lingered in the Detroit Easy Wagon Gear Company. In truth, I almost forgot her. When at last she begged to go, it was all I could to tear away from my study of the axle beds, sidebars, and other ready-made carriage parts available for order.

That night we lodged at a fine hotel in Capitol Park. Saturday midday found us on a boat to the Bass Islands, plowing through Lake Erie's blue-brown expanse. Fishing boats dotted the lake and to the north, puffy white clouds hung like fantasy castles in the sky. We disembarked at Middle Bass Island and stayed in the Wehrle Inn. Elizabeth frowned at the prices, but I pleaded with her that we must enjoy ourselves for once. It would cheer me a good deal, I assured her, as I felt so keenly the loss of my mother.

That June afternoon was exceedingly hot and humid, but the breeze on the island was refreshing. Indeed, I hardly noticed the heat as we strolled amid the grape rows, the vines lush with soft green leaves. My thoughts strayed often to my childhood, and I couldn't help but confess to Elizabeth the romantic ideas these memories stirred in me.

"My dear Elizabeth, once you see Freinsheim for yourself, you'll love it as I do. Perhaps we ought to move there. America has become so warlike, with no end in sight. There may come a time when Freinsheim is the safer place for us."

"*Mann*, you're an American citizen now. Besides, I could never agree to live so far away from my parents."

Her words seemed grossly unfair. I'd given up ever seeing my mother again to marry Elizabeth. I felt determined to make her yield, at least on going to Freinsheim for a visit. "It's not so far as you think. Matthias went back often before the war. He tells me the steamship travel makes the voyage much quicker."

Elizabeth's eyes held a fierceness I'd never seen. "What makes you so anxious to return? Is there a girl in Freinsheim you once knew, with whom you made love?"

I stopped in my tracks. "Why on earth would you think such a thing? I only long to see my father and my brother—they've asked me to come home. If only I'd gone earlier ... to see my dear mother one last time."

Elizabeth pressed her lips together and stared at the ground. An uneasiness feathered in my chest.

"Elizabeth? What is it?"

When she looked up, I saw the tears puddling in her eyes. "The sinful way you are with me in the marriage bed."

"My dear wife!" I felt a deep affection, and surprise, at her naïveté. "You must know there is no sin in it. A man and wife are free to enjoy themselves in the marriage bed."

Elizabeth studied me, her jaw set. "I am not the first."

I forced my eyes to hold her gaze, praying my guilt didn't show. "What can you mean? You are the true love of my heart."

"I believed you to be an upstanding Christian man."

"As I am." Memories of Jean Cody made the heat rush to my neck, but I dared not confess the truth. "Elizabeth, I've made the marriage vows and stand before you as your devoted husband."

I had never seen Elizabeth look so dejected. Was I such a trial to her? Had I already failed to be a good husband? I couldn't bear the thought.

"Charles Rauch had many things to recommend him," she said, "but I didn't trust his moral rectitude. I did not suspect the same of you."

The mention of Rauch punched a hole in my heart so that the wind whistled through. "You wish you had chosen Rauch?"

"You are the man I have married."

The bitterness in her tone stabbed me to the core.

"I think of no other but you, my beautiful wife."

I hoped desperately that my voice didn't sound as hollow to Elizabeth as it did to me. In that moment, I feared I faced years of a marriage to a wife who resented me, who spurned me in bed. I had imagined I'd be able to bend and mold Elizabeth's will to my own liking, but she was made of metal harder than I could have imagined. I was angry, and not a little ashamed.

As we continued our walk, I strove to behave as if nothing was wrong, rambling on about Freinsheim grape harvests and *Kerwe* festivals. But Elizabeth uttered no words of encouragement, and by the end of our time on the island, I had become truly agitated. I was unwilling to contemplate my sin with Jean Cody—it was over, and there was nothing I could do about it in any case.

What's more, I found it a difficult thing that she had called up the specter of my old nemesis, Charles Rauch. Ever since I'd deprived Rauch of Elizabeth Crolly, we avoided each other like poison, an unspoken hatred hanging between him and me. Even so, among wagon-makers, I heard much of his business success. His ice wagons had begun appearing on the streets with regularity, children running behind them to cadge chips from the drivers, riding on the back runners for the refreshing chill that emanated from within. Elizabeth pointed them out whenever we saw one.

I wanted to rail at Elizabeth for her insensitivity about Rauch, for her lack of Christian forgiveness, for refusing to come with me to my homeland and now, for her determination to spoil our one holiday outing. But I kept quiet. In truth, I dared not return to the subject.

Mid-morning on Sunday, Elizabeth and I boarded our steamship back to Cleveland. The previous night in the strange hotel bed I'd turned my back to her. Though I longed for her touch, she did not reach for me. I'd slept hardly at all.

The steamship rattled its way past Johnson's Island in Sandusky Bay, distracting me momentarily from my woes. All the passengers paused as we floated by the prisoner of war camp with its austere wooden fortification. The walls were so tall we could only see the guards in blue uniform, none of the Confederate captives within. It was a gloomy sight, and I wondered again if this war would ever end, if I had made a mistake in coming to America.

By afternoon, a swift wind began to ruffle the waters. Soon large waves were slapping against the steamship's hull. Lightning flashed tree roots across the dark horizon, followed by grumbling thunder and many passengers headed for cover.

"*Mann*, we will surely perish," Elizabeth said, her blue eyes skittish, her pupils large and black.

"Please don't get upset," I urged her. "The sailors will manage."

In truth, my head felt dizzy, swishing and spinning like the gnashing waves all around. The clouds burst with heavy rain, which chased toward us across the open water. I put my arm around my wife to guide her to the covered area.

Elizabeth sagged against me for the first time since our argument. I felt a rush of fondness for her, and remorse.

"I'm so sorry, my little wife," I whispered into her ear. "I didn't mean to disappoint you."

She nestled nearer and I grabbed a post, clinging to it as the boat toppled us roughly onto a bench. Even my prior experience at sea hadn't prepared me for the sudden violence of this gale. As our steamship struggled and tossed against the waves, I felt a deep regret that I'd dragged Elizabeth out here. Today we might die, and it would be my fault. Did Mütterchen even now look down from above, waiting to greet us in a short while? After all my sins and errors, I wondered if heaven even lay in my hereafter.

I hung on to my wife tightly, praying to God to spare us. With sudden ferocity, Elizabeth vomited at my feet, then fell to inconsolable weeping. I shouted my reassurance above the shrieking wind and snarling waves, certain we were about to be swept overboard into the bleak depths. I told her that I loved her, that I was sorry, that her happiness was all I cared about in the whole world.

The storm subsided almost as quickly as it had arrived. By the time the captain and crew steered the steamship up the mouth of the Cuyahoga River to dock, the white-capped waves had softened to choppy gray.

Elizabeth was so bedraggled, I hired a hack to drive us the short distance home. She rode listlessly in the carriage but, as soon as we were safe in the Henry Street foyer, she exploded like a banshee, weeping and wailing.

"I'll never, ever, leave the shore again!" she screamed, hailing me with her fists.

Her mother rushed over to pull her apart from me, circling an arm around her daughter's waist to guide her into the kitchen.

As if Elizabeth were a small child, Frau Crolly helped her out of her soiled dress and commanded me to bring down Elizabeth's housecoat. When I returned, Elizabeth was wrapped in a shawl, rocking back and forth in her kitchen chair, sniffling over a cup of tea. As soon as her cup was drained, my wife retired to bed.

My mother-in-law waited until Elizabeth had climbed the stairs, then crossed her arms and whirled on me as if she intended to throw me from the house.

"For shame, Michael! For shame. I thought you had better sense than to take a woman with child on such a journey."

In this way, I learned I would be a papa. How could I have known? All our time alone together, Elizabeth had never breathed a word. And with my busy days at the wagon shop, I didn't see her often, except early and late. I was a clod, I realized, a male oaf, a reprobate unworthy of my angel.

Chastened and defeated, I went the next day at the noon hour to the Western Union telegraph office to send a wire to Father and Philipp in Freinsheim.

HEARTFELT CONDOLENCES. TRIP IMPOSSIBLE. MARRIED AND EXPECTING CHILD. MICHAEL HARM.

In any event, I'd already missed the laying out of Mütterchen's body, the gathering of the family and villagers to mourn. By now, my mother was three weeks buried in the Freinsheim graveyard under the crumbling chapel tower.

# Chapter 42

———

THAT NOVEMBER OF 1864, AT twenty-three years of age, I cast my vote for the first time for president of the United States. Of course I voted for Abraham Lincoln. In spite of the war, I placed my trust in the high moral principles of this self-made man. The victory celebration for Lincoln this second time was not such a giddy affair, as we faced further carnage with no end in sight.

Shortly afterward, I encountered Matthias Höhn in town. We grasped each other's arms and he extended his condolences on the death of my mother.

"But I was only just going to impart this news to you. How did you know?"

"Konrad Bender came through Akron only a few days ago. He gave me all the news of Freinsheim. He also told me of the wedding of your brother Philipp."

"What? Philipp is married?" My shouts drew stares from passersby.

Matthias laughed, assuring me it was true. The marriage of my brother to Susanna Hisgen had taken place only a few months prior to my nuptials with Elizabeth. In turn, I shared with Matthias that Elizabeth and I expected a child, due any day now. In turn, he informed me about Philipp and Susanna's little daughter Elisabetha, born in March and named after Mütterchen. My mother had held her first grandchild in her arms before going to her eternal rest.

With so much to discuss, and not wanting to stay away long from Elizabeth so close to the birth, I invited Matthias to come for a glass of Rhine wine on Henry Street, but he declined, saying he had come to town on business and would visit another time. As we parted, we shared a laugh, picturing the new religiosity of the Freinsheim Harms now that Susanna stood at the spiritual helm.

Nothing can substitute for being there, when eyes lock in unspoken sentiment and lips speak heartfelt wishes. I proceeded home thinking how, if I had been at the Freinsheim wedding, I would have told my brother I believed Susanna was a good choice for him, with her pious practicality. I'd have reminded Philipp of his tendency to lose his sense of purpose without her. In that light, Susanna was his salvation. I'd have added that perhaps, from time to time, we all squirmed under the absolute authority of Susanna as she quoted her *Heilige Schrift*, but such a moral tongue-lashing every so often did a body good, and in any event, as his heart was already lost, he might as well grow accustomed to this fate.

No doubt Philipp and Susanna had the traditional Freinsheimer wedding, a religious ceremony sealing their bond under the blessing of the Protestant Church. Matthias had told me that Pfarrer Bickes still ruled the parish and so had performed the ceremony. After the vows, my brother and his bride must have made the promenade from the church to the garden where the guests were welcomed, a tall cake carried on a special litter behind them. The Freinsheimers would have dressed in their finest clothes, the children in their excitement rushing ahead and in back of the slow-moving procession. Along the path, wreaths of flowers would have adorned the gates and sandstone walls.

I was sure my brother enjoyed a wedding such as this, his heart bursting all the while with love for his Susanna, for whom he had lost his heart long ago. And in a strange synchronicity, as if living up to the Harm stuff of which we were made, two brothers on either side of the Atlantic married in the same year, settling into our planetary orbits around our god-fearing female suns.

November of 1864

Much loved father, brother and sister-in-law,

I have heard from Matthias, who has seen Konrad Bender, that you are *Gott sei Dank* healthy, after much sadness as the passing of our dear mother. From Matthias I have also received with joy the news of your marriage, dear brother, to Susanna and the birth of your blessed daughter. I will ask God every day that he should let you my dear father and brother and sister-in-law and niece live healthily and contentedly for many long years

The next I must write is that we live here now in a bad time and have to be ready always to carry weapons. The second evil of the war is the inflation which is being felt in all corners of America. All the products like food are twice as expensive as they have been before. As for settling the Freinsheim estate, I trust you, my father and brother, to decide what is best, as due to the war, I am not permitted to travel out of the country just now.

As for me and my new bride, we are both quite healthy and in good spirits after the birth of our first son, Philipp Heinrich Harm. Elizabeth likes to think of you even though she has not seen you face to face. If you have the opportunity, please send us a portrait so she can know you a little better. Also, if you send us a little barrel of 1861, to drink in honor of our marriage, we will drink also to your health and your marriage to Susanna. Brother, it was not right that you didn't tell me for so long from your own writing, but you see I have found out in any case.

Dear brother, Konrad Bender has also come to us, and told us how lucky you were to draw yourself free in the military lottery, for which I'm very glad. I have often wished I would have been with you that one evening when you came home with your number on your hat from Neustadt. I would have been happier than a king. But now I am in America, it is far, but still it is not outside of the world and God's dear sun shines here the same. The one who puts his trust in God has built well, and it is also the same here as there, that he who works has bread, and he who does not work has nothing.

Your true son and your loving brother,

Michael Harm

Here I send you a sample of American small money. Silver money is not to be had anymore. You must wait for the portrait of me and my new wife, since at this moment almost no people travel to Germany.
—Also, many greetings from Adam Crolly and wife and a very heartfelt greeting from me, Elizabeth née Crolly.

At Christmas a reply to this letter came from my brother, informing me of the good health of his wife and child. The paperwork had been filed regarding the estate, the fields divided equally between us. Philipp would get the house in recompense for looking after my father in his old age. My brother declared his intention to buy from me my portion, all but two parcels, which he couldn't yet afford. The plum field that would remain in my name he would farm, and pay me from the profits.

Close to $1,000 was wired to me soon afterward, so I could hardly believe my good fortune, which quickly increased. Just at that time, a new German association had formed, the Concordia Lodge, for the purpose of helping families who lost fathers in the war and such. Another member of this lodge, Herr Butler—a wagon-maker I knew from the old Cleveland Singing Society—informed me that Herr Beach intended to retire, so his shop on Champlain Street was in need of another partner. To enter the partnership, he told me, $2,500 would suffice.

I didn't have the money and told Herr Butler as much. I was feeling dejection on this score and wondering when I might ever have another such opportunity, when that same week, Herr Crolly confided in me he was thinking of selling his cooperage. We were sitting in the parlor at the time, baby Henry snuggling in my arms so Elizabeth could do some mending. It was a never-ending joy, to come home after a long day to my tiny son, so soft and unmarred by the cares of the world.

"The boom times for barrel makers are over," Herr Crolly said.

"But I don't understand. Oil use is on the rise. We even use it to grease the carriage axles."

"Oh, the oil boom continues. It's the coopers who are in trouble. This young whippersnapper John D. Rockefeller, of the Excelsior Oil Works, has found a way to undercut us, to build barrels for half the cost. These last months, I've had to let workers go."

"I didn't realize. What will you do?"

"I'm not a young man anymore, easily changing to a new profession."

I thought of my disappointment regarding the partnership with Herr Butler, and an idea began to form. "I know of an opportunity. You are an excellent woodworker. At Beach & Company, the carriage works on Champlain, Herr Butler is looking for a new partner, but the investment is $2,500, and I have only $1,500 in savings."

Herr Crolly studied me with his pale blue eyes. "You think this carriage works shows promise?"

"I have been to their shop. The work is good, but could be better. If I came in, Herr Butler offered to rename the company Harm & Butler. If you threw in the other $1,000, we could also add your name."

Herr Crolly shook his head, and my heart sank. "I don't need my name on the shop sign. But if I sell my cooperage, I will have the $1,000 you require."

I could hardly contain my excitement. Once I recovered from the shock, we hurried to negotiate the terms. Herr Butler thought it a fine arrangement. Herr Crolly said half in jest that he'd come to work in the wood shop in order to keep a careful an eye on his investment. When I told Herr Hoffmann I was leaving his shop, I expressed my thanks that he had been so kind to me when others had not. He waved my melancholy aside, saying he had anticipated this day and wished me well.

And so to start the new year of 1865, I put my life savings together with that of Adam Crolly and joined in partnership with Ernst Butler to form Harm & Butler carriage works on Champlain Street.

# Chapter 43

Cleveland, Ohio 1865

1 February 1865

M UCH LOVED FATHER AND BROTHER,

I made travels in the end of January to see Matthias Höhn in Akron, and when I returned, what do you think awaited me? On the 24th of January, I have been drafted. Many friends tried to speak for me, but it did no good.

Dear brother, while I was away, out of fear my wife has borrowed $600 to buy my freedom, to keep me out of the military for two years. But the men who serve in one's place now are so expensive that in only a few days the price has gone up, and you can't get someone for under $1,000. No one can describe what happens here. The people are drafted and drafted and fathers are being taken away from their families. And what people have saved for years has to be given for the man to fight for you. In this hard situation, I ask you, brother, if you will get $500. I know you don't have it, but if you can get it, I will pay you back $550. Now the paper money is very low, but the value will rise again after the war. I am sorry to trouble you. I know it is hard for you because you are not someone who borrows and lends. I would have the money myself, but have only just invested in a carriage works here, so we do not have the money otherwise. My bride is beside herself, and insists our baby will not grow up without a father. If you can do this, send it in credit through a secure bank, and don't let anyone know. I work hard at my business, but if the terrible war won't stop, Herr Crolly thinks we must look again for a new homeland.

Love,
Michael Harm

Uncle Jakob is in Cincinnati, trying to go off to California again. From Uncle Rapparlie, I don't hear anymore.

2 March 1865

Much loved father and brother,

I have received the check. I can see from your letter this sum of $500 was too much to ask, but I'm very thankful. Life is very expensive. Pork has gone up from 6 cents to 20 cents. Sugar from 12 cents to 35 cents. Coffee from 19 cents to 55 cents. Boots were once $5, now they are $10-$12. 300,000 more men have been drafted, one out of every sixth man, or 85 out of 500. But we hear the war will soon be over.

Love
Michael Harm

Cousin Scheuermann has married again.

In spite of the anxiety, and the onerous cost, of being drafted, and the constant uncertainty of our finances due to inflation, my experience as a new papa brought me elation that carried me through those bleak winter days. I don't deny Elizabeth's rash actions caused me considerable embarrassment. But my wife's distress on my behalf served as proof to me she still loved me, regardless of my sins. Her courage in the birthing of our son and her skills as a mother made me love her all the more. In those early years of our marriage, we suffered through many such misunderstandings that we never spoke of. In any case, it seemed a fool's errand, this longing for a romantic life, happily idyllic in the imagination, a good deal harsher in reality.

Every hour I was not at home I spent at Harm & Butler as the proud partner of a wagon shop. Each morning as Herr Crolly and I walked to work, I kept a careful eye out for the broughams and victorias, as well as the light buggies drawn by one trotter. During the years of the war, the Greek Revival houses on Prospect and Franklin diminished in importance next to new mansions going up along Euclid street. "Nabobs," we tradesmen called the wealthy Clevelanders, the men who grew rich from mining and timber, and telegraph services, from railroads, iron, and oil. Young elm trees graced Euclid in regular succession, their canopies draping shady boughs over the men in brightly colored jackets and the women in hoop skirts so wide they could hardly fit through doorways. The elegant homes going up were as large as castles, surrounded by carriage houses and outbuildings, shrubberies and circular drives.

Where Euclid intersected with the north end of Public Square, a new grocery that catered to this carriage trade had opened its doors. Chandler & Rudd imported foods from around the world, exotic treats such as caviar from Russia, ginger from Asia, and chocolates from Switzerland. In fact, I first knew of them from Matthias Höhn, who imported the Palatinate beechnuts and beechnut oil for them.

While walking past this grocery one April morning, I observed a gentleman having an argument with his delivery wagon, slamming the back gate up and down, insulting it as if it had ears.

"Sir, I don't believe the timber of your wagon has been properly seasoned," I said in my best, if somewhat stilted, English. I noted the wagon was made at the Rauch factory, no doubt using kiln-dried timber. "The change to warmer temperatures warps the wood."

The man stood back a pace or two, removed his handkerchief, and wiped his sweating brow. "Could be right, there," he said.

I extended a hand. "Harm. Michael Harm. I make the wagons for Harm & Butler, on Champlain."

"William Rudd," the man said, taking my hand and flashing an even set of brownish-yellow teeth.

"Harm & Butler uses the best air-dried hardwoods," I said.

"I'm sure you do, at that." Rudd spurted tobacco juice to one side.

"If you'd like us to do the repair, we can tow the wagon to our shop free of charge."

"Handy, indeed."

I thought perhaps he was laughing at me, so I turned to leave, but the gentleman called after me.

"Say, Mr. Harm, at that shop of yours, might you have a painter able to render a picture of our storefront? If we paint a likeness on the wagon here, Mr. Chandler thinks it will help business."

I studied the Chandler & Rudd letters, an average arrangement on each side of the shiny wagon. Perhaps Rauch's Herr Lehr had been too busy to apply his artistry to this small job.

"I do, Mr. Rudd. My painter can do a fine job on it."

William Rudd looked delighted. "Well. Let's get this wagon over there and see what can be done."

We shook on it, and I agreed to return the next afternoon to tow the wagon for jobbing. But I didn't make it to Chandler & Rudd's the next day, the ninth of April, 1865, as Cleveland's church bells rang out in celebration. "Let us have peace," General Grant declared at Appomattox, upon the surrender of the Confederate General Lee. People did no work that day. Clevelanders swarmed into the streets rejoicing, unfurling red, white and blue flags and bunting at every window and lamp post. At Harm & Butler we hung the star-spangled banner from the second story window to join the celebration for our Union and for our President.

Business resumed in short order, of course, and I sent a man over to Chandler & Rudd's for the wagon. But only six days later, as it stood drying in our paint room, the bells again began their tolling, this time to mourn the death of our extolled President Abraham Lincoln. Such a shock. When I learned of his assassination, I had the overwhelming conviction the world had come to an end. In a daze, I ascended to the shop's second floor, pulled a bolt of black silk from the shelf and unfurled it over the red, white and blue.

Immediately afterward, Harm and Butler closed shop and I headed for home. The streets were a changed landscape, with citizens standing around in groups, or alone, with stunned, vacant stares, some sobbing and openly keening. As I entered the house, the whole family had gathered in the parlor. The sight of my wife and child unplugged the tears and they spilled down my cheeks. I took baby Henry from Elizabeth's arms and clutched him to my breast.

"*Liebes Kind,*" I said in his soft little ear. "*Liebes Kind.*"

"You're scaring him, Papa," Elizabeth said, taking him back from me, her eyes red-rimmed with tears.

In the following days, we learned of assassination attempts also on Secretary of State William Seward and Vice President Andrew Johnson, which did not succeed. It was a dark time, as we feared that our people's government would collapse into chaos once and for all. I awoke every morning with a terrible sense of unease, worried I must return to Freinsheim, or go to Canada, to spare my family if more war should come.

Three days later, the body of our deceased president Abraham Lincoln made its final journey from Washington to Illinois for burial. When the Cleveland officials learned the cortege would pass through Cleveland, a catafalque was specially-built in Public Square. Our deceased hero was laid out for viewing. Elizabeth and I and baby Henry, the Kemps, the Crollys and Uncle Georg Scheuermann and his new wife Amelia and the boys, all gathered at the Crolly home on Henry Street before going to pay our final respects. We spoke in hushed whispers, as if an immediate family member had died. The line to pass the catafalque wound around the Square and down Superior as far as the eye could see, and still the people kept coming, some 65,000, by boat and train, by wagon and on foot, their black clothes shrouding all of Cleveland in a vast tide of mourning.

Booth and his assassins almost sank our ship of democracy, but in the ensuing months, somehow, the country remained afloat. At Harm & Butler, the fast pace of business soon resumed. Mr. Rudd approved Harm & Butler's paint job on his business wagon, and ordered three more.

"Our grocery business is growing fast," he said. "I will need two wagons this fall, and a third in the new year."

The profits from the custom-made vehicles were enough that I was soon able to repay my brother and father for the conscription money, a great relief indeed. I admit to a twinge of discomfort, that I wrested the Chandler & Rudd account from under the nose of Charles Rauch. After all, I had won Elizabeth, so could hardly bear him any ill will. But the Rauch & Company business didn't suffer as a consequence. In addition to business wagons, his factory built a specialty line of victorias and broughams. Of late, the Nabobs favored Rauch & Co. conveyances even over the New England coaches.

I convinced myself I hadn't done Rauch any harm, but apparently, my rival did not see it that way. His animosity became plain to me when a new Cleveland business directory arrived at our door on Champlain. I opened it and searched immediately under the carriage-making heading for our name, but Harm & Butler wasn't listed. Assuming it was an egregious oversight, I put on my hat and went to lodge a complaint with Mr. Stueckle.

"Why have you not included all of the Cleveland carriage-makers in your directory?" I demanded.

Mr. Stueckle blinked, then pawed nervously through papers on his desk. He was a balding man, the last of his thin hair making stripes across his pate. "One moment, please." Mr. Stueckle lifted this and that stack, then turned to the wood cabinet behind him and searched there. Finally, he extracted a sheet and turned to face me. "Right, Mr. Harm, is it? Of Harm & Butler? I have a note here that Harm & Butler Carriage Works would go out of business by the end of this year."

"Wherever would you hear such a thing? We have important contracts, with the U.S. Express Wagon Company, and the Lakeshore Michigan railroad. We never had any idea of closing shop!"

Mr. Stueckle squinted at his paper. "When we visited Rauch & Company on Pearl, I spoke with the proprietor there. Mr. Rauch said I would want to know, as my directory should not look out of date the moment it was published."

I stared at Mr. Stueckle, then put on my hat and departed. It was too late to do anything about it in any case.

With only an hour or two left in the workday, I had no desire to go back to the shop. Nor did I want to go home to my Elizabeth, who'd hinted on Bass Islands she might have preferred Rauch to me after all.

Instead, I went to see Uncle Jakob at House Place. Uncle Jakob had recently been away again for several months, and had only just returned. It was my luck to find him at home.

At first, I didn't confess my state of mind, preferring to relate the latest news at the jailhouse. Right across Champlain from our carriage works, the jailhouse provided a constant source of excitement. This week, activity centered around the Irish Fenian Brotherhood, whose members had devised a plot to make a military invasion of Canada. The headquarters of the attack, it seemed, was an office on Seneca Street. The police had been tipped off and surprised them, ransacking the office and clapping the Irish Brotherhood leaders in chains.

"The Irish hate the English so much, they have lost all reason," I concluded.

"Pure madness," Uncle Jakob agreed, shaking his head. "Never get on the bad side of an Irishman."

"Or a German wagon-maker," I said, and proceeded to confide my latest distress. "It's plain Rauch means to wipe me out if he can," I concluded. "Already everyone thinks first of Lowman, Hurlbut, and Hoffmann for the custom work. Now no new customers will even find me for my light buggies, and I build them of higher quality than anyone around."

Uncle Jakob gazed at me with steady gray eyes. "What do you expect? You stole his woman."

"She chose me over him," I corrected. I felt the sting, that even Uncle Jakob took Rauch's side. I could only imagine what Elizabeth would say if she knew. "So what happened to your plans to go to California?" I asked to change the subject.

Uncle Jakob leaned forward with a shrug. "The only high-paying blacksmithing work was on the transcontinental railroad. I no longer enjoy vagabonding as I once did."

"You finally admit you grow older, not younger, over the years?"

"Not so fast, nephew. I have news." Uncle Jakob grinned. Though the lines were deep in his cheeks and eyes, his face remained ruggedly handsome.

"So tell me."

"It is in part because of you, this news," Uncle Jakob said. "You have set a good example."

Trying to guess, I drained my wine and held out my glass for another pour. "You are going into business for yourself?" I suggested at last.

Uncle Jakob laughed. "See? I'm such an old man, it doesn't even occur to you. But I tell you true: I am to be married in a fortnight."

I stood up so abruptly my chair toppled over. "*Wie bitte?* My old Uncle Jakob, with the gray hairs in his beard? Married?!" I looked around in amazement, righted my chair and plunked down again. "Who is the bride? Hannah Wolff?"

"The same!" Uncle Jakob looked extremely pleased.

I raised my glass over my head. "A more tolerant woman has never graced this earth! Here's to our Hannah, who has caged Jakob Handrich, the migrating bird." We drank to his good fortune. "Uncle, just how old are you, anyway?"

He shrugged. "Forty-two or forty-three. By the time I thought to ask Mother, she couldn't remember the exact year of my birth."

"Forty-three? You marry for the first time at forty-three?!"

I started to laugh then, and could not stop. I laughed and laughed until I had to hold my belly from the ache, until the tears sprang to my eyes and ran down my cheeks. Uncle Jakob laughed with me, a bit more subdued.

As my fit finally subsided, he confided he still had doubts, and asked me about my marriage to Elizabeth. I told him my ill-fated love story from the beginning, of my devotion to Anna Marie which ended in her marriage to Emil Oberholz, of what Elizabeth had said to me on Bass Islands, that she might have preferred to marry Charles Rauch. Uncle Jakob listened carefully, and when I'd finished, shook his head.

"It's a heart-wrenching tale, but I think you misjudge Elizabeth. She looks on you with love, nephew. Don't you see it?"

"Then why will she not agree to visit Freinsheim? I'll never feel as if she truly knows me if she doesn't see my homeland and meet my family."

"It's bad luck, that she now has a terror of the water. But she can't help it."

All my life was I to have bad luck? Even so, I realized, my low mood was going to spoil the evening. "Alla, enough of my whining," I said, shifting upright in my chair. "So what if I'm a dog with my tail nailed in place? Uncle, please forgive me, don't let me howl all the night long. I'm sorry to be morose about marriage on this night of all nights. Elizabeth and I have married young, and so we suffer from our inexperience. This will not be your trouble at all. You and Hannah will have all happiness. I wish you well from the bottom of my heart."

We fell then to discussing Uncle Jakob's plans for the marriage, and if he might, for once, choose to stay in one place for a while.

Later, on my way back to Henry Street, a pensive mood overtook me. I longed for the comfort of my wife, but no doubt Elizabeth would be angry with me when I returned home. It was very late. Now that I thought of it, I'd missed the supper hour without explanation.

"Where were you, husband?" she asked as I entered our bedroom, in just the tone of voice that gave me little hope.

I removed my clothes and slid naked between the laundered sheets. She turned her back to me, but I reached out to her, sliding my hands under her nightdress, tenderly stroking her shoulders and waist, reaching down low along the warm plumpness of her bottom.

"Don't be upset with me," I whispered softly. "I have news you will like. Uncle Jakob is to marry Hannah Wolff."

She twisted around to face me in the silvery moonlight. "Married?! Old Jakob? I don't believe you."

"It's true, I called on him at House Place tonight and he told me so himself." I cupped her breasts in my hands, taking in my wife's beauty, her hair released from its daytime braid to spill along the pillow. "Elizabeth, is it so bad being married to me? Do you wish you had married Charles Rauch?" I held my breath awaiting her reply.

Elizabeth lay still, her eyes black, her gaze holding mine. I could not read her thoughts, and had all but resigned myself to her refusal when she rose from the bed. My wife stood before me in her white nightdress, shimmering. Untying the neck ribbon, she lifted up the hem, pulled the fabric over her head, and climbed naked into bed beside me. As our bodies welded together, I felt the white-hot heat of her forgiveness, and love.

# Chapter 44

19 January 1867

DEAR FATHER-IN-LAW, BROTHER-IN-LAW AND SISTER-IN-LAW,

You have asked my husband to fulfill his duty as a child and write to you, and he agreed to it. But he always says yes, yes, I will do that, and then he does not. But now I think we should start and try to write regularly, so we can build up our correspondence. I received your present, it was very nice.

Elizabeth Harm

Dear father, brother and sister-in-law,

I pick up the pen to write, as your loving son and brother, and according to my wife's bidding, who is right in all things.

As far as my family is concerned we are all quite healthy. The children grow and advance. Philipp Heinrich is already going to Sunday school, and Elizabeth, who we call "Lucy" and baby Emma are healthy and happy.

As for my business, it improves every day. Fred Schuster of Kallstadt came in as a partner when Herr Butler retired, so the carriage works is now called Harm & Schuster. I see Schuster quite often in the evenings as well, as he has married my wife's younger sister Mary Crolly.

Uncle Jakob lives since last year in his house over in town but left last week again for Columbus, thinking to find work there. We have often spent time together, and I greet you many times from him. His wife and his boy are still here, I think he will be coming back soon.

Now I want to close, in hope of a timely answer, I greet you all many thousand times and remain

Yours,

M. Harm

My greetings to Richard Pirrmann and family, to John Fuhrmann and also Anna Maria Oberholz and family

Address: M. Harm 102 Champlain Str. Cleveland O. America

The 14th of September, 1869, dawned with cannon fire. The Cleveland Germans were holding a celebration of unsurpassed extravagance to honor the 100th anniversary of the birth of Alexander von Humboldt, that great explorer, scientist, humanist, and author of *Kosmos*. I marched in the first division of the parade with Concordia Lodge's Harmonie Singing Society. The parade wagons were loaded down with magnificent displays—a replica of a globe, stars floating around it to signify Humboldt's scientific influence around the world, a costumed goddess of Flora amid a glorious bounty of flowers and plants as well as one of Ceres, goddess of plenty, ensconced on a cornucopia spilling over with squashes, fruits, and other products of earth's bounty. All the German gardeners contributed blooms to these floats. The front path on Henry Street had been bare of color as I left that morning. As I marched along the circuitous parade route, I reveled in the number of Harm & Schuster wagons in evidence. The parade concluded at the Rink with grand speeches, a 250-piece orchestra, and many songs. I felt especially connected to my father and Philipp on this festival day that honored Humboldt, the man who had inspired our little family on Wallstrasse with such grand descriptions of the earth and celestial heavens.

In reality, such a lavish reverence for nature was a tribute to bygone days. Oil refineries had sprouted up around Cleveland since the war, and now dominated the landscape until it seemed the interests of industry had overrun nature entirely. Every so often a refinery would catch fire, black smoke billowing upward, rivers of burning oil pouring down to the Cuyahoga so it lit up in flames. When a warehouse with lubricants stored in it caught fire, a thirty foot wall of flame flowed down the middle of Michigan Street, engulfing many buildings, including Herr Hoffmann's wagon shop. I rushed to help where I could, but an entire building of his establishment was destroyed.

Whenever I heard the clang of fire bells in the direction of Public Square, I put on my hat and raced like a mad man to Harm & Schuster to ascertain if my livelihood would turn to smoke and ash before my eyes. So far, *Gott sei Dank*, such a disaster has not been visited upon us.

In the autumn, one year after the Humboldt festival, the stench of the refineries at last drove us out of Henry Street for good. In any event, many German families were settling in the properties along Woodland Avenue to the east. Herr Hoppensack was selling open lots where he had once operated his truck-gardening business. Upon investigation, I discovered it was the same farmland I once enjoyed during my walks up Kingsbury Run. The air was cleaner there, the noise of the factories not so loud. I bought a large tract at the corner of Francis and Tod Streets, and my partner and brother-in-law Fred Schuster bought a parcel next door, in order for the Crolly sisters Mary and Elizabeth to live side by side and care for Herr and Frau Crolly in their dotage.

17 August 1872

Dear Brother and Sister-in-law,

It has been a hard year, with Father gone to his eternal rest and me never coming to see him after all these years. We are sorry that your wife is sick and not coming back to health. My wife thinks she works too hard, and should rest more. Elizabeth says German men don't care if life only means work day in and day out, not only inside the house but also in the field. To that, she says: "I would say 'no, thank you.' "

My business is very good. The demand for work is so strong that we will grow again. No more news except for an election coming. This time it will be shown what the Germans can do, now that the weapons trader U.S. Grant stands against H. Greeley. The former is supported by the English, the latter by the Germans.

Yours,
Michael Harm

December 20, 1875

Dear Brother and family,

Death has cut a hole into your family, and we know how sad that is because on the 13th of August in 1874 our youngest child, Herman, was buried at the age of only one year. He went to the eternal rest after only three days of being sick with the childhood illness called 'summer complaint.'

Aunt Katherina Rapparlie also went to the eternal rest two years ago at 64 years old. Her children have written to give me the news, and tell me that Uncle Johann does a good wagon business in Toledo.

As for me and my family, two years ago I have bought for the children a new piano which cost me $500. All of them can play and sing like larks.

We also have a horse and on summer Sundays drive out to the countryside to visit Matthias Höhn and his uncles. All greet you many times and are very well.

Business life at this moment in America is quite low, and especially the craftsman has to suffer. As far as my business is concerned, there are signs next year will be better.

May the Eternal One heal all of our wounds of this past year.

Yours,
*Michael Harm*

5 April 1880

Dear brother, sister-in-law and children,

We are all healthy and well. Although I had a slight cold last winter, I am healthy again. Business across this country is excellent. Hopefully, after seven lean years, come seven fat ones. Lucy and Emma were both confirmed on Palm Sunday. Henry is now helping with the Harm & Schuster business as a blacksmith apprentice. My in-laws are both still living, and send their greetings.

Dear brother and sister-in-law, after almost 23 years of living in America, today I tell you with full confidence I think you should also come here. America is the land of the future for all people who have a desire to work. I know how dear the Palatinate is to you, I love it myself today even more than when I left it, but I read daily the reports in the newspapers, and hear from the many immigrants arriving, about the growing militarism, about the enormous tax burden that rests upon you, the eternal war clouds. Yet it is so hard to judge what is right, to stay or leave one's dearest land.

I send these lines with my friend Dietz in hopes he will be able to answer for you anything else you wish to know.

With a thousand greetings to you,
M. Harm

Many thousand greetings from Father and Mother to all of you, and we remain your devoted ones, Elisabetha Harm, Lucy, Emma, and Henry Harm

30 May 1882

Dear Brother, Sister-in-law, and children,

The presents that we got from you, especially the hand accordion, were all just following my heart's wish. The wine is exceptional, too. It is a strange feeling when one comes home in the evening and goes to the basement to drink a glass of Rhine wine. Many of my Palatinate friends take advantage of this occasion and visit me. And for all of this, I send my full and heartfelt thanks.

I dream still of visiting Freinsheim, and if we stay healthy for two more years and fate does not forbid it, one beautiful morning I will stand with my wife in front of our old farmhouse and sing "Be Greeted My Heart," which my friends of the Harmonie Choir are convinced no one sings better than me.

As for my business, I have so many orders I do not know where my head is. We have produced alone this winter 22 pieces of fine wagons and buggies, which cost $200 to $500 each, and since the first of February to May, we have repaired and painted 107 wagons. Henry apprenticed as a blacksmith for a time, but the work does not appeal to him. It is not like the old times, when the young knew only work.

Please greet John Fuhrman, Richard Pirrman, and Anna Maria Oberholz.

Your loving brother,
Michael Harm

# Chapter 45

## Cleveland, Ohio, 1893

O N A WARM AUGUST EVENING of 1893, I sat on our front porch on Francis
Street for the evening breezes when Matthias Höhn turned in at our
front gate, travel satchel in hand. My childhood friend still journeyed back
and forth between America and Germany as the frog leaps from one bank of
the ditch to the other. As for me, I lived not fantasy, but reality, toiling away at
Harm & Schuster carriage works, fixed in one place all these years.

"*N'Amend*," I said, reverting to dialect. In truth, I felt a twist in my gut
that my old friend should find me sitting idle. I did not wish to admit my state
of affairs. I didn't like to think of it myself. "Could this be the merchant Herr
Höhn, come to taunt me about another voyage to Germany?"

"*Ja, ja*, I'm on my way," Matthias said with a sigh, climbing the porch steps
and huffing into a wicker chair. "I go in one week's time."

The evening air sang with crickets and cicadas, and began to hold a hint
of coolness. I offered Matthias a glass of Rhine wine, which he accepted, but I
did not rise immediately, as I didn't want to enter the close heat of the house.
I shared the news that I, too, had recently made a journey, to Chicago, for the
Columbian Exposition. Matthias extended hearty congratulations.

"The whiteness of it was amazing, like heaven," I said. "But so expensive. I
don't know how they managed it in such terrible financial times."

The screen door squeaked open and Elizabeth stepped outside, holding
the hand of our little granddaughter.

"*Guten Abend*, Matthias. The sheets are fresh in the guest room," she said.

"So you knew he was coming," I said. "Always, I'm the last to know, behind
all the rest in importance."

"*Tch, Mann*, we pay a fortune for a telephone in the house. Why not use
it?"

Elizabeth was always on me about this expense, but she used the telephone most of all, calling me at Harm & Schuster with every little errand. If she went out at all nowadays, it was for events at church.

Baby Emma crawled onto my lap and leaned her back against my stout belly, the humid heat forming ringlets in her fine brown hair. "*Liebes Kind*," I whispered in her ear, brushing her neck with my beard to make her squirm and giggle. I spoke only German to her, as my daughter and son-in-law spoke only English in their home. All three of our grown children were anxious to speak English, not German, as if they were ashamed of their heritage.

"Our children aren't children anymore, eh Harm?" Matthias observed through a blue cloud of pipe smoke. "When I see them married and having children of their own, then I know I grow old."

"I'm sure it's the same in Freinsheim. If I passed my brother Philipp on the street, I would ask myself: who is that old man?"

Matthias looked from me to Elizabeth, who was just settling into the wicker rocking chair, and clapped a hand firmly on his knee.

"*Alla*, it is time! It is past time. You and Elizabeth must join me for this trip."

"To Germany?" I looked at my wife. "That's impossible. We have no warning."

"Why not? I'm not leaving for a week. I can make the paperwork go quickly. My company does this well."

"What about it?" I asked Elizabeth. "The man invites us to Germany. Will you go?"

In truth, I had suffered disappointment on this score so many times I did not allow hope to enter my heart.

Elizabeth rocked back and forth, not meeting my gaze.

I exhaled a sad chuckle. "You must forgive my wife. She has a fear of the water. She'll never make such a trip."

"Lucy will need me here for the birth," Elizabeth said.

"So you see? It's as I said." I couldn't keep the resentment from my voice.

Matthias puffed at his pipe. "But why not come by yourself, Harm? Surely Schuster can manage the business for three weeks?"

Elizabeth sent me a warning frown, which I ignored.

"It's true, Schuster can manage. And the German Singing Festival is just over, so I'm no longer tied down with the Harmonie."

"*Doch*, what good times we could have! The ocean journey is not as long as before. You shall see! Before you know it, you'll be drinking new wine."

A strong yearning rose in me for the sweet tickling flavor of new wine. And Schuster could handle the business alone, to be sure. The railroad stock had crashed in the spring, so there were no orders for finished work. We had survived the summer with jobbing. But worse times lay ahead, as Sears & Roebuck now sold buggies and wagons in their catalog. All wagon-makers, even the large factories, faced hard times. But if I was going to go, I didn't wish to do so alone.

"I have always wanted to show Henry Freinsheim," I said. "Now would be a good time. Grover Cleveland is happily in the presidency and so doesn't require his services."

"But husband—"

"Wife, I'm sorry for your fears, but I have listened to them enough. You will not go with me, *oder*? I'll speak to Henry tomorrow. If he wants to go, then so will I. How I have missed the *Goldener Herbst* of the Palatinate."

"Wonderful! What good news!" Matthias winked at me, then leaned forward for a better view of Elizabeth. "Excuse me, Frau Harm. I'm truly sorry, as I know the idea of a voyage distresses you. But I couldn't be more delighted. At last, the two Harm brothers will set eyes on each other again. What a grand day that will be!"

But when I suggested the trip to my twenty-nine-year-old son, he pursed his lips as if he had just drunk bitters.

"It's the perfect opportunity," I said. "Your wife Barbara will not miss you, as baby Edna demands all her attention."

"Papa, it is not the perfect time." My son's finely chiseled face and firm jaw resembled his mother's, but he had the blue eyes of my father, tilted up at the outsides. "Schuster and I just went over the books again this morning. Surely it doesn't come as a shock, that if we don't do something immediately, Harm & Schuster must close its doors?"

"Things are slow, I admit, but we have faced hard times before."

"You aren't listening. Schuster has understood for months now we must make a change or fail, but you refuse to face it."

I stared at Henry in disbelief. To him, it was as if times had always been good, and now something dramatic must be done. At nearly thirty, he hadn't experienced the swings of fortune and despair so common in this country.

"Let us give it another month or two. While things are slow, it's our chance to travel. You'll like it in Freinsheim. I have long wanted to introduce you to your Uncle Philipp. It seems he will not come here, so, we will go to him."

"Now is not the time. I must stay and work this out. If it was Paris, or London, I might consider it ... But Freinsheim? No, Papa. I will not travel all that distance just to see a little village in the country."

I felt the heat rise in my neck. "My brother and his family are in Freinsheim. Your German family."

"You said so yourself, they don't come here. Perhaps they don't like us as much as you think."

"You have too much wealth to understand. You think everything is so easy. They are farmers who can't leave the fields and animals unattended."

"It's you who doesn't understand. You pull the wool over your eyes and refuse to believe the carriage works is in trouble. Our only chance is to switch to jobbing, to hire unskilled workers at a lower wage."

"Give it time. People will always need carriages and buggies in this country. You must come with me and meet the family. To know who you are, to see for yourself where you come from."

"Where *you* come from. I didn't come from there. I'm an American."

His disdain seared into me, but I should have known better than to argue. I had lost my power over my son years ago, when I forced him at age sixteen to apprentice as a blacksmith. We had just built our large new shop on Woodland Avenue, with its elevator and twenty-five horsepower steam engines, and a second floor carriage repository to show off our buggies and sleighs. I saw it as the start of his living, to learn all aspects of carriage-making. One day, he could take over Harm & Schuster.

But Henry had attended the English-speaking Central High School and made friends with sons of influential families. Blacksmithing meant nothing to him. Indeed, few people respect this ancient art these days. Henry did the work only grudgingly, with no skill. His sullen attitude maddened me beyond reason. The day I struck him with my fist, I saw I had become my own worst enemy, Lord Rapparlie himself. Within the year, I ended his obligation, assigning him to accounting with the ledgers instead, which was all he ever cared about in the first place. Now he worked as Harm & Schuster's business manager and also as the bookkeeper for the Cleveland Tippecanoe Club.

No matter how hard I pleaded with him to make the trip, Henry would not join me. Regardless, I could stay away from Freinsheim no longer. I missed my brother and longed to see my nieces. In any case, I had to see about the parcel of land, the little plum field I still owned after all these years. Such a chance might not come again. In defiance of Elizabeth's wishes, and with a good deal of excitement and trepidation pumping in my veins, I made plans to voyage with Matthias across the Atlantic, to return to the land of my birth.

IN JUST A FORTNIGHT, AS our ship steamed out of New York Harbor, I stood on the deck looking back toward the west, toward New York City's tall new buildings that crowded the skyline. The green Statue of Lady Liberty had not been here when I first arrived in 1857, but she shone her beacon now. To light my way home?

As Lady Liberty's torch disappeared into the curvature of the earth, I turned my gaze eastward, toward vivid memories of the first fifteen years of my life, a farmer's son hoeing daily in the fields. I glanced at my gold pocket watch, which kept perfect time but lacked the sentimental weight of my first one. According to Matthias, the voyage would be over in a week.

The Columbia steamship with its three towering funnels was a new vessel in the Hamburg-American packet line, built to accommodate over 600 passengers. Matthias and I had all we wanted for comfort and personal hygiene, a far cry from the steerage accommodations on the Helvetia. The lull in physical activity had a soporific effect, so I spent many hours dozing in a canvas chair on deck. All these years at Harm & Schuster, I had never stopped moving. Now my body collapsed in on itself so I could hardly move at all.

Although I looked forward to what lay ahead, my thoughts kept straying back to the carriage works. Fred Schuster had spoken to me just before my departure, confirming Henry's belief that we must change our business methods or fail. In the nearly three decades we had been business partners, Schuster and I'd enjoyed much success, but also the constant sense that any moment we might fall behind. The catalogs arrived at our shop without cease, touting new parts, fittings, the Topliff bow-sprockets, the rubber-coated axles and tires. Each year there was another machine to purchase and learn to operate, new materials to add to our inventory. This summer at the Columbian Exposition, we had witnessed with our own eyes the Studebaker wagon's new styling, its silver-polished aluminum. Harm & Schuster had shifted from the use of wrought iron to cast iron and steel. Was the aluminum yet another material we must add to the manufactory? At what cost? Always we faced such decisions, weighing investments in machinery against the wagon-making craft and the livelihoods of our craftsmen, many of them immigrants who desperately needed the work.

Worse still, Henry kept insisting the horseless carriage was all the young men were talking about. He urged Fred and me to invest in designing one, if we had the money, which he knew we didn't. He had heard the Rauch & Lang factory was experimenting on an electric model. I bristled at this news, but how could Henry know? All these years, I'd never hinted to my son of the animosity between Charles Rauch and me. Even the idea of making motors in addition to carriage bodies was not a change I felt able to manage. Not without a factory.

In truth, as the ship steamed across the Atlantic toward the reunion with Philipp, a part of me began to dread facing him. After all, Philipp had no idea of who I was now, except via letters and reports. The robbery after my arrival in America, the questionable circumstances at the end of my indenture, my plea to borrow a large sum of money to keep from being drafted, all could be interpreted as failure. Now I returned alone, without wife or children by my side, having spent my life building a business that was crumbling before my eyes.

I drifted into a doze and dreamed the seawater rose up around my deck chair to swallow me. I woke with a start.

"Harm, look," Matthias said, appearing over me, his head a dark splotch against the sky. "We've been four days at sea. The sun is out, but you sit with your head in a gray cloud." He flopped down in the chair beside me. "It's not the end of the world that Henry didn't come, *oder?* Every time I make the voyage, I ask my son Frank if he will join me. He always makes an excuse, says he has pressing matters to attend to at home."

"With Henry, it's his mother who put the louse in his ear. Elizabeth is so deathly afraid of water. Plus, my son doesn't know me too well. When he was young, I rarely saw him. I worked day and night all those years, and went often to the Lodge."

Matthias nodded. "The import trade has been a good living, but I also am rarely at home. Even so, I hope to travel west next year, to California."

"How is it so easy for you to get away?"

"Between you and me, my wife seems happier to have me gone."

During the remaining days at sea, for the sake of Matthias, I made an effort to be a more spirited travel companion. Before I knew it, we were stepping on German soil once more.

# Chapter 46

## Freinsheim, Germany, 1893

WHY HAD I WAITED SO long? It seemed so simple to me now. Within a week of leaving Cleveland, I stood blinking in the sunlit streets of Bremen. Without delay, Matthias and I took the train south through the flat lands, then down along the Rhine River. Throughout the winding journey, I kept my eyes pasted on the countryside, the clusters of half-timbered houses tied like knots of yarn on a quilt of green velvet. How ancient this landscape seemed, with its castle ruins and centuries-old cathedrals. In the cities I saw smokestacks of industry similar to what we had in America, but the rural villages appeared unchanged.

At least Freinsheim had its own railway station, which spared us hiking the final distance from Neustadt on foot.

"So, Harm, you're nearly home," Matthias said, flashing a smile at me as we eased our cramped legs off the train.

"Nearly hard at work, you mean?"

From the train window we had glimpsed the backs of villagers bent over the vineyard rows all along the countryside. Somehow, I'd been so caught up in my troubles I hadn't considered that my arrival would coincide with the wine harvest. Of course I must work in the fields.

Matthias gave a mock bow. "My sincerest apologies, but I won't be able to join you. As soon as I see you reunited with your brother, I must be off for my appointment in Dürkheim."

Lugging our satchels, we headed down the red sandstone stairs of the solidly built train station. This area had once been fields, but the village had expanded, with new houses and buildings, even some gaslights, so I hardly knew where I was. On Haintorstrasse, I marveled over the new school, which my nieces had described to me in a letter as 'square like a box' but which impressed me now as being larger in scale than I'd imagined.

Once we'd passed under the archway of the Haintor tower, the narrow corridor of the wall's inner ring appeared exactly the same. How tightly contained Freinsheim seemed compared to Cleveland's broad open avenues. Following the inner perimeter, my eyes danced over the sturdy *Höfe*. I was overcome by how familiar it all felt, as if I'd been away for only a brief span, not thirty-six years. On Wallstrasse, Matthias and I paused briefly at the Harm *Hof* to stow my two travel cases—one carefully packed by Elizabeth with presents for my brother and his family—just inside the stable door. Then we struck out for the vineyard. Without my luggage weighing me down, my feet felt as if they floated on air.

Few people were in the village, as the *Weinlese* pulled every able-bodied Freinsheimer to the vineyards. Matthias and I drew a few open-mouthed stares, but no calls of recognition. In truth, I reveled in my anonymity and my status as foreigner. I had returned at last, transformed from a willowy stovepipe of a boy into a pot-bellied stove, my features thickened with hard work and rich living. I sported a full beard and mustache and wore a suit made of the finest wool, a gold watch chain looping from my silk vest pocket. It occurred to me it had been a good idea to send a telegram ahead to Philipp. Otherwise, I felt certain, he wouldn't recognize me.

We exited the village on the other side, through the ancient *Eisentor*, the hills rising beyond it feathered with soft golden foliage. Clusters of green grapes dangled near the bare ground. Starlings rose scattershot to sweep across the rows. It was late afternoon by now, the September sun drawing long shadows. As I neared the Harm rows, I had trouble making out the features of the workers who were stooped over to pick the grapes. A middle-aged man stood near the wagon that held the wine press, the heavy *Logel* barrel on his back, and all at once I knew him as my brother.

"Philipp!" I shouted.

The man turned in my direction. I broke into a stiff run. "It's Michael! Your brother Michael!"

All around in the vineyard rows, people stood up to stare. If I had been ten years younger, I might have jumped for joy, but as it was, I huffed like a bull as I charged up the last incline to where Philipp stood by the wagon.

"Brother! You have come," he said as we clapped each other on the shoulders. He stepped away and hoisted himself up, in one motion bending at the waist to empty his *Logel* of grapes into the wagon. He jumped down again and unstrapped his burden. "How glad I am to see you!"

"I thought you might need a hand with the wine harvest," I said, grinning.

Philipp eyed me up and down. "You honor us, *Herr Amerikaner*, in our humble field."

He reminded me so much of my father, in the way he set both hands firmly on his hips and looked at me, so forthright and practical. To my astonishment, he wore no beard, only a mustache, and so looked quite cosmopolitan. His thick crop of hair erupted from under his cap just as I remembered it. His body was lean and wiry, his suspenders needed for a real purpose, unlike mine.

I glanced down at my waistcoat and gave a wry chuckle. "Perhaps I'll begin in the morning?"

Philipp threw his arm around my shoulders, knocked off my bowler hat and pawed across my thinning hair with his large hand. Matthias burst out laughing, as did I. I hadn't been a little brother in so long, I could have died of happiness.

Philipp turned to the field. "Susanna! Daughters! Come greet my brother Michael from America."

Matthias and Philipp exchanged greetings as Susanna and my three grown nieces, Elisabetha, Margaretha, and Katharina, lined up before me. The girls looked rugged with outdoor work, but young and beautiful, their faces round, their foreheads broad and clear. My brother introduced me using his terms of endearment for his daughters: Betche, Gretche, and Kätche. In Gretche I saw so much of Mütterchen, in Kätche, my father's eyes.

Several hours of daylight remained for harvesting, but for a brief time we shared the wine-laced water, the traditional refreshment of the *Weinlese*. Around us, the acid-sweet aroma of grape skins bit at our noses. Above us, wispy white clouds laced the blue sky. It struck me full force then, how in Cleveland, we now dwelled beneath perpetually darkened skies. Even at our home on Francis and Tod, the coal-smoked air hovered low to the earth in a murky haze, evening sunsets only a dull red glow in the western sky. I couldn't remember exactly when it had begun, this sooty haze that snuffed out the sun. Amid these yellow-green vineyard rows, clean and bright as if scrubbed by a hard rain, the air was so clear it hurt the eyes.

As Matthias bade us farewell, I promised to meet him in Bremen in a fortnight. The others returned to the grape-harvesting, except for Susanna, who walked back with me to the Harm *Hof* to get supper on the table. On the way, she spoke of the marriages of her two older daughters, Betche and Gretche, and of the ten year difference between these daughters and her youngest, unmarried Kätche, who just that spring had undergone confirmation. I did not mention the other Katherina, the daughter who we learned from the letters had died at just seven years old. Neither did Susanna.

We stepped into the old kitchen, and, for a moment, I felt Mütterchen's aproned form at the stove and Father seated at the table, studying his farm ledgers. The ghostly memories dissipated amid the new scene before me, the additional chairs at a larger table, a collection of gourds and jars of quince preserves on the sideboard, a new cupboard and other amenities. My brother and his family had moved ahead and built a life here, I realized, a whole layer of history I hadn't been present to witness. Only my mind dwelled in the past.

"*Gott sei Dank* you have come back to us at last, brother-in-law," Susanna said. "We have made an extra room in the barn, where for some years a laborer lived. You will sleep there."

I pictured the hayloft where the Prussian and Bavarian soldiers had slept so long ago, but Susanna was referring to an actual room—clean, wallpapered, with rugs to warm the floor. The stairs to reach it were more of a ladder, and scaling it, I felt again how stout I'd become.

It was my hope, at long last, to enjoy face to face conversation with my brother, to ask him the many questions I had about Mütterchen and Father, about what it had been like for him all these years. There was no opportunity that first evening. A stream of visitors began to arrive—the Pirrmans, the Fuhrmanns, and old Frau Reibold.

The front room grew crowded as we drank new wine together and shared decades of news. Many admired my fine suit of clothes. They laughed when I said "*Nein*" instead of "*Nä*," "Yes" instead of "*Ja*," and "*Garten*" instead of "*Gaade*." Until they pointed it out, I hadn't realized how I'd stirred the languages of the Palatinate and Prussia and England into one American bowl.

I asked my friends questions about politics in Germany. Since Bismarck was no longer Chancellor, Pirrmann said, socialist politicians were gaining ground in the *Reichstag*. Most Freinsheimers looked on this movement with concern. But when I suggested a more democratic solution, they said they weren't impressed by American democracy. From what they'd read in their newspapers about labor riots and greedy monopolies, our capitalist system had serious shortcomings. It sounded as bad as a monarchy, Pirrmann said, if the lower class working men were so poorly treated.

Philipp pulled out a letter I'd written years ago, in 1869, on the old Champlain Street stationery.

"What does this mean?" he asked, indicating the top margin, where I'd scrawled "let us hafe pice of ouer Country" in English.

Had I expected Philipp to understand? Or had I not realized I wrote in English? I couldn't recall, but my brother's question made me sad. All this time, he'd wondered what I was trying to tell him. I explained the words of Grant, the deep scars that continued between North and South long after the War Between the States had ended.

For his part, my old comrade Johann Fuhrmann wanted to know about the carriages and wagons, what type of vehicles we made at Harm & Schuster.

"Grade One light buggies, Chandler & Rudd business wagons, express wagons, and also sometimes the fire wagons," I said, thinking of better days. That my carriage works had come to a near standstill this past year, I was loath to confess.

"*Doch*, the fire wagons. Herr Huck now builds the *Feuerlöschspritzen* in Freinsheim. They install hydraulic machines to pump the water."

I inquired the cost of such a wagon. Fuhrmann informed me it was 850 Gulden. *Three hundred twenty-five dollars*! I confessed I couldn't charge over $125 for a fire exercise wagon, or the fire chief would take his business elsewhere. As we discussed these matters, I overheard the old woman, Frau Reibold, explaining to her great grandson about my presence among them.

"It's Michael Harm, the *Amerikaner*," Frau Reibold said, speaking too loud in the manner of old people who are going deaf. "He lived in our village as a boy, but he left his hoe in the field and went off to America with a music band."

Frau Fuhrmann shook her head. "*Tch,* if only he hadn't left the hoe in the field."

The two women gazed sadly at the boy.

"What do you mean?" I wanted to cry out, "That's not what happened!" But then I thought of the day I had, indeed, left the hoe in the vineyard, so many years ago, the time I'd slipped away to listen to the Liedmeister Band. Feeling philosophical, I chuckled to myself. To this day, a part of me defected to the music.

All the same, I didn't want this idea to be the lasting impression of me here.

"Do you know, in Cleveland, we Germans follow the news of our homeland very closely?" I asked. I regaled the whole room with how the German Americans of the Concordia Lodge fretted over the northern Prussian aggression against Schleswig and Holstein in 1867, siding with the Austrians against Bismarck and King Wilhelm, only to turn around and cheer a few years later for the Prussians in the war against France. Even President Grant had sided with the Germans in that conflict. When Napoleon III surrendered in 1871, we German Americans celebrated as if we ourselves had been to battle, waving the black, red, and gold tricolor flag in the streets right alongside the star-spangled banner. "We erected a seventy-foot victory arch on Cleveland's Public Square, and made a long parade. It was quite a sight, that enormous statue of Germania making a tour all through the city."

"*Doch*, we had no idea the Americans cared so much," Philipp said. Indeed, my brother didn't entirely escape military service after all, he informed me. At age thirty-two, he'd been called up to fight in the Battle of Sedan.

"For the German Americans, what happens here is forever in our hearts and minds," I assured my brother. That I never knew of his involvement gave me pause, as I remembered how he and Father had sent the money to buy me a replacement in the American war. If only I could have returned the favor. "In any case, many of the big cities of America have a large population of German immigrants. Politically, President Grant made a good choice to side with Germany, since we Germans favored Greeley. But the cities in America are always changing. Now there is a new *Auswanderung*: Poles, Czechs, Bohemians, Italians, Hungarians all flooding in."

The hour grew late, and our visitors began to take their leave. Thinking of the morrow, I confessed to Philipp I hadn't thought to pack any work clothes to help with the grape harvest. As the clothes of my slim brother obviously wouldn't fit me, Philipp pulled me over to stand next to Richard Pirrmann for measurement. Everyone had a good joke comparing our girths—he was by far the fattest man in the village, they said, but I was fatter still. Pirrmann promised to bring me work clothes first thing in the morning.

In my room in the stable loft, the animals and I shared the fecund odors of manure and sweat. From my window, the starry sky winked down on me. Freinsheim was just as quiet and dark as it had been in my childhood, the only sounds the stirring hooves of the goat and oxen, the clucking of the hens, the thunderous rumbling of the sow.

BEFORE DAWN, A ROOSTER CROWED and then another. A knock came at my door and work clothes were set inside by invisible hands. I pulled on the rough, air-chilled shirt and pants and went to break my fast in the kitchen. "*Moahje*," the family grunted to one another as we chewed our rolls and cold meats and drank our coffee.

Out in the barnyard, light streaked the black hills to the southeast. I strapped a *Logel* on my back, mentally prepared for the weight yet still pulled off balance as it yanked down on my shoulders. When the town bell rang us into the fields, I trudged out with my family and the other Freinsheimers to bend over the vineyard rows and harvest grapes.

It took four days to pick and deliver the crop. Each evening after long days of stooping, more visitors came to see me, longing for news of relatives in Ohio and beyond.

That weekend the *Derkemer Worschtmarkt* began. Philipp's whole family made plans to go. As we packed into the train car with many other revelers, destined for an evening of eating and drinking, music and dancing, I stood in the center aisle staring down at a woman who looked strangely familiar.

She smiled up at me. "*Tach*, Michael Harm," the Frau said, and in that instant I knew her.

"Could it really be Anna Marie Neu— Oberholz?" I stammered. "*Wenn Engel reisen lacht der Himmel.*"

She laughed and turned to the woman beside her. "Do you hear that?

Michael Harm the dreamer has returned to Freinsheim. 'When angels fly the heavens laugh,' he says. What a kidder."

Her silvery voice brought back such memories.

"It's good to be back after so long," I said, longing to turn her attention back on me.

Anna Marie obliged, looking up again with those deep blue eyes I loved so long ago. "I heard a rumor that you had finally returned to us." Her hair showed stripes of gray, yet she held a baby on her lap.

"I feel as if I've never left," I said.

"Well, you shouldn't have. After the Höhns emigrated, not so many people departed anymore. You were among the last to go."

Why did she torture me? Would she have married me, if I'd stayed? Would I wonder my whole life long if it had been a mistake to go in the first place, each mistake that followed adding onto the last, adding up to what never should have been?

"Is this your little one?" I asked, not wishing to grow pensive in the crowded train car.

"*Doch,* this is my grandchild Sylvie, second child of my son Peter."

"I'm sorry, I should have realized," I said. "I, too, am a grandfather."

As I stood balancing against the rocking motion of the train, I learned from Anna Maria the names and ages of her five children, and she of my three. I asked after Emil, and she told me I should visit the Oberholz stand, to taste the finest *Sekt* and *Neu Wein* in the region. In the push of the crowd as we exited the train, we were torn apart. Later in the evening, I went to say hello to Emil, but he was busy with serving, and we exchanged only a few words.

Most of the time, I kept to the benches of the Harm family, squeezed in with many others at the long tables—strangers and friends alike. The strains of music from a Mackenbacher band swirled through the air. Every so often, one or another of us would wander off for a plate of sausage and onions, liver dumplings, pig's stomach, or to fill our jugs with Rhine wine. No doubt Henry would have seen Freinsheim as backward and provincial, but I reveled in the fun-loving simplicity of my people.

The Harm's youngest daughter Kätche didn't like to sit on the bench with her sisters and parents, but stood to one side with girlfriends. Philipp observed her, his expression unreadable, as she went off to dance with various young men.

"I hope those are Freinsheimer boys," I joked.

Philipp did not look amused. "Our Kätche is fond of dancing," was all he replied.

In festival tradition, we laughed and drank and talked with people we had never met and might never see again. From time to time, I thought of how

Anna Marie was somewhere in this crowd, and wondered if I might have had a life with her had I stayed. Then again, seeing her had stirred in me something unexpected. Goosebumps crept over my skin, the kind of sensation that comes at the wedding of a daughter, or the birth of a grandchild. For years and years I'd secretly thought of Anna Marie as the one who could have made me truly happy, even as I blamed Elizabeth for keeping me from returning to my homeland. Now, with dazzling clarity, I realized I was content—with my profession, with my children, with the lovely woman I had married and still loved. No matter what the future held, as scale is polished from steel to bring out a sheen of silver-blue, I saw the beauty of my life with Elizabeth and yearned for no other.

In my remaining days in Freinsheim, I spent many hours with my brother, helping prune in the cherry orchard, raking and mulching the vegetable garden for winter. Philipp told me of the many new industries, where most of the Freinsheimers now worked—the pump factory in Frankenthal and the chemical plant in Ludwigshafen—and I saw with my own eyes how many more fruit trees graced the landscape.

I could hardly believe the quiet in these fields. There were no machines to roar in my ears as they did at Harm & Schuster. As we worked, my brother and I talked over our experiences, about the wars and politics and the loss of our dear children. In addition to his first Katherina, who passed out of this life at age seven, my brother and Susanna had also lost two infant sons. On this heartbreaking subject, we did not dwell overlong.

I stayed in Freinsheim just long enough to remember the natural pace of village community life, the healthy air, the connection to the earth, and the endless drudgery of farm work. My father had been right—it was a good life for my brother. For my part, I would have grumbled every day.

"MY GREATEST REGRET IS THAT I didn't return to see Mütterchen and Father one last time," I said to Philipp one afternoon near the end of my visit. We had entered the gate around the ancient chapel tower to stand over the graves of our parents. Already, I'd made several visits here, meditating with sorrow and unease on the stony silence of the sandstone markers. Had Mütterchen blamed me for not returning to her bedside in her final days? Did Father regret having sent me to America?

"Did Father believe I made good in America, or did he believe I was a *Taugenichts*?" I asked my brother. More than anything, I needed to know this.

Philipp kept his eyes trained on the graves as if he read his answer from the stones. "Worthless? You? Is this what you think? Don't you know, brother? Father had great faith in you. Rapparlie's accusations surely hurt him. We were all confused." Philipp's eyes lit with the old mischief as he turned his gaze to me. "*Hör' mal*, you were much discussed in Freinsheim. But Father was sure there must be some explanation."

I wanted to believe Philipp spoke the truth. I shrugged. "If only I'd taken to the farm work, I wouldn't have been such a trial."

Philipp squinted at me in exasperation. "The only trial was how much our parents missed you. You were always Father's favorite—"

"*Nä, nä*, what can you mean?" I said, astonished. "Father relied on you for everything! He didn't need me. I was just in the way."

Philipp gaped at me then burst into hearty laughter. "Is this what you think? But of course, you weren't around to hear Father brag about his son in America. *Ach Gott*, he didn't see in me the promise he saw in you."

I shook my head. "I'm not convinced, brother. I will always know he loved you best. In any event, I worked hard all these years, to become a blacksmith and wagon-maker, to keep the artisan crafts alive and live up to the Harm name. Even so, in America now we face an uncertain future." I laid a hand on Philipp's shoulder and turned him toward the rooftops of Freinsheim. "Perhaps in the end you will prove the smarter one for not listening to me and coming to America. All the same, you and Susanna must visit us in Cleveland, to see how my life is there. What do you say?"

"Brother, I have traveled as a soldier and later, for meetings for the town council about politics. When I came home, I realized I didn't know who might be here that I could go have a glass of wine with, or what had happened while I was gone. I didn't like it."

"But it's my dearest wish that my children should meet their Uncle Philipp. They are fast forgetting that they are German."

"You said Henry married a German girl."

"Her parents were immigrants, but she and my son only speak English in the home. The young are under this American spell. They don't live for the German culture of poetry and music and plays. At the *Sängerfest* this summer, such a glorious event held in Cleveland, most of those who came had gray hair. The young people weren't so interested. My youngest, Emma, has married a blacksmith, an odd man who believes in this new Christian Science. But at least he keeps the craftsman tradition. You wouldn't believe it, to see my older two, Henry and Lucy. They mix with high society. Lucy has married a man of political importance. They own many fine things. In Cleveland, we have seen wealth I never thought possible." I sobered then, to think of the wrong impression I made. "It's not like it is here. In America, everything changes so fast, and I am growing old. I'm not sure I can change so much anymore."

I lapsed into a reflective silence. I didn't want to confess to Philipp my disappointment that my son was so disdainful of the blacksmithing, that he showed little interest in building carriages, only in racing them. Almost as if he was not a Harm. In the ebbing light, the vineyard rows were turning from yellow-green to gray, and the air was growing chill. Pensively, I looked back at my old village, the steeple of our *Pfarrkirche* rising like a ship's mast above the rooftops.

My brother clapped his arm over my shoulders.

"*Alla*, here is my idea," he said, steering me back toward the Harm *Hof*. "You send your grown children to Freinsheim. Bring them back here yourself, or send them on their own. We'll show them the Freinsheim hospitality, and they'll know how we live here, *oder*?"

I assured Philipp it was a capital idea. After all, since I'd arrived here nine days ago, my whole being felt calmer. I would listen to Henry, let him make the changes to the business as he desired. Once those were in place, I'd insist he take time off, order him to bring his wife Barbara with him to Freinsheim. Elizabeth and I would watch after baby Edna. I'd also convince Billy Hoppensack to bring Lucy to this place. While she was here, she could paint me a picture of the Freinsheim vineyards to hang on the wall in our Francis Street parlor.

Darkness had fallen outside as we entered the Harm kitchen. A lantern glowed on the table, the same lantern my father once lit each night to pore over his farm ledgers, calculating the yield of his crops, his expenses, and income. It dawned on me how Henry did the same thing, scheming day and night with his ledgers. Perhaps he resembled a Harm after all.

The next morning, I signed the documents that would deed my Freinsheim plum field to my brother and turned my sights toward home.

# Chapter 47

---

## Cleveland, Ohio, 1907

I AWOKE TO THE SMELLS OF yeast bread and sweet rolls, knowing instantly it was a Saturday. No doubt Elizabeth had been up since five o'clock mixing and kneading her bread, baking it into warm, fragrant loaves. These days my mind was a bit of a fog in the mornings, so it was not until I'd buttoned up my waistcoat that I remembered it was the 27th of May, 1907, my sixty-sixth birthday.

A venerable age, but no doubt I had more years to live. My dear friends and in-laws the Crollys had departed this life two decades ago now, in 1885 and 1887. Uncle Jakob went to the grave in 1896 at age seventy-three, to his eternal rest in Columbus, Ohio, and old Rapparlie died in Toledo that same year. As for my brother Philipp, I'd outlived him by seven years. I felt his loss keenly, so I could hardly read the news from Germany anymore. As time allowed, I still wrote to his wife and daughters, with faint hopes my children would keep up the correspondence. They had never shown much interest. When Henry went to Paris, he did not even set foot in Germany, although I urged him again and again to visit Freinsheim.

As I came downstairs to the kitchen, Elizabeth and my daughter Lucy greeted me with smiles and birthday greetings. I sat down to a table dusty with flour.

"I declare, Papa, we thought you would sleep the day away," Lucy said, coming over to kiss me on the top of my balding head.

I had been much around the house ever since suffering a bad case of gout. Of the Harm & Schuster carriage works, I did not like to think any more. Just the other day, the German newspaper had gushed once again about Cleveland as the center of the automobile industry. I could make the most beautiful buggies, but even my children no longer wanted them. Some wagon-makers had switched to making automobiles, but Schuster and I didn't have the heart for it.

As I drank my coffee in the kitchen, I could hear birds warbling and caught the sweet scent of daffodils through the open window. Then came the squeaking of metal, no doubt from the brakes of one of those infernal horseless carriages.

"Whoa!" came Henry's voice through the window.

*Can that be Henry driving a motor car?* I pushed away from the table and lumbered to the front door. How much money had he wasted on one of those contraptions? And which kind had he bought? The White steam car? The Baker electric? I came out on the porch in time to see Henry alighting from a shiny new Rauch & Lang vehicle.

"What is this?!"

"Surprise!" Henry said, beaming. My middle-aged son made a dashing figure in his flat cap and long linen driving duster. He had done it again, spending too much of his savings on a fad. He probably bought stock in oil and the railroads, too. Was this what heart failure felt like?

"What is this?" I choked out again. I could hardly breathe from the tightness in my chest.

"Papa, you know what it is," Henry said with the measured patience of a young man talking to one in his dotage. "It's high time for the Harm family to enter the twentieth century. I tested them all, the steam carriage and the electrics, and the Winton gas-powered car. The Rauch & Lang electric is superior to all of them."

My daughter Lucy swept past me, a scent of lavender perfuming the air. "Why Henry, I declare! Will you take me out for a drive?"

"I'm taking Papa first, for his birthday."

My son held the carriage door open for me while Lucy brought me a duster and cap and helped me put them on. Elizabeth came to the porch to exclaim over the car, cautioning Henry not to go too fast. Without a word, I hoisted my stiff body into the open-air vehicle. As Henry powered the motor and propelled us off down Tod, it was all I could do not to grip the front dash. To have nothing but thin air in front of me gave a strong sense of vertigo.

As we jostled along, I realized that a carriage without horse did bring a certain freedom. Our speed was nearly as regular on the hills as the flat places, and the engine didn't tire as a horse would. The stopping and turning capabilities were a marvel. My son had not quite adjusted to the novelty, still clucking to push the car forward, and saying "whoa" when he applied the handbrake.

"Poor horse," I said. "Now he sits neglected in the barn."

"Think how clean the streets will be if everyone rides in these motor cars,"

Henry said. "No piles of manure, no damage to the roads from horse hooves."

Perhaps my son was right. What did I know? I'd never been especially good at predicting the future. In the fine spring morning, Henry drove us to the German garden, idling the motor briefly under the graceful basswoods before the bronze statues of Goethe and Schiller erected only recently, a testament to the lofty ideals of our pioneer days here in Cleveland. No matter if the young preferred to forget. We old German Americans held firm to our ideals of liberty, democracy, science, and the arts.

When we were ready to continue, Henry offered me a chance to drive, but I declined. We rode through Wade Park along Doan Brook, pulling often to the side of the lane to allow the other Saturday drivers to pass. Thank goodness the sun was warm enough in May to dry the damp earth. A bright green hue of leaf buds in the branches, birds warbling, and the sweet scent of wildflowers gave the promise of a new season. As we reached Lake Erie's blank horizon, my head was full of many thoughts, not least of which was the irony of how I came to be sitting in this horseless carriage of Charles Rauch. Wouldn't old Charles get a good laugh, to see me perched in one of his factory-produced marvels? In truth, it was a good joke, and I wished him well.

Here is my secret, a discovery you may make someday in your own way. If you strike hot metal with practiced skill, you reshape its surface to something new. But inside? The material is not so altered. To shape metal to the golden proportions, you must learn to see the space around it. It is not only the song that carries the melody, but the breaths between the notes. Embrace the whole of it, life and death, and you are free.

Dearest children, now is your time.

* * *

Obituary (*Wächter Und Anzeiger* newspaper, Cleveland, Ohio, July, 1910)

Michael Harm passed away on Sunday at the age of 69 after difficult and long suffering from gout, in the home of his daughter Mrs. W.J. Hoppensack, 6204 Francis Avenue. At a large gathering of mourners, among them an imposing number of the oldest German pioneers, the mortal remains of the carriage works owner Michael Harm, a commonly well-known and in many circles well-liked and highly esteemed man, were carried to the grave starting from Köbler's Chapel on E. 55th Street. Pastor August Kimmel memorialized the deceased with a deeply heartfelt eulogy while singers of the Harmonie heightened the impression of the celebration by their prelude of some moving mourning hymns. Members of the Concordia Lodge of the

Freemasons functioned as pallbearers. The funeral took place at Woodland Cemetery.

Mr. Harm, who always showed an avid interest in all German efforts, played an important role within societal relationships. As a singer with the Harmonie, he held all positions of honor of the association and was president for three terms. Additionally he belonged to the Freemasons Lodge "Concordia."

Mr. Harm leaves in addition to his widow one son and two daughters, Heinrich Harm, Mrs. W. J. Hoppensack, and Mrs. P. Becker, in addition to five grandchildren.

\* \* \*

*The descendants of Michael and Philipp Harm have continued to correspond through five generations. The letters, memories, and stories of these Germans and Americans have made this book possible.*

# Endnotes

Letters have been altered to fit the narrative. Original translations from the *Alte Deutsche Schrift* by Angela Weber.

1. Cooper, James Fenimore, *Last of the Mohicans*, Oxford University Press, USA: 2009
2. Schiller, Johann Christoph Friedrich von, "Song of the Bell" Translated by Walter H. Schneider, http://fathersforlife.org/hist/song_of_the_bell. htm
3. Wander, Karl Friedrich Wilhelm, *Auswanderungs-Katechismus (Emigrant's Catechism): Ein Ratgeber fur Auswanderer, besonders für Diejenigen, welche nach Nordamerika auswandern wollen*, Glogau, 1852. (Translation by Hans Dahlke)
4. The words spoken by Jacob Müller about the Republican Convention are quoted from his book *Memories of a Forty-Eighter: Sketches from the German-American Period of Storm and Stress in the 1850s*, translated from German by Steven Rowan, Western Reserve Historical Society: 1996.
5. Browning, Elizabeth Barrett, and H. W. Preston. "SONNET XLIII." *The Complete Poetical Works of Elizabeth Barrett Browning*. Boston: Houghton Mifflin, 1900. 223. Print.

# Glossary

**Note:** Many of the words included in the text are in a dialect unique to the Palatinate region. Where this is the case, the common German word is included in parenthesis beside the Palatinate term.

**Aber** – but
**Achtung** – Attention!
**Ackermann, Ackermänner** (plural) – a farmer (one who primarily plows and cultivates land for grain, fruits and vegetables, as opposed to one who cultivates vineyards for wine-making)
**Aha** – A German interjection meaning *"I see"*
**Alla, Alla hopp** – Palatine expression from the French *"aller,"* meaning *"let's go."* It can also mean *"okay,"* or *"let it go."*
**Altweibersommer** – a German expression like *"Indian summer,"* literally *"old woman summer"*
**Amerikaner** – American
**Amsel** – a common blackbird
**Anzeiger** – Gazette, newspaper
**Aua** – ow
**Auf alten Pfannen lernt man kochen** – German idiomatic expression – on old pots you learn how to cook
**Auf Wiedersehen** – Goodbye
**Auswanderung** – literally, *"out-wandering,"* German term for emigration
**Babbe** (Vater) – father, dad
**Bankert** – bastard
**Bass uff** – watch out
**Bildergeld** – also shortened to *Bilder,* money in paper form with pictures printed on it
**Bitte** – please
**Bengel** – rascal
**Dampfnudeln mit Weinsosse** – steamed dumplings with wine sauce

**Derkemer Worschtmarkt** – a very old festival, going on 600 years, which still takes place in the Palatinate region in the city of Bad Dürkheim
**Deutsch** – German
**Doch** – An idiomatic acknowledgement meaning "on the contrary" or "however"
**du** — you
**du bist ein Narr** – literally, you are a fool. Idiomatic expression meaning, "you must be kidding."
**dummer** – stupid
**Dummbeidel** – (*Dummbeutel*) literally, stupid bag (airhead)
**Dummkopf** – stupid
**Eichelhäher** –jay birds
**Eisentor** – literally, "iron door," the main gate entrance to Freinsheim
**Elwedritsche** – mythical creatures of Palatinate lore, shy, elvish beings with feathers, beaks and fur
**Entschuldigen Sie, entschuldigung** – *Excuse me*
**Es tut mir leid** – I am sorry
**Esel** – donkey
**Feuerlöschspritzen** – hydraulic fire wagons to extinguish fires
**Frau, Frauen** (plural) – woman, wife, Mrs.
**Fräulein, Fräuleins** (plural) – unmarried miss
**Freidenker** – literally, "free thinkers," such as atheists and agnostics
**Frei** – free
**Freiheit** – freedom
**Freilich** – of course
**Friedhofsturm** – an ancient church tower that stands in the Freinsheim graveyard
**Genau** – expression meaning "Exactly!" "Quite!"
**Gesangverein** – singing club
**Goldener Herbst** – golden autumn
**Goldmenschen** – men who hunt for gold
**Gott sei Dank** – Thanks be to God
**Großdeutschland** – large Germany, a term used in arguments for unification including both Prussia and Austria
**Grüße** – Greetings
**Guck mal** – Look
**Gulden** – Guilder, a unit of currency
**Gut** – good
**Gute Brunnen** – literally, "good fountain," a sulfur spring in Freinsheim
**Guten Abend** – good evening
**Guten Morgen** – good morning

**Guten Tag** – hello, good day
**Handwerk** – business where the products are crafted by hand
**Handwerker** – hand craftsman
**Hausmärchen** – folk tales
**Heißen** – to call
**Heilige Schrift** – Holy Bible
**Heimweh** – homesickness
**Herr, Herren** (plural) – Mr.
**Hinnere (Hintern)** – hind end, bottom
**Hof, Höfe** (plural) – village farmhouse (usually with attached stables and a barnyard)
**Ich** – I (*Ich heisse Michael Harm* – I am called Michael Harm)
**Ich liebe dich so inniglich** – song title of the day, meaning: I love you so deep in my being
**Ja** – yes
**Junge** – Boy, kid, lad
**Kaputt** – broken, ruined
**Kein** – no, not any
**Kein König da** – a common expression in the nineteenth century about America, meaning "no king there."
**Kelterwagen** – wagon with a wine press on it
**Kerwe** – Palatinate church fair
**Kirchenlieder** – church hymns
**Kleindeutschland** – little Germany, a term used in political arguments for unification, but with Prussia and Austria separate
**Krug, Krüge** (plural) – a jug for drinking wine
**Kuchen** – cake
**Lagerbier** – a type of beer made with a cold storage process, different from the more common ale of the time. The earliest brewer of lager in Cleveland was Martin Stumpf, who founded The Lion Brewery in 1850. Many more German brewers soon followed. (Musson, Robert A., Brewing in Cleveland, Arcadia Publishing, 2005.)
**Lederhosen** – leather shorts with suspenders traditional in Bavaria
**Leiterwagen** – adjustable wagon made of ladders
**Lieb Kind** – dear child (endearment my grandmother remembers her grandfather Michael Harm saying)
**Lied** – song
**Leck mich am Arsch** – equivalent of English insult: kiss my ass
**Lesesucht** – a passion for reading, or reading addiction
**Logel, Logeln** (plural) – open-topped barrel narrower at the bottom, worn on the back for harvesting grapes

**Luftikus** – easy-going, happy-go-lucky
**Mädchen** – young girls
**Mann** – husband, man
**Markt** – Market square, also a fair
**mit Gut und Blut** – oath meaning "to sacrifice one's all"
**Moahje (Guten Morgen)** – good morning
**Moin, moin (Guten Tag)** – low German for good day
**Mütterchen** – term of endearment for mother
**N'Amend (Guten Abend)** – Good Evening
**Nä (Nein)** – No
**Narr** – fool
**Neu Wein (neuer Wein)** – a grape hard cider only available in September and October
**Oder** – or – when used at the end of a sentence, it means "is it not?"
**Oma** – grandmother
**Onkel** – uncle
**Opa** – grandfather
**Palais de l'Industrie** – an enormous glass, stone, and iron exhibition hall erected in Paris under the reign of Emperor Napoleon III in 1855 (destroyed in 1897)
**Pfarrer** – pastor
**Pfarrkirche** – parish church
**Pfennig-Magazin** – literally, "penny magazine," a weekly magazine
**Polizei** – police
**Putte** – cherub, in art, a chubby-faced, winged child
**Tach (Guten Tag)** – Good Day
**Tannenbaum** – evergreen Christmas tree
**Rathskeller** – a bar or tavern below the street
**Reichstag** – political parliament in Germany after 1871 unification
**Sag mal** – idiomatic expression meaning "Say," or "Tell me,"
**Sängerfest** – singing festival
**Sau** – pig
**Saumaa (Saumagen)** – a pork, potato, vegetable and spice mixture fried in a sow's stomach casing
**Schnorranten** – vagabond, or "beggar" musicians
**Schlachtfest** – pig butchering feast
**Scheiße** – shit (expletive)
**Schmeck'** – taste
**Schnell** – quickly, hurry
**Schwanger** – pregnant
**Schwarzbrot** – German bread of dark rye

**Schwören** – to swear
**Sekt** – Palatinate sparkling wine
**Simsaladim Bamba Saladu Saladim** – nonsense words in a song
**Stadtmauer** – a fortified wall around a village
**Sprechen Sie Deutsch?** – Do you speak German?
**Tante** – aunt
**Taugenichts** – worthless
**Törichter** – foolish
**Turnverein** – gymnastics club
**Vorsichtig** – careful
**Wächter am Erie** – name of a Cleveland German newspaper meaning, literally, "The Guard on the Erie," a wordplay on a Mannheim German newspaper for democracy – *Der Wächter am Rhein* – "The Guard on the Rhine."
**Wanderbuch** – a passbook carried by a craftsman journeyman
**Wanderlied** – traveling song
**Weinlese** – grape harvest for wine-making
**Weihnachten** – Christmas
**Wenn Engel reisen lacht der Himmel** – German idiomatic expression: When angels fly the heavens laugh.
**Weltschmerz** – world-weariness, heaviness of heart
**Wes Brot ich ess, des Lied ich sing** – old German proverb – whose bread I eat, his song I sing.
**Wie bitte?** – German expression for "come again?" or "please repeat that."
**Wingertsleit** (Wingertsleute) – wine-growers
**Worscht (Wurst)** – German sausage
**Zum Schifflein Christi** – the little boat of Christ, name of an early Cleveland German church
**Zwei** – two

# Acknowledgments

———✳✳✳———

THIS NOVEL WOULD NOT HAVE been possible without the dedicated assistance of my German relatives, especially Angela Weber, who translated nineteenth century family letters from *Alte Deutsche Schrift* and made important research contacts before, during, and after my visit to the Palatinate in 2010. Matthias Weber too has been generous with his time, giving me tours of Freinsheim and of castles of the region, not to mention history lessons, a vineyard bicycle tour and colorful stories. Thanks to Bärbel Weber for opening her home for an extended stay while I researched this book. Heartfelt thanks to all my German relatives and friends who have been so hospitable and supportive: Wolf Bielstein, Ina Dörr-Mechenbier, Inge Faber, Gretel and Otto Kopf, Markus Kopf, Hannah and Helen Mechenbier, Christoph, Carlotta and Luzi Otterbeck, Armin Schlachter, Sigrid Steil, Marliese Weber, Hans-Günter and Stephanie Weber, Manfred, Heike, Stephanie and Kristina Weber.

While researching in Cleveland, I received expert help from Vicki Catozza and Ann K. Sindelar of the Western Reserve Historical Society, Heidi Stelmach of the Cleveland Metroparks Canalway Center, Martin Hauserman, archivist of Cleveland City Records, and William C. Barrow, of Cleveland State University library. A later visit to the Ohio Historical Society in Columbus was also invaluable. On the research trail in Germany, thanks to Monika Eisenbart, Dr. Hans-Helmut Görtz, Roland Paul, Dr. Inge Preuss, and Freinsheim's retired Evangelical Protestant Pastor Herr Walter.

What I know of the ancient art of blacksmithing I owe to Tim Middaugh of Old West Forge in White Salmon, Washington and to The Northwest Blacksmithing Association, especially for their terrific lending library. What I know of wagon-making comes in large part from *The Carriage Trade*, an impressively thorough, well-written book by Thomas A. Kinney. Professor

Kinney also extended the favor of reading an early version of my manuscript. His encouragement and feedback are deeply appreciated. Thanks to Dr. Hans-Helmut Görtz, Freinsheim historian for his expert assistance on Palatinate history and dialect. The map graphics are thanks to Maria Brown of Kroll Maps. Thanks to Jerry Bowman for an enthusiastic tour of The Northwest Carriage Museum in Raymond, Washington.

For family genealogical research, much credit goes to my father Clyde Patterson, now deceased, and also to the following persons: Angela Weber, Dr. Hans-Helmut Görtz, David Williams and Sarah Thorsen Little. At The Northwest Institute of Literary Arts, I am indebted to my thesis advisors Kathleen Alcalá, Wayne Ude, and my second reader William Dietrich. I have been helped, inspired, and cheered by faculty and classmates at The Northwest Institute of Literary Arts MFA program. Thanks to all who have supported me there, especially Janet Buttenwieser for her careful reading of my manuscript and great suggestions at a time I felt stuck, and to Ana Maria Spagna, whose encouragements came at a time I needed them most.

Heartfelt thanks to Jo Gustafson, who instilled in me the courage to give up my day job and write and has been there for me throughout this journey, and to Michele Genthon for being my writing partner and constant inspiration.

I am incredibly fortunate to have found Coffeetown Press, especially my outstanding editor Catherine Treadgold. Thanks also to Jennifer McCord for her incredible book expertise and encouragement and to Jennifer Richards for her counsel and insight.

As they say, it takes a village. My writing group has offered able feedback and faithful support all along. Thanks to my book group, the Women Who Sleep with Books, with whom I've spent two decades discussing books, keeping alive my passion for a good story.

This book would not have been possible without my grandmother Emma Patterson who told me stories of her favorite grandpa Michael Harm when I was a child. Emma also corresponded faithfully with Anna Faber and Helena Weber until she reached her nineties, which has kept the Harm and Handrich descendants together for five generations. Heartfelt thanks to Craig Patterson for scanning family photos, organizing family mementoes, and being a true friend as well as brother.

Finally, my love and thanks go to my husband Dave for his trust and belief in me, and my children George and Vivian Gebben, for their patient good humor as I sat for hours on end at the computer wrestling this book into being.

# Author's Note

---

T HE WRITING OF *THE LAST of the Blacksmiths* began in the spring of 2007
with the discovery of a packet of old German letters as I helped my father
move to assisted living.

My father, Clyde A. Patterson, Jr., was a lifelong resident of Cleveland,
Ohio. Just two months after my birth, in 1958, he moved our family into
a house of his own design (he was an architecture professor at Kent State
University), in a suburb called Moreland Hills. Growing up on the southeast
side of Cleveland in the 1960s and 1970s, I knew my hometown metropolis as
a center of steel manufacturing, oil refineries, automobile plants, and a river
so polluted it caught fire. My family and I would sometimes ride the Green
Road Rapid Transit to Cleveland's downtown Public Square to shop at the
then-signature department stores Higbee's, Halle's, and The May Company.
The view out the windows was of a rustbelt landscape, tall smoke-belching
stacks on the horizon, crumbling houses and brick buildings closer in. The
area along the tracks was overgrown and littered with corroding girders,
broken appliances, scraps of tarpaper, cast off cement blocks, and shards of
glass.

Emma Hoppensack Patterson, my paternal grandmother, had an entirely
different image of Cleveland. In the 1960s, my father designed and built a
house for her (and my grandfather, who died soon after the move) on our
property in Moreland Hills. During my childhood, I often visited my
grandmother on my walks home from school. We would sit across from each
other at the kitchen table, and—while pork chops and onions bubbled in their
own gravy on the stove—she would conjure scenes of Cleveland in years past.

My grandmother had grown up in downtown Cleveland, on Francis
Avenue near present-day E. 55th, under the same roof as her grandparents.

She said they spoke only German, to each other and to her sister Olga. She remembered how her Grandpa Harm, legs swollen painfully with gout, would pull her to him, his scratchy beard tickling as he whispered *"Liebes Kind"*— dear child—in her ear. She reminisced about visiting her grandfather's Harm & Schuster carriage works, where she and her sister would sit in the new carriages in the second floor display room for the view out the window as parades processed down Woodland Avenue. About winter sleigh rides in the open air, bundled up under a heavy lap robe, hands toasty warm in her sleek beaver-skin muff.

Every Christmas during my childhood, my grandmother would write letters in German "to the relatives" in Freinsheim, Germany. In 1988, on my first trip to Freinsheim (my parents and brothers had already visited several times) I fell in love with the picturesque town and surrounding vineyards and orchards, but especially with the relatives. By the time I made it to Freinsheim, my grandmother was already gone; she had died two years earlier. It felt amazing, and not a little sad, to meet Anna Faber and Helena Weber, the sisters with whom my grandmother had corresponded all those years, yet never met. I wished my grandmother could have been with me to meet them, to hold their hands, hear their voices and gaze into their kind faces.

The many descendants of Anna and Helena welcomed me warmly. Although my German was poor, the younger relatives spoke excellent English, and we shared much conversation over *Kuchen*, coffee and wine. Because the last names of these relatives were Weber, Faber, and Kopf, I did not readily make the connection between my grandmother's childhood stories of Grandpa Harm and these Freinsheimers.

In 2007 when Dad and I came across the letters dating back to the 1920s and written by Anna Faber and Helena Weber, Dad decided the descendants of these now-deceased women would probably like to have them, so we mailed them off without much thought.

A year later, my cousin Angela Weber, granddaughter of Helena Weber, came to visit me in Seattle, hand-carrying a surprise—over a dozen letters found in Tante Inge Faber's Freinsheim attic, dating from 1841 to 1907. That these letters were written in nearly indecipherable *Alte Deutsche Schrift* (Old German Script) did not dissuade my cousin at all. Angela had already tackled that old, flowery handwriting and begun to read the oldest letters. She said they were all written from Cleveland and must be from our ancestors. Honestly, I had only a mild interest at the time, but at her bidding, I sat down to puzzle over the contents.

Angela had already compiled an inventory. Letters written in and after the 1860s were all penned by Michael Harm, whose name was familiar to me. Even earlier ones had been penned by men named Handrich and Rapparlie.

Who were they? Angela had studied my father's family tree, which he had shared with the Freinsheimer relatives. The tree indicated the Handrichs were also related to us, on Michael's mother's side. Johann Rapparlie, it seemed, was related to the Handrichs by marriage.

As Angela and I proceeded with the translations, enlightenment gradually dawned. In the mid-1850s, two brothers became separated by the broad Atlantic, as a result of need, or ambition, or some other explanation lost to time. Angela was descended from the older brother Philipp Harm, who had remained in Freinsheim. I was descended from Michael Harm, who had come to Cleveland in 1857.

The letters were a revelation to us both, as they imparted copious information about the lives of people unknown to us. Our great-great-great-grandfather, grandmother, uncles, and aunts. We learned Michael Harm did not arrive without any connections, as we had previously assumed, but to be with family—his uncles and aunts on his mother's side, who had immigrated to Cleveland in 1840. Michael Harm had come to apprentice as a blacksmith, that much we knew from my father's notes on the family tree. What we had not realized was that he apprenticed under his uncle in the family wagon-making business. And so on.

Sometime after Angela returned to Germany, I visited the National Archives and Records Administration (NARA) on Sand Point Way in Seattle to see if I could find the actual date, not just the year, of Michael Harm's arrival in America. The letters had offered quite a few clues about port of departure (Havre) and of arrival (New York). I expected to find a smattering of passenger lists per week in New York's harbor in 1857. Instead, there were a number of rolls of microfilm to scroll through. Three, sometimes four boats, carrying upwards of 400 passengers, arrived in New York daily in that era, from all over Europe, but especially from England, Germany, Ireland, and Scotland. The magnitude of the story took hold, and I was hooked.

As I began writing a novel based on the life of my great-great-grandfather Michael Harm, I did so in total naïveté. I knew next to nothing of nineteenth century history, philosophy, theology, and culture. To get started, I turned to Dickens, Melville, James Fenimore Cooper, George Eliot, Isabella Bird, and other nineteenth century authors. About blacksmithing, information was harder to find. There are a few books, such as Alden A. Watson's *The Blacksmith,* and a chapter in *Moby-Dick* explores the role of the blacksmith on board a whaler. But in our late twentieth and early twenty-first century reality, the ancient art of blacksmithing is not part of everyday experience. To gain a better understanding of this artisan craft and what Michael Harm experienced, I enrolled in a four-day beginning blacksmithing course at Old West Forge in White Salmon, Washington. Under Master Tim Middaugh, I hammered with five other novices from morning till evening each day, crafting tools, fireplace pokers, a wreath hanger, and a sign bracket. The experience could only approximate blacksmithing in my great-great-grandfather's day. In modern times, most blacksmiths work with bar steel and propane forges, not wrought iron and coke fires. It was an approximation, a mere glimpse. The time-honored artisan skills lost to the machine age can never be fully known.

About a year into the project, after having written about 150 pages, after having read and reread Johann Rapparlie's and Michael Harm's letters so often I heard their voices in my dreams, I traveled to Freinsheim for a research visit. I stayed near the heart of that ancient walled village with Angela's mother Bärbel. My relatives the Webers, the Fabers, and the Kopfs, many of whom still live there, treated me royally, taking turns ushering me around the Palatinate to meet with historians and visit castles, museums, and even a working blacksmith shop in nearby Friedelsheim. They wined and dined me on the regional cuisine and led me on gorgeous hikes, including the Freinsheim annual Wine Hike. I had the opportunity to attend the ages-old Dürkheimer Wurstmarkt and go on a bicycle tour through the golden-leaved vineyards. I even managed to harvest grapes by hand with the Freinsheim City Council. After staying for over a month, I returned to Seattle and began writing the book over again, from page one, this time in the first person voice of Michael Harm.

While *The Last of the Blacksmiths* is heavily researched and based on a true story, some characters are entirely invented. Michael's immediate relatives, as well as Pfarrer Bickes and Pfarrer Holderied, are real historic figures. The Catholic priest Holderied was indeed sentenced to death, freed only at the last moment by the arrival of the Prussians in Dürkheim. On the other hand, the schoolteacher Herr Glock and his family, Gerhard Becker the blacksmith and family, Emil Oberholz and Anna Marie Neufeld, Herr Adler and Herr Franck and the Liedmeisters, are all figments of my imagination.

At NARA, I identified Michael Harm—Michel Harne (after much searching, I must conclude that "Michel Harne" is a misspelling of Michael Harm)—as Passenger Number 262 on the Helvetia, captained by Lewis Higgins. His ship arrived in New York on June 30, 1857, on the same weekend as one of the infamous riots in New York's Five Points Slum. A U.S. citizen Philipp Haenderich (I call him Franz Handrich in the novel) is listed quite near Michel Harne on the Helvetia register. Was this person Michael's relative, charged with bringing him across to America? I have no evidence to that effect, but for this novel, surmise that it was so. Other names listed near Michael Harne were: Barbara Metzger (17), August Haas (15), Margaret Haas (17) as well as Louis Sparer (20) and Christian Winner (21). For the record, I have no confirmation that the individuals listed near Michel Harne traveled intentionally as a group, that Handrich married Metzger, etc.

In Cleveland, Johann Rapparlie was indeed Michael's uncle, the master blacksmith to whom he was apprenticed those many years ago. In the historical letters, Rapparlie writes to Freinsheim about losing his leg, although it is unclear how the accident occurred. Also according to Michael's letters, he and Rapparlie had a serious falling out, although the reasons are only hinted at. I drew the names of the workers in the Rapparlie wagon shop from the 1860 census, but invented their characters and relationships. I have no evidence Michael had an affair of any kind, let alone with a Manx woman named Jean Cody. However, quite a few persons from the Isle of Mann did immigrate to Cleveland in that era, as evidenced by census records. As for the Crollys, Scheuermanns, and Jakob Handrich, I have rendered them as close to historical fact as possible, but in the end, have made up many details. Regarding Matthias Höhn, I have evidence that a Michael Höhn traveled to Freinsheim with Michael Harm in 1893, that they were at that time good friends, and that a large Höhn family emigrated from Freinsheim in the 1850s. The first name I changed so as not to confuse the narrative. But again, I have mostly invented the details.

As for Charles Rauch, there was indeed a Jacob Rauch who ran a Wayside Smithy on Columbus Road, whose son Charles took over the business when his father was killed in the Civil War. Charles Rauch, under Rauch & Co. and later Rauch & Lang, did make fine carriages—victorias, cabriolets and broughams—and his design for an ice wagon won a bronze medal in 1876 at The Centennial Exhibition in Philadelphia. In the early twentieth century, the Rauch & Lang factory developed and produced Rauch & Lang electric cars, marvels of workmanship in their day. Coincidentally, a Charles Rausch (15) crossed the Atlantic, his name found on the passenger manifest quite near that of Michel Harne and Philipp Haenderich. Were Rauch and Rausch one and the same person? I doubt it. I am a writer of historical fiction, so for the sake of story, there comes a point where the facts must end and the imagination take flight.

Writing *The Last of the Blacksmiths* has literally and figuratively changed my life. In the three years it took to research and write this book, I've been outwardly breezing through twenty-first century life, while inwardly inhabiting the pre-petroleum nineteenth century. This parallel existence has allowed me to perceive my real-time world through a new lens. Having considered in depth how people lived 150 years ago, I now perceive our culture as fast losing its grip on essential survival knowledge as technology hurtles us at an ever faster pace, for better and worse, into the material, global age. After this experience, I am quite certain I will never tire of research adventures, which entertain and enlighten and always keep me thinking. Finally, I have discovered at my core a strong sense of family and place, from where and from whom I have come into being.

It never ceases to amaze me that—for all of the many times I stepped off the Cleveland Rapid Transit into the Terminal Tower—I never realized I was arriving at the former location of Champlain street, where the carriage works of Harm & Butler, then Harm & Schuster, once stood. As for the Rapparlie Wagon Shop, on a recent visit to downtown Cleveland, I went on a quest to locate the former corner of Seneca Street (W. 3$^{rd}$) and Michigan. According to my best guess, the shop where Michael Harm apprenticed stood at the present-day site of a paved over parking lot, the closest landmark being Cleveland's Hard Rock Café.

My family's past would have been buried forever had it not been for the existence of the letters, which started me on such an astonishing odyssey. For five generations now, the descendants of Philipp and Michael Harm have continued to correspond. Will there be a sixth? I hope and believe there will.

—*Claire Gebben, January, 2013*

# Discussion Questions for Book Groups

---

1. How do the various immigrants in *The Last of the Blacksmiths* adapt to their new country? What surprised you about the German immigrant experience? Do you think immigrants today experience something similar? What might the differences be?

2. On the transatlantic voyage, Christian Wiener says, "In America, I will change my luck." In what ways might this have been possible? Was Michael able to take his destiny into his own hands? What circumstances in his life were beyond his control?

3. If Michael had lived in different times, would he have married the same woman? How do you think Michael's childhood experiences influenced his choices?

4. Did Michael "become" an American or did he hold on to his German past?

5. What are some of the parallels between the fast pace of change during Michael Harm's life and this modern era where technology is changing society?

6. How did the experiences in *The Last of the Blacksmiths* compare to your own ancestors'?

7. How did religion impact Michael's life? How did the religion of your ancestors affect your life and the life of your family?

8. Have your family members found anything surprising while researching their ancestry? Did any of the documents not back up the "official" story?

9. Close to one-fourth of Americans have all or partial German ancestry, but many families are not even aware of their German ethnic heritage. Is this because of the World Wars and the concentration camps? In what ways have German immigrants been an important influence in American culture?

CLAIRE GEBBEN WAS BORN AND raised on the southeast side of Cleveland in Moreland Hills, Ohio. She penciled her first novel at age ten, 101 pages on blue-lined notebook paper. She is of German and Scottish descent, but notes that the German side of the family were more meticulous record-keepers. A fan of the outdoors, she took both summer and winter mountaineering expeditions through the National Outdoor Leadership School in Wyoming.

In 1980 Ms. Gebben earned a BA in Psychology from Calvin College in Grand Rapids, Michigan. Shortly thereafter, she traveled through Ecuador, Peru, and Bolivia for several months on an extended honeymoon. Returning to the U.S., she and her husband moved seven times in seven years, living in Grand Rapids, Ann Arbor, Cleveland, and Buffalo before landing in Seattle, Washington.

Ms. Gebben's hobbies include skiing, dance, hiking, photography, singing, and travel. She has worked as a resource center manager, newspaper columnist, newsletter editor, ghostwriter, in desktop publishing, multi-media, and communications, all the while raising a family and pursuing her love of reading and writing. In 2011, she earned an MFA in Creative Writing through the Northwest Institute of Literary Arts on Whidbey Island, Washington.

Ms. Gebben's stories, essays, and articles have appeared in *Soundings Review*, *The Speculative Edge*, *The Fine Line*, *Shark Reef* and other publications. She is the archivist of her 160-year-old Methodist Church. On a 2010 research visit to Germany, Ms. Gebben was featured in the local newspaper *Die Rheinpfalz* harvesting grapes in the Freinsheim community vineyard of her ancestors.

Ms. Gebben serves on the board of the Northwest Institute of Literary Arts, the Whidbey Island MFA Alumni Association, and the professional writers organization Seattle Freelances. In 2013, she served as fiction editor of *Soundings Review* literary magazine.

Ms. Gebben is married, has two adult children, and lives on Mercer Island, Washington. *The Last of the Blacksmiths* is her first novel.

You can find Claire on the Web at www.clairegebben.com.

CPSIA information can be obtained at www.ICGtesting.com
Printed in the USA
BVOW02s2051150114

341625BV00005B/25/P